HOSTS

ALSO BY F. PAUL WILSON

Repairman Jack novels:
The Tomb
Legacies
Conspiracies
All the Rage

Healer
Wheels Within Wheels
An Enemy of the State
Black Wind
Soft & Others
Dydeetown World
The Tery
Sibs
The Select
Implant
Deep as the Marrow
Mirage (with Matthew J. Costello)
Nightkill (with Steven Spruill)
Masque (with Matthew J. Costello)
The Barrens & Others
The Christmas Thingy

The *Adversary* Cycle:
The Keep
The Tomb
The Touch
Reborn
Reprisal
Nightworld

As editor:
Freak Show
Diagnosis: Terminal

HOSTS

A Repairman Jack Novel

F. PAUL WILSON

A TOM DOHERTY ASSOCIATES BOOK • NEW YORK

HOSTS: A REPAIRMAN JACK NOVEL

Copyright © 2001 by F. Paul Wilson

A Forge Book
Published by Tom Doherty Associates, LLC
175 Fifth Avenue
New York, NY 10010

www.tor.com

Forge® is a registered trademark of Tom Doherty
Associates, LLC.

Library of Congress Cataloging-in-Publication Data

Wilson, F. Paul (Francis Paul)
    Hosts : a Repairman Jack novel / F. Paul Wilson.—1st ed.
      p. cm.
    "A Tom Doherty Associates book."
    ISBN 0-312-87866-4 (alk. paper)
    1. Repairman Jack (Fictitious character)—Fiction.   2.
Microbial mutation—Fiction.   I. Title.

    PS3573.I45695 H67 2001
    813'.54—dc21

                            2001040288

First Edition: October 2001

Printed in the United States of America

0 9 8 7 6 5 4 3 2 1

ACKNOWLEDGMENTS

Special thanks to Charlotte Abbott for her many valuable insights.

And thanks to the usual crew for their enlightened and discerning input: David Hartwell, Coates Bateman, Elizabeth Monteleone, Steven Spruill, and Albert Zuckerman.

HOSTS

TUESDAY

1

Kate Iverson stared out the window of the hurtling taxi and wondered where she was. New York was not her town. She knew certain sections, and if it were daytime she might have had some idea as to her location, but here in the dark and fog she could have been anywhere.

She'd started the trip thirty minutes and who-knew-how-many miles ago in the West Twenties with a follow-that-cab scenario—*I still can't believe I really said that*—that moved across town and up the FDR Drive. The East River had served as a comforting landmark for a while, but as twilight had faded to night, the river fell behind, replaced by dark shapes and fuzzy lights looming in the fog beyond the roadway.

"What road is this?" she asked the driver.

Through the Plexiglas barrier came the accented reply, double-rolling the *r*'s: "Bruckner Expressway." The driver's ID tag showed a dark mustached face with glowering black eyes and indicated he was Mustafah Salaam.

She'd often heard "the Bruckner" mentioned in the incessant traffic reports on New York City radio but had no idea where it was.

"This is Bronx," the driver added, anticipating her next question.

Kate felt a quick stab of fear. The Bronx? Visions of burned-out buildings and rubble-strewn lots swirled through her brain.

Oh, Jeanette, she thought, staring ahead at the cab they were following, where are you going? Where are you taking me?

Kate had stashed her two teenagers with her ex and taken a short leave from her pediatric group practice in Trenton to stay with Jeanette during her recovery from brain tumor therapy. The experimental treatment had been a resounding success. No ill effects . . . at least none that would be apparent to Jeanette's treating physician.

But since completion of the treatment, Kate had noticed a definite personality change. The Jeanette Vega she'd come to know and deeply love over these past two years was a warm, giving person, full of enthusiasm for life, with an opinion about everything. A delightfully edgy chatterbox. But slowly she had changed. The new Jeanette was cold and distant, rarely speaking unless spoken to, leaving her apartment without a word about where she was going, disappearing for hours at a time.

At first Kate had chalked it up to an acute reactive depression. Why not? What medical diagnosis can rock the foundations of your world more deeply than an inoperable malignant brain tumor? But depression didn't quite explain her behavior. When Jeanette should have been depressed—when she'd been told she had a literal death sentence growing in her brain—she'd remained her upbeat self. Now, after a miraculous cure, after regaining her whole future, she'd become another person.

Maybe it was a stress reaction.

Or a side effect of the treatment. As a physician Kate prided herself on keeping current with medical progress, so she was familiar with medicine's cutting edge; but the experimental protocol that had saved Jeanette seemed damn near science fiction.

Yet it had worked. The tumor was dead, and Jeanette would live on.

But would she live on without Kate?

That, Kate admitted, was what was really disturbing her. Nearing middle age—in darn good shape for forty-four, she knew, but still six years older than Jeanette—she couldn't help worrying that Jeanette had found someone else. Someone younger.

That would be so unlike the old Jeanette. But this new Jeanette . . . who could say?

Jeanette had been put on notice that her remaining time on earth was numbered in months instead of decades; she'd believed she'd seen her last Christmas tree, tasted her last Thanksgiving dinner. And then it was all given back to her. How could anyone's psyche survive that sort of trauma unscathed?

Perhaps the ordeal had caused Jeanette to reassess her life. Maybe she'd looked around and asked, *Is this what I want?* And perhaps, in some new back-from-the-brink perspective, she'd decided she wanted something else. More. Different.

At least she could tell me, Kate thought. She owes me that much.

Jeanette hadn't asked her to leave—she had the right since it was her apartment—but she had moved out of the bedroom they'd always shared on Kate's visits and into the study where she slept on the couch. No amount of questioning from Kate had elicited a reason why.

The not knowing gnawed at her. So tonight, when Jeanette had walked out the door without a word, Kate had followed.

Never in a million years would she have imagined herself trailing the woman she loved through the night. But things change. It hadn't been all that long ago that she never would have imagined herself loving another woman.

Up ahead, Jeanette's cab turned off the Bruckner and Kate's followed it onto a road the signs identified as the Bronx River Parkway. And after a few miles the city suddenly disappeared and they were in the woods—in the Bronx?

"Stay closer," she told the driver. "You're letting them get too far ahead."

She didn't want to come all this way just to lose her.

Then Kate saw signs for the Bronx Zoo and New York Botanical Gardens. More turns, each new road smaller than the last until they were traveling a tree-lined residential street.

"Are we still in the Bronx?" she asked, marveling at all the well-kept homes trailing by on either side.

"Still Bronx, yes," the driver told her.

How come it never looks like this on TV? she wondered.

"Keep going," Kate said when she saw Jeanette's cab pull into the curb before a neat brick colonial.

Her anxiety soared as a thousand questions cascaded through her mind. Who lived there? Another woman?

She had the driver stop half a block beyond. She watched Jeanette's cab leave her on the sidewalk and pull away. As Jeanette started up the walk toward the house, Kate opened her own cab's door.

"Wait here," she said.

"No-no," the driver said. "You must pay."

Nice neighborhood or not, this was still the Bronx, and a long way from Jeanette's apartment. Kate did not want to be stranded here. She glanced at the meter and fished the exact amount out of her wallet.

"Here," she said, keeping her voice low as she handed him the money. "You'll get your tip when we get back to the city."

He seemed to accept that, nodding without comment as he took the money.

She pulled her raincoat tightly around her. A chilly night for June. The fog was thinning and the wet street glistened in the glow from the streetlights; every sound seemed amplified. Kate was glad she'd worn sneakers as she padded along the street, keeping the parked cars between her and Jeanette.

When she'd approached as close as she dared, she stopped behind a tree trunk and watched Jeanette walk up the front steps of the house. Kate's heart ached at the sight of her: a yellow rain slicker and loose jeans hid her feminine curves; a Yankees cap hid much of her straight, jet black hair, but Kate knew those curves, remembered the strawberry scent of the shampoo Jeanette used to wash that hair.

Suddenly Kate wished she hadn't come. Who was going to open that door? Forty minutes ago she'd been dying to know, now she was terrified. But she couldn't turn away. Especially not now, because the door was opening and a man stood there, a heavyset fiftyish man with a round face and small eyes and a balding melon head. He smiled and opened his arms and Jeanette embraced him.

Kate's stomach lurched.

A man? Not Jeanette! Anyone but Jeanette! It simply wasn't in her!

Stunned, she watched Jeanette follow him inside. No, this couldn't be. Kate moved out from behind her tree and approached the house. Her sneaker slipped on a wet tree root and she nearly fell, but kept going, stumbling on until she reached the foot of the front stoop. She saw the name *Holdstock* on the mailbox and fought a mad urge to hammer on the door.

Then she noticed silhouettes moving back and forth within the front windows. More than two. What was going on in there?

Kate started toward the nearer of the two windows but changed her mind. Too much light out here. Wouldn't do to have a neighbor pass by and catch her peeking in. She backed away and moved around to the shadowed side of the house. There she crouched between a pair of azalea bushes and peered through the screen into the Holdstock living room.

Six . . . seven—no, eight people in the room. Three men, five women, of varying ages, shapes, and sizes, all taking turns embracing Jeanette as if she were a long-lost relative. And Jeanette was smiling— oh, God, how Kate missed that smile. Days since she'd seen it, days that felt like a lifetime.

An odd group. And even odder that no one seemed to be speaking. Not a word. Apparently they'd been waiting for Jeanette, for immediately after greeting her they all seated themselves in the circle of chairs set up around the room. And still no one spoke. Everyone seemed to know what to do: they joined hands, closed their eyes, let their heads fall back . . . and smiled. Jeanette and all the rest wore beatific smiles, so full of peace and contentment that Kate, for an instant, envied them. They looked as if they were viewing God herself.

And then they began to hum. Not a transcendental "oum," this was a single note, and it went on and on, without a trace of harmony. Everyone humming the same note.

What are you into, Jeanette? A prayer group? Is that what's happened? Your old pantheism couldn't handle a malignant glioma so now you've joined some rapturous fundamentalist sect?

Kate heard a sob and realized it had come from her. She sagged against the bricks, weak with relief.

This I can handle, this I can deal with. As long as you don't reject me . . . us . . . what we've built over the years, I know we can come through this.

She backed away from the window, turning when she reached the front lawn. She gasped as she found a woman standing not two feet away.

"You have had fears, and now they are eased, yes?" A deep voice with a Russian accent.

She looked middle-aged and wore a white hooded cape that fell below her knees. Dark hair framed her face. Kate stepped back when she saw the big white dog standing at her side. It looked like some sort of husky. Its eyes reflected light from the street as it stared at her, but she sensed no hostility.

"You startled me," Kate stammered, not sure how to explain her presence here. "I . . . I was just—"

"You think is perhaps religious group? At worst a cult, yes?" Her dark eyes flashed, her lipsticked gash of a mouth tightened into a thin line as she raised a crooked index finger; she used it to emphasize her words by jabbing it at Kate. "Not cult. Worse than cult. Much worse. If you wish to save the loves of your life you must stop them."

"What?" Kate said, baffled. What was she talking about? "I can't—"

"Of course not. You will need help. Here is number to call." Her other hand wormed from under the cape and held out a card.

Kate hesitated, not knowing what to make of this woman. She seemed composed but her patter was paranoid. And yet . . . she seemed to know about her . . . and Jeanette.

"Take it," the woman said, thrusting the card at her. "And do not waste time. Time is short. Call him tonight. No one else . . . only him."

Kate squinted at the card in the dim light. Getting so hard to read lately—the price to pay for passing forty—and her glasses were tucked away in her bag. She pushed the card to arm's length and angled it for a better view. A phone number and a name, handwritten in an old-fashioned cursive style. She couldn't make out the number but the name was written larger: *Jack.*

That was it—no last name, no address, just . . . Jack.

"Who—?"

She looked up and found herself alone. She hurried out to the sidewalk but the woman and her dog were nowhere to be seen, vanished as if they'd never been.

Am I going crazy? she wondered. But the card in her hand was real.

The woman's words echoed back to her: *If you wish to save the loves of your life . . .*

She'd said *loves,* hadn't she? Yes, Kate was sure of it . . . the woman had used the plural. Kate could think of only three loves in her life: Jeanette, of course, but even before her came Kevin and Elizabeth.

Something twisted in Kate's chest at the thought of her children being in some sort of danger . . . needing to be *saved.*

But how could that be possible? Kevin and Lizzie were safe in Trenton with their father. And what possible danger could the hand-holding, regular middle-class folks in the Holdstock living room pose to her children?

Still the mere hint from someone, even an addled stranger, that they might be in danger jangled Kate's nerves. Danger from what? Attack? They were both teenagers now, but that didn't mean they couldn't be molested.

She glanced back at the house and thought she saw a curtain move in one of the front windows. Had one of the worshipers or whatever they were been watching her?

This was too creepy. As she turned and hurried back toward her waiting cab, more of the old woman's words pursued her.

And do not waste time. Time is short. Call him tonight.

Kate looked at the card. *Jack.* Who was he? Where was he?

2

Riding the Niner.

Sandy Palmer wondered what percentage of his twenty-five years he'd spent bumping and swaying along this particular set of subway tracks back and forth to Morningside Heights. And always in the last car, since that left him a few steps closer to his apartment.

Got to save those steps. He figured everyone was allotted only so many, and if you use them up too fast you're looking at early death or a wheelchair. Obviously marathoners and the hordes of joggers crowding the city parks either were unaware of or gave little credence to the Sandy Palmer theory of step preservation and reclamation. They'd regret it later on.

Sandy glanced around the car at his fellow passengers. Seven years now riding either the Nine or the One, starting with his first semester at Columbia Journalism and the frequent trips down to the Village or SoHo, now every damn day getting jammed in on the way down to midtown and back for his job with *The Light*. And in all that time his fellow riders still looked pretty much the same as they always had. Maybe a few more whites in the mix these days, but not many.

Take this car, for instance: Relatively crowded for a post-rush-hour run, but not SRO. Still a couple of empty seats. Working people— nurse's aides, bus drivers, jackhammer operators, store clerks, short order cooks, garment workers. Their skin tones ran a bell curve, starting with very black, peaking in the mid-browns, and tapering off into lily- white land. After growing up in Caucasian Connecticut, Sandy had had to get used to being a member of a minority on the subway. He'd been a little uneasy at first, thinking that people were staring at him; it took months before he felt comfortable again in his white skin.

The white guy dozing diagonally across from him on the L-shaped plastic bench they shared mid-car looked pretty comfortable. Talk about generic pale male—if Sandy hadn't been thinking about white people he probably wouldn't have noticed him. Clean shaven, brown hair stick- ing out from under the dark blue knit cap pulled down to his eyebrows, an oversized white Jets shirt with a big green 80, jeans, and scuffed work boots. The color of his eyes was up for grabs because they were closed.

Sandy wondered what he did for a living. The clothes gave no clue other than the fact that he wasn't white collar. Clean hands, not overly callused, though his thumbnails seemed unusually long.

The train slowed then and about a third of the passengers rose as signs announcing FORTY-SECOND STREET / TIMES SQUARE started slip- ping past the windows. The generic pale male opened his eyes to check the stop, then closed them again. Mild brown eyes. Definitely a GPM— an infinitely interchangeable example of the species.

Not like me, he thought. With my blond hair, hazel eyes, thick glasses, this big nose, and acne scars left over from my pre-Accutane teenage years, anyone could pick me out of a lineup in a minute.

New riders replaced those debarking almost one for one, spreading through the car in search of seats. He saw a slim young woman move toward a double seat at the very front of the car, but the man in it, a scraggly-bearded Asian guy in a stained fatigue jacket, with wild hair and wilder eyes, had his gym bag and a boom box on the empty half and he brusquely waved her away.

Wisely, she didn't argue—he looked like the sort who was heavy into soliloquies—and went elsewhere in search of a seat. Sandy figured that was a potential blessing in disguise because she was moving toward the middle of the car, toward him.

Keep coming, he thought, wishing he were telepathic. I've got your seat—right here next to me.

She looked about twenty or so, all in black—sweater, tights, shoes, even the wire rims on her tiny funky glasses. She'd done one of those shoe-black dye jobs on her short, Winona Ryder-style hair, which made her pale face—not Winona Ryder's face, unfortunately, but still pretty—look all the paler.

Sandy slid to his left, leaving half of his butt off the edge of the seat to give her plenty of room. She took the bait and slipped in next to him. She didn't look at him, simply opened her book and began to read.

Instead of rejoicing, Sandy felt his insides tighten. What now? What to say?

Relax, he told himself. Just take a deep breath, figure out what you can about her, and see if you can find some common ground.

Easy to say, but so hard to do. At least for Sandy. He'd never done too well with women. He'd been to a couple of the campus counselors when he was a student and they'd both said the same thing: fear of rejection.

As if someone needed a Ph.D. to tell him that. Of *course* he feared rejection. Nobody in the whole damn world liked rejection, but that didn't seem to stop people from courting it by coming on to each other with the lamest, sappiest lines. So why did the mere possibility of rejection paralyze him? The counselors liked to tell him the *why* of the fear didn't matter so much as overcoming it.

Okay, he thought. Let's overcome this. What have we got here? We've got a book-reading Goth chick heading uptown on the 9 express. Got to be a student. Probably Barnard.

As the train lurched into motion again, he checked out her book: *Hitchcock* by François Truffaut.

Bingo. Film student. Columbia.

Okay. Here goes.

He wet his lips, swallowed, took that deep breath . . .

"Going for your film M.F.A., right?" he said.

And waited.

Nothing. She didn't turn her head, didn't even blink. She did move, but just to turn the page of her book. He might as well have used sign language on a blind person.

But he knew he hadn't imagined speaking, knew he must have been audible because the GPM opened one of his eyes for a two-second look his way, then closed it again. Reminded Sandy of Duffy, their family cat: a one-eyed glance—two would require too much energy—was the only acknowledgment that chunky old tom granted when someone new entered his presence.

So now what? He felt like he was back in high school after asking some girl if she wanted to dance and she'd just said no. That had happened only once but that once had been enough to stop him from ever asking anyone again. Should he retreat now? Slink away and hide his head? Or push it?

Push it.

He raised his voice. "I said, are you going for your film M.F.A.?"

She looked up, glanced at him with dark brown eyes for maybe a whole millisecond, then went back to her book.

"Yes," she said, but she spoke to the book.

"I like Hitchcock," he told her.

Again to the book: "Most people do."

This was going nowhere fast. Maybe she'd warm up if she knew he'd gone to Columbia, too.

"I graduated from the School of Journalism a couple of years ago."

"Congratulations."

That did it, Sandy, he thought. That broke the ice. She's really hot for you now. Shit, why didn't you just keep your mouth shut?

He racked his brain for another line. He'd already been given the cold shoulder; nothing left to lose now. He'd swum beyond his point of no return, so he had to keep going. She was either going to let him drown in a sea of rejection or send him a lifeboat.

He smiled. Just the kind of crappy imagery his journalism professors had tried to scour from his brain. One had even told him he wrote the most cliché-ridden prose he'd ever read. But what was the big deal about clichés? They served a purpose in journalism, especially tabloid journalism. Readers understood them, *expected* them, and probably felt something was missing if they didn't run across a couple.

The sudden blast of music from the front of the car cut off the thought. Sandy looked around and saw that the wild-haired guy in the fatigue jacket had turned on his boom box and cranked it up to full volume. It was pumping out a sixties tune Sandy half knew—"Time Has Come Today" by the Something-or-other Brothers.

Back to the film student. Maybe he should dazzle her by mentioning his great job at the city's most infamous weekly tabloid, *The Light*, where his degree from one of the country's great journalism programs landed him an entry-level position one step above the janitorial staff— except in pay. Or how he's been doing interviews at every other paper around the city trying to move up from *The Light* and no one's calling back. That'll impress her.

Oh, hell, go for gold and let her put you out of your misery.

"What's your name?"

Without missing a beat she said, "Lina Wertmüller."

Not just unfriendly, she thinks I'm an idiot. Well two can play that game.

Sandy stuck out his hand. "Glad to meet you, Lina. I'm Henry Louis Mencken, but you can call me H. L."

To Sandy's shock she lifted her head and laughed. He'd made a funny and she'd *laughed*. What a wonderful sound, even if he could barely hear it over the blasting music.

And then the name of the group behind the song came to him: the Chambers Brothers.

Suddenly—other sounds. Shouts, cries, screams, and people stumbling, scrambling past him in a mad rush toward the rear end of the car.

"It's time now!" cried a voice. "Yes, it's time."

Sandy turned and saw the Asian in the fatigue jacket standing before the door at the front end of the car. His black eyes were mad, endlessly, vacantly mad, and he clutched in each hand a black pistol that seemed too long and too thick in the barrel. Then Sandy realized they were equipped with silencers.

Oh, Christ, he thought, shock launching him to his feet, he's going to start shooting.

And then he saw the bodies and the blood and knew that the shooting had already begun. Images flashed through his instantly adrenalized brain as he turned to run—not everyone from the front of the car had made it to the rear; the first to be shot lay where they'd fallen . . .

. . . like the Korean guy, maybe Sandy's age, with rust-colored hair and a Nike swoosh on his cap, sprawled on the red-splattered floor, facing Sandy with his headphones still on his ears, blood leaking from his nose, and black eyes staring into the beyond . . .

. . . like the heavy black woman in the two-piece sleeveless gray suit over a black polka dotted white blouse with starched pristine cuffs, lying face down, still twitching as the last of her life ran out from under her wig and stained the copy of *Rolie Polie Olie* that had spilled from her Barnes and Noble bag . . .

. . . or the others who'd hit the deck and now huddled and crouched and cringed between seats, holding up their hands palm out as if to stop the bullets, and pleading for mercy . . .

But they were asking the wrong guy, because the man with the guns was tuned to some other frequency as he shuffled along the aisle, swinging his pistols left and right and pumping bullets through the silencers. *Phut! . . . phut! . . . phut!* The sounds barely audible through the music as slugs tore into heads and tear-stained faces, sometimes right through the supplicating hands. He moved without the slightest hint of urgency, looking for all the world like a suburban homeowner on a sunny Saturday morning strolling his lawn with a can of herbicide and casually spraying the weeds he passed.

And somewhere up there, up front, someone's bowels had let loose and the stink was filling the car.

Brain screaming in panic, Sandy ducked and swung around and saw the GPM crouched behind his seat, facing the rear of the car, and he must have lost it because he was shouting something that sounded like, "Doesn't anyone have a goddamn gun?"

Yeah, asshole! Sandy wanted to say. The guy standing in the aisle has two, and he's coming your way!

Turning further Sandy came face to face with Lina or whoever she was and knew the naked fear in her blanched face must have mirrored his own. He looked past her at the rest of the screaming, panicked riders crammed like a mass of worms into the rear of the car, the nearer ones wriggling, kicking, biting, clawing to get further to the rear and the ones at the very back battling with all they had to stay where they were, and suddenly Sandy knew what the others had already discovered—that once you got back there you had nowhere to go unless you could find a way to open the rear door and jump onto the tracks at who-knew-how-many-miles an hour and hope that if you were lucky enough not to break your neck when you hit, you wouldn't land on the third rail and get fried to a cinder.

He saw a brown hand snake upward at the rear of the press, grip the red emergency handle, and yank down . . .

Yes!

Saw the handle come free as the cord snapped.

And just then the Fifty-ninth Street/Columbus Circle station lit up around the train but it didn't slow because oh shit it was going to skip Sixty-sixth Street as well and not stop until Seventy-second.

Seventy-second! No wonder the gunman was in no hurry. He had his prey cornered like cattle in a stockyard pen and could slaughter them at will—kill just about everyone before the train reached its next stop.

Sandy saw only one chance to save his life. If he could get to the rear there, worm his way through the massed crowd, even if he had to do it on hands and knees—he was thin, he could do it—and get as far back as he could and crawl under a seat, maybe he could survive until Seventy-second Street. That would be the end of it. When the doors opened the gunman would take off or blow his own brains out, and Sandy would be safe. All he had to do was survive until then.

Another glance at the gunman showed him pointing one of his pistols down at someone Sandy couldn't see. The only visible part of the next victim was a pair of hands raised above the back of a seat, a woman's hands, mocha colored, nails painted bright red, fingers interlocked as if in prayer.

Even more frightening was the realization that this faceless woman and the GPM appeared to be the last living people between Sandy and the killer. Panic took a choke hold on his throat as he turned and lunged toward the rear of the car—oh sweet Jesus he didn't want to die he was too young and he hadn't really begun to live so he couldn't die now oh please not now not now—but the film student was there, half in, half out of a crouch and he slammed against her, knocking her over, and they both went down, Sandy landing on top as they hit the floor.

He was losing it now, ready to scream at the bitch for getting in his way, but more important than screaming was knowing right now, right this instant where the gunman was, so he looked back, praying he wouldn't see that impassive bearded face looming behind the muzzle of a silencer. Instead he saw the GPM, whose face was set into grim lines of fury and whose eyes now were anything but mild, and he was muttering, "Shit-shit-shit!" and pulling up the cuff of his jeans where something leather was strapped and then he was yanking a metallic object from the leather and Sandy saw it was a tiny pistol. At first he thought it was one of those old-fashioned Derringers women and gamblers carried in westerns but when he saw the dude work the little slide back and forth he realized it was a miniature automatic.

And now the GPM—Sandy was finding it hard to think of him as generic anymore but didn't have any other handle for the guy—was on his feet and moving toward the killer and Sandy wondered, What's he think he's going to do with that little pop gun? and then it went off and after the dainty little *phuts* of the killer's guns the sound was like a cannon in the confines of the subway car and the bullet must have caught the killer in the shoulder because that was where his fatigue jacket exploded in red, knocking him back and spinning him half around. He screamed in pain and stared with eyes full of shock and wonder and fear at this guy coming at him from out of nowhere. Sandy couldn't see the GPM's face as he worked the slide to his pistol again, just the back of his head and not much of that thanks to the knit cap, but he did see the woman who'd been the next intended victim crawl out from where she'd been cowering on the floor and scrabble past the dude on her belly, her teary eyes showing white all around, her lip-sticked mouth a scarlet O of terror.

Then the killer started to raise the gun in his good hand but the GPM was still moving toward him like an eagle swooping in on a field mouse, had that little pistol raised and it boomed again, the recoil jerking his hand high in the air, the second bullet detonating another explosion of red, this time in the killer's other shoulder, knocking him back against one of the chrome hang-on poles in the center of the aisle where he sagged, both arms limp and useless at his sides, and gaped at the relentless man moving ever closer. He roared and lunged forward, whether to head-butt or bite the GPM no one would ever know, because without pausing, without the slightest hint of hesitation the GPM leveled that toy pistol at the killer's left eye and let it boom again. Sandy saw the killer's head snap back and the impact swing him halfway around the pole before he lurched free to do a loose-kneed pirouette and collapse, half sitting, half sprawled against one of the doors, very, very, very dead.

And then the GPM was working the little slide on his little gun again, and a fourth boom, this into the tape player, reducing it to a thousand flying black fragments and stopping its incessant cries about time having come today.

Stunned silence in the car after that final report—only the rattle of the wheels and the whistle of the wind racing past.

Saved!

The word batted around the inside of Sandy's head, bouncing off the walls, looking for purchase on the disbelieving, rejecting surfaces. Finally it landed and took root as Sandy accepted the glorious possibility that he would see tomorrow.

And he wasn't alone. Cheers and cries of joy arose from the multitude packed like sardines at the rear of the car. Some were on their knees, tears on their faces and hands raised to heaven, thanking whoever or whatever they called god for deliverance; others were laughing and crying and hugging each other.

"We're alive!" the film student under him said. "What—?"

Abashed, Sandy rolled off of her. "Sorry."

She sat up and stared at him. "God, I can't believe you did that!"

"Please," he said, looking away to hide his shame. He saw the GPM in a crouch, picking up something from the floor, but couldn't focus on what he was doing. Sandy had to frame an answer. How could he explain the terror that had taken control of him? "I don't know what came over me. I—"

"You shielded me with your own body!"

What? He turned and found her staring at him, her chocolate-brown eyes wide and wonder filled.

"I've heard of it and, you know, seen it in films, but I never believed—I mean, you were like some Secret Service agent!"

And then her face screwed up and she started to cry . . . huge racking sobs that shook her fragile body.

Sandy's befuddled brain finally registered that she thought he'd knocked her down and landed on her to protect her. What did he say to that?

But before he could respond he heard a voice call out behind him.

"We've got a lady who's still alive here! Somebody get up here and help her!"

Sandy turned and saw that the GPM had turned to face the rest of the car, but he'd first stretched his knit cap down to his chin. The effect might have been comical but for that deadly little pistol still clutched in his hand. What was going on here? A few moments ago he'd had his face out in the open for everyone to see. Why hide it now?

"Come on!" he shouted through the weave. "Someone move their ass up here, goddamn it!"

A young black woman with cornrowed hair, wearing white pants and a blue sweater stepped forward.

"I'm an OR tech. I know a little—"

"Well, come on then! Maybe you can save one of your fellow ewes!"

She edged forward, giving Sandy an uneasy look as she slipped past him and hurried to a woman who was moaning and clutching her bloody head. He understood her uncertainty. What he didn't understand was the anger in the GPM's voice.

"Why me?" the man shouted. "Why do I have to save your sorry asses? I don't know you, I don't care about you, I want nothing to do with you, so why me? Why did I get stuck with it?"

"Hey, mister," said a tall lean black fellow who could have been a minister. "Why you so riled at us? We didn't do nothing."

"Exactly! That's the problem! Why didn't one of *you* put him down?"

"We didn't have no gun!" someone else said.

"And this creep knew that. He knew he'd be dealing with a herd of human sheep. Losers! You make me sick—all of you!"

This was scary. The dude seemed almost as crazy now as the mass murderer he'd just killed. Sandy was beginning to wonder whether they'd traded one maniac for another when the train roared into the Seventy-second Street station. He saw the GPM pocket his pistol and turn toward the door. As soon as the panels parted he leaped through and dashed across the platform. In a flash he was lost among the crowd.

3

Keeping his head down, Jack dodged through the people waiting on the narrow platform. Pulled his cap up as far as the bridge of his nose and kept one hand on his face, rubbing his cheeks and eyes as if they were irritated.

Of all the luck! Of all the lousy goddamn luck! Why on my train, in my car?

Someone in that car had seen his face, would remember it, give out a decent description, and by tomorrow his likeness would be on the front page of every paper in the city and flashing across TV screens every hour.

Maybe I should leave town tonight. And never come back.

But his face would be plastered all over the national news as well—*Time, Newsweek*, the network and cable shows. He'd be on every newsstand everywhere. Even if the likeness wasn't good, sooner or later someone would make a connection and point a finger.

And then life as Jack knew it would be over.

Yanked off the cap as soon as he hit the stairs, taking them two at a time while he pulled off his football jersey. Stuffed that into the hat and wadded it all into a tight little bundle. Hit street level as a bare-headed guy in a white T-shirt carrying something blue.

Keep your head, he told himself. You've still got options.

But did he? At the moment he hadn't a clue what they were. Knew there had to be some but right now his adrenaline-addled brain was too wired, too pissed to think of them.

The Seventy-second Street station opened onto a wrought-iron fenced island in the middle of the perpetual vehicular chaos where Broadway forced its way on a diagonal across Amsterdam Avenue. His

27

instincts wanted him in a full-tilt sprint away from the station, urged him to jump the fence and skip through the traffic, but he forced his legs to keep to a walk.

Don't attract attention—that was the key here.

Vibrating like a nitro-fueled hotrod at the start line, Jack stood with half a dozen other pedestrians and waited for the walking green. When it came he crossed and headed east on Seventy-second, which was perfect because, as one of the handful of two-way cross streets in the city, it was busy at this hour. No one else here seemed in a hurry, so he adopted a loose-limbed but steady amble to blend in. He slipped through the shoppers and the locals hanging out on this mild June night, all unaware of the bloody horror in the subway car a few dozen feet below. Two blocks ahead lay Central Park. The anonymity of its cool shadows beckoned to him.

What a horror show. He'd read about that sort of thing in the papers but never expected to be an eyewitness. What drove someone to that sort of mad carnage?

Damn good thing he rarely traveled without the Semmerling, but still he raged that he'd been forced to use it in front of all those citizens. Not that he'd had a choice. If he'd waited for someone in that crowd of sheep to save *his* ass, he and a lot of others would be as dead now as the poor souls splattered all over that subway car.

Why me, damn it? Why couldn't someone else play hero?

Hero . . . no doubt that was what they'd call him if he'd hung around, but that would last only the proverbial New York minute—right up until they escorted him to the cooler for illegal possession of an unregistered weapon and carrying said weapon without a permit. And sure as all hell some shyster would dig up the shooter's family and have them sue him for wrongful death and excessive use of force. And how long before the papers learned that he didn't have a job, or a known address, wasn't registered to vote or licensed to drive—hell, didn't even have a Social Security number? Then the tax boys would want to know why he'd never filed a return. On and on it would go, spinning out of control, engulfing him, ensuring that he never took another free breath for the rest of his life.

Jack picked up his pace a little once he crossed Columbus, leaving the shops and restaurants behind and walking through the ultra-high-rent district. Almost to Central Park West, he passed the two liveried gatekeepers outside the Dakota who kept watch on the spot where another gun-wielding lunatic had done his bloody work in 1980 and ended an era.

He crossed CPW and stopped at the mossy, soot-encrusted, rib-high wall of textured brownstone. The park lay just beyond . . . tempting . . . but if he entered here he'd have to exit somewhere else; his best bet would be to get out of sight as soon as possible. His apartment was less than half a mile from here. An easy walk. But first . . .

He stepped through an opening in the wall and entered the shadowed underbrush. Once out of sight he pulled his shirt from the cap and dropped it in a puddle. A dozen feet farther on he shoved the cap into a tangle of vines, then angled around and made his way back out to the sidewalk.

Keeping to the park side, he lengthened his stride and headed uptown. To his left, echoing along the concrete canyons, sirens began to wail.

4

Sandy Palmer crouched in an uptown corner of the Seventy-second Street subway platform with *The Light*'s editor on the other end of his cell phone. The connection was tenuous from this underground spot, and he feared losing it at any second.

George Meschke's voice growled in his ear. At first he'd been pissed at being disturbed at home, now he was all ears. "You're sure you've got that number right?"

"Absolutely."

"Six dead?"

"As doornails. Two men and four women—I counted them twice before I left the car." Sandy peered through the controlled chaos farther down the platform. "A seventh victim, a black woman, was still alive but with an ugly head wound. The EMTs are just taking her away."

"You're amazing, kid," Meschke said. "I don't know how you kept your cool. I'd've lost it after going through what you've just told me."

"Cool as a cucumber," Sandy said. "That's me."

He neglected to mention that he'd given up dinner soon after the train had stopped. Even now—what, fifteen minutes later?—his hands were still shaking.

Those first moments were something of a blur. He remembered seeing the GPM run out, and his abrupt exit had seemed to throw a switch in the crowd. Suddenly everybody wanted out—immediately if not sooner. Sandy had had to pull aside the still sobbing film student from the mass exodus to keep her from being trampled.

As he'd helped her to her feet he'd realized he had a golden opportunity here: he was a trained journalist who'd witnessed a front-page crime. If he could gather his senses, focus on the details, and make the most of the fact that he was his own primary source, he could accomplish something here, something big.

"What's your name?" he'd asked the shaken young woman. "Your real name?"

"Beth." Her voice was barely audible, her skin so white she looked almost blue.

"Come on. Let's get you out of here."

As he'd moved behind her, guiding her, half supporting her, he turned and checked out the front end of the car . . . the sprawled bodies of the victims . . . the killer, whose upper half had fallen through the doors when they opened, lying half in and half out of the car . . . the OR tech still tending to the wounded woman . . . and the blood, good Christ, the blood—the whole end of the car was awash in pools of it. Who'd have thought people could hold so much blood? And the smell— books always described the smell of blood as coppery, but Sandy had no idea what the hell copper smelled like, only that the whole car reeked of death and unimaginable violence and suddenly he couldn't breathe and the hot dog and Mountain Dew he'd wolfed down on the run after work couldn't stay where they were, wanted out of him as urgently as he'd wanted out of that charnel house on wheels.

And so as he propelled Beth ahead of him and stepped into the marginally fresher air of the station, his stomach heaved and ejected its contents in a sour, burning arc that disappeared into the dark chasm between the train and the edge of the platform.

Wiping his mouth Sandy looked around and hoped that no one had noticed. No one seemed to. After what they'd all been through, vomiting was a nonevent.

He'd then become aware of the noise that filled the station—the cries, the moans, the wails of the survivors who'd just escaped mixing with the screams of the waiting would-be passengers as they got a look inside and turned away with wide eyes and slack jaws. He noticed some getting sick just as he had, or collapsing onto benches and weeping, or simply slumping to the concrete platform.

He'd also noticed others hightailing it up the stairs, those who either didn't want to be questioned by the police, or didn't want to get involved in any way.

Sandy very much wanted to be involved—up to his eyeballs.

He'd found an empty spot on an initial-gouged wooden bench and eased Beth into it. Behind him he heard the automatic doors hiss closed after their programmed interval. He whirled, afraid the train would leave, but no chance of that: the killer's body was blocking one set of doors from closing—they kept pincering his corpse, then rebounding, closing again, and rebounding . . .

A conductor trotted down, his annoyed expression melting to horror, his forward charge stuttering to a halt when he saw the carnage, reversing to a wobbly-kneed retreat as he staggered away for help.

Sandy noticed a woman nearby sobbing into her cell phone. "Nine-one-one?" he asked.

She nodded.

Good. That meant the cops would be here in minutes. Scanner-equipped stringers and reporters wouldn't be far behind. He didn't have much time to get ahead of them.

"You'll be okay if I leave you here for a bit?" he'd said to Beth.

She'd nodded but said nothing. She was sobbing again. He felt bad leaving her but . . .

"I'll only be a couple of minutes."

Sandy had hurried then down to the far end of the platform where he could have some privacy and hear himself think. He wondered why he wasn't coming apart like so many of the others. He had no illusions about his inner toughness—he'd had lessons in piano, tennis, even karate, but none in machismo. Maybe it was because he had a job to do, and when he'd finished he too would fall apart. He hoped not.

That was when he'd got hold of George Meschke. He hadn't been sure what he'd accomplish. *The Light* was a weekly, published on Wednesdays, and tomorrow's issue had already been put to bed. But Meschke was the editor, this was news, and he seemed to be the one to call.

Cops and emergency teams had flooded into the station and he related everything as he'd seen it.

"This is great stuff, Palmer. Amazing stuff."

"Yeah, but what can we do with it? This week's issue is set." Never before had Sandy wished so fiercely that he worked for a daily.

"Not anymore. As soon as I hang up with you I'm calling everyone in and we're going to scrap the first three pages. Redo them top to bottom. I'm going to rough this out pretty much as you told it to me. It'll be your story—your first-person account—under your byline with a front page go-to."

"My byline—front page? *My* byline?" Sandy resisted the urge to jump up and do an arm-pumping victory dance. This was not the time or place. "You mean that?"

"Damn right. Now get off the phone and nose around there. Pick up as much as you can. The *Times*, the *Post*, and the *News* will be stuck up on street level. You're the only one down below, Palmer, so milk this dry. Then rush down here and we'll see about doing a box feature. Hell, with an eyewitness on staff, we're going to be *the* paper on this story."

"You got it, George. But listen. I've thought of a headline."

"Give it to me."

" 'Underground Galahad.' "

"I don't think so."

"How about 'Nightmare on the Nine'?"

"Better. But let's leave the headline for later. Concentrate on your first-person opportunity down there."

"Sure. Talk to you soon."

Sandy snapped the phone shut and leaped up from his crouch. His nerve endings sang. Front page . . . his own byline . . . on a major story—the story of the year! This was better than sex!

As he started back toward the chaos, he realized he was probably grinning like a nerd who'd just lost his virginity. He wiped it off. And slowed his bounding pace. Had to be professional here. This was a monster leg up for his career and he'd better not blow it.

The NYPD had swarmed in and taken command. Plainclothes detectives and uniforms were everywhere, sectioning off the platform with yellow crime scene tape, stretching more between columns and across stairways.

They'd herded the survivors into one area. As Sandy approached he noticed some looking dazed, some still sobbing, one hysterical, a few trying to hide the large wet spots on their pants, all coming down from the adrenaline overload of fearing for their lives as cops tried to take statements from the more coherent ones.

Sandy wove slowly through the crowd, pausing to listen whenever and wherever he could.

". . . and then out of nowhere, this savior appeared," said a stooped old woman in a wrinkled blue dress.

"What did he look like, ma'am?" said the female officer bending over her with notebook in hand.

"Like Jesus."

"You mean he had long hair?"

"No."

"Short, then?"

"Not exactly."

"Can you tell me what he looked like?"

"We were not to look upon his face . . ."

Sandy moved on, pausing again by the tall ministerial black man he recognized from the death car.

". . . and so then I spoke to him."

"Spoke to who? The second shooter?"

"We think of him as the Savior."

" 'We'?"

"We who were blessed enough to survive. When we were freed from the train, someone said, 'Who was he? Who was our savior?' And that's how we now refer to him."

"Can you give me a description of this 'savior,' sir?"

"Medium build, brown hair . . . I can't tell you much about his face because I didn't see it. He had this hat, you see, and he pulled it down to hide his face."

"How tall was he?"

"I'd say average height. Shorter than me, anyway."

Sandy kept moving, taking a circuitous route back to Beth, and along the way he kept hearing his fellow survivors trying and failing to describe this man they were calling 'the Savior.' He understood their problem: a guy so unremarkable seemed virtually invisible. Sandy had tagged him GPM for that very reason: he was a paradigm of the generic pale male.

He found Beth again but now she wasn't alone. A plainclothesman was seated next to her, his notebook held at the ready. Beth had her hands stuffed stiff-armed between her knees and was still shaking. Sandy knelt beside her. She jumped when he laid a hand on her shoulder.

"Oh, it's you," she said with a nervous flicker of a smile.

"And you are . . . ?" said the detective.

"Sandy Palmer. I was on the train with Beth."

"Have you given a statement yet?"

The word *no* was approaching his lips when a subliminal warning from somewhere in his subconscious made him pull it back.

"Who's that policewoman back there?" he said, trying to avoid getting caught in a lie later. "I forget her name."

The detective nodded. "Were you able to get a look at the second shooter?"

"You mean the Savior?" Sandy replied.

"Whatever."

To avoid a direct answer Sandy turned to Beth. "You saw him, didn't you, Beth?"

She shook her head.

"But you were right there, just a couple of feet from him."

"But I wasn't looking at him. I barely looked at you, if you remember."

Sandy smiled. "I remember."

"I mean, I saw his back when he went after the killer—wait! He had a name on the back of his shirt!"

The detective leaned forward, his pencil poised over his pad. "What did it say?"

Beth squeezed her eyes shut. "It was all such a blur, but I think it said 'Sherbert' or something like that that."

"Sherbert?" the detective said, scribbling. "You're sure?"

Sandy rubbed a hand over his mouth to hide a smile. "Chrebet," he offered. "I remember now. He was wearing a green-on-white Jets jersey. Number eighty."

"Christ," the detective muttered, shaking his head as he scratched out a line on his pad with hard, annoyed strokes. "I think we can figure it wasn't Wayne Chrebet."

"You know him?" Beth said.

"Wide receiver for the Jets," Sandy replied, then added, "That's a football team."

"Oh." She seemed to shrink a little. "I hate football."

"You didn't see his face?" the detective said.

"No. He had it covered when he turned around." She turned to Sandy. "You didn't see him either?"

Sandy wet his lips. An idea was forming. Its boldness tied his gut into knots but its potential made him giddy. It meant going out on a limb—far out on a very slim limb. But then, nothing ventured, nothing gained . . .

"I saw what you saw," he said.

"Shit," the detective muttered and slapped his notebook against his thigh. "What was this guy—invisible?"

"When can we leave?" Beth said. "I want to go home."

"Soon, miss," the detective said, softening. "Soon as we get names and addresses and statements from all you witnesses, we'll see that you all get home safely."

As the cop moved off, Sandy leaned close to Beth and whispered, "I'm getting stir crazy. I've got to move around. You'll be okay for a few minutes?" He didn't know why but somehow he felt responsible for her.

"Sure," she said. "Not like there aren't any cops around."

"Good point."

He left her and edged back toward the death car where flashes from the forensic team's cameras kept lighting the interior like welders' arcs. He noticed a cluster of three plainclothesmen and one uniform gathered outside one of the open sets of doors. Farther on, a man wearing latex gloves—from the forensics team, no doubt—examined the killer where he'd fallen through the doorway.

Sandy needed to be over there, needed to hear what these cops were saying, but he couldn't get his feet to move. One step past that tape and he'd be sent scurrying back with his tail between his legs to stay put with the rest of the survivors. But he wasn't just a survivor, he was the press too, damn it—the people's right to know and all that.

He tried to remember techniques from that assertiveness training course he'd taken last year but came up blank except for the old bromide about how the worst that could happen was that someone simply would say *No.*

But fearing rejection, of all things, seemed more than silly after what he'd just been through.

Sandy pulled his press card from his wallet and palmed it. A quick glance around showed no one looking his way. He noticed that one of the plainclothes cops was pretty big. Huge, in fact. Choosing an angle of approach that used the big guy's bulk as a shield, Sandy ducked under the yellow tape and sidled up to the foursome, listening, taking mental notes.

". . . like the second shooter knew what he was doing."

"How you mean?"

"According to what we're hearing he got the crazy in the shoulders first, then blew him away."

"Fucking executed him's more like it. But what was he carrying? Nobody can tell us anything about his gun except it was real small."

"And holds at least four rounds."

"Not a .22, I can tell you that. Not a .32 either from the size of the crazy's wounds. Guy took his brass with him so we can't use that."

"The whole thing's weird—including the way he blew away the crazy. I mean, why not just do the head shot and have it done with?"

" 'Cause if you miss that first head shot—and if we're talking about a tiny little barrel, there's a damn good chance you will—you're a goner because this Colin Ferguson wannabe's got a pair of nines and he's going to blow you away. So if you're smart you do what our guy does: you go for an arm and—"

"Seems low percentage to me. I'd go for center of mass."

"Fine—unless he's wearing a vest. And witnesses say the crazy was turned sideways when he took the first hit. An arm's bigger than a head, and even a miss has got a good chance at the torso, vested or not. So our guy goes for an arm and makes the shot. Now there's one less gun to deal with, and he's also a few steps closer. So now it's easier to take out the other arm."

"Sounds like he's been trained."

"Damn straight. Taking his brass with him says he's a pro. But trained by who? With both arms messed up, the crazy wasn't going to do any more shooting. Could've left him like that. But he finished him off."

"But good."

"Probably didn't want to hear about 'yellow rage' for the next two years."

"Like I said—a fucking execution."

"You got complaints about that, McCann?"

"Maybe. Maybe I don't like executioners running around loose."

"Which is probably just why he took off. He—"

The black plainclothesman speaking caught sight of Sandy over the big guy's shoulder and pointed at him. "*You* are in a restricted area."

"Press," Sandy forced himself to exclaim, holding up his card.

Suddenly he found himself the object of an array of outraged expressions.

"How the hell—?"

"And an eyewitness," he quickly added.

That mollified them somewhat, until the big detective, the one they'd called McCann, florid faced with thinning gray brush-cut hair, looking a little like Brian Dennehy, stepped in for a closer look at his press card. His breath reeked of a recent cigar.

"*The Light*? Christ, he's from the fucking *Light*! Aliens and pierced eyeballs! Oh, shit, are you guys gonna have a ball with this!"

"That was the old days. We're different now."

It was true. The new owner had moved *The Light* away from the shock-schlock format that had made it notorious decades ago—every issue with an eye injury on page three, with photo if possible, and an alien story on page five—into a kinder, gentler scandal sheet, concentrating on celebrity foibles.

"Yeah? I wouldn't know."

"Of course not," Sandy said, feeling braver now. "Nobody but nobody reads *The Light*. Yet somehow the issues keep disappearing from the newsstands."

"Probably those aliens," McCann said. "Tell me, did your journalist's powers of observation happen to register a description of the second shooter's face?"

Sandy had already settled on how to play this. He shook his head. "No. But I know someone who did."

He was suddenly the center of attention, all four of the cops *who*-ing like a chorus of owls.

Sandy pointed to the killer. "Him."

"A wise-ass," McCann said. "Just what we need." He gave Sandy a dismissive wave. "Get back on the other side of the tape with the other useless witnesses."

Sandy managed not to move. He couldn't let this happen. What could he say? One of his therapist's remarks about every relationship being a negotiation of sorts filtered back to him. Negotiate . . . what did he have to offer?

The gun. They'd been talking about the gun, wondering what kind, and Sandy'd had the best look at it.

"Okay," Sandy said, turning and staring to move away. "I came over here because I got a good look at his gun. But if you're not interested—"

"Hold it," said McCann. "You better not be playing any games here, newsboy, or you're gonna find your ass in a sling."

Again he had their attention. Now he had to play this just right. Negotiate. Give them something they needed, something real, and in return get to hang here where the action was. But he sensed that a direct quid-pro-quo offer would only land him in hot water. Damn, he wished he had more experience at this.

Okay, just wing it and hope they're grateful.

"He pulled it out of an ankle holster."

The detectives glanced at each other. The black one nodded. "Go on. You know the difference between a revolver and an automatic?"

"It looked like an automatic. I saw him pull back the slide before he started toward the killer, but . . ."

"But what?"

"Maybe it wasn't working right because he pulled the slide back before every shot."

"I'll be damned!" said the lone uniform. "Could be a Semmerling."

"A what?" McCann said.

"Semmerling LM-4. Supposedly the world's smallest .45. Saw one at a gun show once. Would have picked it up if I'd had the dough. Looks like a semi-auto—has the slide and all—but it's really just a repeater."

"How small?" McCann wanted to know. He was looking Sandy's way.

Sandy tried to remember. "Everything happened so fast . . . but I think"—he straightened his fingers and placed his palm against his hip—"I think I could cover it with my hand."

McCann looked back to the uniform. "That about right?"

A nod. "I'd say so."

"Sounds like a stupid piece to me," the black detective said.

"Not if you want maximum stopping power in a little package."

"C'mere," McCann said to Sandy, motioning him to follow.

Sandy stayed right on the big detective's heels. Oh, yes. This was *just* what he'd been hoping for.

But when they came upon the killer's corpse he wasn't so sure. Close up like this he could see that the man's shoulder wounds were worse than he'd thought. And his face . . . the right eye socket was a bloody hole and the remaining eye was bulging half out of its socket . . . his face was all swollen . . . in fact his head seemed half again its normal size.

Be careful what you wish for, Sandy thought, averting his gaze as stomach acid pushed to the back of his throat.

He swallowed and looked again at the corpse. What a photo that would make. He felt in his pocket for the mini-Olympus he always carried. Did he dare?

"Hey, Kastner," McCann said to the gloved man leaning over the killer. "Your best guess on the caliber—and I won't hold you to it."

"Don't have to guess. If these wounds aren't from a .45, I'm in the wrong biz."

McCann nodded. "Okay. So our second shooter wanders around with something called a Semmerling LM-4 strapped to his ankle."

"Not exactly government issue," the black detective grunted. "And hey, if the crazy was hit with a .45, how come his brains aren't splattered all over the car?"

"Because the second shooter was using frangibles," Kastner the forensics man said.

"Whoa!" said the uniform.

"Frangibles?" Sandy asked. "What's a frangible?"

"A bullet that breaks up into pieces after it hits."

"*Lots* of pieces that bounce all over," Kastner commented. "They're going to find puree du brain when they crack this guy's cranium."

McCann turned to the black detective. "Which brings us back to what I said before, Rawlins: an execution."

With McCann not looking, Sandy had his chance. Carefully he wormed his camera out of his pocket and pointed it toward the corpse. He couldn't risk a flash but the lights looked bright enough. He covered the flash with a thumb. A quick glance showed Rawlins and the others facing McCann.

"Doin' a crazy who's just blown away half a dozen good people and on track to do a dozen or two more?" Rawlins said, pursing his lips and shaking his head. "That's not an execution, that's putting down a mad dog. That's steppin' on a cockroach."

Keeping his face toward the cops, Sandy held the camera at hip level and started shooting.

"Maybe," McCann was saying. "But I like to know who's doing the stepping."

After half a dozen quick frames Sandy slipped the camera back into his pocket. He was sweating. He felt as if he'd just done a two-mile sprint.

"Easy enough in this case," Rawlins said, breaking into a grin. "We just roust all the average-height-medium-built-brown-haired white guys in the five boroughs and check their ankles for holsters."

"We'll find him," McCann said. "Guy does something like this, saves a carload of lives, he thinks he's a hero. He's gonna tell someone. No way he'll be able to keep his yap shut. And then we'll have him."

"And then what?" Sandy said, alarmed. They were talking about the man who'd saved his life. "What'll you do to him?"

McCann squinted at him. "Probably nothing. A lot of people are gonna want to give him a ticker-tape parade—I know you and everyone else on that car sure as shit will—but plenty of others won't be so keen. He may have saved lives, but he's also probably some sort of gun nut, and as of tonight he's a killer. Not exactly the perfect poster boy for civic responsibility."

"You want to lock him up?" Sandy said.

McCann shook his head. "Not particularly. But I do want to know who he is. Anybody who wanders through my precinct carrying that kind of firepower and who's able to use it to such deadly effect, I want to know about."

"But you have no description beyond average-height-medium-built-brown-haired Caucasian, right?" Sandy asked. The answer was crucial.

"Don't even have his eye color," Rawlins said.

Sandy almost blurted *brown* before he caught himself in the nick of time.

"Think the survivors could be protecting him?" the uniform said.

McCann narrowed his eyes and scrutinized Sandy. "How about that, Mr. Newspaperman? You and your friends here wouldn't be obstructing justice now, would you?"

Sandy's tongue took on a leathery taste and texture. He swallowed and tried to muster some indignation.

"If you mean did we all get together and cook up a useless description, how could we? None of us was in any state of mind for that kind of thinking. If you want to see what I had for dinner, detective, check out the tracks over there. We were all too sick with relief at just being alive."

"Even if they'd wanted to," Rawlins said, "I doubt they'd've had time. Let's face it: this second shooter was an average white male who hid his face and took off."

"Yeah, I guess so," McCann said. "Doesn't matter much anyway. Like I said: he'll turn up. Just a matter of time."

But I'm going to find him first, Sandy thought, as visions of talk shows and book contracts danced in his head.

The Savior . . . the second shooter . . . the GPM . . . whatever he was called, only one person in this whole city could identify him. And Sandy Palmer wasn't about to fritter that away. Simply having survived that death train would earn him a moment in the journalistic sun tomorrow. But what about the next day, and the day after that? He'd be—quite literally—yesterday's news.

But not if he held onto this ace in the hole . . . and played it right.

Mama Palmer didn't raise no dummy. A once-in-a-lifetime golden opportunity had been dropped into his lap, a chance to parlay his eyewitness status into an even bigger media coup: he'd find the Savior, wrangle an exclusive to his story, then bring him in.

He thought of reporters linked for all posterity with the sources of their greatest story: Jimmy Breslin and his Son of Sam letter, Woodward and Bernstein and their Deep Throat.

How about Sandy Palmer and the Savior?

5

Jack sat in the dark, sipping a Corona and watching his TV, terrified of what he might hear and see, but he couldn't turn it off. Started with Channel Five which kicked off its nightly news at ten, but tonight it didn't matter which New York station he chose; they'd all interrupted their regular lineups to cover the subway mass murder.

But the big hook, the story within the story that made this must-see TV, was the mystery man who had killed the killer and then faded away. Everyone wanted to know who he was.

Jack chewed his lip, waiting for the eyewitness description, the artist's sketch. Any moment now a likeness of his face would flash onto the screen. He cringed when he saw some of the survivors, people he recognized from the train, snagged by the cameras and microphones. Most hadn't much to say beyond how grateful they were to be alive and how they owed their lives to the mystery man, someone they'd labeled "the Savior." As to what this fellow looked like, none of those on camera had anything to add to the previously broadcast description of a brown-haired white male between twenty-five and fifty years old.

Relieved, Jack let his head fall back and closed his eyes. So far so good. But he wasn't in the clear yet. Not even close. Someone had to have got a good look at him; that kid trying to pick up the film student, for instance; he'd been sitting only a couple of feet away. Probably pouring his guts out to a police sketch artist right now.

Finally the newscasters moved on to other stories and Jack found himself up and moving about the apartment, wandering through the rooms. Had a stack of videotapes set up for his Terence Fisher festival. He'd planned to start tonight, opening with *Curse of Frankenstein*, but knew he wouldn't be able to sit still through it. His two-bedroom place usually was plenty of room for him, but tonight it felt like a noose around his neck. Slowly tightening.

Got to get out of here.

And go where? He ached for Gia but she was out of town. As soon as school let out she'd packed up Vicky and flown to Ottumwa, Iowa, for a week-long visit with her folks, part of her ongoing effort to keep Vicky in contact with her extended family. Hated that the two women in his life were so far away, resented sharing them with other people even if they were blood relations, but he never mentioned that to Gia. Who knew how many more years Vicky's grandmother would be around?

Maybe just wander over to Julio's, stand at the bar, have a beer, and pretend it was just another night. But the TV would be on and instead of the Yanks or the Mets everyone would be watching the special reports about the subway murders and that was all they'd be talking about.

How about simply going for a walk?

But what if—he knew this was ridiculous, but the thought stuck with him—what if he passed somebody from the train on the street and they recognized him?

Possible, yes. The least bit likely, no.

And let's face it, he thought. Tonight I'm safe. No sketch yet. Tomorrow might be a whole different story.

Tonight could be his last chance to wander the city at will. Might as well get out there now and take advantage of it.

He showered and dressed in a completely different look: khakis, a light blue shirt with a button-down collar under a cranberry V-neck sweater to hide the Glock 19 in his nylon small-of-the-back holster.

On the way to the door he stopped and looked around the cluttered front room where he kept all his stuff. Old stuff. Neat stuff. Most people would call it junk—premiums, giveaways, and kitschy tie-ins from the pulp magazines, comic strips, and radio shows of the 1930s and '40s displayed on century-old furniture. Another generation's nostalgia.

What about his own childhood growing up through the seventies?

He remembered little and cared less. Why keep a Brady Bunch lunch box when you could have one with The Shadow staring at you from under his black slouch hat? A Radio Orphan Annie decoder, an official Doc Savage Club certificate . . . nothing from his own past was anywhere near as neat as those.

Gia, perpetually baffled at his attraction to this stuff, had often asked him why—why a lunch box or magic ring or cheap plastic doo-dad from *any* era?—and he'd never been able to come up with an answer. Didn't care to try. Some shrink-type could probably fabricate a deep-seated reason for his compulsion to accumulate ephemera with no connection to his own past, but who cared why? He liked it. Enough said.

But if forced to cut and run he'd have to leave all this behind. Strangely it didn't matter. It was stuff. Neat stuff, but still just stuff. He could walk away with barely an instant's regret. Gia and Vicky, though . . . being separated from them would be a killer.

Not going to happen, he told himself as he headed down the stairs for the street.

He'd do whatever it took to keep this one lousy incident from disrupting his life and his business.

His business . . . he hadn't checked his voice mail in a while.

Walked over to Broadway, found a phone booth, and tapped in his codes. One call. From a woman who said she'd been referred to him as someone who could help her with a problem involving a friend and a cult. Left her cell phone number but didn't say who'd referred her or any details about the cult or her problem with it. Decided she was worth a call back. An indefinable something about her voice appealed to him, made him want to work on her problem.

Glanced at his watch: 11:20. Might be late to call her, but he needed something to do and this could be it. A new customer with a new fix-it job would occupy his mind and time while waiting for the fallout from tonight's fiasco.

Dialed her number. When she answered he said. "This is Jack, returning your call."

"Oh. I didn't expect you to call back so soon." A nice voice; soft and mature. Not too old, not too young.

Good start, Jack thought.

"Some problems can wait," he said, "some can't. You didn't say anything about yours. I can meet you tonight if necessary."

"Gosh, it's late but . . ."

"Where do you live?"

"I . . . I'd rather not say."

"Not your street address, your section of the city."

"Oh. It's called the Flower District. It's—"

"Know it." Upper Twenties around Sixth, above Chelsea. "I can meet you anywhere you want down there in about fifteen minutes."

"Tonight? Gee, I don't . . ."

"Lady, you called me."

A pause during which he swore he could hear her chewing her lip.

"Okay. But someplace public."

Someplace public . . . could meet her on Forty-second Street. Few places in the city more public than the Deuce since Disney moved in. Maybe too public. Better to make it closer to where she lived . . .

Considered the Seventh Avenue Papaya on the corner of Twenty-third, but that was usually a madhouse this time of night. He grinned. Maybe he should freak her out and suggest La Maison de Sade, the S-and-M supper club next to the Chelsea Hotel. Wait—that was it.

"How about the Chelsea Hotel?"

"Where's that?"

Something not right here. "Thought you said you lived in the Flower District. You live down there and don't know the Chelsea?"

"I'm visiting. I'm from . . . from out of town."

"Okay then. It's right down Seventh from you. On Twenty-third. I'll meet you in the lobby. Is that public enough?"

"I don't know . . . this is so strange."

Hesitant. Jack liked that. He'd take a hesitant customer over a gung-ho out-for-blood type any day.

"Here's how we'll work it: I'll hang out there until midnight. If you change your mind and don't show, fine. If you see me and don't like what you see, just turn around and go back home and we'll forget the whole thing."

"That sounds fair, I guess."

"And you should know up front that I don't work cheap."

"I think it's a little early to haggle about fees. How will I spot you?"

"No problem. I'll stand out."

"How?"

"I won't be wearing black."

A tiny laugh. "I've spent enough time here to appreciate that!"

Her laugh . . . something vaguely familiar there . . . an echo of a laugh from long ago, but damned if he could remember who or when.

"Do I know you?" Jack asked.

"Oh, I doubt that. I doubt that very, very much."

Probably right. She said she was from out of town and Jack didn't leave the city much.

She added, "I only heard of you a couple of hours ago."

"From whom?"

"That's the strangest part. This woman I've never seen before gave me your number and said you could help."

"A stranger? What's her name?"

"I don't know. She had a Russian accent and a big white dog. She said to call you tonight . . . only you."

Got his number from a stranger . . . that didn't sit right, especially since the only people he knew with Russian accents were members of a Brighton Beach crew he'd had a brush with last year, and they weren't too fond of him.

A little extra caution might be in order here.

"You call someone you've never heard of on the recommendation of someone you don't know. You must be a very trusting person."

"No, I'm not. I'm just a very upset person. Maybe even a little frightened."

Thought he heard her voice threatening to crack at the end there. Okay. She sounded genuine. He could figure out later who the mystery woman was. For now . . .

"All right. I'll be dressed like Joe Prep; no way you'll be able to miss me in that crowd." Thought of something. "And remember, it's the *Chelsea* Hotel, not the Chelsea Savoy which is a couple of doors away. You want the big old red building with wrought-iron balconies all up and down its face and a red-and-white-striped awning over the entrance. Got it?"

"Got it."

"Okay. See you then."

Hung up and flagged a cab. As the driver headed down Broadway,

Jack wondered why he felt so determined to involve himself in fixing this woman's problem, whatever it was. He knew he was looking for a distraction, but it went beyond that.

Shrugged it off. Important thing was he was on the move, doing something instead of hanging around his apartment like a prisoner in a cell.

6

Sandy sat before one of the workstations in the darkened editorial pool, cursing as he tried by trial and error to decipher the workings of the unfamiliar program.

Once he'd figured he'd learned all he was going to at the crime scene, he got McCann to spring him and made a beeline for *The Light* offices just off Times Square. Immediately he'd had a face-to-face with George Meschke and the rest of the staff during which they'd listened with wide eyes as he recounted his tale. What a buzz getting the rapt attention of all those hardened pros.

Only Pokorny, good old smart-ass Jay Pokorny, the only other reporter on the staff anywhere near his age, had tried to rain on his parade.

"You sure you didn't stage this, Palmer?" he said, looking down at him along his long, thin, patrician nose. "You know, hire some guy to off people in front of you just so you could make the front page?"

"Only you'd think of that, Jay," he'd said.

"I could be home getting laid," Pokorny mumbled, and wandered away.

After Sandy had written up his first-person eyewitness account—sans the GPM's description, of course—he zapped it to Meschke's computer. From there it would go to the printers who were standing by, readying a double run of tomorrow's edition.

All he needed now to make this incredible evening complete was just one usable frame on that roll he'd given the photo lab.

At the moment, Sandy was on his own time, doing his own thing. That involved a program called Identi-Kit 2000. He'd seen a reporter using it once and learned it was loaded onto the mainframe. Tonight he'd found and accessed it, and was now trying to get it to work for him. A manual existed somewhere in the building, he was sure, but he couldn't go asking for it. Anyone hearing about a witness to a major crime who wanted to know how to use the computer equivalent of a police sketch artist would catch on fast to what Sandy was up to.

He wasn't doing too badly without the manual, but the program offered so many variations on facial features that he felt his mind going numb. He'd wasted a lot of time trying to guess the hairline, then realized that was a mistake. He'd never seen the GPM's hairline and if he got it wrong it would work against him. So he had the program stick a knit watch cap on the head and that solved that.

A truly amazing piece of software. Slowly, steadily, through trial and error, hit and miss, he'd seen the GPM's face emerge and take shape on the screen. Except for the damn eyes. He'd worked the chin, the nose, the lips until they were pretty close to what he remembered. But the eyes—when he raised them they looked too high, yet when he lowered them they looked equally wrong.

He closed his own eyes and tried to remember the man's face as he'd looked past Sandy's shoulder to check the station stop . . . brought it into focus and zeroed in on those mild brown eyes . . .

Wider. That was it.

Back on the screen, Sandy widened the eyes then moved them up just a tad.

It's him! he thought, feeling his fingers tingle. Damn me, it's him!

He saw a world, a *universe* of possibilities bursting open before him.

But only if he kept it to himself. If anybody else got hold of this he'd lose his exclusive . . . lose that glorious future.

Sandy glanced around. No one nearby. He mouse-clicked PRINT, typed a "10" into the COPIES box, then turned off his monitor. He rose, stretched, and made his way as casually as he could to the printer. There he watched the sheets with that face, that wonderful generic face, sliding into the tray.

When all ten were done, he folded them once and buttoned them inside his shirt, then returned to the workstation.

Now . . . what to do with the Identi-Kit file? His first instinct was to delete it. But what if he needed to come back to it, maybe revise it? He didn't want to have to start from scratch all over again. He decided to label it GPM and leave it in the Identi-Kit folder. That way it would have no connection to him, and anyone finding it would think GPM stood for the initials of the guy in the drawing. Gerald P. Mahoney perhaps.

Sandy grinned as he closed out the program. *Sometimes I'm so sneaky I scare myself.*

He headed for the exit, gliding like a dancer through the maze of empty desks. A little shut-eye, then he'd be up early to catch the morning edition with his first byline. Maybe a call to the folks to make sure they picked up *The Light* so they wouldn't miss seeing how all those years of tuition were finally bearing fruit, even if he was working for a sleazbloid.

And then later tomorrow . . . starting the search.

Only problem was, he wasn't the least bit tired. In fact he was still totally wired. He wished he could drop into a bar where all his friends hung out and hoist a few beers while he blew their minds with his story of the subway ride to hell and back.

Trouble was, he didn't have a gang of friends. Not even one good friend, to tell the truth. Hell, he didn't even have a roommate. He still lived alone in the co-op his parents had bought in Morningside Heights when he'd entered Columbia. They still owned it and had been letting him live on there rent free since graduation—a great perk for him and a solid investment for them with the relentless rise in West Side property values.

Most of the time he didn't mind not having close friends. Acquaintances were perfectly adequate. But tonight . . . tonight he wished he had one person—just one—he could share this with. That film student, for instance. Beth. What was her last name? He could kick himself now for not getting her phone number. And the least he could have done was to have found her and said good-bye before he'd dashed back to *The Light*.

Typical me, he thought. *A brown thumb with relationships.*

And face it, what did he have to offer? Not as if he was setting the world on fire like some of the guys he'd known in undergrad. A few of his fellow English majors had gone on to brokerage houses and investments banks and mega-bonuses—*English* majors without a single business course to their names! And don't mention the computer geeks who spent every waking moment of their college years playing Ultima Online and then joined dot-coms in the Flatiron District to haul down six figures plus stock options. The market collapse had stifled their brags, but financially they remained light years ahead of Sandy.

When's my turn? he'd asked himself.

Well, he'd got the answer tonight. Sandy Palmer's turn was *now.* He'd always dreamed of breaking a big story, and now that dream was about to come true.

He kept flashing back to Woodward and Bernstein. Who were they before they connected with Deep Throat? Nobodies. But afterward they were household names. This story wasn't the caliber of Watergate, but it had the same potential for hooking public interest, and not just locally—nationwide eyeballs could be staring his way.

He tried to rein in the fantasies—never paid to get your hopes up too high—but he could feel them taking off, soaring in a high, jet-fueled arc.

Fifteen minutes of fame? Screw that. He'd do a network *hour* with Charlie Rose, be on *all* the talk shows. He'd be the man to know, the guy to be seen with, his name would pop up in gossip columns, his face a regular on "The Scene" page of *New York Magazine* as he's spotted attending film premieres, gallery openings, and literary receptions, and don't forget parties in the Hamptons where his dalliances would be mentioned in the "Sunday Styles" section of the *Times.*

Dalliances . . . oh, yeah. Those models and starlets just throw themselves at famous writers and journalists. No more worrying about relationships, *everybody* will want to know Sandy Palmer.

But first he'd have to find the guy.

That sobering reality brought him back to earth. This was not going to happen by itself. He had some work ahead of him. Hard work.

Out on the street Sandy flagged a cab. He'd already decided to splurge on a taxi home. He didn't think he could handle another subway ride tonight.

7

Jack knew it was her the moment she stepped through the door.

He'd been sitting in the Chelsea's intimate, marble-tiled lobby on an intricately carved sofa situated between the equally intricately carved fireplace and a metallic sculpture of some sort of jackal sitting atop an undersized elephant. He'd spent the waiting time admiring the vast and eclectic array of art festooning the walls.

The Chelsea had been a fabled haunt of artists and entertainers for decades, and nowadays most of them seemed to own clothes of only one color: black. So when this woman in beige linen slacks and a rose sweater set stepped through the door she stood out among the leather and lingerie habitués as much as he did. Her head was down so he didn't see her face at first, but the style of her curly honey blond hair and mature figure jibed with the voice on the phone.

Then she looked up and their eyes met and Jack's heart stuttered and missed a beat or two.

Kate! God, it was *Kate!*

Her voice, that little laugh—now he knew why they'd sounded familiar. They belonged to his sister.

Kate looked as stunned as Jack knew he must, but then her shock turned to something like fear and dismay.

"Kate!" he called as she started to turn away. "My God, Kate, it's me! Jack!"

She turned toward him again and now her face was more composed but hardly full of the joy one might expect at seeing her younger brother for the first time in a decade and a half.

Jack hurried up and stopped within a foot of her, staring.

"Jackie," she said. "I don't believe this."

Jackie . . . Christ, when had he last heard someone call him that? The word sundered an inner dam, loosing a flood of long-pent-up memories that engulfed him. He'd been the last of three kids: first Tom, Kate two years later, and Jack eight years after her. Kate, the natural nurturer, had half-raised him. They'd bonded, they'd been pals, she'd been the coolest person he knew and he'd fairly worshipped her. And then she'd gone off to college, leaving a hole in his ten-year-old life. Med school and pediatric residency after that. He remembered her wedding day . . .

Most of all Jack remembered this face, these pale blue eyes, the faint splash of freckles across the cheeks and nose, the strong jawline. Her hair was shorter and faintly streaked with gray; her skin had aged a little with a hint of crows feet at the corners of her eyes; and her face was a bit fuller, her hips a tad wider than he remembered, but her figure wasn't that much different from the one that had kept the boys calling all through high school. All in all his big sister Kate hadn't changed much.

"I don't believe this either," he said. "I mean, the odds are . . ."

"Astronomical."

He felt they should kiss, embrace, do something other than stand here facing each other, but they'd never been a huggy clan, and Jack had dropped out of his family and never looked back. Hadn't spoken a word to Kate in fifteen years. Until tonight.

"You look great," he said. And it was true. Even with very little make-up she did not look like a forty-four-year-old mother of two. She'd always been fair haired, but now she was a darker shade of blonde than he remembered. What a mane she used to have. "I see you've stopped straightening your hair. I still remember watching you use Mom's iron to flatten out your waves."

"Eventually you get to the point where you have to stop fighting your nature and just go with it." She glanced away. "Look. This was a mistake. If I'd had the slightest inkling you were the Jack I was calling, I never would have . . ." She let it trail off.

"Why not? If you've got a problem you should call family."

"Family?" Kate's eyes blazed to life as she turned back to him. "What would you know about family, Jackie? You vanished from our lives without even saying good-bye! Just a note saying you were leaving

and not to worry! As if that was possible. For a while we didn't know
if you were dead or alive. Do you have any idea what that was like for
Dad? First he loses Mom, then you drop out of college and disappear.
He almost lost it!"

"I'd already lost it, Kate."

Her eyes softened, but only a little. "I know how Mom's death—"

"Murder."

"Yes, you always insisted on calling it that, didn't you. It hit us all
hard, and you the hardest perhaps, but Dad—"

"I've been back to see him."

"Only rarely, and only after he tracked you down. And I sent you
all those letters, invited you to christenings and graduations and an-
niversaries, but you never responded. Not even to say no. Not once."

Jack's turn to look away, focus on a painting of a Manhattan street
scene, but viewed at a crazy angle. Kate was right. She'd made a major
effort to keep in touch, tried hard to bring him back into the family,
and he'd snubbed her.

"Jackie, you've got a niece and a nephew you've never even met.
They used to look at the wedding pictures and point to this young
stranger who was one of the ushers and ask who he was."

"Kevin and Elizabeth," he said. "How are they?"

He knew them only from their photos. Kate was one of those people
who sent out an annual here's-what-we've-been-doing-all-year letters
with her Christmas card, usually accompanied by a family photo. At
least she used to. Nothing at all from her for the last few years. Since
the divorce.

"They're wonderful. Kevin's eighteen, Liz is sixteen, as if you give
a damn."

Jack closed his eyes. Okay. Deserved that. He'd seen her kids grow
up long distance, on Kodak paper.

But after he'd cut himself off and reinvented himself here in New
York, how could he go back? He could never explain who he'd become.
Tom, Kate, Dad especially—they'd never get it. Be horrified, in fact.
Took enough to live his own life; didn't want to have to invent another
life just for their approval.

"Look, Kate," he said. "I know I hurt people, and I'm sorry. I was
just starting my twenties and coming apart at the seams. I can't change

the past but maybe I can make up just a tiny bit of it to you now. Your friend and this cult you mentioned . . . maybe I can help."

"I don't think this is in your field."

"And what field would that be?"

"Appliance repairs, right?"

He laughed. "Who told you that?"

"Dad."

"Figures."

His father had called one of Jack's numbers years ago and heard an outgoing message that went: *This is Repairman Jack. Describe the problem and leave a number and I'll get back to you.* Naturally he'd assumed his son was some sort of appliance fixer.

"He's wrong?"

"I make my living fixing other things."

"I don't understand."

"No reason you should. Let's go someplace where we can sit and talk."

"No, Jackie. This won't work."

"Please, Kate?"

He reached out and gently gripped her wrist. He felt at the mercy of the vortex of emotions swirling around him. This was Kate, his big sister Kate, one of the best people he'd ever known, who'd been so good to him and who was still smarting from the awful way he'd treated her. She thought badly of him. He had to fix that.

She shook her head, seemed almost . . . afraid.

Afraid of him? That couldn't be. What then?

"Look. This is my city. If I can't help out your friend, I'll bet I know someone who can. And if that doesn't work out, at least we can talk. Come on, Kate. For old times' sake?"

Maybe his touch did it, but he felt a change in her muscle tone as some of the resistance seeped out of her.

"All right. Just for a little while."

"Great. What are you up for—coffee or a drink?"

"Normally I'd say coffee, but right now I think I could do with a drink."

"I hear you. Let's hunt up a place without music."

He took his sister by the elbow and guided her out to the street, then up along Seventh Avenue, wondering how much he dared tell her about himself, his life. He'd play it by ear. The important thing was he had her with him now, and he wasn't letting her go until he'd done something to make up for the hurt he'd caused.

8

Kate stared at the man sitting across the table from her. Jackie . . . her little brother . . . though he was hardly little anymore. She supposed she should start calling him Jack now.

They'd come upon a place called The Three Crowns that Jack had said looked good. A fifty-foot bar ran down the right side, a row of booths with green upholstery along the left, all of it oak. Oak everywhere. But not too crowded. The patrons seemed a mix of straight couples and gay males of varying ages, par for the course in Chelsea. The lights and the sound from the TVs over the bar were low and they'd found an empty booth in the rear. No table service, so Jack had made the trip to the bar and just returned with a gin and tonic for her and a pint of Harp for himself.

She quickly downed half her drink, hoping it would help dull the shock still vibrating through her. Jackie! Of all people! And worse, she'd mentioned "my friend" and the cult on his voice mail. She couldn't let him know about her and Jeanette. Nobody could know. Not yet.

Jackie . . . Jack. A part of her wanted to hate him for the pain he'd caused everyone. Well, not everyone. Tom was too self-involved to worry much about anyone a few inches beyond his own skin. But damn, she and Dad had gone half crazy with worry over Jack.

Yet she looked at him now and felt an urge to smile, to laugh aloud. This might be a terrible time to run into him, but despite everything that had happened—*not* happened, actually—between them, she couldn't deny this heart-swelling joy at seeing him again. Jackie . . . she'd helped feed him and change him when he was an infant, read him stories and baby-sat for him into her teens. And look at him now. Lord, how he'd changed. He'd been a boy the last time she'd seen him—a senior at Rutgers, one semester to go, but still a boy. A dark and brooding boy after Mom's death.

She still sensed a darkness in him, but he seemed comfortable in his skin now. And how he'd filled out that skin. Jackie had been so skinny as a kid, now she could sense sleek muscles coiling under his shirt. But was that a healing laceration running from the edge of his hairline into his right frontal scalp? Yes, definitely. It looked about four weeks old. She wondered how he'd got it.

He'd said this was his city and she could believe that. He seemed to belong here, moved so easily down its streets. She couldn't tell whether it had adopted him, or he'd adopted it. Whatever the case, they seemed made for each other.

Little brother or not, she had to keep this brief. One drink, promise to keep in touch, then get out of here. Keep the talk on the family, the good old days when Mom was still ruling the roost, keep it off Jeanette and the cult. Kate would find another way, sans little brother, to deal with that.

So they talked.

Actually Kate found herself doing most of it. Mostly about Kevin and Lizzie; she touched—a very glancing touch—on her divorce from Ron, mentioned a few details about her pediatric group, and then ran out of steam.

"See much of Tom?" Jack asked after a lull.

She shook her head. "No. He's a judge in Philly now, you know."

"I'd heard."

"He's on his third wife now. Saw him briefly over Christmas. I didn't see it when you were younger, but you and he look amazingly alike. Put on ten years and twenty pounds, add a little gray to your hair, and you could be twins."

"My big brother," Jack said, frowning as he shook his head. "Of all things, a judge."

Wondering at Jack's tone of chagrin, she raised her glass for another sip but found only ice cubes.

"Time for another," Jack said, taking it from her.

Before she could protest he was up and moving away from the table.

Moves like a cat, she thought as she watched him go.

Time to change the subject. So far the conversation had been pretty much a one-way street. Now it was his turn.

"So," she said as he set the second drink before her. "Enough about me. I need some answers from you. Most of all, I want to know why you simply disappeared from our lives. Was it what happened to Mom?"

Jack nodded. "Indirectly."

I knew it! Kate thought. Knew it, knew it, knew it!

"We were all devastated, Jack, but why—?"

"You weren't there in the car when that cinderblock came through the windshield, Kate. You didn't see the life seep out of her, see the light fade from her eyes."

"Okay. I wasn't there. Neither was Tom. But Dad was and he—"

"Dad didn't do anything about it. I did."

"I don't understand," she said, baffled. "Did what?"

He stared at her a long moment, as if weighing an important decision. Finally he spoke.

"I found him," he said softly. "Took me a while, but I found the guy who did it."

"Who did what?"

"Who threw the cinderblock off the overpass."

The words jolted her. Jackie had gone out looking . . . hunting . . . by himself?

"How come you never said anything? Did you tell the police?"

He shook his head. "No. I took care of it myself."

"What . . . what did you . . . ?"

Suddenly it was as if a mask had dropped from Jack's face. She looked into his eyes now and for an instant, the span of a single agonized heartbeat, she felt as if she were peering into an abyss.

His voice remained low, flat, as cold as that abyss. "I fixed it."

And then the mask was back in place and an old memory flashed though Kate's brain . . . a newspaper article about a dead man, battered beyond recognition, found hanging upside down from a Turnpike overpass not too long after Mom's death, and she remembered wondering if it might be the same overpass, and if so it should be torn down because it must be cursed.

Could that have been the "guy" Jack said he'd tracked down? Was that why the body had been hung from that particular overpass?

No . . . not Jackie . . . not her little brother. He'd never . . . he couldn't kill. It had been someone else hanging from the overpass. And this man he'd mentioned . . . Jack had simply beaten him up.

Kate wanted very much to believe that. She turned her mind from the other possibility, but it lingered like a shadow across the table.

"Did . . . what you did solve anything? Did it make you feel better?"

"No," he said. "I'd thought it would, I was so sure it would, but it didn't do a damn thing for me. And after I . . . afterward nothing seemed to make much sense. College seemed particularly pointless. I had to get away before I exploded. I dropped out, Kate—*way* out. Spent years in a blind rage, and by the time I'd blown off some of it and locked up the rest, I'd burned too many bridges to go back."

"Maybe you told yourself that. Maybe that made it easier for you, but it wasn't true."

"It was. And is. My life and your life . . . they're different worlds. No way you'd understand."

"Understand what? This repair business of yours? Just what is it you fix?"

"Hard to say. Situations, I guess."

"I don't get it."

"Sometimes people have problems or get themselves into situations where the legal and judicial system can't help, or they're involved in something they can't bring to the system. They pay me to fix it for them."

An appalling thought struck her. "You're not some kind of . . . of hitman, are you?"

He laughed—a real laugh, the kind you can't fake—and that reassured her. A little.

"No. Nothing so melodramatic as that."

"Do you pay people off?"

"No, I just sort of . . . it's hard to explain. And not the sort of thing I can advertise on a billboard."

"Is it legal?"

A shrug. "Sometimes yes, sometimes no."

Kate leaned back and stared. Who was this man across from her? He'd said he lived on a different world, one she'd never understand,

and she was beginning to believe him. He was like a stranger from a faraway planet, and yet in many ways he was undeniably still her little brother Jackie.

First Jeanette, now Jack . . . her own world, never a comfortable place these past few years, now seemed to be crumbling. She felt unmoored from her life. Wasn't there anything left she could rely on?

Jack said, "Now can you see why I thought it best for all concerned that I keep to myself?"

"I don't know." Earlier tonight Kate would have said no—nothing you could have done would have changed the way we felt about you. She wasn't so sure anymore. "Maybe."

"I think Dad has scoped that I'm hiding something. Know what he asked me last time we talked?" Jack grinned. "Wanted to know if I was gay."

Kate gasped. She couldn't help it. She felt as if someone had just dashed a bucket of cold water in her face.

❖

"It's not all that bad," Jack said, seeing Kate's shocked look.

He wondered at that. As a pediatrician she must have run into her share of teenagers who thought or knew or feared they might be gay. Maybe that was still a big deal in Kate's white-collar, middle-class-citizen world. Around here it was no deal at all.

"He flat-out asked you?" she said, her eyes still wide. "Just like that? When?"

"Couple of months ago. It was when he was planning to come up from Florida and visit you and Tom. I was trying to deflect him from including me in his itinerary."

"What did he say? Exactly."

Jack wondered at her sudden intensity.

"He said something about how he realized there might be aspects of my life I didn't want him to know about—which was dead-on right—and then he said that if I was gay . . ." Jack had to smile here. "He could barely get the word out. Actually he said if I was gay 'or something like that'—he never got into what the 'something like that' might be—it was okay."

"He said it was *okay*?" Kate couldn't seem to believe it. "We're talking about our father, the Reagan Republican, the Rush Limbaugh fan. Dad said it was okay?"

"Yeah. He told me, 'I can accept it. You're still my son.' Isn't that a killer?"

Not that it changed a thing. His father might be able to accept a gay son, but he'd never accept how Jack made his living.

He saw tears in his sister's eyes and asked, "Something wrong?"

She quickly wiped them away. "Strange how some people can surprise the hell out of you." Eyes dry again, she looked at him. "Well, are you?"

"What?"

"Gay?"

"No. Strictly hetero."

"But you never married?"

"No. I kicked around a lot when I was younger, but I'm pretty much settled with one woman now."

"Pretty much?"

"Well, *I'm* settled, but let's just say she's got some issues about my work. How about you? I'll bet a lot of guys came around after the divorce. Seeing anyone?"

"Yes." A little nod, a little smile, but very warm. "Someone special."

"Are we going to hear wedding bells again?"

And now a sad look. "No."

Strange answer. Not at all tentative. Unless she was seeing a married guy. That didn't fit with the straitlaced Kate he remembered, but as she'd just said: people can surprise the hell out of you.

He'd never thought of his sister as a sexual being; she'd always been just . . . Kate. But smitten enough to be making it with a married guy . . . a sure recipe for hurt. He hoped she knew what she was doing.

"So much of what we do comes down to sex, doesn't it," he said. "Sometimes too much, I think."

"How so?"

"I mean it's a part of life, a really wonderful part of life, but not *all* of life. There's work, play, food, mind, spirit—lots of things. But I tell you, I run into so many people who seem to define themselves by their sexual preferences."

" 'So many'?"

"Let's just say I don't hang with too many members of the middle class, and no members of the upper class. So yeah, *many* of the people I know do not have what might be considered 'normal' lifestyles."

" 'Normal' being within two standard deviations from the mean?"

"Sure, why not. Everything's a bell curve, right? I'm talking about people on either fringe of the curve."

"Give me a for-instance."

He thought a moment, then remembered Ray Bellson.

"I did a fix-it for this guy once who was totally into bondage. Always wore black leather, had a belt made out of handcuffs, paintings of tied hands and feet on his walls, furniture made out of chromed chain . . . it went on and on. You'd sit and talk to him and he'd be tying and untying knots in this piece of cord he always carried around. It had completely taken over his life."

She sipped her G and T, then said, "Where do you think I'd fall on that curve?"

Weird question for his big sister to ask her little brother.

"Never thought about it, but I assume somewhere right in the middle. I mean, I don't see you squeezing into black vinyl and brandishing a whip."

She laughed—her first real laugh tonight. "I don't see that either. But I'm just wondering what qualifies someone for 'normal' on your bell curve."

Jack shrugged, not comfortable with pigeonholing people. "How did we get on this subject anyway?"

"You brought it up."

"Actually Dad brought it up."

"How did you feel when he asked you if you were gay?"

Jack noticed her eyes fixed on his, as if the answer were very important.

"I remember being sort of glad he wasn't wondering if I was a rapist or a pedophile."

"But you've never been attracted to a man?"

"Never. I'm as attracted to guys as I am to sheep, goats, and chickens. Which is to say, not at all. Zero chemistry there. In fact the idea of getting cozy with a guy—*blech*."

"But you're not a gay basher."

"I figure everybody's got a right to their own lives. You may own nothing else, but you own your life. So if you don't tell me how to live mine, I won't tell you how to live yours."

"You've got no problem with lesbians either?"

"Lesbians are cool." He tried to draw out the *c* like Beavis. Or was that Butthead? He always got them confused.

"Really." An amused smile played around her lips.

"Sure. Look at it this way. I've got a number of things in common with lesbians right from the get-go: we both find women attractive, and neither of us is interested in having sex with a man. Now that I think about it, I've got definite lesbian tendencies."

"You know many?"

"A few. There's a lesbian couple who're regulars at this bar where I hang. It's a workingman's place and a couple of the guys weren't exactly welcoming at first; but these gals weren't about to let that stop them, so they kept coming back and now they're part of the family. Anybody tries to hassle them now will find himself nose to nose with those very same guys who gave them a hard time at first. Carole and Henni. I sit with them now and then. I like them. They're brainy and funny, and you can, I don't know . . . relax with them."

"Relax?"

"They know I'm not coming on to them, and I know they're not the least bit interested in me. Take sex off the table and a lot of games disappear."

"So being with them is sort of like being with the guys."

"Not quite. Guys have a whole different set of games. No, it's more like . . . like sitting here with you."

Kate's eyes widened. "Me?"

"Well, yeah. We may have a lot family baggage between us, but neither of us is trying to slap a move on the other."

She narrowed her eyes and gave him a sidelong look. "You're absolutely sure about that?"

"Hey, don't go weird on me, Kate," Jack said, laughing. "I'm the family weirdo, and one is enough."

"You still haven't told me where you think I fit on your curve."

"You're not going to let this drop, are you?'

"Not until you tell me."

"Okay. Let me ask you a couple of questions first. You can have love without sex, and sex without love, agreed?"

"Of course."

"What if you had to choose between them? What if you had to live the rest of your life with either no sex or no love? And by no love I mean loving no one and no one loving you. Which would you give up?"

Kate barely hesitated. "Sex."

"There you go. That's normal."

"That's it? That's your sole criterion for normal?"

"Not mine—yours."

"I never said it was mine."

"You chose love over sex, and the very fact that love is your choice makes it normal, because you're one of the most decent, honest, *normal* people I've ever known."

"That's not just circular reasoning—it's spherical."

"Works for me, Mrs. Wife-mother-pediatrician."

"Ex-wife."

"Which is probably even more the norm these days. Hey, if I'm wrong, prove it."

Kate opened her mouth, looked as if she was about to say something, then closed it again. She glanced at her watch.

"I've got to go."

"But what about your friend and the cult?"

"I'll work something out."

She seemed afraid. Of what? What was she hiding?

"Is your friend into something illegal?" He couldn't believe Kate would be involved with someone who was but . . . you never knew. "Because that's okay. Most of the people I know—"

"No-no, nothing like that. She's recovering from cancer therapy and she's acting strangely. It's more psychological than anything else."

"Some of these cults can play rough if you interfere."

"It's nothing like that, Jackie . . . Jack. Really. I was upset when I called; now I think I was overreacting. I don't think I need to get you involved."

"Involve me," he said. "I'm here for you." Before she could put him off again, he grabbed a cocktail napkin and said, "Got a pen?"

"I think so." She fished one out of her shoulder bag and handed it to him.

"I'm putting down my number and the numbers of two people I've worked for recently—both women and, coincidentally, both doctors.

Before you write me off, you call them and see what they say. If you still don't want my help, I won't like it, but at least it'll be an informed decision."

She took the napkin but didn't promise to make the calls.

"Come on," Jack said. "I'll walk you home."

"I'm practically there already."

"Little brother does not let big sister walk the mean streets alone at night."

"Jack—"

"I can walk beside you or six feet behind you, but you might as well resign yourself to the fact that I'm seeing you safe home."

Kate sighed, then smiled thinly. "Let's go then."

Out on Seventh they walked and talked about getting together again during her stay in the city and keeping in touch afterward until a neon sign down one of the streets caught Jack's eye: FYNYL VYNYL. He thought he knew all the used record shops in the city but this was a new one. Almost 1 A.M. and it was still open. He couldn't pass this up.

"Mind if we stop in here for a sec?" he said.

"Not at all."

Inside, a guy with a shaved head and huge muttonchop sideburns looked up from behind the counter as they entered. "We're closing in about fifteen minutes,"

"We'll only need one of those if you really know your stock," Jack told him.

"What I don't remember, this baby does," he said, patting the Mac to his left.

"Great. It's a single from 1971. A&M Records. 'Tried So Hard' by the Flying Burrito Brothers."

The guy snorted. "Yeah, right. The Dutch 45? I've got a waiting list for that one. Still haven't seen a copy."

Jack waved and turned back toward the door. "Thanks anyway."

"Flying Burrito Brothers?" Kate said as they returned to the sidewalk. "They're from my time. How'd you get interested in them?"

"You."

"Me?"

"Sure. You had all those Byrds albums."

"Oh, right. Back when I was horse crazy. They did that song 'Chestnut Mare' and that got me into them and buying up all their old records. But how—?"

"You played their stuff so much I got to be a fan. And my favorite Byrd was Gene Clark. Still love his songs. So a couple of weeks ago, after buying myself a dual-deck CD burner, I decided to make the ultimate Gene Clark disk. And I want the version of 'Tried So Hard' that he sang with the Burritos. Trouble is, it was only released in Holland on a 45. The group took his voice out when they put the song on their third album."

"So you're hunting a 1971 record that wasn't even released on this side of the Atlantic. Kind of obsessive, no?"

"All your fault. The enduring influence of my big sister."

"Wow. Should I feel pleased or guilty?"

"Guilty."

"Thanks a lot. As if I don't have enough . . ."

She never finished the thought because someone behind them said, "Hey."

Jack turned. He was pale, dressed in dusty black jeans and a rumpled long-sleeved shirt; looked all of twenty.

He said, "A spear has no branches."

Jack stared at him, baffled. "What?"

The guy blinked, as if coming out of a trance. "I need some money."

"Sorry about that," Jack said.

"You don't get it." He raised a shaky hand, showing a box cutter. "I need some money *now*." His desperation was palpable.

Jack heard Kate's sharp intake of breath. He guided her behind him with his left hand while slipping his right under his sweater and pulling the Glock from the small of his back. He held the pistol against the front of his right thigh where Kate couldn't see it.

"Look," Jack said, "I've had a bad day, a *very* bad day, and I'm in no mood for this. Try it somewhere else."

Looking as if he couldn't believe what he'd just heard, the guy waved the box cutter before him. "Money, man, or I start cuttin'."

"You don't want to start this, pal," Jack said. "You really don't. 'Cause if you do it's not gonna go down the way you were thinking." He raised the Glock a few inches and waggled it to make sure the guy couldn't miss it. "You see what I'm saying? So do yourself a favor and take a walk."

The guy's eyes angled down to the pistol, then back to Jack's face. He backed up a step.

"Hey, forget it, okay?"

"Forgotten," Jack said.

The guy turned and hurried away. Jack watched to make sure he kept going, then he turned Kate around and guided her ahead of him back toward Seventh, tucking away the pistol as they moved.

"I've never been so frightened in my life!" she said, looking over her shoulder. "My goodness, Jack, he had some sort of razor blade and you . . . you just talked him out of it! How on earth—?"

"I think that even though he was a mugger, he must be one of those naturally empathetic people."

"An empathetic mugger?"

"Sure. I told him I'd had a bad day and really didn't want to be bothered, and he understood."

"That's crazy! I've never heard of such a thing!"

"Happens now and then. You'd be surprised how many people like him respond to reason if given a chance."

Kate talked about the encounter non-stop until they reached the place where she was staying, an apartment in the mid-Twenties. Jack took one look and fell in love with the building. Its five-story brick front was lined with intricate terra cotta friezes, two per floor, one running along the floorline, the other arching over the windows, and in the keystone spot atop each window was set an open-mouthed face of some sort—animal or human Jack couldn't be sure in this light.

"What a neat building!" he said.

It stood out like a polished gem amid the debris of an otherwise purely commercial block of parking lots, print shops, frame galleries, and businesses dealing in wholesale fabric and sewing machine repairs.

"It's called the Arsley," Kate said. "The name's not anywhere on the building, at least not that I've seen, but that's what people who live here call it."

"I'll have to add this to my collection."

"You collect buildings?"

"Only neat ones. And this one is very neat."

"You're still saying 'neat'?"

"Never stopped." He snapped his fingers. "Hey, how about I take you on my Neat Building tour sometime?"

"I don't know, Jackie."

"I want to get together with you again before you go back to Trenton, Kate. I want Gia and Vicky to meet you too."

The need to reconnect with Kate was an ache in Jack's soul. He'd just got her back and couldn't let her slip away again.

Finally she smiled. "Okay. I think I'd like that. You have my cell number. Set it up and call me."

"I'll do that."

His delight was blunted as his mind darted back to the very real possibility that she was in some sort of trouble. She'd felt threatened enough to call a perfect stranger for help. Something was going on, something more serious than a friend acting strangely. Kate might say she didn't want his help, but that didn't mean she didn't need it. And if she needed help, like it or not, he'd see that she got it.

Then the briefest of hugs but the contact filled him with a protective fire.

Kate was his sister, damn it. Nobody was going to play games with his sister. Not on Jack's watch.

9

"Why did you follow me?"

Kate jumped at the sound of Jeanette's voice, turned and saw her standing at the end of the apartment's short front hallway. Kate had left Jack down on the sidewalk and had been expecting an empty apartment.

Jeanette was dressed for bed in her usual—an XXXL T-shirt that hung off one thin shoulder and reached almost to the knees of her long slim tanned legs; tonight's was emblazoned with the cover of the Indigo Girls' *Come On Now Social* album. Her dark shoulder-length hair was pulled back in a short ponytail. Her brown eyes fixed Kate with a reproachful stare.

Kate's first thought was, How does she know? Then she remembered the figure she'd thought she'd seen at the window of the Holdstock house. She'd had the impression it was a man but it must have been Jeanette.

And then guilt scalded her. She'd sneaked out behind the woman she loved and followed her like a cop tailing a criminal. But she'd done it out of concern.

"Because I'm worried about you, Jeanette. You're just not yourself and I—"

"You shouldn't have done that."

Kate sensed no anger in her voice, no threat, yet something in the words, a subliminal note in her tone, raised gooseflesh along her arms.

"I couldn't help myself. I'm so worried."

"Don't be. I'm fine. In fact I've never been better."

"But we never talk, and—"

"We'll talk soon," Jeanette said. "We'll talk as we've never talked before. I promise."

And then she turned and walked away toward the study at the rear of the apartment.

Kate trailed after her. "How about now?"

"No. Not now. But soon."

"Please, Jeanette. I'm . . . lonely without you."

Jeanette stopped and turned at the study door. "That's only temporary. Soon you'll never be alone or lonely again."

Kate was struck dumb. Before she could respond Jeanette closed the study door. Kate heard the click of the lock, just as she'd heard it every night since Jeanette had moved out of the bedroom. She felt her throat tighten.

I am not going to cry. I am *not*.

She was a grown woman, a mother of two, and a seasoned physician. She was an expert problem-solver, and she would solve this one. Somehow. And she would do it without tears.

Trouble was, she couldn't find a handle for this problem. Perhaps because her heart was breaking.

Kate stood in the center of the living room and looked around. Hardwood floors, an oriental rug, functional furniture, paintings by local artists picked up at street fairs—some they'd picked out together. The kitchen-dining area at the far end, which was not very far at all. A small, two-bedroom apartment with the second small bedroom converted to a study/office where Jeanette worked when she telecommuted to Long Island. She worked for a software company that designed custom databases for businesses. She could do a stand-up routine with her store of quips about the underdeveloped bodies and overdeveloped brains of the nerdy twentysomethings she worked with. A good dozen years older than most of them, she'd said she felt like a den mother most of the time.

But now her home office was back to being a bedroom. Four nights ago Jeanette had moved out of their bed to sleep on the couch in the office. No fight—they never fought—not even a mild disagreement. She'd simply picked up her pillow and moved out of the room. When Kate had asked—begged—for an explanation, all Jeanette would say was, "It's only for a little while. We'll be back together again soon."

Kate wandered into the little kitchen and saw the edge of a crumpled-up white paper bag sticking out of the garbage pail top. As she pushed it farther down to allow the lid to close she spotted the red and yellow McDonald's logo and froze.

McDonald's?

She pulled out the bag and found a Big Mac container inside and her heart sank. More proof of the change in Jeanette who'd lived her entire adult life as a strict vegetarian. She wouldn't even eat eggs. Until now.

Kate leaned against the counter and ran the events of the past week or so through her head again, trying to make some sense of it all.

Jeanette had come home from the hospital her cheerful, acerbic old self, so wonderfully upbeat that the experimental protocol had worked. Like a condemned prisoner with an unexpected reprieve from death row.

But slowly she'd begun to change. Kate hadn't noticed it at first, but looking back now she could identify the subtle initial signs of Jeanette's progressive withdrawal. Sitting and staring out a window instead of rattling off her usual running commentary as she read the paper; gradually she abandoned the paper altogether, stopped listening to music, lost interest in TV. Originally she'd said she wanted to use her medical leave to work on her pet project—a CD-ROM-based in-

teractive drama for women—but spent less and less time at her computer with every passing day; even stopped mentioning her plans for
Int-HER-active, Inc., the company she hoped to start someday.

Silence. It gave Kate the creeps because this little apartment had
always been filled with the sounds of life: music, the TV, sound clips
from the computer—a multimedia melange combined with constant
chatter. At thirty-eight Jeanette was a quasi-activist lesbian who had
been out since her teens; Kate was a middle class mom of forty-four
who still wasn't ready to come out. Their different perspectives had
made for endless hours of lively discussion.

Until now.

And food. Whenever Kate was up from Trenton, and that was every
other weekend, they'd always gone out of their way to whip up at least
one elaborate meal. But now Jeanette had lost all interest in cooking,
leaving it to Kate. Not that Kate minded—after all, she was here to
help all she could—but Jeanette could at least show some interest in
the food. She consumed hearty portions but didn't seem to care what
was on the plate. Homemade eggplant rollatini and Kraft macaroni and
cheese straight out of the box were non-greeted as equals.

And then Jeanette had begun her disappearing acts, leaving without
a word of explanation, without even saying good-bye.

Kate sighed. She felt helpless, and she wasn't used to that. An alien
feeling . . .

Alien . . . that was what Jeanette had become. This was like an
episode of the *X-Files*, or *Twilight Zone*. Jeanette seemed to be turning
into someone else, a remote being who sneaked out to prayer meetings
or whatever they were.

And tonight the surreality had been compounded by a strange
woman giving Kate a phone number that turned out to belong to her
brother.

Jack . . . he'd become someone else too, an unsettling someone else.

Was the whole world going mad, or just her?

But at least she still recognized her brother. Some of the old Jackie
she'd known was still part of the new Jack; she wished she could say
the same about Jeanette. And despite all his changes she'd found something intensely likable about the new Jack, something solid and de-
pendable. She sensed that the boy she'd known had grown into an
upright man, one who'd do what he said he'd do, honor his word, stay

the course . . . all those old-fashioned virtues that might seem corny and hokey in this city, in this time.

The incident with that razor-wielding youth had left her shaken, but when Jack had put his arm around her on the walk home she'd felt so . . . safe. Was that the right word? Yes. Safe. As if an impenetrable transparent shield had slipped over her.

Feeling as if her limbs were cast in lead, Kate dropped into a chair. She grabbed the remote and thumbed the POWER button, not caring what was on so long as it broke this unbearable silence.

Fox News . . . and someone talking about a mass murder on the subway. Her first thought was of Jack, fear that he might have been caught in the gunfire, then she realized they were talking about something that had happened hours ago.

She shook her head . . . big sister still worrying about little brother, when it had been abundantly clear tonight that little brother was quite capable of taking care of himself.

But what about big sister? She wasn't doing too well.

Something Jeanette had said tonight sifted back to her.

We'll talk soon . . . we'll talk as we've never talked before. I promise.

It had sounded so sincere . . . a ray of hope. Why didn't it make her feel better?

And what else had she said?

Soon you'll never be alone again.

What did that mean?

One day at a time, Kate thought. That's the way I'll have to deal with this . . . one day at a time.

10

The pain wrenched Kate from sleep.

A sharp stabbing sensation in her hand—and the feeling that she wasn't alone in the room.

"Jeanette?"

No answer.

Terrified, she rolled over and fumbled for the switch on the bedside lamp. Finally she found it and turned it on. She blinked in the sudden glare and scanned the room.

Empty. But she'd been so sure . . .

The bedroom door stood open. From down the hall came a sound . . . the click of the study door closing. And locking.

Kate looked at her stinging hand and found a small drop of blood leaking from a puncture wound in her palm.

WEDNESDAY

1

Sandy was up and out at the ungodly hour of 6:03 A.M., but the sun was ahead of him, peeking around the granite Gothic spires of St. John the Divine as he bounded along the sidewalk. He skidded to a stop before the newsstand and there it was: *The Light*. The headline took up the top half of the page:

SIX-GUN
SAVIOR!

A blurry photo of the dead killer occupied the bottom half. His photo! They'd found something usable on his roll.

And below that, the banner: *EXCLUSIVE EYEWITNESS REPORT INSIDE! (see pg. 3)*

"Yes!" he shouted and pumped his fist.

He snatched up an issue and opened it to page three and there he was: his first-person account boxed with his picture. Oh, no! They'd used the geeky photo from his HR file! But he forgot about that as soon as he started reading.

Butterflies fluttered up from his stomach and into his chest. This was his first Ferris wheel ride, his first look at the Magic Kingdom, his first kiss all rolled into one. He felt as if his head were about to float away.

"That is one dahlah," said an accented voice.

"Hmmm?"

Sandy looked up and saw the swarthy newsstand owner holding out his hand.

"You must buy to read. One dahlah."

"Oh, yeah." He fished singles out of his pocket. "I'll take four."

He'd have access to virtually unlimited free copies at work but that wasn't the same. The ones in his hand came from a newsstand, from the street, and somehow that made them more real.

"Oh yeah, and I'll take a copy of that subway map too."

He checked out the front pages of the competition. The *Post* head-line was okay—"SUBWAY SLAUGHTER!"—but he liked the *News* headline better: "NIGHTMARE ON THE NINE!" As expected, the *Times* was more sedate with "SIX DEAD IN SUBWAY MASSACRE." But both ran photos from above ground, mostly of the survivors as they emerged from the subway station. He looked at *The Light* again with his photo and its banner about his story. His story. A laugh bubbled up inside and he let it loose. When the newsstand owner gave him a strange look Sandy pulled open one of his copies and pointed to his picture.

"That's me, my man! Me!"

"Yes," the man said. "Very nice."

Sandy got the feeling the guy thought he might be scaring away his customers and wanted him to move on. So Sandy moved on, feeling lighter than air. Nobody could bring him down this morning. Nobody.

2

"Yo, Stan."

Stan Kozlowski lowered his copy of the *Times* and looked across the table. His shorter, heavier younger brother Joe had a copy of *The Light* folded in half and was pinning it to the table with the index finger of his good hand. Usually he bought the *Post* but *The Light*'s front page photo of the dead gunner must have caught his eye this morning.

They occupied their usual table near the front window of Moishe's kosher deli on Second Avenue. The kosher part didn't matter—they'd been raised Catholic—but Moishe's was convenient, the coffee free-flowing, and the bagels unbeatable.

"What?"

"You been reading about this guy on the train last night?"

"Some."

He'd skimmed the stories to see if the *Times* knew more than last night's TV news. It didn't. And the mystery about this "Savior" guy had the whole city buzzing. Moishe's was no exception: Didja hear? The Savior this, the savior that. Whatta y'think? Blah-blah-blah. The story wasn't a day old and already Stan was sick of it.

"Yours say anything about his gun?"

"No. Not that I recall. I—"

"You guys figured out who he is yet?" said a squeaky voice with a Brooklyn accent sharp enough to cut steel.

Sally, their usual waitress at this, their usual table, had returned with her usual pot of coffee. Seventy if she was a day and built like a hunchbacked bird, she dyed her hair flame orange and applied eye make-up with a trowel.

Stan noticed how Joe slipped his scarred hand off the table and onto his lap. An automatic move. Seeing it caused something to twist inside Stan. Joe shouldn't have to hide any part of himself.

Two years now since the accident . . .

Accident, hell. He and Joe had called the fire an accident and stuck to the story so well that Stan caught himself every now and then believing it really was an accident. But the fire that had ruined their reputations and put them both out of business and scarred Joe for life had been no accident.

Joe hadn't been the same since then. Before the fire he'd been Joe Koz, top torch in the Northeast, maybe the whole coast, and no slouch with C-4 either. Now . . . well, he was damaged goods, and his ruined hand was only the visible part; he'd been damaged inside as well. He'd stopped caring. He never worked out anymore. Must have put on forty pounds while Stan had maintained his fighting weight. He was four years younger but now looked a good ten years older.

Stan looked up at Sally. "Who? This Savior guy? Why should we care?"

"We might," Joe said. "We might care a lot."

Something in his voice made Stan give his brother a closer look; he noticed that Joe's face was set in grimmer lines than usual.

"Sure you do," Sally said, refilling their cups. "Especially if they offer a reward."

"If the city doesn't," Joe said, "I just might offer one myself."

Sally laughed. "You do that, Joe. You do that."

As she moved on, Stan stared at his brother. "What's up, Joe?"

"It doesn't say nothin' in the *Times* there about the kind of gun he used to whack the crazy?"

"No."

Joe smirked. "I guess bein' a college boy has its drawbacks. Even us lowbrow dropouts hit pay dirt once in a while."

They'd had a long running rivalry about who read the better paper. Joe had never finished high school. Stan had gone to college after Nam, earned a B.A. in English from Pace, not that he ever used it. All he'd ever needed to know he'd learned in Nam.

"Get to the point."

"One of *The Light*'s reporters was on that train last night—right in the car where it all went down—and he says here this Savior guy used a tiny little .45 that he pulled out of an ankle holster."

Stan went cold. The *Times* articles had said the killer had used 9mm pistols with homemade silencers but hadn't mentioned a thing about the caliber of the Savior's gun or his holster.

"That doesn't mean it's him," Stan said.

"Yeah. I bet there's fucking thousands of guys running around with teeny-tiny .45s strapped to their ankles."

For the first time in two years Stan saw that old spark in his brother's eyes. He didn't want to douse it.

"You've got a point. It could be him. But don't get your hopes up."

"*Get* them up?" Joe grinned, showing yellow teeth. He'd never been much for dentists. "They're already up—*way* up. I hope to God it's him, Stan. And I hope if he doesn't show himself they track him down and drag him into the spotlight. Because then we'll see him, and then we'll know if he's our guy, and if he is he's gonna die!"

"Easy, Joe," Stan said. "You're getting loud."

"Like I give a steaming wet brown cruller! Damn fuck right I'm getting loud!"

He held up his left hand and waved it in Stan's face. Mottled shiny pink scar tissue gleamed under the ceiling fluorescents; it enveloped his index and middle fingers, fusing them into a single digit, and it swathed his ring and pinky fingers, joining them as well. The thumb too was scarred but remained separate.

"We've got issues with this guy, Stan. Serious business issues. But for me it's personal too." He began pounding the table with his good hand. "I've been lookin' for him two years, and if this is him, he's gonna die! I'm gonna blow him off the face of the fucking earth!"

Joe's final words echoed off the hammered tin ceiling of Moishe's kosher deli where patrons and staff alike stared at him in stunned silence.

I'm going to have to make some assumptions here, Sandy Palmer thought as he leaned over his subway map. He sat at his cluttered desk in the front room of his apartment and traced the Broadway line through the Upper West Side.

One indisputable fact: the Savior had taken off at Seventy-second Street. But had that been his intended stop or had he been forced by the circumstances? Had he been heading home or heading to work or on his way to his girlfriend's? Trouble was, the Nine went all the way to Van Cortlandt Park up in the Bronx.

Sandy stared at the face on the Identi-Kit printout propped up against the computer screen before him. Who are you, my man? Where do you live? Where do you hang? Where do I find you?

He couldn't see much choice in where to search. He'd have to assume that the mystery man either lived on or frequented the West Side around Seventy-second Street or somewhere above that.

He leaned back and rubbed his eyes. A *lot* of territory. Millions of people.

Well, no one said fame and fortune would come easy. Good journalism sometimes required a lot of legwork. He was up for it. He just had to hope he got lucky and—

The phone rang. Oh, no. Not his mother again. He'd called his folks last night to tell them about the shooting and his story in the morning edition. Bad move. Mom had lost it, crying for him to come back home where he'd be safe; Dad had kept his composure but agreed that Sandy should come home, at least for a few days. No way. He wasn't a college kid anymore. He was twenty-six and this was where he lived and worked. The conversation hadn't ended on a happy note.

He debated letting the answering machine pick up but decided against it. He got out half a hello when a gruff voice cut him off.

"That you, Palmer?"

Sandy recognized McCann's voice. And he didn't sound happy. Oh, shit, he was going to come down on him for sneaking that photo.

"Detective," he said. "Good to hear from you."

"I thought we had an understanding about that gun, Palmer."

"What gun?"

"The second shooter's. We were gonna keep certain things out of the press."

"I haven't breathed a word about it being a Semmerling."

"Yeah but your piece mentions that he used 'a miniature .45.' That kind of narrows the field, don't it?"

Shit. He hadn't spilled that on purpose. Sandy felt like saying, I thought you didn't read *The Light*, but he wanted to keep McCann on his side. He could be a valuable resource.

"I'm sorry, Detective. I didn't know. I don't know anything about guns."

"Well, you should start learning."

"Look, I'm sorry. I'll be more careful in the future."

"See that you are."

And then he hung up, but Sandy thought he'd detected the slightest softening of the detective's tone before the connection broke. Good. He couldn't afford to burn any bridges. And McCann hadn't even mentioned the photo.

The intercom buzzed. Someone calling from the foyer. What now?

"Yeah," he said, depressing the button.

"Is this Sandy Palmer?" said a woman's voice. Young, Tentative.

"That's me. Who's this?"

"Beth Abrams. From the . . . the train last night?"

Oh, wow!

"Beth! Come on up!"

He buzzed her in, then surveyed his apartment. What a sty! He scrambled around picking up the dirty clothes and junk mail that littered the place. He tossed everything into the bedroom and closed the door on it. The place still looked a shambles.

Should've showered, he thought. He gave each armpit a quick sniff. Not great, but not offensive.

The printouts! Shit, he didn't want her seeing those. He slipped them into a manila envelope just as she knocked. He pulled the door open and she looked awful as she stood on the threshold, her pale face tear-streaked and shadowy half moons under her big dark eyes.

"Beth," he said. "How in the world—?"

And then she was tight against him, her arms locked around his back, sobbing her heart out. Oh, man, did that feel good. When had any woman, let alone an attractive one like Beth, thrown her arms around him? He closed the door and held her as she cried, absorbing her shaking sobs.

It took her a good ten minutes to regain control. He wished she'd taken more time. He could have stood there all day.

"I'm so sorry," she said, backing up a step and wiping her eyes on her sleeve. She was still all in black, dressed in the clothes she'd worn last night. "I didn't mean to do that, it's just that I'm such a wreck. I mean, I can't sleep, I can't eat, I wanted to go back to Atlanta last night but there were no flights that late and besides no one's home because my folks are touring Scandinavia and are somewhere in fucking *Oslo* right now and I tried to talk to my boyfriend about it and I thought he understood but after a while he let it slip that he thought it was awesome. Can you *believe* that? He thinks it would have been so *awesome* to have been there! So I just walked out and I need to talk to someone who understands what it was like, someone who was there too."

"That's me," he said. "But how did you find me?"

"I saw your picture in the paper and remembered you saying you'd graduated from Columbia so I called the alumni office as soon as it opened and they gave me your last address. I hope you don't mind."

"Mind? Are you kidding? I was trying to figure out how to get in touch with you but I never got your last name."

"And I realized I never really thanked you for what you did."

"What I did?"

"Stop being modest. You shielded me with your own body. I'll never forget that."

"Oh, that," he said as guilt spiked him. "Let's not make too much of that."

"How can you be so calm?" she said, staring at him. "How come you're handling this and I'm not?"

He'd been asking himself that same question. "Maybe because I was able to write about it. I had to confront my terrors; maybe focusing and putting them down on paper was some sort of exorcism."

Not to mention how my being there is going to make my career.

"There's another way to look at it," he added—this had just occurred to him and it was pretty good. "You have to figure, with all the millions of people in this city and all the subway lines and trains that run every hour, what are the chances of being caught on a subway car with a gun-toting madman? A zillion to one, right?"

Beth nodded. "I guess so."

"So what are the chances of getting caught twice? Think about that. The odds of either of us ever having a gun pointed our way again has got to be *eighty* zillion to one. So the way I look at it, I just survived the worst moment of my whole life. Everything from here on is a cakewalk."

"I never thought of it that way." She took a deep breath. "I can't believe this, but I think I feel better already. Just seeing you so together after going through the same thing I did makes it easier to handle."

Did that mean she was going to leave? Hello, have a good cry, feel better, then back to the boyfriend? No way.

"Want some coffee? Tea? I've got some good green tea."

"You know," she said with a twist of her lips which, on a day like today, had to suffice for a full-fledged smile, "all of a sudden that sounds good."

He started toward the kitchenette. "How about something to eat? I don't have much but—"

"No. I still can't think of eating. Just some tea would be great."

Good, he thought, because unless you're into chunky peanut butter and stale Ritz crackers, I'm afraid you're out of luck. The cupboard is bare, babe.

"Have a seat on the couch there and I'll start the water boiling."

What do I do now? he asked himself as he filled the kettle.

He'd been planning to start canvassing the Upper West Side with his printout. He'd called in sick at work, telling them he was still too shaken up to make it in. They'd all been understanding, even going so far as to offer him stress counseling, which left him feeling guilty.

But what he needed far more than stress counseling was a big follow-up story.

Then George Meschke himself got on the line and went on about how sales of this week's issue were going through the roof. Lots of the outlets had squawked at first at the double shipments they received, but now they were calling to say thanks—they'd sold out.

So Sandy was the man of the moment down at *The Light*, but that wasn't going to help him here at home. As much as he needed to find the Savior, he so wanted to make the most of this chance with Beth too. She'd come looking for *him*, damn it, so he'd be a real jerk to blow her off. Turn her away now and he might never see her again.

Shit. Why couldn't anything be easy?

"Do you take yours with sugar?" he called as he checked the bowl.

He usually snagged a packet or two from the coffee shops and delis when he remembered to, but it looked like he hadn't remembered in too long. Just a few white granules speckling the bottom.

Beth hadn't answered him so he headed back toward the front room.

"I hope you don't need—"

And as he moved, for a second, just a second, he had a vision of her lying on the couch, stripped of her clothing, her white skin stark against the dark fabric, open arms reaching for him as she offered herself in grateful repayment for what she considered an act of unparalleled bravery. After all, if he'd been willing to sacrifice his life for her safety, the least she could do was . . .

And there she was, lying on the couch . . .

. . . limbs akimbo . . .

. . . fully dressed . . .

. . . sound asleep.

Got to hand it to you, Palmer, he thought. You sure do have a way with women. A real knack for riveting their interest.

And then it hit him that this was perfect. She could sleep here while he started canvassing.

Yes! Like having his cake and eating it too.

He tiptoed into his bedroom and grabbed a pillow and blanket, then returned to the couch where he slipped the former under her head and tucked the latter around her body.

He found a pad and scratched out a note.

> *Beth—*
>
> *Had to go down to the paper. If you wake up before I'm back, please don't leave. We have LOTS to talk about!*
> *Sandy*

He placed the pad where she had to see it, then leaned over and kissed her on the cheek.

"You're safe here," he whispered.

He grabbed the envelope with the printouts, tucked them into his knapsack along with his note pad, pens, and tape recorder—be prepared, as the Boy Scouts say—then eased himself out.

Life hadn't been great before, but it was definitely getting better. Not a bowl of cherries yet, but on its way.

4

"All right already!" Abe said when he finally opened the door in response to Jack's insistent knocking. "My hundred-yard sprint days are long past."

"It's known as the hundred-yard *dash*, Abe."

"Dash, sprint, whatever—I can't do it anymore."

Jack doubted that Abe Grossman, the balding proprietor of the Isher Sports Shop, whose belt length probably equaled his height, had ever sprinted or dashed a hundred consecutive yards in his life. He strode by him and headed down one of the narrow, canyonesque aisles teetering with hockey sticks and basketballs and safety helmets, heading for the counter in the rear. His nose started to itch from the dust that layered everything. Abe didn't do high volume in sporting goods. His real business was in the basement.

"Got the morning papers?"

Silly question, Jack knew. Abe read every issue of every local English language paper—morning, evening, weekly.

Behind him he heard Abe's mocking tone, " 'Good morning, Abe, my good and dear friend.' And a very good morning to you, Jack. My, but it's early, even for you. 'Yes, Abe, so sorry to barge in on you like this—' "

"Abe," Jack said. "I'm feeling just a bit frazzled this morning and I could use your help."

He hadn't slept well. The combination of the subway mess and running into Kate on the same night had kept him turning and pounding his pillow until dawn.

" 'Frazzled,' says he; cranky, says I. But I should be one to quibble? He wants help but he asks for the morning papers."

"Yeah. I need another pair of eyes to help me go through every article on last night's subway killings word by word and—"

"For why? To see if the police got an accurate description of you?"

Jack stopped and turned so fast he almost lost his balance. He felt his blood congealing as he stared at Abe.

"You know?"

"What's not to know?" Abe said, slipping his considerable bulk past Jack—no easy feat in these confines. He waddled on and led Jack back to the scarred counter where the morning papers lay scattered. "A gun-toting crazy gets blown away by this nondescript *mensch* with a .45 the size of a *kreplach* and I should think it's Senator Schumer? Or Bernie Goetz back on the job?" He grinned. "So where's your halo, Mr. Savior?"

"But . . . but how?"

This was bad, very bad. If the connection was that obvious to Abe, how many other people had made it?

"The Semmerling, of course. You forget already who sold it to you?"

"Could've been another make. An AMT Backup or—"

"Could've, shmoud've. Who else but my dear friend Jack would go up against two autoloaders with a five-shot double-action piece?"

"Not like I had much choice."

"And you did have five shots, didn't you?" Abe's eyes narrowed as he scrutinized Jack. "A round in the chamber and four in the clip, right?"

Jack shrugged and glanced away. "Well . . . not exactly."

"Please don't tell me you started off with an empty chamber."

"I know it's safe but a loaded chamber bothers me."

"What if four hadn't been enough, Jack? What if you'd needed that fifth round? Where would you be now?"

Jack noticed a shift in Abe's tone. He glanced at his old friend's face and saw real concern there.

"Point taken."

"So tell me: how close did he come to killing you?"

"What makes you think he came close at all?"

"You were outgunned and you had to work that *farkuckt* slide for every shot." Abe visibly shuddered. "You could have wound up in a body bag like the rest."

"To tell the truth, I think he was so shocked to see someone else with a gun that he didn't know what to do. Never occurred to him that he might have to defend himself."

"So you didn't need a fifth?"

"Didn't even need the fourth." Jack dropped the spent casings from last night on the counter. "Here's the brass."

"Very considerate of you. I'll recycle these and—wait: there's four here. I thought you said—"

"Used it to kill his boom box."

Abe winced. "Don't tell me: playing rap. Dr. Schnooky Ice or somebody."

"Nah. An old song I used to like, but I don't think I'll want to hear it again for a long while. Can we go through the papers now?"

"*Newsday* and the *Times* I've been through already. No detailed description in either."

That was a relief. "All right, you take the *News* and I'll take the *Post*." As Abe settled on his stool behind the counter, Jack scanned everything pertinent in the *Post* and found nothing.

"So far, so good."

"Nothing in the *News* either," Abe said.

Jack felt the tension coiled in his shoulders and along the back of his neck begin to ease. He spotted the *Village Voice* in the pile. No need to bother with that—a weekly wouldn't have a fast-breaking story like the massacre—but he couldn't resist a dig at Abe.

He tapped its logo. "I'm surprised, Abe. I didn't think you stooped to freebies."

"For the *Voice* I make an exception—but only because of Nat Hentoff. Even when it wasn't free, I bought the *Voice* for Nat. Such a *mensch*."

"Right. Like I used to buy *Playboy* for the articles. 'Fess up. You read the *Voice* for the personals."

"You mean those ads that show pictures of beautiful woman but feel the need to have a banner reading FEMALE plastered across her *tuchis* to assure me that what I'm looking at is what I'm looking at? That I don't need."

The logo of *The Light* was visible at the bottom of the pile but Jack gave no sign that he'd seen it.

"Got any scandal sheets?"

"Feh! Never!"

"Not even *The Light*?"

"Especially not *The Light*. Grant me a modicum of taste."

"Not even as paper to line Parabellum's cage?"

"Parabellum wouldn't allow it. Never. Not fit for his droppings."

"But here it is."

"Where?"

"There. *The Light*—right in front of you."

"Oh, that. Well, I can explain. You see, I was looking for birdcage paper this morning and Parabellum spotted the headline and liked it so he made an exception. A momentary aberration on the part of an otherwise splendid and tasteful bird."

"He's forgiven."

"Parabellum thanks you, I'm sure. But please don't tell anyone. He's very sensitive, and even those *shlub* park pigeons would laugh at him if they knew."

"My lips are sealed." Jack looked around as he tugged *The Light* from beneath the pile. "Speaking of Parabellum, where is the blue-feathered terror of the skies?"

"The perfect parakeet is sleeping in. You miss him? You want I should—?"

"No, let him sleep until we're finished. With my luck he'll drop one of his little packages right on some crucial para—oh, no!"

"SIX GUN SAVIOR" and "Exclusive Eyewitness Report" screamed at him. He opened to page three, almost tearing the paper in his haste. His gut clenched as he found a face he recognized staring back at him.

"Christ!"

"Nu?" Abe said, leaning forward to get a look. "What's up? What is it?"

Jack's memory colorized the grainy black-and-white photo—dark blond hair, hazel eyes, fair skin, gold wire on the glasses.

"This kid! He was sitting a couple of feet away from me on the Nine last night."

The byline identified him as Sandy Palmer. Jack felt his palms growing moist as he read Palmer's first-hand account, dreading each new paragraph, certain that here was the one that would describe his features; and if not this paragraph, then the one after it. Palmer had nailed the shoot-out pretty much as Jack remembered it, but when it came to describing the so-called Savior, the kid came up empty.

"He was looking right at me," Jack said. "And I know I looked at him right before I made my move. He had to have seen me."

"You think maybe he left it out for some reason?"

"But why?" Jack didn't know what to think.

"Here, look," Abe said, rotating the paper so he had a better angle. "He's got an excuse. Listen: 'I know I saw his face at one time or another during the trip, but it made no impression on me. Neither did any of the other faces I saw before the shooting began. Ships passing in the night, every night, night after night. And that's sad, don't you think? This man saved my life and I can't remember his face. Perhaps this is a lesson for us all: look at the faces around you, really look at them. They're not just faces, they're people. Remember them. You may wind up owing your life to the person behind one of those faces.' " Abe grimaced. " 'Ships passing in the night.' *Oy.* So original. This is journalism?"

"Do you believe him?"

Abe shrugged. "I should think that if he'd been able to sit down with a police artist and give him anything useful, your *punim* would be on page one of every paper in town."

"Good point." Jack was starting to feel better. "You know, I just might get through this."

"Let's hope so. But the vultures already are swarming. Senators, congressmen, councilmen pushing and shoving to see who can be first to climb on top of those dead bodies to get better seen. Their stomachs should burst. They yammer about stricter gun control but what we're getting is stricter victim disarmament. Next thing you know one of the dead folks' relatives will be running for office on a victim disarmament platform, arguing for more of the same kind of laws that left their dead loved one defenseless."

"Irony ain't always pretty."

"It goes further. These *shlubs* like to hit up small businesses for donations. They don't know how good their *farshtunken* laws are for my real business, but they shouldn't come to me looking for donations. A *krenk* I'll give them."

Jack thought about Abe's real business, about the scores of pistols and rifles racked in the basement. He hesitated, wondering if he should ask, then plunged ahead.

"You ever wonder when you hear about something like this if it was one of your guns that did the killing?"

Abe sighed. "Yes, I do. But I'm careful who I sell to. That's no guarantee, obviously, but most of my customers are solid citizens. Of course, their buying a gun from me automatically makes them criminals. Felons even. But mostly they're decent people looking for a little extra protection who shouldn't want to be awakened in the middle of the night by stormtroopers when someone decides to collect all the city's registered weapons. Lots of ladies I sell to. These victim disarmers would rather have a woman raped and beaten to death in some back alley than let her carry a little equalizer. A *broch* on all of them!"

Uh-oh, Jack thought as Abe's face reddened. Here he goes.

"Gun laws they want? Make me king and gun laws they'll get! Random checkpoints day and night! If you're not carrying a weapon— *bam!* A fine! Three offenses and we lock you up! Last night would never have happened in *my* city! That *meshuggener* would have thought twice, three, maybe four times before trying what he did, and even if he'd gone ahead he'd have got off one, maybe two shots and then everybody would have opened up on him and a lot fewer bodies would've been dragged out of that car. And just imagine what the body count would have been if you'd been delayed a few minutes and wound up on the next train. Think about that."

"I have. And I'm also thinking you're crazy. You have any idea what this city would be like if you gave everyone a gun?"

Abe shrugged. "A period of adjustment there'll be, of course, during which a lot of defective genes will be removed from the pool, and during which I might maybe think about going on vacation. But when I came back I'd be living in the *politest* city on earth."

"Sometimes I wish the gun had never been invented."

"No guns?" Abe put his hand over his heart. "You mean a world where I'd have to make my entire living selling this sporting junk? *Oy!* Wipe such a thought from your brain!"

"No, seriously. I wouldn't mind a world where no guns existed."

But if one gun existed—just one—Jack wanted to be the man to own it. And since lots of guns already did exist, he wanted to own his share, and he wanted to own the best.

"Enough sky blue," Abe said. "You have plans for the day?"

Jack thought about that. Hadn't made any because he hadn't been sure he'd be able to show his face on the street. Now the whole day had opened up. Gia wouldn't be back until tomorrow but . . .

"Maybe I'll get together with my sister."

Abe's elevated eyebrows wrinkled his forehead all the way up to where his hairline used to be. "Sister? I remember you saying once you had one but since when are you in contact?"

"Since last night."

"What's she like? She'd like a good deal on a .32 maybe?"

Jack laughed. "I doubt that. Tell you the truth, I'm not sure yet what she's like. It's been a lot of years. But I hope to find out . . ."

5

Sitting alone in Jeanette's sunny kitchen, Kate cradled the phone after the last of three calls she'd made this morning.

The first had been to Kevin and Elizabeth—one of her twice-daily calls—before they ran out to school. They were sixteen months apart in age but, because of the timing of their births, only a year apart in school. The school year was drawing to a close and neither could wait for it to end, especially Kevin who, as a junior, thought he knew it all. She hoped he wouldn't muff his final exams. Liz was a sophomore and practicing like mad for her big flute solo in Telemann's Suite in A Minor with the school orchestra, nervous but handling it pretty well. Kate had promised again for at least the hundredth time to be back home next Monday to hear her.

And of course the lies continued—about how the person she was nursing back to health was a dear old college sorority sister who'd been living in Europe and had returned for cancer treatment.

So many lies . . . lies to everyone. Sometimes she wondered how she kept track of them all. She was so sick of lies, but she couldn't quit quite yet. She'd have to go on with this double life for two more years. Just hang on until Liz was eighteen and heading for college. Then she'd come out. With a bang.

But until then . . .

Kate ached to be back with the kids but knew she couldn't leave Jeanette in this state. She'd have to find some resolution to the situation before she headed back to Trenton this weekend.

The next two calls had been to complete strangers. She had no intention of involving Jack in her problems, but hadn't been able to resist the opportunity to peek through a window into her brother's life and perhaps learn something about the enigma he'd become.

The first had been to a fellow pediatrician, an infectious disease specialist working not far from here in a clinic for children with AIDS; the second to an endocrinologist named Nadia Radzminsky.

Kate hadn't let on that Jack was her brother, saying only that he'd offered their names as references. Both women had been effusive in their praise, but evasive when Kate had pressed for details about what he'd done to earn their regard. Alicia Clayton, the pediatrician, had said something to the effect that Jack didn't come cheap, but was worth every penny. Each had made it clear, though, that she could trust Jack with anything. Even her life.

Her younger brother was sounding a little scary. He was known as Repairman Jack . . . and for a price he fixed things . . . problems. How bizarre.

Not that my circumstances are exactly run-of-the-mill, she thought as she rubbed the healing puncture in her palm.

It hadn't been a dream. Something had pricked her palm last night. It couldn't be a spider or insect bite because she saw no tissue reaction. It looked like a needle had stabbed through the skin.

The thought gave her chills. With HIV and hepatitis C and who knew how many other as yet unrecognized diseases floating about, a puncture wound was not something she could brush off. She couldn't imagine Jeanette doing anything to harm her, but then she'd never imagined Jeanette behaving as she had the past few days.

Kate looked up at the sound of the study door opening and saw Jeanette, mug in hand, crossing the living room. She'd been hiding away all morning. Dressed in a loose red T-shirt and jeans, her feet snug in her well worn Birkenstocks, she looked wonderful. If only she'd smile . . .

"More coffee?" Kate said, putting on a hopeful grin.

"Just need to heat this up," Jeanette replied, her tone and expression neutral.

At least she doesn't seem as angry as last night, Kate thought. I suppose I should be grateful for that.

"What are you doing in there? Working?"

Jeanette didn't look at her as she placed her cup inside the microwave and started jabbing the buttons. "What's wrong—couldn't see enough through the keyhole?"

That stung. "Darn it, Jeanette, that's not fair! I'm not snooping on you!"

Jeanette turned toward her with a sneer twisting her lips, but then her whole expression changed, flashing from smugness to wide-eyed terror.

"Kate, oh please, Kate, help me!" she cried, staggering forward against the counter and gripping it with white-knuckled intensity.

Kate was out of her seat, moving around the counter. "Dear God, Jeanette, what's wrong?"

"Something's happening to me, Kate! I think I'm losing my mind!"

She grabbed Kate's forearms, her trembling fingers digging deep into her flesh, but Kate didn't mind. She could see in her eyes that this was Jeanette—*her* Jeanette—and she was terrified.

"You're okay! You've got me! I'm here for you!"

"You've got to do something, Kate! Please don't let this happen to me! Please!"

"Don't let what happen?"

"It's taking over!"

Oh, Lord, she sounded so paranoid. "It? What are you talking about?"

"Please, Kate! Call Doctor Fielding and tell him it's taking over!"

6

Wonderful things, buses.

Rarely during his fifty-two years had the old Terrence Holdstock used mass transportation, unless of course one included jetliners in the category. He had never ridden a bus. But the One Who Was Terrence loved buses. Took them everywhere. The more crowded the better.

He'd boarded one on Fifth Avenue—didn't know which line, didn't care. One was as good as another. He bided his time during the stop-and-go progress downtown, edging toward the rear, waiting to make his move. The packed bodies in the aisle, the smorgasbord of odors would have bothered the old Terrence, but the One Who Was Terrence didn't mind at all.

Finally he saw his chance: the skinny black woman who had been occupying his favorite seat—right side, by the window, next-to-last row—rose and debarked. Quickly he slipped past her seatmate, nestled his stocky frame into her vacated seat, and settled down for a nice long ride.

Yes, this was by far the best seat. From here he could watch nearly all the packed humanity within, and observe the streaming crowds of hosts on the sidewalk beyond the glass. He would spend much of today here, just as he had spent much of yesterday, and the day before.

The old Terrence, before he'd finally faded away, had been baffled by this behavior. And he'd been upset, incensed even, when the new Terrence had quit his job at the agency without so much as a good-bye to his accounts. But he'd never been terribly fond of that job anyway. And besides, what would being an ad exec matter after the Great Inevitability? There would be no such wasted activity as advertising in the future, but the old Terrence was too stubborn and, in the end, too frightened to realize that.

The One Who Was Terrence looked forward to the glorious new world. Of course he should: he was going to be instrumental in bringing it about. And then—

A sudden ripping sensation—not in his clothing, not in his viscera, but in his mind—jolted him. Something was wrong. Who—?

Alarmed, he searched and realized that Jeanette was missing; gone without a trace. Was she dead? This was terrible. He knew her address. He had to go there!

The bus was gasping to a stop at just that moment. The One Who Was Terrence lurched from his seat and fought his way down the aisle to the exit doors. He caught them as they were starting to close and slammed them back. He jumped to the pavement and immediately stepped into the street, looking for a cab.

He was frightened. Nothing like this had ever happened. It wasn't in the plan. It might ruin everything!

Just as suddenly as it began, it was over.

Jeanette released Kate's arms and staggered back to lean against the counter, as if dizzy. She blinked and looked at Kate.

"What just happened?"

"I don't know," Kate said, as baffled by this new shift in mood as she was by the first. Like turning a switch. "Don't you?"

"No. I think I must have blacked out. First you were standing over there and now you're right in front of me and I don't remember you moving."

"But you were talking to me, shouting, in fact. Something about 'it's taking over.' "

Shock mixed with uneasiness on Jeanette's face. "I said that? No, I . . . couldn't have said that. I'd remember."

"Why would I make that up, Jeanette?"

"I don't know. Taking over what?"

"You didn't get to it, but you seemed terrified." Kate stepped closer and placed a hand on Jeanette's arm. "Jeanette, I think you had a seizure."

She pulled away. "What? Epilepsy? Don't be ridiculous! I've seen seizures. I know what they're like. I wasn't shaking, was I? I didn't fall down and start foaming at the mouth."

"That's a grand mal seizure. But there are all kinds of seizures. Temporal lobe seizures can cause personality changes, bizarre behavior. I—"

"I did *not* have a seizure!"

"It could be the tumor, Jeanette. Maybe it's not responding as well as we thought. Or maybe this is an aftereffect of the treatment. We've got to call Dr. Fielding."

"No. Absolutely not."

"But just a moment ago you were begging me to."

"You must have misunderstood. Why would I want to see Dr. Fielding? I'm fine. Never felt better."

"Jeanette, please." The more Kate thought about what she'd just witnessed, the more concerned she became. She'd never seen such a dramatic personality shift—a real-life Jekyll and Hyde without the smoking potion. She felt the nape of her neck tighten. "This could be serious."

"It's nothing, Kate. Don't trouble yourself about it. Just leave me alone. I—" She turned her head sharply, as if listening. "Wait. Someone's coming."

Jeanette slipped past her and headed for the door. Before she was halfway across the front room the door swung open. A man stood on the threshold. Kate recognized him as the one who'd welcomed Jeanette into the house in the Bronx last night.

"How did you get in here?" Kate blurted.

His eyes briefly fixed on her—Kate hadn't been close enough until now to notice how small and cold they were—then flicked away. Neither he nor Jeanette bothered to answer her, but she noticed something metallic in his hand.

The realization that Jeanette had given him a key to her place made Kate queasy.

He stepped into the room and closed the door behind him. He held out his hands to Jeanette. "What happened to you?"

She shook her head and placed her hands in his. They stood staring at each other.

"Concerned," the man said.

Jeanette only nodded. They stared a few seconds longer, then Jeanette said, "Seizure."

With that they both glanced at Kate.

"What is going on here?" Kate said. "And who *are* you?"

"This is Terrence Holdstock," Jeanette said. "A friend."

"All right?" Holdstock asked Jeanette.

"Not sure."

"See myself."

More staring, then Jeanette turned to her. "We're going for a walk."

A panicky voice inside was telling Kate not to let Jeanette go off with this man. She had this terrifying and wildly unscientific impression that there were two Jeanettes, and the one she'd known and loved was trapped inside this stranger and trying to claw her way out.

"I'll come along."

"No," Jeanette said. "We need to be alone."

Without another word, not even good-bye, they turned and left.

At any other time, Kate knew, she would have been crushed. But she was too shaken for that. Something was terribly wrong. The problem was neurological. It had to be. And the man who had worked on her brain was her oncologist, Dr. Fielding.

Her hand shook as she reached for the phone. She had to call Fielding. But after that . . . what? What could Fielding do if Jeanette refused to see him? That man Holdstock seemed to have some mesmerizing influence over her.

Which meant she should make another call. To her brother. Much as she'd wanted to keep him out of this, she couldn't discount how the two women she'd called this morning had said they'd trust Jack with their lives. Maybe someone like him was needed here, because Kate found the coldness in Holdstock's eyes as unsettling as Jeanette's behavior.

Could she trust Jack with Jeanette's life? She didn't have much choice.

God, she hoped she wouldn't regret this.

8

With aching legs and burning feet, Sandy plodded toward his apartment door, grimly certain that he'd find the place empty, Beth gone. Which would be in perfect synch with how he'd come up after a day of trudging through the Upper West Side: empty.

Can't expect to strike it rich first time out, he kept telling himself.

But he couldn't deny that the hope of a lucky lightning strike, however unreasonable, had nestled in his brain when he'd set out this morning.

So much for hope. By five-thirty he'd had it. He knew he should keep pushing but he'd run out of gas. The streets and sidewalks were jammed and he couldn't take any more suspicious looks or negative headshakes. He was tired of hearing "Never seen him before in my life," and even more tired of lying about why he was looking for the man in the drawing. So he'd packed it in.

Tomorrow was another day.

But what about tonight?

I could sure use some company now, he thought. Female company with big brown eyes and short black hair. Beth company.

But he couldn't allow himself to hope that she'd still be there. She'd probably awakened, maybe hung around a little, got bored, and went back to her boyfriend.

And then Sandy heard the music, the spellbinding strains of "It Could Be Sweet" from Portishead's first album filtering through his door. He keyed it open and stepped inside. The music engulfed him along with an odor. Food. Someone was cooking.

"About time you got back!" Beth said, smiling from the kitchenette. "I was getting worried."

Sandy tried to take it in. Bottles and jars and boxes on the counter—wine, Ragu, Ronzoni. A candle burning, the blinds drawn, music playing . . .

Beth's face fell. Something in his expression maybe.

"Is this okay?" she said. "I hope you don't think I'm horning in but I woke up and there was no food so I thought I'd cook us dinner. If you're not cool with that . . ."

Sandy couldn't speak so he held up his hand to stop her.

"What's wrong?" Beth said. "Say something. Look, if I've over-stepped my bounds . . ."

What to say? Sandy thought. Then it hit him: try the truth.

"Sorry. I was kind of afraid to speak. I'm so happy you're still here I thought I'd cry."

Her smile lit the room. She ran to him and threw her arms around his neck. She hugged him, gave him a quick kiss on the cheek, then stepped back.

She said, "Jesus, you're something, you know that? So sweet! I've never met anyone like you."

"Well, I—"

"And I can't believe you like Portishead—at least I assume you like them because you've got all their albums. I *love* them. And not just because the lead singer and I have the same first name."

Lead singer? Sandy thought, still dazed. Oh, yeah. Beth Gibbon.

"You bought food?" he said. So lame, but it was the best he could do at the moment.

"Yeah. Are you anorexic or something? I mean, there was *no* food in this place."

Sandy's head was spinning and Beth was talking at light speed. Could she be a crankhead or something?

"I eat takeout a lot. Look, uh, Beth, are you all right?

"All right?" she said, laughing. "I'm miles better than all right. I don't think I've been so all right in years!" She dashed to the couch and picked up a handful of yellow sheets from his legal pad, the one he'd left the note on. "Look at this! Notes, Sandy! It's just so pouring out of me!"

"Notes about what?"

"About what? What else? Last night. I woke up and found your note and remembered what you'd said this morning and suddenly it was like *wow!* Insight! I am *so* psyched!"

"What'd I say?"

She grinned. "Oh, so you like Ray Charles too."

"Huh?"

"Never mind. You said maybe you were able to handle what happened because you had to write about it. That the writing forced you to confront your reactions, that putting it all down on paper was some sort of exorcism. Remember?"

"Yeah." He vaguely recalled saying something like that. "Sort of."

"So that's what I've been doing! For months now I've been going crazy trying to decide what to do for my thesis film, and when I woke up this afternoon I remembered what you said and there it was, staring me right in the face!"

"Your film?"

"Yes! It's going to be about what happened on the train last night. Not literally, of course, but metaphorically about having your mortality so shoved right in your face. And you know what? Ever since I started writing down these notes, I'm not afraid anymore."

She tossed the yellow sheets back toward the couch. They never made it. They fluttered instead like dying birds and fell to the carpet.

She threw her head back and shouted. "I'm saved!"

They drank the wine and talked as she cooked the spaghetti and spiced up the Ragu in some wonderful way. And they talked while they ate. Beth was twenty-four, from Atlanta, with an English degree from Baylor. Her folks were the sort who valued stability, she told him, and weren't all that crazy about her going for a film degree; it wasn't a career that guaranteed a steady income and benefits—like teaching, for instance.

And all the while Sandy ached for her but couldn't say so, couldn't make the first move.

Finally the wine and the food were gone. Sandy cleared the table with Beth. They were both standing at the sink when she turned to him.

"Can I ask you something?"

"Sure. Anything."

"Have you got something against sex?"

Sandy blinked in shock, tried to say no, but found himself stuck in a Porky Pig stutter. "M-m-m-m-me? No. Why would you say that?"

"Because I'm here and I'm as willing as I'll ever be and you haven't made a move. Not a single move."

That fear of rejection shit again, Sandy thought. Damn me! How do I get out of this?

"Well, look," he said. "I mean, after you gave me such a brush-off last night I thought maybe you might be, you know, playing for the other team."

He hadn't thought that at all, but it was a good cover.

Her grin split her face. "Me? A lez? Oh, God, that's such a riot!"

"It is?" It was the best he could come up with on such short notice.

"You were just a stranger on a train then." She nudged him. "And hey, how about that—I was reading a Hitchcock book no less. But now . . ."

Beth slipped her arms around Sandy's neck again and pulled his face down to hers.

"Now you're a guy who saved my life, or at least was willing to take a bullet for me, and then you calmed me down when I was so freaking out, and then you inspired my student film. Where the hell have you been all my life, Sandy Palmer?"

"Waiting for you," Sandy said.

And then her lips were sealed over his and she was hooking her right leg around him and tugging at the buttons of his shirt.

She wants me! he thought, his heart soaring. Wants me as much as I want her.

What a difference a day makes.

9

Kate was waiting outside on the front step as Jack neared the Arsley. She wasn't alone. In the fading light he could make out a tall, thin, stoop-shouldered man in a suit.

Who's this? he wondered.

He'd figured the easiest way to get to Pelham Parkway and back was to drive, so he'd offered his services. But he'd expected only Kate as a passenger.

Felt a smile start at the sight of her, and was struck again by what a good-looking woman she was. Dressed simply and casually in a fitted white shirt and black slacks, she still managed to project taste and style. Guy with her looked to be about her age, but on the homely side. Jack hoped this wasn't the "someone special" she'd mentioned last night. She could do a lot better.

He pulled his two-year-old black Crown Victoria into the curb before the pair. Kate leaned in the passenger window.

"Jack, this is Dr. Fielding, Jeanette's oncologist. He wants to come along."

Swell, Jack thought sourly.

Didn't know what Kate was getting him into, and a third party might tie his hands. She'd told him about Jeanette Vega, a dear friend from college recovering from brain tumor therapy with no one to care for her. And she'd told him about this Holdstock guy popping into Jeanette's unannounced with a key; that plus his apparent influence over Jeanette earned him a high creep quotient. Hopefully tonight's excursion would run smoothly, but Jack found cults generally creepy. Too unpredictable. Jonestown and those Hale-Bopp weirdos were prime examples.

But he smiled and said, "Sure. Why not?"

The doc slipped into the back seat and Jack noticed his dark hair, over-gelled and frozen into long shiny black rows left by his comb. He stretched a bony, long-fingered hand toward Jack. "Jim Fielding."

"Jack," he said, shaking Fielding's hand. "An oncologist who makes house calls. Am I witnessing an historic event?" He turned to Kate who was belting herself in next to him. "Hope you didn't use any illegal means of coercion."

"As opposed to legal means of coercion?" Kate said. "No, Dr. Fielding insisted on coming along."

"Really."

"I'm concerned about Jeanette's bizarre behavior," Fielding said, "particularly the possibility that she might be developing a seizure disorder. She's fortunate a trained observer like Dr. Iverson was there as a witness."

Dr. Iverson? Jack wondered, then realized he was talking about Kate.

"I'd like to do a little first-hand observation myself. And if Jeanette won't come to me, then I'll go to her."

Sounds like a good guy, Jack thought.

Kate patted the seat between them. "Big car. Reminds me of Dad's."

"He's got a Marquis, same car but sold by Mercury. It's the state car of Florida."

"I wouldn't have thought you were a big-car type, Jack."

"I'm not."

"You rented this just for tonight? Jack, you should have told—"

"No, it's mine. Sort of."

"Sort of how?"

"Just . . . sort of." Should he explain how he'd paid for the car but it was registered under someone else's name? Nah. "Don't worry about it."

"I'm not worried about it—just you."

"It's okay."

Cars were an ongoing problem for Jack. With no officially recognized identity, he couldn't own one in the conventional manner. At least as a city dweller he had little call for one, but on those rare occasions when the need arose he wanted immediate access. Used to keep an old Buick registered under Gia's name but that arrangement had led to a dicey situation where Jack had been linked to the car and the car had been traced back to Gia.

Wasn't about to let that to happen again. He made a point of learning from his mistakes and so he'd hunted around for another way to have access to wheels that couldn't be traced to him. Came up with a beaut: find a guy equipped to field whatever a disgruntled target of Jack's work might toss his way, then clone his car.

After weeks of careful searching, Ernie, his documents guru, found just the man: Vinny the Donut Donato.

Vinny D supplied muscle for a Bed Stuy shy; lived in Brooklyn Heights and drove a recent model Crown Vic—black, of course. Jack would have figured Vinny as more a Cadillac kind of guy, but when he looked in the Crown Vic's trunk he understood: big enough to hold three, maybe four bodies.

So Jack had Ernie make him up a set of tags and a registration identical to Vinny's; and a driver's license which, except for its photo, was a perfect match of Vinny D's. Then Jack went out and bought a Crown Vic like Vinny's—a banged-up version that he never washed, but the same make and model.

The thing Jack liked most about Vinny D was his perfect driving record. Ernie's probe of the DMV computer showed no points. Whether this was due to diligence and skill behind the wheel, or a liberal application of grease in official places, Jack neither knew nor cared. The important thing was that if Jack ever got stopped he wouldn't be hauled in as a scofflaw.

It wasn't perfect. Always the possibility of Jack and Vinny D winding up on the same street at the same time and Vinny just happening to notice that their tags were identical. But since Vinny kept his car in Brooklyn and Jack garaged his in Manhattan, and hardly used it, he figured the chance of that happening was practically nil.

"Do we have a plan?" Jack said. "Do we even know she's at this address?"

"It's the only place I can think of to start," Kate said. "She left with that man this morning and hasn't been back since."

Jack said, "I'm feeling a little left out here. You both know this woman and I've never met her. What's she like?"

Kate cleared her throat. "The Jeanette you'll meet tonight—if you do meet her—is not the same woman she was before her treatment."

"And just what was this treatment?"

"For a brain tumor—an inoperable malignant glioma."

Fielding added from the rear: "By far the most common primary tumor developing in the human brain and too often refractory to current therapeutic approaches."

Kate went on. "So when the diagnosis was made I did some research and found Dr. Fielding and his clinical trial. Jeanette qualified for his study and—" She turned in her seat toward Fielding. "Perhaps you can tell it best."

"Of course." Fielding leaned forward. "Jeanette's tumor was treated with a stereotactically administered recombinant adenovirus vector carrying the herpes simplex thymidine kinase gene, followed by intravenous ganciclovir."

"Oh," Jack said. "That clears that up." He glanced at Kate. "Anyone care to translate?"

Kate smiled. "I watched the whole operation. Under x-ray guidance, Dr. Fielding threaded a tiny catheter into the tumor in Jeanette's brain. He then injected the tumor with a special virus, a recombinant strain of adenovirus that's had a specific gene from a herpes virus spliced into it."

"Wait. Doc, you injected herpes into this woman's brain?"

"Not the herpes virus per se," Fielding said. "Just a piece of it. You see, the altered adenovirus is called a vector virus. I'm oversimplifying, but let's just say it's attracted to dividing cells, and wild cell division is what makes a tumor a tumor. When the vector virus meets the tumor cells it does what all viruses do: it adds its own genetic material to the tumor's."

Kate said, "Think of the vector virus as a Trojan horse, but instead of Greeks it's carrying this tiny piece of a herpes virus—"

"Thymidine kinase gene H5010RSVTK, to be specific," Fielding added.

"—which gets incorporated into the tumor cells along with the virus's own genes. Now, there's no specific drug that will kill malignant glioma cells, but we do have medications that will kill viruses. And one of them, ganciclovir, kills by destroying a virus's thymidine kinase gene."

"Exactly," Fielding said. "And so, after injecting Jeanette's tumor with the virus and giving it time to combine with the tumor cells, we flooded Jeanette with high intravenous doses of ganciclovir."

"Which made a beeline for the tumor," Jack said, getting the picture now. "The herpes gene acts as a homing device for the gan- whatever guided missile."

Fielding laughed. "Homing device and guided missile—I like that. I'll have to remember it next time I'm explaining the protocol to a patient."

Kate said, "The ganciclovir not only kills the tagged virus, it kills any cell carrying the thymidine kinase gene. And since the tumor cells now carry that gene . . ."

"Blammo," Jack said, filled with wonder. "No more tumor. Sounds like science fiction. Or maybe horror fiction. What kind of mind dreams up something like this?"

"I wish mine had," Fielding said. "But I'm merely following in others' footsteps."

"But who volunteered to be the first patient to have a virus injected into his brain?"

"Someone with nothing to lose. But lots of lab animals paved the way."

"So Jeanette is cured."

"Not completely," Fielding said. "At least not yet. Malignant gliomas are tough, resilient tumors. Her last MRI showed a marked reduction in the tumor's size but she'll probably have to undergo another course of therapy to finish it off once and for all."

Kate turned in her seat and looked at Fielding. "And you still don't see any possible link between the protocol and Jeanette's personality changes?"

Fielding paused before answering. "Getting a reprieve from what is in a very real sense a death sentence has been known to cause enormous psychological turmoil."

Which isn't exactly answering the question, Jack thought, but maybe he's worried about a malpractice suit.

Kate had given him Holdstock's address but Jack hadn't had the faintest idea how to get there. He'd checked out a map before leaving tonight and had the route pictured in his head.

Night had settled in by the time he reached Astor Avenue. He slowed to a crawl, watching for a number.

"There it is," Kate said, pointing to a brick house ahead. "The lights are on. I know Jeanette's in there."

"Okay," Jack said, pulling into an empty spot half a block down. "Now that we're here, what do we do? How do we confirm she's there?"

He was mildly uncomfortable with the situation. Too ad lib. Normally he'd have checked out the house in advance and have a plan in place. And he never would have brought anyone else along. But this was Kate's gig. He was along for the ride and to provide some back-up if necessary.

Kate said, "I looked through the living room window last time."

"That's a little risky, don't you think? A neighbor could report us as peepers."

"That would be catastrophic," Fielding said. "My entire career would be in jeopardy if I were even charged as a Peeping Tom."

Your *career*? Jack thought. If Jack got hauled in for anything—from shooting a crazy on a subway to littering—he could kiss his freedom bye-bye.

"Just a quick look," Kate said, opening her door. "I'll go myself. I've never heard of a woman being charged as a Peeping Tom."

No way Jack was letting Kate do it on her own. He got out on his side, and Fielding did the same. Career or not, curiosity must have got the better of him.

"Let's make this quick, people," Jack said as he caught up to Kate on the sidewalk. "One look, then back to the car to discuss our next move."

"I'll bet they're having that ceremony or seance or whatever it was I saw last night," Kate said.

When they reached the house Kate didn't break stride. She trucked right across the lawn toward the lighted window on the side. Jack slowed, letting Fielding go ahead of him. He brought up the rear, doing a three-sixty scan of the area. A few neighboring windows facing this way but no sign of anybody at them. All probably watching TV. Okay.

Kate reached the window, went up on tiptoe, and stared inside.

Jack heard her excited whisper: "There she is."

As Jack approached, Fielding came up behind Kate and peered over her shoulder. Jack saw him lean closer, then jerk back as if he'd received a shock.

"Oh, no!" he cried. Jack winced at the volume. "Oh, dear God, this is worse than I thought!"

He lurched away from the window just as Jack got there. Through the glass—thankfully it was down—Jack saw eight people sitting in a circle holding hands. And that was it. No one appeared to be speaking. The eight of them just sitting there with these goofy smiles on their faces. He was about to ask Kate which one was Jeanette but she'd slipped away.

"Dr. Fielding!" he heard her say. "Where are you going?"

Jack looked and spotted Fielding heading around the front of the house.

"Inside! I'm not leaving here until I find out what this is about!"

Kate followed Fielding and Jack followed Kate and the three of them wound up on the front steps. Jack went to grab Fielding to try to calm him down and find out what had set him off, but too late; he began pounding on the front door.

Kate looked at Jack and he jerked a thumb toward Fielding with a questioning look. She shrugged her shoulders, obviously as baffled as he.

"Take it easy, Doc," Jack said. "We don't need to wake up the whole borough."

Fielding looked as if he was about to speak when the door opened. A heavyset man with thinning blond hair and eyes too little for his face—his looks fit Kate's description of Terrence Holdstock—stood gaping at his three visitors.

"Why, Dr. Fielding. What a surprise!"

"What's going on here, Terrence?" Fielding said.

"Just a meeting. A support group, you might say."

"Support for what?"

"For the ordeal we've been through, and for the wonderful future that awaits us. All thanks to you, Dr. Fielding."

"Yes, well, I'm glad you feel that way, but how did you all meet? I have strict confidentiality procedures. If someone in my office—"

"Nothing like that, I assure you. We met quite by accident."

"*All* of you?" Fielding took a step forward. "Look, may I come in? I'd like to—"

Holdstock didn't budge. "I'm afraid not, doctor. We're right in the middle of our meeting. Perhaps some other time."

"No, please, I must talk to you, all of you."

Holdstock shook his head. "We're fine, doctor. And getting better every day, thanks to you."

"I want to see Jeanette!" Kate said.

"She will be home later. As for now, please let us be."

So saying, Holdstock stepped back and closed the door.

"No!" Fielding cried.

He raised his hand to hammer the door again but Jack caught his wrist before he could land the first blow.

"I don't think that's going to get us anywhere."

Fielding resisted for a second, then dropped his arm. "I guess you're right."

"That's it?" Kate said. "We're giving up? Just like that?"

"We're regrouping," Jack said. "Holdstock has the law on his side at the moment. This is his house and he's invited a bunch of guests over to hold hands. He can have the local boys in blue haul us off for disturbing the peace here. So I say we go back to the car and settle down and let Dr. Fielding here tell us why he hasn't been straight with us."

Fielding stiffened.

Kate looked at Jack as if he were crazy.

"Look at him," Jack told her. "Look at his expression. And that conversation with Holdstock. Could you make sense of that?"

She turned back to Fielding and her eyes narrowed. "What aren't you telling us?"

Fielding's eyes were haunted. "I know those people in there. They're all my patients. Every single one of them!"

10

"Jeanette is not the first in my clinical trial to exhibit personality changes," Fielding said.

Kate bit back her anger. She sat half turned in the passenger seat as Jack slowly cruised the empty, tree-lined streets. Fielding was a dark blob in the rear, lit occasionally by a passing street lamp.

"What do you mean?"

She could feel her emotions running wild, tugging her in all directions. She wanted to charge back and drag Jeanette from that house; but she also wanted to hear what Fielding had to say. That might be more important right now.

"Over the past month or so I've had calls from the families of a number of patients in the study. They all complained of personality changes or strange behavior."

"Why didn't you say that when I called you this morning?"

"Because I didn't want you jumping to conclusions. And I couldn't handle a barrage of questions for which I had no answers."

"That's why the house call," Jack said, and Kate picked up on his tone . . . disdain or disappointment, or perhaps a little of both. "It wasn't for Jeanette's sake. It was for yours. There's been a screw-up somewhere and you're trying to cover your ass."

"I did it for many reasons," Fielding said. "I needed a first-hand look at this strange behavior that was being reported. I figured I'd start with Jeanette, then see if I could observe others. I never dreamed I'd find everyone in the trial in one room."

"Everyone?" Kate said. The night was warm but she drew her legs up under her to ward off a sudden chill.

Fielding was nodding. "All eight."

"What's the big deal about that?" Jack said. "They all went through the same thing, so—"

"They shouldn't know each other," Kate told him. "It's standard procedure in clinical trials to keep the patients anonymous. So, if they've never met during treatment and don't know each other's names, how did they get together?" She turned back to Fielding. "Any ideas?"

"Holdstock said by accident, but that's impossible. And how all eight recipients of the same vector strain managed to—"

"*Same* strain?" Kate exclaimed. "You mean they all were treated with the same virus?"

Fielding didn't reply.

Jack said, "I believe she asked you a question, doc."

"All right, yes," Fielding sighed. "Terrence Holdstock was the first, Jeanette the most recent."

Kate swallowed. She had an uneasy sense about where this was going. "What's different about that strain?"

"I have no idea."

"He's lying," Jack said.

"I am not!" Fielding sputtered.

"Trust me," Jack said, his eyes on the road, his voice flat. "He's lying."

How can he be so sure? Kate wondered. Or is he just guessing and trying to goad Fielding? Kate decided to weigh in with her own prod.

"One way to find out," she said. "Go to your medical center's practices and standards committee and ask for a full review."

"That won't be necessary," Fielding said quickly. "I've already reported it to the hospital board and to NIH."

"NIH?" Kate felt a wave of nausea. He wouldn't contact NIH unless it was something major. "Why?"

"That's the National Institutes of Health?" Jack said. "Down in DC?"

"Bethesda, actually," Fielding replied. "You see . . ." His voice shook and his words seemed to dry up. He wet his lips.

This is going to be bad, Kate thought. She gripped the edge of her seat, squeezing it. Oh, Lord, this is going to be terrible.

"You see," Fielding went on, "after connecting the complaints to the same vector strain, I took out the cultures and ran an analysis on the virus. It . . . it has mutated into two separate strains."

"Mutated?" Jack said. "Does that happen a lot?"

"No," Fielding replied. "That is, some viruses mutate frequently, but not adenoviruses. This was totally unexpected."

Kate closed her eyes. "Mutated how?"

"The original strain remained but the mutation had altered the thymidine kinase gene."

Kate groaned.

"That's bad?" Jack said.

She said, "It means the mutated strain was injected into the tumor along with the original vector virus. But without the thymidine kinase gene the mutation is immune to ganciclovir. The drug killed off the vector virus and the infected tumor cells—"

"But not the mutation," Jack said. "Oh, hell."

"Right. That means that Jeanette and the others have a mutant adenovirus running through their brains."

"Is it contagious?" Jack said.

"Yes and no," Fielding said. "Adenoviruses usually cause mild infections—pinkeye is a common one—but are caught only from people shedding the virus. These people are not shedding the virus."

Kate turned to Fielding. "We've got to do something!"

"I told you: I've contacted NIH and they in turn should be contacting Jeanette within a day or two."

"I mean *now!*"

"What do you suggest?"

"Find a way to kill the mutation!"

"I've already begun testing various virucidal agents against it. I'm confident we can find an effective cure."

"But in the meantime," Kate said, "what about other complications?" She envisioned the viral particles invading Jeanette's neurons, multiplying inside, then rupturing the cell membranes and moving onto other cells, their numbers growing exponentially. "What about meningitis? Encephalitis? What about an abscess eroding into an artery and hemorrhaging? She could die, Dr. Fielding!"

"I'm working as fast as I can," he said. "But even if I had a cure in my pocket right now, it might not help us."

"What are you talking about?"

"Consider: why am I here instead of home? Because Jeanette refused to come in to be checked. How do we cure a patient who refuses treatment?"

Kate's stomach knotted as she remembered Jeanette's words this morning: *Why would I want to see Dr. Fielding? I'm fine. Never felt better . . .*

"It's a gray zone," Fielding was saying. "If the patients aren't complaining, if they deny anything's wrong and don't want treatment . . . you can see the problem, can't you."

Yes, she could.

A wave of fatigue swept over her, leaving her chilled and achy.

Fielding said, "I'll keep testing the mutation while we wait to hear from NIH. I'm sure a call from them will convince Jeanette and the others how serious this is and that they all need help."

But as far as Kate was concerned, Jeanette already did want help—she'd told Kate so this morning. Pleaded with her for help. And Kate was darn well going to see that she got it.

THURSDAY

1

"Easy, Joe."

Stan Kozlowski had watched his brother becoming more and more agitated as he tore though the morning papers at their tiny kitchen table. By unspoken agreement they'd decided to eat breakfast at their pad this morning. Joe's outburst at Moishe's yesterday had drawn too much attention. They'd been just two of the regulars, Stan and Joe, no last names. Now Joe had no doubt become the regular with the scarred hand who'd gone into a screaming rage about blowing somebody off the face of the earth. With outstanding federal and state arrest warrants on each of them, discretion said to lay low.

"Nothing!" Joe said, tossing the *News* onto the floor where it landed in a heap next to the similarly discarded *Post* and *Newsday*. "You'd think *one* of the assholes on that subway car would have gotten a good enough look at their fucking Savior to give *some* kind of description. What about your *Times* there? Anything?"

"Lots of psychobabble about the personality types of the two shooters." With one man dead and the other missing, Stan was amazed at the bull these "experts" could sling without speaking word one to either man. "But if you mean anything like a police artist sketch, no."

"Shit!" He leaped up from his chair and gave the papers on the floor a vicious kick, sending them into fluttering flight against the far wall. Which wasn't very far at all. "It's him, I tell you. This Savior is our guy!"

Stan wasn't going to say, Easy, Joe, again. He'd already said it too often since yesterday morning.

"I know you want it to be him, Joe, but—"

"Oh, it's not just *want*, Stan. I can *taste* him. I can smell his *stink*! My palm started to itch the minute I read about that tiny .45. He's our guy, Stan. He's the reason we're living in this shit hole. He's our fuckin' guy!"

Shit hole is right, Stan thought as he surveyed their crummy one-bedroom apartment.

How the mighty had fallen: from Upper East Side condo owners to fugitive Alphabet City renters—literally overnight.

All because of "our guy."

Whoever he was he'd come out of nowhere. And he came smart and tough. Whether he had a personal grudge or was hired for the job, who knew? Stan figured he was hired. A pro. Just like the two of them.

Fires and explosions—the Kozlowski brothers' specialties. All thanks to the U.S. Army and a tour in Nam.

Stan hadn't wanted to go to Nam, and if he'd stayed in college the war would have been over by graduation day. But when he'd flunked out in year one the draft board wasted no time scooping him up. Over in the provinces Stan learned all about C-4, became a gonzo expert at blowing up Charlie's booby-traps with the white clay-like substance. And he brought all that training home with him. He finished college after the war but the economy sucked then, so he'd gone into a business of his own, taking in Joe in as a partner, teaching him all he knew.

Together they'd made a good living. It was never personal. Somebody not making payments, somebody skimming too much, somebody talking too much, somebody at a point where he figured he'd been paying into his fire insurance policy long enough and decided it was time to make a withdrawal, they called Stan and Joe Koz.

They'd been a perfect team: Stan planned, Joe planted, and they took turns fashioning the bombs or mixing the accelerant.

Then "our guy" came along, interfered with their latest job—which turned out to be their last—causing a major botch that made them look worse than no-talent amateurs.

But that hadn't been the worst. Somehow he'd followed them back to their farm up in Ulster County and torched the house and the barn where they stored their C-4 and accelerants. And most of their cash.

Joe had ruined his hand and almost got killed trying to save that. And he'd failed.

But things got even worse. An investigation showed that the barn had housed a bomb-making operation; BATF was brought in and that was when the warrants started. Stan and Joe had owned the place in another guy's name but he'd rolled over in a heartbeat when the feds came knocking. RICO statutes got invoked and everything they'd owned wound up impounded.

Plus Joe couldn't get his hand fixed because that kind of plastic surgery wasn't exactly done in back rooms, and hospitals asked too many questions.

Finally, now, no one would hire them. Like they were dead. Worse than dead. Like they'd never existed. Like, the Kozlowski brothers? Who they? Never heard of them.

All because of one guy. Our guy.

But Stan was not convinced that he and this so-called Savior were the same.

"I want him too, Joe. And if this Savior guy turns out to be him, fine. We'll get him. Together. But not in a way that's going to point a finger at us. We'll do him the way he did us: mess him up and then disappear without a trace."

"You're worried about attention? I *want* attention. I want everyone to know who did him and why. Because he took *everything* from us, Stan. Remember how we used to be? We was hot. We was Tiffany. We wore Armani to the fucking gym! We used to watch our ankles through our socks. Remember that?"

Stan remembered, but why dwell on it. "At least we're not doing time."

"Time? We *are* doing time! A jolt in the joint would be better'n this. This isn't living, it's fucking hell. No, wait. If hell was a shit-filled toilet with a broken flusher in the dysentery capital of India, I'd take it over this. You got that?"

"Joe—"

"A guy with a combo of AIDS, brain cancer, and a colostomy's got it better'n us. No, Stan. I call the shots on this one. This gives me first dibs."

He held up his maimed left hand, thumb extended, the scar-fused fingers forming a shiny pink V. Someone seeing him do that on the

street once had called out, "Live long and prosper," and Stan had had
to pull Joe off the guy before he killed him.

"When I find the fucker I'm gonna tie him in a chair and get me
a blow torch and make his whole face look like this."

2

Kate stood in the bedroom doorway and blinked at the sight of Jeanette
smiling at her from the rocker in the sunny front room.

"Look who's a sleepyhead," Jeanette said pleasantly.

"Jeanette . . . you're . . ."

"Sitting and having coffee. Want some?"

Which Jeanette was this? Friendly though she seemed, it wasn't
Jeanette number one, the one she loved; and it wasn't the silent and
sullen number two. Could some third personality be emerging?

"No thanks. My stomach doesn't feel so hot."

In fact Kate's entire body didn't feel so hot. Chilled, rather. And
achy. She'd been exhausted when she returned last night and had fallen
into bed almost immediately. She still felt tired. She blamed that on
the weird dreams that had haunted her all night. She couldn't recall
any details beyond the fact that she'd awakened several times sweaty
and unsettled.

"I thought you'd be upset about last night. I didn't mean to pry,
but I'm concerned. I'm more than concerned, Jeanette. I'm worried
sick."

"I know you are," Jeanette said. "I was pretty angry the other night,
but now I realize you're doing it out of love. But don't worry yourself,
Kate. I'm fine, really I am. And I've never been happier."

"But Jeanette, you're not . . . you."

Jeanette smiled warmly. "Who else could I be? I know it seems confusing now, Kate, but soon you'll understand. Soon everything will be made clear."

"By whom?" Kate said, wandering over to the kitchen area.

"It will come from within." She began to laugh—a good-natured laugh without a hint of derision.

"What's so funny?"

"I just made a joke."

"I don't get it."

A beatific smile. "You will, Kate. You will."

Kate noticed a jar of Sanka on the kitchen counter.

"Decaf?" she said. "Since when?"

"Since today. I think I might be drinking too much caffeine. Maybe that's what happened to me yesterday. I got a little wired."

The Jeanette Kate knew could barely move until she'd had her morning coffee.

"That was a lot more than caffeine overload."

"Kate, how many times do I have to tell you I'm fine?"

"But you're *not* fine. Dr. Fielding told me the vector virus mutated and you and the others may be infected with it."

She went on to explain the details of Fielding's story.

Jeanette seemed blithely indifferent. "A mutation? Is that what he thinks? How interesting."

"It's not *interesting*, Jeanette," Kate said, restraining herself from screaming the words. "It's potentially catastrophic! How can you just sit there? If someone told me I had a mutant virus crawling around my brain I'd be on the next plane to Atlanta and the CDC!"

"Has it occurred to you that Dr. Fielding might be wrong?"

That brought Kate up short, but only for a second. "A mutation in a recombinant vector virus is so unusual, I'm certain he wouldn't have told us if he weren't one hundred percent sure."

"But wouldn't I be sick?"

You *are* sick, Kate thought.

"Poor Kate." Jeanette smiled sympathetically. "Getting yourself all worked up. Why not just calm down and let Dr. Fielding worry about it?"

"Well, at least he won't be worrying alone. He's called NIH; you should be hearing from them soon. And he's already working on a way to treat the new infection."

"Kill the virus?" Jeanette said. She lost her smile.

"Of course."

"Even if I'm suffering no ill effects?"

"He infected you with the virus, so he's got to eradicate it. He can't very well leave you infected."

Jeanette sat silent, staring at the wall.

Is it finally sinking in? Kate thought. She prayed Jeanette was appreciating at last how serious this was.

Finally she looked at Kate again. "Who was that other man with Dr. Fielding last night?"

The abrupt shift of subject left Kate a little dizzy. "Man? Oh, that was my younger brother Jack."

Jeanette smiled. "Your brother . . . not much of a family resemblance."

How would Jeanette know? She hadn't come to the door with Holdstock. Had she been peeking through a window?

"Will he be working with Dr. Fielding?" Jeanette said.

"I don't think so."

She don't know much about Jack's talents, but she doubted they lay in virology. He might wind up helping in other ways, though. She could see now how she might need him to come between Jeanette and Holdstock.

"I'd like to meet him," Jeanette said. "Does he know about you and me?"

Kate shook her head and felt that familiar tightening in her chest whenever she considered the prospect of coming out to anyone, especially a member of her family. She'd felt it last night when Jack had said that he thought it was about time he met this Jeanette. Kate had agreed but ducked setting a time and place.

"No. And I'd rather he didn't."

"Okay. We'll just be friends then."

More proof that Jeanette was not herself. The real Jeanette would have launched into a mini-lecture. She'd been out since her teens and fervently believed the closet should be a thing of the past. Not that Jeanette didn't appreciate the risks for someone in Kate's position, especially where child custody might be an issue. But here in this big city far away from Trenton, she'd have wanted Kate to come out to her brother, or at the very least consider it.

Okay. We'll just be friends. Uh-uh. That wasn't Jeanette. Not even close.

Jeanette added, "Why not invite him over for dinner tonight?"

"You're sure you don't have to go out?"

To another seance with your cult?

"I'd much rather meet your brother."

This third Jeanette was certainly easier to deal with than the second . . . but she still wasn't the real one, and Lord how Kate missed her.

"Jack's seeing a woman," Kate said. "He might want to bring her."

"Sure. I love to meet new people."

This could make for one strange evening, Kate thought. But on the positive side, she'd get to meet—what was her name? Gia. Such a warm light in her brother's eyes when he'd mentioned her. Kate wanted to meet the woman who had captured his heart.

3

Sandy felt good as he walked the West Eighties. No, check that, he felt totally fabulous. Life was da bomb. His ship was coming in. He could sense it just over the horizon, steaming his way.

Yesterday he'd been trudging door to door, store to store, dogged by a cloud of futility and a subvocal dirge droning on and on through his head about how he was attempting the impossible. Today he was bouncing along past the brownstones on the side streets and the endless variety of restaurants and shops along the avenues, grinning like an idiot.

"Beth," he whispered. He loved her name, the sound of it, the feel of it on his lips and tongue. "Beth-Beth-Beth-Beth-Beth."

They'd made love last night. Not just sex—love. Sweet and tender.

Not just two bodies, but two people with a connection. This morning they'd made love again, and it was even better.

After sitting in a coffee shop where they'd talked and talked, they'd split: Beth to a workshop and Sandy to the streets—he was still on sick leave; he just had to hope he didn't run into anyone from *The Light* while he was pounding the pavement.

He hated to leave her but all play and no work would very definitely make Sandy a dull boy. Very dull. But he and Beth would reunite tonight for dinner . . . and more.

As for the last forty-eight hours, Sandy could draw only one conclusion: anything was possible. And all things do come to those who wait.

That didn't make the task of finding the Savior any less daunting, but today he felt sure he'd succeed. He didn't know how long it would take but if he kept plugging he'd win the respect and renown he'd dreamed of. All he had to do was be patient. Rome wasn't built in a day.

He stopped before a bar named Julio's that sported a bunch of dead plants hanging in the window. The door stood open so Sandy stepped through. The dim interior, redolent of tobacco smoke and spilled beer, was bigger than he'd expected. The short bar curved around on his left; a sign hung over the stacked rows of liquor bottles: FREE BEER TOMORROW . . . He smiled; he liked that. But what was with all the dead plants?

Despite the early hour nearly half a dozen men stood at the bar smoking and sipping drafts. Sandy hesitated, then stepped up and placed his Identi-Kit printout before the nearest drinker.

"I'm looking for this man."

The fellow glanced at Sandy, then down at the printout, then back at Sandy. He had a worn middle-aged face, wore dusty work pants and a faded T-shirt that might have once sported a logo of some sort. A shot and most of an eight-ounce draft sat before him on the bar.

"Who the hell are you?"

Sandy was used to suspicious reactions. He went into his patter.

"I've been hired by the executor of his uncle's estate to find him. He's come into some money."

The man's eye's narrowed. "What's in it for me?"

Sandy couldn't count how many times he'd been asked that since he started searching. He'd finally come up with a reply that worked.

"Nothing from me, I'm afraid. I'm paid by the day. But that doesn't mean you can't work something out with this guy if you know him."

The man leaned toward Sandy. "You came to the right place," he whispered, his eyes shifting back and forth, his breath so sour Sandy had to grip the bar to keep from recoiling. "He's here right now."

Sandy jerked up straight and looked around. Oh, Christ! He's here? Right here?

But he saw no one who even vaguely resembled the man on the train.

"Where?"

"Right next to me!" the man said, then burst into a raucous laugh as he grabbed the printout and turned to his neighbor. "Ain't this you, Barney? Tell this fella here it's you and we'll both be rich!"

"Yeah that's me!" Barney cried. " 'Cept I'm better lookin'!"

Bastards, Sandy thought as they passed the sheet down the bar and back. Some of the others laughed, others just stared at him.

He held out his hand. "Very funny. Can I have it back now?"

"Naw," said the first drinker. "We're gonna keep this. Maybe start doin' our own search. Got any more?"

"That's my only one." Sandy had four more folded in his pocket but he wasn't about to let them know. "Please. I need it."

Barney said, "Hey, Lou, you know what I think? I think we should put my phone number on this, take it over to Staples, and get a hundred copies made. We plaster them all over the place and collect the reward."

No! Sandy thought, feeling a surge of panic. He couldn't lose control of that picture. It was his key!

"There *is* no reward! Now give it to me!"

He tried to grab the printout, reaching for it, but Lou roughly shoved his arm away.

"Watch it, kid. You spill my beer and I drink the next one out of your empty skull!"

"That's mine and I want it back!" Sandy said, his voice rising of its own accord. If he had to fight these old bastards he would. No one was going to screw up his future.

"Hey-hey!" said a new voice. "What's going on, meng?"

Sandy looked around and saw a short muscular Hispanic in a sleeveless sweatshirt.

"Hey, Julio," Lou said, handing him the printout. "Fella here's lookin' for this guy. You ever seen him?"

Julio—Sandy assumed he was the Julio this dive was named after—said nothing for a long time, slowly smoothing his pencil-line mustache with his free hand as he stared at the paper. Then, without looking up, he began peppering Sandy with questions about who and why and what reward. Sandy gave his standard replies but they didn't seem to be flying.

"Yeah, I seen him," Julio said, finally looking at Sandy. His eyes were piercingly dark.

Sandy saw truth in those eyes and felt his heart pick up tempo.

"Where?"

"Not sure. Around. Tell you what, meng. I do you a favor. I hang this up by the bar and if anybody knows him, they call you. What your number?"

Sandy was about to give it to him when he noticed that Barney and Lou had somehow managed to position themselves between him and the door. And the three other men at the bar had all stopped talk and were staring his way.

Menace writhed through the air . . . something going on here . . .

"I . . ." Think. *Think!* "This is kind of embarrassing . . . I've been a little short lately and so my service was canceled."

"Too bad. You got more of these?"

"Not on me."

"Where you live?"

Sandy was alarmed at where these questions were going . . . they all seemed aimed at pinning down *his* location when they should have been about locating the man on the printout. What had he stumbled into here?

"I'm staying with a friend. She . . . she wouldn't like me giving out her address."

Oh, shit! he thought, wishing he could take that back. That didn't go with his story about his phone being turned off.

"I thinking now," Julio said. "I think I remember seeing this guy a lot in the park."

"What park? Central?" That wasn't much help.

"No. Riverside."

That was even worse. Riverside Park ran along the Hudson for miles, from the Seventies up past the GW Bridge.

"Any particular area of the park?"

"Yeah. I think I seen him playing basketball a couple time. Right down here."

"This end of the park? Great."

"Yeah. You look there. Maybe you run into him."

"Thanks a lot." Sandy reached out a tentative hand. "Can I have my drawing back?"

"No," Julio said, folding it and sticking it in his back pocket. "I think I keep this one."

Sandy was about to protest but something in the little man's face told him that would be futile.

"I'd appreciate it if you wouldn't show that around until I find that man and talk to him."

"If that is your wish."

The reply startled Sandy. Why so agreeable all of a sudden?

Julio made a tight, almost imperceptible sweeping motion with his right hand and Sandy heard Lou and Barney move back to the bar.

Julio grinned. "And when you find this guy, you tell him Julio sent you and he wants ten percent, you hear?"

"You got it," Sandy said.

He turned and practically leaped through the door to the safety of the sidewalk. He headed west without a look back.

Glad to be out of that place. All sorts of undercurrents flowing through it. Probably something illegal going on and he'd riled their suspicions.

But no matter. He'd got the break he'd been praying for. And Riverside Park was only a few blocks ahead.

Anticipation spurred him into an easy trot.

4

"Your *sister?*" Gia said, her blue eyes wide.

"The one and only."

Jack tapped the Crown Vic's steering wheel in mild frustration; they'd zipped out of the airport parking area but now the Grand Central Parkway was moving at a geriatric pace.

He'd picked up Gia and Vicky at LaGuardia after their flight in from Des Moines. Jack was stirred at how much these two meant to him. The anxiety he'd felt before the plane landed, his impatience when they weren't the first off, and then the throat-tightening burst of pleasure when they appeared: Gia, trim and leggy in jeans and a pink T-shirt, and eight-year-old Vicky running to him, dark brown braids bouncing behind her; picking her up, swinging her around, then hugs and kisses from both of his ladies. He still carried the glow.

"You've got a sister, Jack?" Vicky said from the back seat. "I didn't know you had a sister. Can I play with her?"

"Sure. She's my big sister, you know."

"Oh." Vicky's voice fell. "You mean she's *old.*"

Jack drew in his lips, covering his teeth, and hoarsened his voice to sound like an old codger. "Yesh, she'sh sho old she'sh got no teeth, jusht like me."

Vicky laughed and said, "Is that a joke, Mom?"

Gia said, "Very loosely defined, yes."

"Goody! That means I can give you the present I brought you from Iowa."

"A present?" Jack said, exaggerating his surprise. "For me? Oh, you shouldn't have."

While Vicky was fumbling in her backpack, Jack's beeper chirped.

126

Only three people had the number, and one of them was sitting next to him. Had to be Abe or Julio. Checked the display: it read simply, *J.*

That bothered him. Julio usually left messages on Jack's voice mail. This was the first time he'd ever used the beeper. Something must be wrong.

"Got to call Julio."

"Want to use my cell phone?"

He shook his head. "Never know who else is on the line. I'll find a gas station."

Until recently Gia might have made a remark about his being paranoid. But a few weeks ago someone had traced the tags on her car thinking it belonged to Jack and she'd wound up with a couple of Bosnian goons hanging around outside her door.

"Where's my present?" he cried out, raising his right hand over his shoulder and thrusting it backward, palm up. "Gimme, gimme. I can't wait!"

A fusiform shape in a papery sheath landed in his palm. He glanced at it.

"Corn? You brought me an ear of corn? I'm at a loss for words, Vicks. No one's ever, *ever* given me a gift like this."

"Mom thought of it. She said to give it to you next time you told one of your jokes."

"Oh, she did, did she?"

He glanced at Gia who was staring straight ahead, wind fingers from the open window running through her short blond hair as a barely perceptible smile played about her lips.

Jack had been teaching Vicky to tell jokes. One of the many wonderful things about an eight-year-old was that even the hoariest, lamest one-liners got a laugh. She loved puns, and a joke the caliber of *What's the difference between a fish and a piano? You can't tuna fish!* was the absolute funniest thing she'd ever heard. Trouble was, Vicky practiced her act on her mother who had to listen to the same joke again and again and be expected to laugh every time.

"I think this calls for a new knock-knock, Vicks," Jack said. He had a really bad one he hadn't told her yet.

Gia groaned softly. "No. Please, God, no."

"Knock-knock," Jack said.

Vicky replied, "Who's there?"

"Banana."

"Banana who?"

"Knock-knock."

"Who's there?" she repeated with a giggle.

"Banana."

"Banana who?"

"Knock-knock."

Vicky was laughing now. "Who's there?"

"Banana."

"Not again! Banana *who?*"

"Knock-knock."

"Who's *there?*" She made "there" a two-syllable word this time.

"Orange."

"Orange who?"

"Orange you glad I didn't say banana again?"

Vicky dissolved into belly laughs. A child laughing—Jack couldn't think of a more wonderful sound. She went on so long that he began laughing himself. Only Gia seemed to miss the humor. She'd closed her eyes and thrown her head back against the headrest.

"The only good thing about knock-knocks," she said in a low voice, "the *only* thing, is that they're short. But now you've gone and taught her one that's triple length. Thank you, my love."

Jack pressed the ear of corn against the side of his head. "What's that? Your voice sounds husky. I can't ear you."

Vicky burst into another laugh so loud and hard that even Gia had to smile—though she hid it behind her hand.

"I got a million of 'em, Vicks. Want to hear another?"

"Let's talk about your sister instead," Gia said quickly. "How on earth did she find you?"

Jack took a moment to allow himself to switch gears. "It's complicated but in the end it comes down to this: this friend she's babysitting after brain tumor therapy has been acting weird and got herself involved with some sort of cult. A stranger gave her my number."

Gia frowned. "A stranger just happens to give *your* sister *your* number. Do you buy that?"

"I know it's one hell of a coincidence, but it happened. What else could it be? I know I was the last person on earth Kate was expecting to meet. You should have seen the look on her face when she saw me. Looked like she'd been poleaxed."

"Still," Gia said, shaking her head. "Very strange. What does she look like?"

"Not too much like me. She takes after my father's side. But you can see her in person tonight if you want. She called this morning and invited us over for dinner."

"Us?"

"Yeah, well, I told her about you. Are you up for it?"

"Are you kidding? Pass up an opportunity to get first-hand dirt about you when you were in knickers?"

"I never wore knickers."

"I wouldn't miss it for the world!"

"Swell."

He spotted an Exxon sign and pulled off. Called Julio and heard what he had to say. When he returned to the car he must have looked as ill as he felt.

Gia took one look at him and said, "What's wrong?"

Time to tell her. "We had an incident on one of the subways while you were gone," he said, trying to be oblique.

"The bang-bangs," Gia said, catching on that he wanted to keep Little Miss Big Ears in the back seat out of the loop. With practice they'd managed to raise vagueness to an art. "That made the news even in Ottumwa."

"Then you've heard about the man they're looking for."

"The one they're calling the Savior?"

Jack looked at her and nodded. "Uh-huh."

Gia met his eyes, then she paled and jammed her hand against her mouth. "Oh, God, Jack, no!"

"What is it?" Vicky said from the rear. "What happened?"

"A car came too close, honey," Gia said.

"Oh." She went back to her Harry Potter book.

Gia stared at him. "I heard about it on the news. I worried about you, if you were one of the victims, but that lasted only an instant because then they were talking about someone who'd stopped the, um"—her eyes flashed toward the rear seat—"carnage and then taken off, and the first person I thought of was you, because you wouldn't let something like that happen, and you certainly wouldn't hang around afterward." She took a breath. "But I never really *believed* it was you. It must have been awful!"

"It was. But it's getting worse. Julio says someone was flashing what looks like a police artist's sketch of me around his place this morning. And from Julio's description it sounds like this kid from *The Light* who was sitting near me when it went down."

"*The Light?*" Gia made a face. "What are you going to do?"

"Not sure yet. But I've got to do something."

Jack drove on with a cold weight in his stomach. Couldn't let this kid go on flashing his picture around the Upper West Side. Sooner or later—sooner, Jack bet—someone would recognize the kid as the eyewitness reporter from *The Light* and two and two would add up to him.

5

The good thing about the lower end of Riverside Park, Sandy had decided, was that it was narrow enough to allow him to see from one side to the other. Luxury midrise apartment houses climbed to the east, and the Hudson sparkled in the late morning sun to the west beyond the trees and the highway. The bad part was that the man he was looking for was nowhere to be seen.

He'd wandered from the Eleanor Roosevelt statue all the way to the Soldiers and Sailors Memorial and back. The mild weather was drawing more and more people outdoors. He checked out the basketball courts, the sunbathers, the readers, the snoozers, the frisbee tossers, the dog walkers, even the baby carriage pushers, showing his printout to anyone he could collar.

No luck. Zero. Zilch.

A beautiful day but he wasn't in the mood to appreciate it as he stood near the bronze statue of a very young-looking Eleanor and wondered, Have I been had?

Could this Julio guy have sent him on this wild goose chase just to get rid of him so he could start his own search?

Sandy looked around, trying to decide whether to leave or hang in a little longer. He'd shown the printout to everyone in sight . . .

. . . except the man on the bench downslope from where he stood. When had he arrived? He slouched on the seat, chin on chest with his arms folded and a baseball cap pulled low over his face, catching forty winks.

Sandy walked toward him. He felt a brief flutter of apprehension about disturbing a sleeping man but he was determined to leave no stone unturned.

"Excuse me, sir," he said as he reached him. "Can I ask you a question?"

What happened next was a blur: the man did not look up but his hand darted out to grab the collar of Sandy's T-shirt, twisting it tight about his throat as he yanked him nearly off his feet to land in a half sprawl next to him on the bench.

Now the head turned and Sandy knew this face, the face he'd been showing people for two days, but he didn't know the eyes because the mild brown seemed so much darker now and so full of fury. He opened his mouth to cry out but the index finger of the man's free hand was in his face, an inch from his left eye, and he was talking through his teeth.

"Not a word! Not a sound!"

Sandy nodded four, five, six times. Sure, sure, he'd say nothing. That was easy. Couldn't speak if he wanted to with his tongue glued to the dry roof of his mouth.

Sandy's brain screamed: What did I do wrong? Why's he so mad? He's not going to hurt me, is he?

The man, the Savior, transferred his grip from the front of Sandy's shirt to the back, jerking him upright on the bench. He snatched the printout from Sandy's grasp and stared at it.

Maybe he's unbalanced, Sandy thought, feeling his body begin to quake. His thoughts flew in wild directions. Maybe he's as psycho as the killer on the train. Maybe he was going to start killing the passengers himself but the other guy started first and that's why he killed him because *he'd* wanted to do it.

Sandy struggled to calm himself. Stop being an idiot. The Savior had had that tiny little pistol. Hadn't been equipped for mass murder.

But sure as hell there was murder in his eyes now.

Sandy looked around. He was in a public place, people all around. Nothing was going to happen to him here.

But then anyone on the last car of the Nine the other night might have said that too.

"Where'd you get this?" the Savior said.

Sandy's attempt at a reply came out a croak.

The Savior shook him roughly. "Tell me!"

"I-I made it."

"You drew this?"

"Computer."

"Who else knows about it?"

"Just me. Look, I don't know what you're so mad—"

"How many copies?"

Sandy figured he'd better tell the truth. "A couple more on me. A bunch more at home."

"And where's that?"

He saw where this was going and didn't like it. He realized he was in the grip of a very dangerous man who was royally pissed. Detective McCann's words from that fateful night rushed back at him.

. . . fucking executed him . . . he's a pro . . .

Sandy's bladder squeezed. What had he got himself into? He needed some insurance, and fast.

"I left one in an envelope in my desk!" he blurted. "To be opened in case something happens to me."

Now he wished to hell he had.

The Savior stared at him for what seemed like an eternity, then released him with a shove. "Yeah, right." He held out his hand. "Give me the rest of them."

Sandy fished out the printouts and handed them over. The Savior folded them, then stared out toward the Hudson.

"Go home, shred those other copies, and mind your own business."

"But this *is* my business!"

"Dogging my ass is your business?"

"I'm a journalist. I'm not out to hurt you—"

"That's a relief."

"I just want an exclusive."

The Savior looked at him again. "A what?"

"When you come in, I want an exclusive on your story."

"You've heard the expression 'when hell freezes over'? Satan will be figure skating when I come in."

Sandy was stunned. Could he believe this? He'd figured the Savior was consulting with a lawyer and waiting for the media buzz to build to a howling frenzy before coming forward. That he might have no intention of coming in at all had never occurred to him.

"You can't be serious! You're a hero! You'll be on the cover of every newspaper and magazine in the world. Instant celebrity"—he snapped his fingers—"like *that!* Any restaurant, any club in town—*zip*—you go right to the head of the line."

"Yeah? Is that how Bernie Goetz is being treated these days?"

The Goetz case—was that why the Savior was hiding? It did make sense. Goetz had wound up bankrupt with his life turned upside down and inside out by the trials and suits. But that wasn't going to happen here.

"Look, I'm no lawyer, but there's no parallel. Goetz's attackers hadn't killed anybody and they had no guns when he opened up on them. The guy you shot had two guns, had just murdered six people, and was only getting started. Goetz saved himself from getting mugged and maybe cut up, you saved *other* people's lives—lots of them."

"Including yours."

"Yeah. Including mine. For which I'll be eternally grateful."

"Well, in return, you forget you ever saw me and we'll call it even."

Low-grade terror still crawled through Sandy's gut, but something in him refused to let him cave.

"Look, I can't. I've got a higher calling: the people's right to know."

"And your exclusive right to tell them? Cut me a break, kid. If I show up, I face a gang of charges: owning an unregistered weapon and carrying a concealed weapon without a permit, just for starters. You and those others are alive today because of multiple criminal acts on my part."

Criminal acts . . . what a great hook.

F . P A U L W I L S O N

"Hey, don't worry about that. You'll be such a hero, what DA would dare bring you to trial? Instant celebrity! Think of it! Every door will be open to you. People dream about an opportunity like this!"

"Some people don't."

Didn't this guy realize what he was throwing away?

The Savior rose. "Like I said before: shred the drawings and forget about this."

He turned and started to move away.

"I *can't* forget it!" Sandy heard himself cry out. "This is my life! My future! I can *make* you come in! I can have that drawing in tomorrow morning's paper!"

The Savior stopped, turned, and Sandy quailed when he saw the look in his eyes. Maybe he'd overdone it; maybe he'd pushed this man just a little too far . . . pushed a man who shouldn't be pushed.

"You know . . . you make me wish I'd waited just a little bit longer before taking that guy out."

The realization of how much he owed this man slammed into Sandy now with the force of a runaway train.

He saved my life.

Talk about clichés. How many times had he heard people say that about saving just about everything *but* a life? Somebody finds a lost set of keys, helps finish a paper or report, provides a breath mint before an important meeting: *You saved my life.*

Not even close.

But with this man, it was a fact. Sandy knew he should be saying, You saved my everything. Sandy owed him his boxed byline in the paper yesterday, owed him last night with Beth, owed him the big fat hairy future he envisioned, a future he'd been planning to ride to on this man's back.

The Savior said, "Do your damnedest," and started to turn away again.

"Wait! Please! I'm being a shit."

"No argument here."

"Can't we work something out?"

"I doubt it."

"But there's got to be a way I can get my exclusive and you stay out of the spotlight."

Out of the spotlight . . . Sandy was still baffled by the man's reluctance to take credit for his heroism, but he owed him too much not to try and honor his wishes, no matter how shortsighted.

"I don't see how," the Savior said. "If you get your exclusive it means you've seen me. Then the pressure for a description is on, not just from your bosses, but from the cops—especially the cops."

"I could claim I'm protecting the confidentiality of my source."

"And then you're slapped with obstruction of justice. How many nights you think you'll last in Rikers before you cave?"

Sandy hated to admit it, but he doubted he'd hang on through an *hour* at Rikers. And then an idea struck.

"Not if I say you called me and I got the story over the phone!"

The Savior seemed to be considering this as he stood silent and stared at Sandy.

Finally he nodded. "That'll work. You go ahead and make up something—whatever you want. Say I said it and that'll be that."

"No-no. That won't cut it. I want this to be real. The truth."

They were talking about his future here. He couldn't base it on a fabricated story.

"The truth? Since when does anyone care about that?"

"I do. Pretty much."

The Savior stared at him. "You're not going away, are you."

Sandy mustered all his courage and shook his head. Would the man who'd saved his life, take it? He thought not.

"Sorry. I can't drop this. I just can't."

A long silence with the two of them standing statue still, facing each other, while growing moisture soaked Sandy's armpits.

Finally, "What do you want, kid?"

"I'll need *some* background, but I'm sure people will be mainly interested in how you learned to shoot and why you were carrying a pistol that night, and most important, what was going through your mind before and after you killed the killer."

Another pause, then, "Jeez, this is stupid, but if it'll make you go away—and I mean that: you go away and forget you ever saw me." He held up the printouts he'd taken. "And you get rid of the rest of these."

"Deal," Sandy said. Easy promise to make—the Savior had no way of checking.

"And I don't mean burn them. Burning causes suspicion and you'd be amazed what can be reconstructed from ashes these days. Tear them up into one-inch squares and flush them. Nothing more anonymous than a sewer system with eight million contributors."

"But there's one I can't get back. It's at a place called Julio's and—"

"I'll take care of that one."

And then it was suddenly clear what had happened this morning. Of course! The men in Julio's had recognized the man in the printout. Julio had sent Sandy here to the park, then called the Savior and told him where he'd be.

His excitement building, Sandy pulled the tape recorder from his knapsack. "Let's get started."

"Put that away. No recording. And we're not sitting out in the open here either. I've got a car nearby. I'll drive and talk, you take notes."

"Fair enough," Sandy said.

This is it! he thought as he followed the Savior out of the park. His blood tingled like champagne through his arteries. It's happening! It's all coming together! I'm on my way!

6

"You're retiring the Semmerling?" Abe said. "This I don't believe."

Jack didn't want to believe it himself. He'd kept the tiny .45 strapped to his ankle for so long it felt part of him. This was like carving out a piece of his flesh. But in light of what he'd learned from Sandy Palmer, he knew it had to go. So after ditching Palmer he'd come straight to Abe's and told him about his "interview."

"The kid knew all about it from listening to the cops on the scene. One of them identified it from its description."

Bad enough to be caught with any weapon in this town, but to be caught carrying a gun the cops had issued a BOLO for . . .

Abe raised his. "A gun *maven* cop. Such luck you have."

"Yeah. Mostly bad lately."

He worried about this cub reporter or whatever Sandy Palmer was. Not that he was a bad kid, but too damn ambitious. He might make the wrong kind of compromises to get ahead—the kind that could land Jack in a lava pit.

And he lacked simple common sense. He'd got into Jack's car without an instant's hesitation. If Jack were more impulsive, or maybe had enough screws loose that he didn't care if Palmer had one of those drawings tucked away with a note, he easily could have killed him in the car and dumped him in any one of a dozen spots he knew around the city where he wouldn't be discovered for days, maybe weeks.

But he hadn't. The only thing he'd done to Sandy Palmer was lie.

Jack had led him to his car—making sure they approached from the side so he didn't get a look at the tags—and driven him around for nearly an hour while he filled the car with pure bullshit. Pretty good bullshit, he thought, considering it was created on the fly.

Palmer had taken copious notes, stopping Jack along the way for questions and clarifications. Finally Jack managed to scrape him off at a subway station, but not before the human remora had extracted his voicemail number just in case he had some "follow-up questions." Jack figured the number was safe—billed to a credit card registered to a nonexistent person.

"So what did you tell this crusading reporter?"

"I told him that the Savior was an orphan, in and out of foster homes and trouble until a cop gave him a choice of either getting booked on a B and E or joining the army."

"I see a movie already."

"I think it's been done. And Pat O'Brien probably played the cop. Anyway, Young Savior joined the U.S. Navy instead of the army and qualified for SEAL training. He received a medical discharge due to a back injury."

"And now he's a *farbissener* who—"

"Whoa. You lost me on that one. A farbiss-what?"

"A bitter, cranky person—you know how you get sometimes. The way I see it, such hatred this Savior has for society he's a recluse."

"Do you mind?" Jack said. "This is *my* life story I'm telling here. Let *me* tell it."

"So I can't add a little flavor, a little color?"

"An ex-Navy SEAL isn't colorful?"

"You a SEAL?" Abe laughed. "Obeying a drill sergeant? That I'd like to see."

"I wasn't a SEAL, but the Savior was."

"Do you even know what SEAL stands for?"

"Haven't a clue. But I'm sure an ex-SEAL like the Savior does. And although he has no official status with the government, he still freelances for certain government agencies."

"Is one known by three letters, the first of which is a C and the last an A, maybe?"

"He's not free to tell. But because of the nature of his government work he's always armed. Always. As a result he was able to save lives the other night. Also because of the nature of his work, he cannot allow his face to be made public."

"This is good. Such a screenwriter you would have made. A derivative hack, maybe, but that shouldn't disqualify you."

"But here's the icing: The Savior is baffled as to why he should be called a savior or a hero or anything of the sort. He only did what any other decent citizen would have done, had they been equipped to do so."

"That'll stir some talk."

"Right. Talk about something other than the Savior, I hope. Boy Reporter has his exclusive, making him happy so he goes away and leaves me alone. The cops try in vain to match the background described by El Savior to a real person, making them unhappy. They go back to watching and waiting, time passes, people forget about the Savior dude, and life gets back to normal."

Abe's eyebrows rose again, higher this time. "You're smoking something that potent and not offering any to your old friend Abe?"

Jack sighed. "Yeah, I know." No way this was going to fade away that smoothly. "But I can dream, can't I?"

"Dream away, but in the meantime I can offer you a true autoloader, better than your Semmerling."

"In .45?"

"No. But you load an AMT Backup .380 with a half dozen MagSafe sixty-grain Defenders—keeping one in the chamber, please—and you'll have almost as much stopping power as you had with the Semmerling.

A new ankle holster you won't need because this will fit in the one you have, and best of all you'll need only one hand to keep firing because you won't have to work that *farkuckt* slide for every shot."

Life without his Semmerling . . . Jack supposed he was going to have to get used it. Wouldn't be easy.

He sighed. "Okay. Get me one."

7

Sandy sat in his cubicle at *The Light* and looked around. Finally he was alone and nobody close enough to see what he was doing.

He'd shown up early and received an astoundingly warm welcome that took him totally by surprise. People he barely knew had shaken his hand and clapped him on the back, asking him how he was doing, what it had been like, how he'd felt, how he was handling it, and on and on. Any other day he would have basked in their attention, but not now when he had a pad full of notes from the interview of his life burning a hole in his knapsack. It took a good half hour before he was left on his own.

And now, just when he was ready . . .

"Hey, Palmer," said a voice on his left. "When do you expect to be kicked upstairs?"

Sandy looked up to see Pokorny gazing over the top of the divider that separated their cubicles. With his long thin nose and thinning hair he looked like one of those old time *Kilroy Was Here* doodles.

"Funny, Jay."

"Seriously," he said, ambling around the divider to slouch his bean-pole bod against Sandy's desk, "your story's all anybody's talking about around here."

Sandy shrugged, tried to be humble. "Yeah, well, I thought that night on the train was the worst of my life. Now it looks like it might turn out to be the best thing that ever happened to me."

"You spun some gold, man." His envy was tangible.

"I don't know about gold. Someone handed me a lemon and I've been making lemonade."

He saw Pokorny wince and wanted to kick himself. I don't believe I just said that.

"What are you going to do for your second act?"

The question took Sandy by surprise. "Second act?"

"Sure. Now that you've got everyone's attention, how are you going to keep it?"

"I . . . don't know," Sandy said, playing dumb. "I never thought about it."

"You'd better think of something, my friend." He straightened from his slouch and patted Sandy on the shoulder. "You don't want to be a flash in the pan."

Condescending bastard, he thought as Pokorny slithered from sight. Flash in the pan was probably his fondest wish for Sandy.

But Pokorny didn't know that Sandy already had his second act scripted. All he needed was a little privacy to put it into production.

It took Sandy another half hour before he dared to pull out his cell phone and begin. He dialed *The Light*'s main number and punched his way through the options tree until he got to an operator. Then he cupped his hand over the receiver and lowered his voice.

"I need to speak to Sandy Palmer."

"Do you know his extension?"

"No. But I must speak to him now."

"Here it is. I'll connect you."

The Savior was supposed to have gone though this same routine from three different pay phones during the first thirty minutes after he'd dropped Sandy off. It was his idea. He thought Sandy's walking in after two days off just in time to get a phone call from the city's number one mystery man was a little too pat. Sandy had to agree. So the Savior was to make sure he talked to a live operator each time and then leave hang-ups on Sandy's voicemail to show that someone had been trying to get in touch with him for a while.

Sandy jumped as his desk phone rang. He picked up the receiver, turned off his cell phone and began the charade of pretending to be talking and taking notes.

The Savior . . . Sandy wished he knew his name so he could call him something else. But what a cool guy. And what a life he'd led. This would make a great piece even if he weren't the Savior.

And that might be a problem. How to convince the editors that this was the real deal and not just some kook? The only way he could see to verify the caller's bona fides was the pistol. Sandy would say that the man on the phone named the make and model and explained how he'd used it. Only Sandy and the cops knew about the Semmerling.

Then the next question would be: Why you, Palmer? Why a nobody like you instead of some network anchorman or nationally syndicated columnist?

Easy.

The Savior and I were on the death train together. There's kinship there. We're blood brothers.

That should work, Sandy thought. Sounds reasonable.

The editors would check with McCann about the Semmerling. Once that was verified, they'd believe. Because they'll *want* to believe. They'll be dying to run the story.

Of course that would mean another call, or maybe even a visit from McCann.

Sandy felt his sweat begin to run. That was when the going would get rough. McCann would want all the details. Sandy had only one lie to worry about. Just one. But it was a whopper.

He prayed he wouldn't slip up.

8

So this is Jeanette Vega, Jack thought, glancing at the slim brunette in fitted shorts and pale blue tank top as he stood in her kitchen and opened the second of the two bottles of merlot he and Gia had brought. Her hair was her striking feature—glossy black, parted on the left and severely pulled back into a single tight braid that reached below the nape of her neck; warm brown eyes, no make-up, a fading tan. Not the prettiest woman Jack had ever seen, but not bad looking. Kind of quiet, but nothing so abnormal about that.

Although he usually drank beer—and he'd had a couple at Gia's before cabbing over here—Jack was determined to do the wine thing tonight. And do it with gusto. Because after the day he'd had he felt he deserved an ambitious blood alcohol level, even if it meant reading tomorrow's *Light* with a hangover.

Maybe a hangover was the only way to go, because God knew what that kid was going to write.

But that would have to wait till morning. At the moment he meant to concentrate on Jeanette. And Kate too, of course. But Kate and Gia had their heads together in the living room, discussing Jack's boyhood he was sure. He hoped Kate wouldn't spill anything embarrassing like his bed-wetting problem.

Jack had filled Gia in as best he could on Jeanette's brain tumor treatment and subsequent personality change. That hadn't deterred her; she still wanted to meet Kate. Sitting at Gia's and sipping beer as he watched her work on a painting commissioned for a paperback cover had eased his Sandy Palmer-jangled nerves.

He glanced at Kate now and sensed that her nerves could do with a little easing. She wore a sleeveless cotton jumper and the humidity had made her honey blond hair curlier than usual, but she didn't look well tonight. Tired and worn. And jumpy. Something was eating her.

Jeanette on the other hand was cool and serene. She leaned against the kitchen side of the counter, physically three feet away, mentally somewhere at sea off Bora Bora. Seemed to be watching him open the wine, but her gaze was unfocused.

Jack rated his small-talk skills with those of the average geranium, and usually counted on others to carry the conversation load. But Jeanette was barely here. Had he bored her into a trance?

He glanced longingly at the couch. He'd much rather be over there where he could try and censor whatever Kate was telling Gia . . .

❖

Kate said, "Our folks worried about him sometimes."

"Imagine that," Gia said with a wry smile. She wore a long summer dress that brought out the intense blue of her eyes.

Kate had taken an instant liking to Gia. She'd sensed that here was someone not only very pretty and very bright, but also very much her own person.

"He was something of a loner."

Gia sipped her wine. "He's still not much of a team player."

"He was on the track team but he ran cross-country. Not a lot of friends, either. But it was the movies that most concerned our folks. He couldn't get enough of those junky old horror and sci-fi movies."

"That hasn't changed."

"It would be a sunny Saturday afternoon and Jackie would—"

Gia grinned. "*Jackie*? Oh, I love it!"

"That's what our mother called him and we all sort of picked it up. Anyway, on a beautiful Saturday he would say he was going to the park but if you drove by the local theater you'd see his bike chained to a post nearby. Every Saturday the Lenape would show two old horror-sci-fi movies in a double feature and he'd rather sit there alone in the dark than play with the other kids."

"That child was definitely father to that man." Gia said, pointing to Jack.

Jack and movies . . . Kate remembered when he was nine she heard Jack's alarm go off at two in the morning, then heard him pad downstairs in the dark. When ten minutes passed and he hadn't returned, she went down to see what he was up to. She found him wrapped in his bedspread cross-legged on the floor before the TV with the sound very low, entranced by some cheap black-and-white movie. She told him to get back up to bed but he pleaded with her, saying he'd been trying to catch *Invasion of the Saucer Men* forever but it never played in the movies or on TV or anywhere anymore until tonight. He *had* to see it. He might never get another chance. Pleeeeease?

So she'd sat next to him under the spread, her arm protectively around his shoulders, and watched with him. She soon knew why no one showed it any more: *Invasion of the Saucer Men* was awful. But to Jack it was some sort of grail he'd finally found and he loved it. Looking back now it was a special shared moment, a closeness fated for extinction with the advent of the VCR.

Kate glanced over to where Jack stood with Jeanette. Would that life were still so sweet and simple.

And then she remembered: "The dip. I forgot to heat the dip."

❖

The extended silence was getting awkward. Jack noticed that Jeanette's tank top revealed lean, muscular arms. Good deltoids, the kind that come only with weight training.

That looked like a conversation opener.

"You work out, Jeanette?"

"Hmmm?" She blinked and returned to North America.

Jack cocked his arm in a bodybuilder's pose. "Do you work out?"

She smiled. "I used to, back when I thought that sort of thing was important." A shrug. "Now it seems kind of silly. So many things seem silly now."

Jack could see how being told you were going to die long before your time could change your perspective on just about everything. Especially working out. Not much point to a well-toned body if the next stop was a casket.

"You were at the house last night," she said, staring at him. "Why?"

Pretty damn direct question. How much could he say and not contradict anything Kate might have told her?

"I was just tagging along. Kate was worried about you and doesn't know the city, so I ferried her around."

"Everything's fine now," Jeanette said with a smile. "And getting better every day."

"Great," he said, holding up the open wine bottle. "Can I pour you some?"

Jeanette shook her head. "No, thank you. I don't need that anymore."

Good, he thought. That leaves more for me. And I *do* need it.

"Do I take it that means you've found a replacement?"

Another smile. "In a way."

Jack hoped this might provide a segue into this cult of hers, but his sister bustled into the kitchen before he could move on it.

"The dip," Kate said, pulling open the refrigerator door. "Hot avocado. Forgot all about it. And yes, Jack, I'll have another glass of that. So will Gia, I'm sure." She shoved a covered dish into the microwave and began jabbing buttons. "Just let me nuke this on reheat for a few minutes to warm it up. There. Now, where's that—?"

"Kate!" Jeanette wailed, her voice a terror-laden plea. "Oh God, Kate, why haven't you done anything?"

Her cry was so abrupt, so heartrending, that Jack nearly dropped the wine bottle. He stared at her agonized features and saw that her earlier remoteness was gone. The woman on the far side of the counter now was reaching out with her eyes, with her hands and arms, panic radiating from every pore.

"Jeanette!" Kate cried, turning Jeanette to face her. "What is it? What's happening!"

"I'm losing, Kate! I can't hold out much longer. Pretty soon there'll be nothing left of me! You've got to help me, Kate!" Her voice rose to a scream. *"For God's sake help me!"*

And then her knees buckled. As she fell against Kate, Jack started around the counter to help but Gia was already there.

"Get her over to the couch!" Gia said.

The three of them helped the barely conscious Jeanette across the room where they stretched her out. Kate placed Jeanette's ankles on the arm rest, positioning them above the level of her head, then took her pulse. Gia ran back to the kitchen and started running water over a dish towel. Jack stood back and watched, a little shaken.

"This is what happened yesterday morning," Kate said. "Jeanette, are you—?"

"What's going on?" Jeanette said, shuddering and starting to sit up.

Kate tried to hold her down. "You had another one of those spells. Just rest for a moment."

"No." She struggled to a sitting position. "That can't be. How did I get over here?"

Jeanette was back to the remote woman Jack had met when he'd arrived; she seemed concerned but not as much as Jack thought she should be.

"We helped you," Gia said. Her face was pale, she looked shaken. "You almost passed out."

"This is the second time now, Jeanette," Kate said. "You can't go on like this. You've got to let Dr. Fielding check you over."

"He's an idiot."

"Then let's see someone else."

"What for? I'm fine." She shook off Kate's hand and rose to her feet. "Everybody just give me some space."

Kate and Gia stepped back.

"Jeanette—"

"Please, Kate, would you ask Jack and Gia to go. I'd like to be alone."

Kate blinked. "Do . . . do you want me to leave too?"

"No, of course not. This is your home too." She turned to Jack. "I'm sorry. It was nice meeting you both. I know we'll meet again soon."

She turned and headed for a doorway at the far end of the room.

"I don't know what to say," Kate said when the door closed behind Jeanette. "She did this yesterday morning, and now again . . ."

"For a few moments there," Gia said, "she seemed like another person."

"A terrified one," Jack added.

Kate nodded. "I know. A true multiple personality disorder is so rare it's almost nonexistent . . . but I don't know how else to explain this."

"And why does she refuse to see a doctor?" Jack said. "If I'd just become another person for a few minutes and didn't remember it, I'd be on the phone demanding an appointment yesterday."

"Look," Kate said. "Why don't you two go on. I'm really sorry about this but—"

"Not your fault, Kate. Why don't you come out and catch a bite with us?"

"No. I should stay here in case she needs me. You two go ahead." She hugged Gia and kissed her cheek. "It was wonderful meeting you." Then she turned to Jack and hugged him.

He wrapped his arms around his sister and held her close. Had he ever done this? He couldn't remember. If not, he shouldn't have waited this long. It felt good, and would have felt better if not for a nagging fear for her.

"You're sure you don't want to come along?"

She stepped back and nodded. "I'll be fine. Call me tomorrow."

Jack didn't feel right about leaving her but didn't see any options. He opened the door.

"Okay. I will. First thing. And you have my home phone number. If you need me, you call, no matter what the hour."

In the kitchen the microwave oven dinged. The avocado dip was ready.

9

Jack and Gia took the stairs down.

"Did you see how Jeanette changed?" Gia said. "Isn't that the strangest thing you've ever seen?"

He knew they'd both seen stranger things, but . . .

"Yeah. Pretty damn strange. Creepy."

"I'll say," she said as they reached street level. She laid a hand on his arm. "And by the way, how come you never told me your sister was gay?"

"*What?*" He was stunned. His big sister, the pediatrician mother of two, a lesbian? Was Gia nuts? "How can you even *think* that?"

"Well, there may not be Melissa Etheridge posters on the wall, but there's a whole collection of Cris Williamson CDs in the rack, and if she and Jeanette aren't a couple, I'll remarry Richard when he returns."

They both knew her ex was gone for good—as in dead and digested. But Gia was way off here.

As they pushed through the front door into the night air Jack said, "Kate's not—"

And then it all came together. Of course she was. Kate was a giving person, but Jack suddenly realized she'd never take a leave from her practice and her kids to nursemaid some old sorority sister. When she'd said she was seeing someone special but foresaw no wedding bells, it wasn't a married man, it was a woman.

Jack turned and stared through the glass doors into the vestibule of the apartment building. "I didn't see it. How could I miss it?"

"With any other pair of women I'm sure you would have, right off. But your brain wasn't offering you options for your big sister's sexual orientation. So unless Kate showed up on a motorcycle with a shaved head and 'Bitch On Wheels' tattooed on her arm, you weren't going to see it. Her being a lipstick lesbian just made it harder."

"No wonder she seems to be walking on eggs when I'm around. Kate . . . I can't get over it."

"Does it bother you?" Gia said. "Come on, Jack, talk. You keep things in and stew about them. Don't do that here. Talk to me."

"Okay. Am I bothered? No. Anything Kate wants to be is fine with me. But am I shocked? Yes. Because I never saw it coming. I grew up with her, Gia. Never a sign, never a hint."

"At least not that you saw."

"Granted. I was a kid and I wasn't looking. But she always had boyfriends and . . . Gia, it's like the direction I always thought was north has suddenly become south. Should I go back and talk to her? Tell her I know and it's all right? Maybe that way she can relax around me."

Jack was used to knowing what to do in most situations, but here he was foundering.

"Since you asked," Gia said, "yes. Otherwise the two of you will go on dodging each other: she'll be hiding who she is and you'll be hiding that you know what she's hiding. But it's not my decision. And whatever you do, save it for tomorrow. Kate's got enough on her plate tonight, don't you think?"

Jack slipped his hand around the back of Gia's neck and kissed her lips. What would he do without her?

"Thanks."

She brushed her fingers against his hair. "Not a good day for Repairman Jack, hmmm?"

"Lousy."

"Well, Vicky's sitter is good till midnight. We could go back to your place and maybe, just maybe, if we think real hard, we might come up with a way to help you forget your troubles."

It had been a whole week. Jack felt more than ready.

"I think that's a perfectly wonderful—"

He noticed a woman standing across the street, staring. Not at them. Above them. She seemed to be in a trance. Something familiar about her face.

"What's wrong?" Gia said.

"Check out that blond woman over there. Do we know her?"

"Never seen her before."

Jack followed the line of the woman's stare and felt a stab of uneasiness when he realized she'd drawn a bead on the west corner of the third floor.

Gia whispered, "She's staring at Jeanette's apartment."

He looked at the woman again and now he recognized her. From the seance or whatever it was in the Bronx last night.

"I don't like this," Jack said. Not with Kate in that apartment.

"Look over there," Gia said, cocking her head to the left. "Down on the corner."

Jack spotted the man immediately. Although Jack didn't recognize him—a number of people at the seance had had their backs to him when he'd peeked in—he felt sure he was with the cult. Because he too was staring up at Jeanette's apartment.

How many more weirdos out tonight? he wondered as he scanned the block. He spotted none beyond these two.

Jack stepped to the curb for his own look at Jeanette's windows and spotted a human silhouette standing in one of them. A Bates Motel chill rippled across his shoulders. The open-mouthed terra cotta head glaring down at him from atop the window arch frieze only added to his unease.

Then the shadow disappeared from the window. Jack did a quick review of the apartment layout and decided it had to be Jeanette's study. Was she coming out to join the others?

"Let's move over here," Jack said, guiding Gia away from the vestibule's light wash and into the shadows.

Sure enough, minutes later Jeanette emerged. She crossed the street and joined the other two. The trio glided off toward Seventh Avenue.

"This is creepy," Gia said. Jack could feel her shiver as she clutched his arm and leaned against him. "Like some of those movies you make me watch. Where do you think they're going?"

"Looking for a cab to take them to the Bronx, I'll bet." But he didn't care about them. It was his sister who concerned him. "I've got to check on Kate."

He stepped back to the apartment house door and pressed the button labeled J. VEGA. Three times. Finally Kate answered.

"Yes?"

"Kate, it's Jack. I just saw Jeanette leave. Are you all right?"

"Of course." Even through the tinny little speaker Jack thought her voice sounded thick with emotion. "Why wouldn't I be?"

"Can I come up, Kate?" He glanced at Gia for approval and she gave him a combination shrug-nod. "I'd like to talk to you."

"Not tonight, Jack. Maybe tomorrow. It's been a long day and I'm not feeling that great."

"You're sure you're all right, Kate?"

"I'm fine, Jack. Fine."

That last word, couched in a sob, tore his heart.

"Kate . . ."

But she'd broken the connection.

Jack turned to Gia and slipped his arms around her. "I can't stand this," he said, pulling her close and resting his cheek against hers.

She caressed his back and whispered, "I know. You're the fix-it man and you can't fix this."

"I don't even know where to start."

"Let's go home. Things may look different in the morning."

"Yeah."

But he doubted it.

FRIDAY

1

Sandy found Beth in the kitchen making fresh coffee when he burst into the apartment with the morning edition.

"Ta-daaaa!" he cried as he held up the front page.

Beth shrieked and ran to him. She'd moved some of her clothes into his apartment yesterday; she was barefoot in tight little shorts and a T-shirt and she looked so good Sandy wanted to grab her and hug her, but she snatched the paper from him and held the tabloid at arms length, staring at the three-word headline large enough to read from a block away.

THE
SAVIOR
SPEAKS!

" 'An exclusive interview for *The Light* by Sandy Palmer'!" she said, reading the italic refer running along the bottom. "Sandy! Your name's on the front page!"

"I know, I know! Isn't it awesome!"

"Totally! I've so got to read this!" She opened to page three. " ' "Call me anything you want," the man known as The Savior said. "The one thing I'm not telling you is my name." ' " She looked up at him and smiled. "What a great opening line!"

While Beth stood there reading, Sandy wandered about the front room, unable to sit or even stand still. Every giddy nerve in his body was singing a joyful tune and his stomach tingled, almost to the point of nausea. Today was without a doubt the best day of his life, and the best moment of this day was when he'd stopped in front of the newsstand and gaped at that front page. For a full minute at least he'd stood frozen, couldn't even reach into his pocket for the change to buy a copy. And during that minute he'd seen one person after another pass up the *Times* and the *News* and the *Post* and go for *The Light*.

Mine. My *Light*.

He'd sure as hell earned it. Yesterday he'd thought he was home free after weathering an intense grilling by George Meschke and the other editors; then McCann showed up and put Sandy in the hot seat, firing questions from all angles, obviously hoping he'd contradict himself. He pushed Sandy almost to the breaking point.

"Am I on trial here?" he'd finally shouted. "All I did was answer the goddamn phone! Since when is that a crime?"

And that had brought Meschke to his rescue. He'd told McCann they were satisfied with the story's authenticity and were running it in the morning. McCann reluctantly backed off.

"Well, at least we know he was a SEAL," the big detective had said. "Or at least he says he was. That's a boost. Only so many guys make it all the way through SEAL training. We'll get the Navy on this."

He'd extracted a promise that the make and model of the Savior's pistol would not be mentioned, then stormed off.

But beyond the front page, beyond the interview, was the fact that *The Light*, for the first time in its fifty-year history, was putting out a second issue in the same week. They'd contacted their advertisers, pulled out all the backlogged restaurant and book and theater reviews and packed them into the back pages to fill out the count. Then they'd contacted their distributor for delivery of a Special Edition that would be four times their usual run.

All because of *moi*, he thought. I'm making this paper go.

"Awesome!" Beth said, lowering the paper and fixing those big brown eyes on him. " 'We're all alive today because of a criminal act.' Totally, totally awesome!"

"You like it? You think it was well written?"

Sandy hung on her answer. Beth admired him, she made love to him, but he wanted her respect, too.

"Absolutely! But it must have been so weird talking to him on the phone. I mean, he saved our lives. I wish I could remember what he looked like, don't you?"

The question put Sandy on alert, blunting his high. He'd been dying to tell Beth about his meeting with the Savior, and a couple of times last night he'd caught himself just as he'd been ready to blurt it out. He was afraid he'd explode if he didn't tell someone soon.

But he couldn't risk it. Not even with Beth. If she let it slip, he would come under relentless pressure. Maybe he could tell her later, after things cooled down a bit. Or maybe he'd save it for his book on the Savior; what a great hook to be able to reveal that he'd actually sat and talked face to face with the mystery man.

"What would you do if you could remember?" Sandy asked.

"You mean, like if someone hypnotized me and suddenly I could see his face?" Her eyes lit. "Hey! That might be something I could use in my film!"

She jumped to the cluttered table he used as a home desk and jotted a few lines on a pad.

"But if you could remember," he repeated, "what would you do?"

She looked at him. "Tell you the truth, I'm not sure. Yesterday I would have told the world. But just a few minutes ago, while you were out, I was channel surfing and came across *To Kill A Mockingbird*. I love black-and-white films and I've seen it at least two dozen times. It was the scene where Scout and Jem are attacked in the woods, and then someone they don't see kills their attacker. Turns out it's Boo Radley, but Atticus decides not to tell anyone because it would ruin Boo's life. And it hit me: maybe the Savior is like Boo Radley—an otherwise harmless recluse who jumped in when he was needed, but whose life would be ruined by publicity."

"This guy's not harmless," Sandy said. "And no way anybody's going to mistake him for a mockingbird."

"Maybe not, but . . ." Beth shrugged. "What's he sound like?"

"Like a regular guy. No real accent I could identify." No lie there. He glanced at his watch. "I'm expected at the office."

Sandy had decided to get down to *The Light* so he could bask in the buzz. He expected some of the other reporters, especially the older ones, to be jealous, but he hoped most everybody else would be happy for him. Another round of handshaking and backslapping would be in order. And this time, without an interview to write up, he could relax and enjoy it.

And leaving now also meant he wouldn't have to tell Beth more lies.

"Okay," Beth said. She gestured to his desk. "Do you mind if I use your computer to start the treatment for my film?"

"Sure." Sandy considered the chaos of notes, newspaper clippings, envelopes, folders, and CD cases that littered the surface. "If you can find the keyboard."

Beth giggled as she started to sift through the mess. "I'm sure it's in here somewhere." She lifted a manila envelope and peered inside. "This anything important?"

"Yes!" Sandy said, louder and quicker than he wished. He knew that folder: the remaining Savior printouts. He tried to laugh it off as he reached out with forced casualness and eased it from her hand. "Notes for an article I'm planning. My editor'll kill me if anything happens to them."

Beth looked mildly offended. "I wouldn't let anything happen to them."

"Only kidding." He crossed his arms, trapping the envelope against his thudding heart. "The place is yours. Really. Rearrange that stuff any way you want."

The Savior had been right. These printouts were a liability. Sandy's session with McCann yesterday had driven home how badly the detective wanted the Savior. If he got him, bye-bye exclusive.

No question—the printouts had to go. He couldn't see any further use for them anyway. If he ever needed another copy all he had to do was call up the Identi-Kit file from *The Light*'s system and print it out.

Beth picked up the newspaper from the desk and stared again at the headline.

"I still can't believe how lucky we were that a man with his training was on that train and in that car with us. I used to think I'd love to meet him—you know, give him a hug and say thanks—but after reading this I'm not so sure."

"Why not?"

"Well, he doesn't exactly come across as the warm cuddly type."

"He's not." Sandy remembered the murderous look in the man's eyes. "In fact . . ." A vague impression had just congealed into a suspicion. He stood silent, trying to get a grip on it.

"What?" Beth said.

"I wonder how much of what he told me I should believe."

"You think he was lying?"

"Not completely. I'm pretty sure the part about being a Navy SEAL is true. I remember one of the cops on the scene saying things about the second shooter being well trained, but I don't know about doing secret work for government agencies. He hinted that he's involved in black ops and showing his face will blow his cover. But what if he's not undercover? What if he's hiding for another reason?"

"Such as?"

"Like he's a wanted man."

"If that's true, I hope they never catch him."

"Even if they did catch him I bet I could get him off."

"You? I think you're great and all, Sandy, but how on earth would you manage that?"

He grinned. "By mobilizing the people. The pen is mightier than the sword, my dear. Never underestimate the power of the press."

"This is our guy, Stan."

Not this again, Stan Kozlowski thought as he looked up from his bagel and shmear.

They'd returned to Moishe's this morning and were back at their usual table. His brother Joe was hidden behind *The Light*'s screaming headlines, with only his hands visible. Both of them. Joe wasn't bothering to hide the scarred left this morning.

"Where's it say that?"

Joe lowered the paper. His dark eyes glittered in his puffy face. "Right here where he says he freelances for government agencies but can't say which ones or what he does for them."

"So?"

"Think about it, Stan." He leaned forward and lowered his voice. "Maybe ATF traced the components of one of our little devices back to a point where they suspected us but couldn't make a case. So they hire this ex-SEAL to find our stash and blow it. That happens, what's the first thing the locals do? Call in ATF of course. Bang. They've got their case. Works for me."

Stan thought about that. He had a sense, what with how Waco took so long to go away, that ATF would be a bit shy about burning or blowing up buildings. But if the job was done by an outsider, someone who couldn't be connected to them . . .

"That would be illegal, Joe," he said, deadpan. "I refuse to believe that an agency of our government would stoop to something like that."

Joe smirked. "Yeah, of course. What was I thinking?"

"What *are* you thinking?"

Joe pulled a newspaper clipping from the breast pocket of his shirt and unfolded it on the table. Stan recognized the article from the other day—the eyewitness account. Joe stabbed a finger onto the photo of the writer.

"See this guy? Same one as talked to this fucking Savior in today's paper. What I'm thinking is I go hang around *The Light* offices and see what this microturd's up to."

"You mean follow him?" Sounded like a major waste of time.

"Yeah. Why not? Not like I got much else goin' on in the toilet I call my life these days."

Wasn't that the truth. For both of them.

And now that Stan thought about it, maybe this would be good for Joe. Even if he came up empty handed—as he most likely would—at least he'd be out and about instead of sitting in his chair in that litterbox apartment staring at the TV all day.

"Maybe I'll tag along," Stan said. "Just to keep you out of trouble."

He said it lightly, but he was dead serious. Joe was like a carelessly wired block of C-4 these days. No telling what might set him off.

3

"You look awful," Kate said to her reflection in the bathroom mirror. Pale, dark circles under her eyes . . . at least her eyes showed no signs of conjunctivitis. She'd been worried about adenoviruses lately, and that was a common symptom.

She checked her palm. The tiny puncture had healed. For a while, with the aches and malaise Kate had experienced two days after the wound, she'd feared she'd been infected with something. But today the aches were gone.

Not so the fatigue. The dreams had something to do with that, she was sure. Last night's had been the strangest by far. She'd spent the night flying over a landscape of coins—pennies, nickels, dimes, and quarters, all the size of sports arenas, and all face down. And droning in her head a babble of voices, mostly unrecognizable except for Jeanette's and one that sounded like Holdstock's, drifting in and out, calling her name.

And then the dream had stopped.

Not too long afterward she'd heard Jeanette come in and go directly to her room.

And now here she was facing another morning feeling exhausted— physically, mentally, emotionally.

Part of her wanted to run. The emotional abuse from Jeanette— she'd found a way to make silence and indifference abusive—was almost more than Kate could stand. But she kept telling herself this was not Jeanette. Somehow her brain had been affected and her true self was crying to get out. The need to rescue the real Jeanette was the only thing keeping Kate here.

A buzzing sound . . . she opened the bathroom door. The vestibule

bell. Someone down front wanted to get in. Jeanette had stopped answering bells of any sort—phones, doors—so Kate knew it was up
to her.

Who on earth? she thought as she pressed the button and said,
"Hello?"

"Kate, it's Jack. We need to talk."

Do we? she thought.

"Okay. Come up for coffee."

"Can you come down? We'll find an Andrews or something."

He sounded so serious. What was on his mind?

"Let me throw on some clothes."

Minutes later, dressed in jeans and a sweater, she stepped out of
the stairwell into the building's lobby. Kate had left a note to Jeanette
saying where she'd be. Not that Jeanette would care.

She found Jack, also in jeans but wearing a flannel shirt, waiting
outside on the sidewalk. He didn't look too well rested himself. He
stepped up to her and enfolded her in his arms.

"I know about you and Jeanette," he said in a low voice, "and it
doesn't change a damn thing. You're my sister and I love you."

And suddenly Kate found her face pressed against his chest and
she was crying—quaking with deep-rooted sobs. She tried to stop them
but they kept coming.

"It's okay, Kate," he said. "Don't be afraid. I won't tell a soul."

She pushed free and wiped her eyes. "That's not why I'm crying.
I'm *glad* you know. You can't imagine what a relief it is to stop hiding
it from you, to come out to *someone*."

"Oh . . . good. I spent half the night trying to figure the best way to
word it. I didn't know how you'd react. I—"

She stretched up on tiptoe and kissed his cheek. "You did just
fine."

She clung to him a moment longer, almost dizzy with relief and
lighter in heart than she'd felt in years.

"Let's walk," he said. "I'm not yet properly caffeinated."

"But just let me hear it again, Jack," she said as they ambled arm
in arm toward Seventh. "Does my being a dyke really not change a
thing for you or were you just trying to make me feel better?"

He made a face. "You're not a dyke."

"Sure I am."

"No. When I hear 'dyke' I see a fat broad in work clothes and boots with a bad haircut and a load of 'tude."

She laughed. "It doesn't mean superbutch anymore. It's what we call ourselves. As Jeanette says, 'We're taking back the word.'" Or what Jeanette used to say, Kate thought as a wave of sadness brought her down. "But you're not answering the question."

"Okay, the question seems to be since I lie about myself to just about everyone every day, how can you be sure I'm telling you the truth."

"Not at all—"

"Or is it about whether I'm one of those politically correct liberal types who knee-jerks to this sort of thing?"

Had she offended him?

"Jack—"

"So let's get a few things straight, Kate. I'm not PC and I'm not liberal—I'm not conservative or Democrat or Republican either. I operate on one principle: you own your own life, and that means you're free to do anything you want with that life so long as you don't interfere with other people's freedom to live their lives. It means you own your own body and you can do anything you want to it—pierce it, fill it with drugs, set it on fire—your call. Same with sex. As long as there's no force involved it's none of my business how you get off. I don't have to approve of it because it's not my life, it's yours. I don't have to understand, either. Which, by the way, I don't."

As he paused for breath Kate jumped in. "But that doesn't tell me how you feel."

"Feel? How does surprised and baffled sound? If you'd been a tomboy all your life and had never dated I could see it. But you had one boyfriend after another."

"Right. But no steady."

"Is that significant?"

"I didn't think so then, but I do now."

They found a little place on Seventh called The Greek Corner. She saw no one looking even vaguely Greek behind the counter, but the coffee smelled good. They took a table in a largely deserted glassed-in bump-out that would have been a solar oven if the sun had been out.

Jack sighed. "To tell the truth, Kate, I don't understand same-sex attraction. I know it exists and I accept that, but it's alien to me. I'm not wired for it. And then, of all people, you."

"You can't be more surprised than I was, Jack. But it's here. It's me. And there doesn't seem to be a darn thing I can do about it."

"But how? When? Where? Why? Help me here, Kate. I'm completely at sea."

"I'm still trying to figure it out for myself, Jack. You want to know when? When I knew? I'm not sure. Gay guys seem to know much earlier. With women it's not so easy. We're much more fluid in our sexuality—not my term, something I read. But it's true. We're much more intimate with each other. Sure I liked boys when I was a teenager. I liked dating, being courted, pursued. I even liked the sex. But you know what I liked more? Pajama parties."

Jack covered his eyes. "Don't tell me there were teenage lesbian orgies going on just a few feet down the hall from my bedroom and I didn't know."

Kate gave him a gentle kick under the table. "For crying out loud, Jack. Cool it, okay? Nothing ever happened. But there was a lot of contact—the pillow fights, the tickling, the laughing, the sleeping three to a mattress, two to a bedroll. Back then that was all considered normal teenage behavior for girls, but not for guys."

"I'll say."

"And it was normal for me. I loved the closeness to the other girls, the intimacy, and maybe I loved it more than the others, but I never connected it with sex."

"When did that happen?"

"When did I know I was a dyke?"

Jack drew in a breath. "That word again."

"Get used to it. I found out about two years ago."

"Two years? You mean you never once . . . ?"

"Well, in France—you remember my junior year abroad—"

"I missed you terribly."

"Did you? That's nice to know. I had no idea."

"Big boys don't cry."

"And that's a shame, isn't it. But anyway, I had an 'almost' or a 'pretty near' experience there but never gave it much thought afterwards because things are different in France. You remember that Joni Mitchell song, 'In France They Kiss On Main Street'?"

"Vaguely."

"Well, it's true. In France the *girls* kiss on main street—straight girls. They kiss, they hug, they walk down the street hand in hand, arm in arm. It's just a natural thing there."

It's February and her name's Renée, dark hair, dark mysterious eyes, tall, long-limbed and, at twenty-two, a year older. She's invited Kate to her family's country place in Puy-de-Dôme for the day. The two of them are wandering one of the adjacent fields, talking, Renée so patient with Kate's halting French, when it begins to pour. They're drenched and half frozen by the time they reach the empty house. They strip off their sodden clothes, wrap themselves in a huge quilt, and huddle shivering before the fire.

Renée's right arm snakes around Kate's shoulders and pulls her closer . . . for extra warmth, she says.

And that's good because Kate wonders if she'll ever feel warm again.

Your skin is so cold, Renée says. And she starts to rub Kate's back . . . to warm her skin.

And it works. Only a few rubs and Kate is flushed and very warm. She returns the favor, sliding her hand up and down Renée's smooth back, her skin as soft as a baby's. Renée's long arm stretches to where her hand can rub Kate's flank, stretches farther still until it reaches her breast. Kate gasps at the electric sensation of Renée's finger's caressing her nipple and holds her breath as lips nuzzle her neck and the hand trails down along her abdomen. She feels as if something deep inside her is going to burst—

And then the sound of tires on the gravel outside—Renée's mother and little brother, back from the market with the makings for tonight's dinner. The spell shatters with shock and then a mad laughing dash to Renée's room where she lends Kate some clothes to wear until her own are dry. They go down to greet Renée's mother . . . and neither of them ever speaks of that afternoon again.

"What 'almost' happened?" Jack said.

"The details aren't important. It all receded into my subconscious—or maybe it was pushed, I'm not sure which—but the end point was that when I allowed myself to remember it, I looked on it as nothing more than an interesting but anomalous event. After all, I was free, white, and almost twenty-one, and it was the seventies when it was cool to experiment. I saw it as a brush with lesbianism but I knew I wasn't a lesbian. I moved on."

"To medical school."

"Where I met Ron. He was a good-looking, sensitive man and we had so much in common—middle-class backgrounds, similar families, both headed for medical careers. And he was crazy about me so it seemed a perfect match. I loved him, maybe not as much as he loved me, but there was a genuine attraction there and getting married was what was expected of me. So that's what I did. Ron's a good guy. A lot of formerly married women who've come out can tell horror stories about abusive relationships. I don't have that. I can't say I finally came out because I was mistreated. If anything, I mistreated him."

"As I heard it from Dad, he cheated on you."

"And I don't blame him. After Elizabeth was born I lost interest in sex. It's not that unusual, at least on a temporary basis, but for me it went on and on. Ron and I had a good marriage for a long time. I was a good wife and he was a good husband. But as the years went by, I kept feeling less and less fulfilled. That's a terrible word, but it's the only one that fits. Something was missing, Jack, and I didn't know what it was. Until I met Jeanette."

"You mean Sybil."

"Please don't do that, Jack," she said, feeling a flush of anger. "You didn't know her before this virus thing. She's the most exhilarating person I've ever met."

"All right. I'm sorry. You're right. I only know the Moony version of Jeanette. But still, is she worth all this turmoil in your life?"

"Jack, you can't imagine what I was like. I was no fun. Seeing my patients and doing okay as a mother, but I wasn't cutting it at all as a wife. Ron's a good man, and he was a considerate lover, but no matter what he did, it wasn't right. And I wasn't giving Ron what he needed, so finally he went elsewhere. I don't blame him, but he blames himself. And that breaks my heart. We'd been best friends. He thinks he broke up our marriage, but really, it was me."

"You, or Jeanette?"

"I didn't meet her until after Ron and I were separated. My pediatric group had decided to computerize and I knew *nothing* about computers—Ron was into them and so were the kids, but somehow the things never appealed to me. I figured I'd better get up to speed, so when I saw an ad for a computer course at the local Marriott designed for women novices, I signed up."

"Let me guess: Jeanette was the instructor."

"She moonlights from her programming job to do stints with a firm that runs seminars all over the country. She designed her own course, aimed strictly at female computerphobes. It's a bit of a cause for her, so women won't be relegated to the sidelines during the digital revolution."

Kate felt her throat tighten at the memory.

"You should have seen her, Jack. She was wonderful. Took control of the room with her presence. She kept it light but we could sense how she truly cared. And she was so funny, Jack. Hard to believe from what you've seen, I know, but she cracked us up with tales from the days when she worked for a computer problem hotline."

"Was there some sort of instant chemistry?"

"I couldn't take my eyes off her. She tended to wear tennis shirts and slacks and sandals; her hair was shorter then—she looked more butch than now, but at the time I chalked that up to computer geekiness. I wouldn't say I was in love, but when the class was over that first night, I was so captured by her I couldn't bear the thought of leaving her and going home. I wanted more. I approached her and asked if she gave private lessons . . ."

Jeanette gives her a long look, a little half smile gently twisting her lips.

"Lessons in what?"

"Why, um, computer lessons." What a question. "I need some sort of accelerated course."

"Why don't we discuss it over dinner?"

Kate loves the idea. The kids are home; she left them money for a pizza delivery. A hot meal with this fascinating woman is so much more enticing than snacking alone on a leftover slice or two when she gets home. She'll just have to let them know that she's going to be a little later than she'd planned.

"Sounds good," she tells Jeanette. "I just have to make a call first."

They settle on the Italian restaurant right in the hotel. Jeanette starts with a light beer while Kate has a Manhattan. Jeanette protests when

Kate orders a veal dish so she settles for spaghetti puttanesca. Over the meal, during which they split a bottle of Chianti, Jeanette does a lot of asking and Kate does a lot of answering.

When they're through she invites Kate up to her room where they can use her laptop to determine how much she knows and how much tutoring she's going to need. Wonderful idea. Kate's feeling so warm and relaxed and comfortable with this woman that she doesn't want the night to end yet.

She steps into Jeanette's room, dark except for the glowing screen saver on the laptop. She starts forward but never reaches it. Hands grip her upper arms, turn her around, soft lips find hers. Kate stiffens, instinctively begins to recoil, then gives in to those lips. Jeanette's hands move from her shoulders to the buttons of Kate's blouse, tugging at them, freeing them, slipping the fabric off her shoulders. She's insistent, will not be denied. And Kate has no will to deny her or to fight her rising heat, for a new sensation is filling Kate, something she's never fully experienced. Lust.

She lets Jeanette guide her to the bed, lets her take her on the flowered spread, and feels transported to a place she's never been before, another realm. And for the next two hours she has her first private lesson from Jeanette, but not in computers, as a patient, expert teacher tutors her in the ways of warmth and wetness.

"One thing led to another and . . . we became lovers. Then partners. And I began my double life. A very eligible divorcée in Trenton; half of a luppie couple here in New York."

"Luppie?" Jack said, then waved his hand. "Never mind. I just got it."

"Jeanette said her gaydar picked me out during class—she called me 'a Talbot's dyke'—but had no inkling that she'd be my first."

"But she's been good for you?" Jack asked, and she saw real concern in his eyes.

"I don't think I've ever been happier or felt more . . . whole. Jeanette has been wonderful to me and *for* me. She's so tuned in. She's been my guide into this world I barely knew existed, while I've smoothed some of her rough edges and taught her to take a longer view on some things."

After coffee and sweet rolls they left the Greek Corner and wandered up to the urban garden that defined this length of Sixth Avenue, the Flower District.

"Where do you go from here?" Jack said as they threaded through the foliage.

Potted greenery lined the curbs, everything from rubber plants to oversized ferns to small royal palms. The storefronts were riots of color—reds, yellows, blues, fuchsias—and behind them, inside, dimly glimpsed through condensation-layered glass, lay deep green pocket rain forests.

Last week Kate might have picked out some flowers for the apartment, but not today . . . not in a flower mood today.

"In two years, when Lizzie's off to college, I'll tell the kids and Ron. After that it won't take long for the news to leak to my patients, and then the you-know-what will hit the fan. I'll lose a fair share of them. Trenton may be the state capital but it's a small town at heart. People will decide they'd rather not bring their kids, especially their daughters, to a lesbian pediatrician. Especially when there are five other straight doctors in the same office. And that won't make my partners happy."

"So come to New York," Jack said, slipping his arm around her shoulder. "*Lots* of kids here whose parents won't care how you spend your off hours. And it'll be great having you close."

She leaned against him. "You can't imagine how much I appreciate being able to talk to you like this. And I'm sorry for going on so. Listen to me: the love that dare not speak its name cannot shut up. But I've had this bottled up for so long and I feel so . . . so alone right now."

"But you and Jeanette must have some friends. I mean, there's a huge gay community down here that—"

"Yes, but I'm a forty-four-year-old babydyke who isn't out. That makes me a sort of pariah to the younger dykes, the *grrrls*, the twenty-somethings who've been out since their teens. They think we all should be out and eff anyone who doesn't like it."

" 'Eff'?" Jack grinned. "Did you say '*eff*'?"

"I always have trouble saying the F-word."

"That's because you're a square. Always were."

Kate sighed. She couldn't take offense. It was true.

"I'm still a square in so many ways. A square dyke—can you imagine? A walking, talking oxymoron. Born square, doomed to die from terminal squareness. It's just that I was always trying to set a good example—for you when we were growing up, and later for Kevin and Liz."

"And you did," he said softly. "Just as I'm sure you still do."

"I don't want to change the world or be part of a movement. I just want to be me. It's taken me so long to get to this point that I just want to relax and enjoy it. And I never cared what others thought as long as I had Jeanette. We're both a little old for the gay club scene; we'd have dinner at Rubyfruits once in a while, but mostly we cooked in and just enjoyed being with each other."

"No dressing up and going out on the town looking like *Wild One* Marlon Brandos?"

"Just being a vanilla dyke more than fills my deviancy quota."

"Don't call yourself a deviant."

"It means deviating from the norm. And that's what we dykes do."

"Can't help how you feel. Not as if you're hurting anyone."

"Not yet at least. But when I finally come out . . . who knows?" She shook her head. "All because of a chromosome . . . one lousy chromosome."

"There's a gay gene?"

"Maybe. But I'm talking about the Y-chromosome, the one that makes you male. We females have two X-chromosomes, but if I could change one chromosome, change just one of my X's to a Y, my feelings for Jeanette would be considered perfectly normal."

Jack gave a low whistle. "Jeez. You put it like that, what's all the fuss about?"

"Exactly. One chromosome. And if I had it, I wouldn't have all this terrible angst and dread about letting people know."

He grabbed her shoulder. "Just thought of something. Are you going to tell Dad?"

Kate shuddered. She had no idea how her father would react. She loved him. They'd always been close, but he had no idea. No lesbians in his world. What words could she use to tell him that his only daughter was one?

"I haven't decided whether he should be before or after the kids. Either way, that's when the you-know-what hits the fan."

"Would that be 'ess' hitting the fan, or doo-doo?"

Kate laughed and hugged Jack. "Both!"

She loved the man he'd become. What great luck running into him. And what a wonderful feeling to be out to him. It had been so easy.

She looked around and realized they were back at the Arsley. She almost dreaded going back upstairs and facing Jeanette. Who would she be today?

"Mind if I come up with you?" Jack said.

Does he read minds? she wondered.

"I'd like that."

She keyed her way through the front door but stopped Jack in the lobby. She had to make one thing absolutely clear to him.

"No one else can know what we've discussed this morning, Jack. Not till Kevin and Liz are both eighteen. It's not just for my sake but for theirs too."

"Okay, sure, but—"

"No buts about it, Jack. Ron doesn't know and I can't predict how he'll react. He's a good man and I think he'll be okay, but you never know. If he feels his masculinity has somehow been compromised, he may try to get back at me through the kids. We have joint custody now but he might sue, claiming that as a lesbian I'm an unfit parent—"

"No way."

"It happens all the time, Jack. The courts can be rough on lesbians. But even if Ron accepts it, what about Kevin and Liz? The news will sweep through their school in minutes, and you know how cruel kids can be. Adolescence is hard enough. I can't add that to the load. When they're both in college I'll sit them down and tell them. Until then I've got to stay in the closet. Just like you."

"Me?" He looked shocked. "What—?"

"Yes, you. You're leading a double life just like me. You've got one face you show to the public but then there's this other side, this Repairman Jack thing that you've been hiding all these years—from Dad, from Tom, from me, and I'm sure from the police, since you've as much as said some of what you do isn't exactly legal. You've got your own closet, Jack."

He stared at her a moment, then nodded. "Never thought of it that way but I guess I do. Except I can't come out of mine. Ever."

"You did to me."

He shook his head, raised a hand, and waggled his pinky finger.

"I opened the door a crack and showed you this much. The rest stays inside."

"Why?"

"Because my closet's way deeper and lots darker than yours."

She expected to see sadness in his eyes but found only flat acceptance. He'd made choices and he'd live with them.

Just as she'd live with hers.

4

Jeanette was not in sight when Jack and Kate came in.

"She might still be asleep," Kate said.

Jack hoped not. He wanted to see what mental shape Jeanette was in before he left Kate alone with her. He also wanted another look at this woman who meant so much to his sister. He couldn't help but see her differently now. She was no longer Kate's friend, she was her lover.

"Who's asleep?" Jeanette said, stepping out of her room with a mug in her hand.

She wore an Oberlin sweatshirt and cut-off shorts. Nice legs. Great quads. She definitely worked out.

"How are you feeling?" Kate asked.

Jeanette beamed. "Absolutely wonderful. How about you? And Jack. So good to see you again. How *are* you?"

Jack glanced at Kate, saw the tight line of her lips, and knew how she was feeling. They were in the presence of Mary Poppins without the accent. Or maybe the Stepford Dyke.

"Just fine," Jack said. "We had a walk and a talk."

"I'm out with Jack," Kate said. "He knows everything."

Jeanette glided into the kitchen. "Isn't that nice." She placed her mug into the microwave and began punching buttons. "Not that it's going to matter."

Kate looked as if she'd been slapped. "What do you mean?"

"Oh, nothing." Her smile broadened. "And everything."

She punched the START button and her grin died. Slack-faced and staring, she swayed.

"Jeanette?" Kate started forward.

Jeanette began mumbling, slowly, extracting the words like corks from wine bottles. "Kate . . . I . . . we . . . no . . . Kate, I'm almost gone. Can't hold out—"

And then the microwave oven chimed.

And Jeanette blinked and regained her smile as abruptly as she'd lost it.

"What?" Jeanette said. "Why are you staring?"

"You had another of those spells," Kate said.

"Don't be silly." She removed her reheated cup from the microwave and took a sip. "Mmmm."

"Jeanette—" Kate began as Jeanette brushed by her on her way out of the kitchenette, but Jeanette cut her off.

"Any plans for today, Kate?" She plopped herself in the rocking chair and smiled.

As Kate began another attempt at convincing Jeanette to make an appointment with Dr. Fielding, Jack stared at the microwave. Wasn't sure, but thought he remembered Jeanette having her 'spell' last night while Kate was nuking the dip. And now while reheating her coffee.

Could microwaves trigger these spells? Didn't know a lot about them, but if people with pacemakers were supposed to keep their distance, who knew what other effects they might have?

"Anyone mind if I make myself a cup of coffee?" he announced to the room.

Kate gave him an odd look and he knew what she was thinking: after all the coffee he'd drunk at the Greek place he should be floating.

But Jeanette said, "Sure, be my guest."

Found a mug, filled it with water, and stuck it inside the oven. This gave him a chance to look it over. Noticed the door wobbled on its hinges, and he found a crack in the lower right corner of the glass. Had it been dropped at some time?

Closed the door, set it for five minutes on high, and punched START. As it hummed to life he turned to Jeanette.

Nothing. She sat in the front room sipping and rocking and shaking her head no to everything Kate was suggesting.

So much for that theory.

But wait. Jeanette had been standing in the kitchen both times. Proximity could be a factor.

Hit the STOP button.

"Something wrong here," he said. "The microwave won't stay on."

"Sometimes the door doesn't catch," Jeanette said. "Make sure it's closed all the way."

Jack made a show of opening and closing the door, and pretended to press START.

"Nope. Still won't go."

"Men!" Jeanette said with an exasperated sigh as she rose from her chair. "You're only good for one thing."

Jack stepped aside to allow her to reach the microwave. "And what's that?"

"Procreation."

Weird thing for a lesbian to say. Wasn't *breeder* a derogatory term among gays?

Watched her press START.

She dropped her cup, splashing Jack's ankles with hot coffee, and now her face had that slack look again, and she started mumbling.

"No . . . yes . . . this helps . . . what are you . . ."

"Jeanette!" Kate cried, rushing into the kitchen area. "It's happening again!"

"Easy, Kate."

She grabbed Jeanette's hand. "What's happening?"

"It's the microwave oven. Seems to have some effect on her."

"Then turn it off!"

"No," Jeanette gasped. "Leave . . . it on."

"Listen to her, Kate. It's a good effect. Like it's snapping her out of whatever spell she's under."

"The virus," Jeanette said. "The virus . . ."

"What about the virus?" Kate gripped Jeanette's shoulders and gently rotated her until they were face to face. "Tell me."

Jack retreated a step. Three people strained the tiny kitchen's occupancy limit. Let Kate handle it. She was the doctor.

Jeanette's tone changed—same voice, but suddenly more focused. "We do not want to speak of this."

"What do you mean, 'we'?"

Fractured again: "Wasn't me . . . don't listen to them. It's the virus . . . changing us."

"Changing you how?"

"My brain . . . our brains . . . reaching critical mass . . ." Another shift in tone. "No! We will not speak of this!"

Jeanette squeezed her eyes shut, seemed to be making a heroic effort to exert control. Might have been funny on a stage or in a comedy club, somebody doing a parody of a bad horror film about demonic possession or warring multiple personalities, but the fear-sweat streaming from Jeanette's pores was real. Jack sensed a once indomitable personality clawing for a fingerhold on her identity and his heart went out to her. He wanted to help her but hadn't a clue as to how.

"Tell me, Jeanette!" Kate said. "What's happening to you?"

"Eaten . . . eaten alive. Every minute . . . every second . . . less of me . . . more of them."

"Jeanette, that sounds so—"

The microwave went *ding!* Jeanette stiffened, blinked.

Damn! Jack quickly reached around Kate, punched another ten minutes into the oven and got it running again.

"E pluribus unum! E pluribus unum! E pluribus unum! . . ."

She kept repeating the phrase and Jack couldn't be sure which Jeanette was responsible. It seemed like a prayer, or a mantra, something you might repeat endlessly to drown out a sound or a frightening thought.

"Jeanette!" Kate still had hold of her shoulders and was shaking her. "Jeanette, stop that and listen to me!"

But she kept droning the same damn phrase.

And then Jack turned at the sound of the door opening and saw Holdstock rush into the room.

"What's going on here!" the pudgy man cried. He wore a gray, three-piece suit; his face was flushed and sweaty, as if he'd been running. "What are you doing to her?"

"Hey-hey!" Jack said, stepping toward him and straight-arming him to a stop. "Where do you get off barging in here?"

"I have a standing invitation," he puffed. He held up a key. "See? More than you have, I'm sure."

He tried to slip past, but Jack wasn't about to let that happen. He grabbed him by his suit vest.

"Whoa, pal. Just stay where you are."

And behind Jack the "e pluribus unum" chant continued.

"You take your hands off me! And stop torturing that woman or I'll call the police!"

"Will you?" Jack said. "I wonder."

But the threat did hold weight for Jack. Last thing he wanted was a couple of cops at the door.

"Let me go to her! Please!"

"Let him, Jack," Kate said. "Maybe he can explain what this is about."

Jack released Holdstock who lunged past him toward Jeanette.

"Listen to her," Kate said as Holdstock neared. "Do you have any idea what that means?"

"Of course," he said.

But instead of explaining he reached past Kate and unplugged the microwave.

"Hey!" Jack said as the chant stopped.

Jeanette sagged against Kate, then straightened and pushed away. "What . . . ? Where . . . ?"

"It's all right, dear," Holdstock said, guiding her from the kitchen. "I'm here now."

"Get your hands off her," Jack said.

"Should I take my hands off you, Jeanette?" Holdstock said.

"No. No, of course not."

"You're coming with me," he told her, steering her toward the door. "It's not healthy for you here."

"Not so fast," Jack said, blocking their way.

Jeanette glared at Jack. "You! You're an enemy! You're evil! Get out of my house!"

"Jeanette!" Kate said. "Please!"

"I want you to stay, Kate," she said, keeping her eyes fixed on Jack, "but if your brother is here when I come back, I'm calling the police."

Jack didn't move. His gut told him he shouldn't let her go—for her sake—but if she said she wanted to leave, he couldn't see he had much choice but to let her.

Reluctantly he stepped aside. But only a little. Just enough to let them squeeze by.

As Holdstock brushed past, one arm around Jeanette's shoulders, Jack felt something sharp scrape against the back of his hand. He glanced down and saw a fine scratch. How had that happened? Holdstock's near hand had been in his coat pocket as he'd passed.

He shrugged. Nothing serious. Probably just a pin from a cleaning tag. Barely bleeding.

He turned to Kate and found her still standing in the kitchen, a lost, confused look on her face.

"What just happened here?" she said.

"Damned if I know. You're the doctor. Have you ever seen anything like that?"

"Never."

"Has to be the microwaves. But I know as much about microwaves as I do about string theory."

"I know they're a form of radiation—non-ionizing radiation. Depending on the wavelength, they're used for everything from radar to cell phones to cooking. But I can't believe Jeanette has a personality change anytime she gets near a microwave oven."

Jack took Kate's hand and brushed her fingers over the crack in the glass on the oven door.

"This microwave oven happens to leak."

Kate shook her head. "I still don't understand . . ."

"I've got a whole list of things I don't understand about this. And Holdstock is high on it. You told me he showed up right after Jeanette's first personality change, right? And now he pops in again. You think he's got the place bugged?"

Kate rubbed her upper arms. "Don't say that. I've read articles about people becoming ill from exposure to microwave snooping devices."

"A couple of months ago I spent a whole weekend with a group of paranoids who had crazy stories about any subject you could name. Among them were tales about CIA and KGB experiments using microwaves for mind control. Maybe they're not so paranoid."

"You're giving me the creeps."

"And what was she saying about the virus changing her brain? You think that could be?"

Kate looked miserable. "Jack, I don't know. It doesn't seem possible. It's an adenovirus. Even mutated I can't imagine an adenovirus changing someone's brain."

Microwaves, multiple personalities, mutated viruses—Jack felt as if he'd stepped off a ledge into an underwater canyon.

"Maybe not, but I think the guy to contact is Fielding. I don't know about you, but this is way out of my league. Maybe you'd better get back to him."

"I'll do that right now."

"And while you doctor-talk with him, I'm going to run an errand. Be back in no time."

Jack had an idea he wanted to try. But he'd need some hardware first.

5

Sandy sat at his desk in a daze. This had to be the greatest morning of his life. He still couldn't believe the reception when he'd walked into the press room two hours ago—cheers and a standing ovation. George Meschke had met him in the middle of the floor to shake his hand and tell him that his edition—yes, they'd called it *his* edition— had been selling out all over the city.

And now his voicemail. He'd just finished listening to the last of nine messages. People he hadn't heard from in years—a former roommate, old classmates, even one of his journalism professors—had called to congratulate him. What next?

"Hi, Sandy."

He looked up and blinked. Patrice Rawlinson, the perpetually tanned silicone blonde from the art department. Sure, she was faked and baked, but with those painted-on dresses she was everyone's dream babe.

He struggled for a reply. "Oh, uh, hi."

Brilliant.

In the past when he'd said hello to her in the halls she'd always looked through him. A real Ralph Ellison moment. But now she'd come to him. She'd walked that gorgeous body all the way to his cubicle and spoken words to him. She'd said his name.

"I just wanted to say how much I enjoyed your interview with the Savior. I hung on every word. That must have been so exciting to talk to him."

"It was." Please don't say anything stupid, he told himself. "It's a moment every journalist dreams of."

"You've got to tell me *all* about it sometime."

"Gladly."

"Give me a buzz when you're free."

And with that she swayed off. Sandy resisted sticking his head outside his cubicle for an extended look at her, as he'd done so many times in the past. He was above that now.

"Tell me that wasn't Patrice's voice I just heard," said Pokorny from somewhere on the far side of the partition.

"It was, my man. It most certainly was."

Pokorny groaned. "I'm going to kill myself."

Does it get any better than this? Sandy thought, grinning.

No. It was positively intoxicating. Like a drug. And just as addicting. He didn't want to let this go. Couldn't. He needed more, a steady fix.

But what next? He couldn't let this be the pinnacle of his career— talk about peaking too soon! He had to come up with something equal or better. And the only thing he knew for sure that would fit that bill was another interview with the Savior.

But what was left to cover in a second interview? Rehashing the same old material wouldn't cut it.

But what if I challenge the initial material? he wondered.

He suspected that some of it wasn't true. In fact the more he thought about it, the surer he became that the Savior wasn't doing undercover work for the government. That was a little too glamorous, a little too Hollywood.

So what other reasons could he have to stop him from stepping forward to be acclaimed as a hero?

And then he remembered his earlier conversation with Beth. He'd been blue-skying with her but—

Sandy slammed his hand on his desktop. Christ, I bet that's it! The man has a criminal record. He's a fugitive! Some sort of felon with a warrant out for his arrest. And that's why he was armed!

He had his next hook: get the Savior to talk about his crime. Maybe he was an innocent victim, on the run because of a crime he didn't commit—

No, stop. You're getting Hollywood again.

Maybe he'd committed just one crime, or maybe he wasn't bad all the way through. He certainly did the right thing on the train. Maybe . . .

And then it all came together, driving Sandy to his feet, gasping like a fish out of water. He had it! A fabulous idea!

He fumbled a slip of paper from his pocket—the phone number the Savior had given him. He reached for his phone, then stopped.

No. No calls from here. Somewhere he was sure the paper kept a record of all outgoing numbers. Better a public phone.

Sandy hurried for the street. He was a man on fire, a man with a mission. He was going to do something wonderful, something that would repay the mystery man for saving his life. Talk about advocacy journalism! He'd be pulling off a journalistic coup to make today's story look like a weather report. Not just your common everyday, run-of-the-mill journalistic coup—*the* journalistic coup of the new century!

Can you spell *Pulitzer*?

6

Jack struck out at a hardware store and an appliance store, but finally found what he wanted at the Wiz. On his way back to Jeanette's apartment he stopped at a pay phone to check his messages. He groaned aloud when he heard Sandy Palmer's voice.

"Good morning, 'Jack.' Yeah, like I'm supposed to believe that's your real name."

Jack? How did he know—?

And then Jack remembered: the outgoing message on his voicemail began, "This is Jack . . ." He'd forgot all about that. Not that it mattered. Palmer thought it was phony anyway.

"Listen, we have to talk again. I've come up with an idea that's going to transform your life. We've got to meet. And don't blow this off, because what I've got to say to you is vitally important. Another reason you shouldn't blow me off is I've still got the drawing. Now don't get me wrong, because I don't want you to think I'm trying to blackmail you, but I'm pretty sure you weren't completely straight with me the other day—about your past, that is—so I don't feel bound by our little agreement to destroy the drawing. But we can let bygones be bygones and straighten all this out with one little meeting. Call and tell me where and when. And trust me, Jack, or whatever your name is, you'll be ever so glad you did."

He left his number and extension at the paper.

Jack slammed the receiver against the phone box. Then did it again. And again.

Now I don't want you to think I'm trying to blackmail you . . .

What else am I supposed to think, you rotten little bastard?

He had this frenzied urge to get his hands around Palmer's pencil neck and squeeze until . . .

Easy. Step back. Look at it again . . .

But short of killing the kid, Jack saw no quick and easy way to take command of the situation. Palmer controlled the deck. Jack would have to play it his way. For now.

He called Palmer's number and extension. With an effort he kept his voice low and even when he reached his voicemail.

"Same place. Noon."

Then he hung up.

He'd cooled a little by the time he reached Jeanette's apartment, but his mood was still cooking over a low flame.

Kate took one look at him and said, "What's wrong?"

"Nothing to do with this."

"Need to share?"

Jack considered that, almost gave in to the urge to tell her, but decided against it. The fewer who knew, the better.

"I'll be all right. But thanks." He opened his Wiz bag and produced a little white gizmo. "Looky. A microwave tester."

He set the oven for five minutes and started it, then ran the little tester along the edges of the door. The indicator started flashing red immediately and went into high gear when he reached the lower right corner with the cracked glass.

"That confirms it. Leaky oven." He hit the off switch. "How dangerous is that?"

"I did a search on Jeanette's computer while you were out."

"I'd think a doctor would know all about microwaves."

"Why? I haven't found a use yet for radar in my practice."

"Radar?"

"That's why the first microwave ovens were called radar ranges. Microwaves are radiofrequency radiation—somewhere below infrared and above UHF in the frequency spectrum."

That meant nothing to Jack. "I know they're used for cell phone transmission. But what's the downside—besides brain tumors?"

"That's never been proven, and it seems unlikely since it's non-ionizing radiation. The main effect is heat. The guy who discovered the microwave oven was playing with different frequencies, looking for new radar applications, when he melted the candy bar in his shirt pocket."

"A true 'Eureka!' moment."

"I suppose so. The ovens work by causing vibrations in water molecules, creating heat. The strength of the transmitter and the frequency of the waves determine the depth of penetration and the amount of heat generated. The best documented ill effects in humans are cataracts and sterilized testicles."

Jack stepped away from the oven. "But no brain tumors."

"Not a one. But my search popped up lots of hits involving central nervous system effects—everything from memory loss to mind control. I don't know how factual they are though."

"So if this virus is having an effect on Jeanette's brain—"

"Which is the heart of the central nervous system."

"—maybe the microwaves disrupt that."

"But what about Holdstock? He was dosed with the virus too, but he walked right up to the oven and turned it off."

"Right. Forgot about that. Damn. So much for that theory."

"Pretty far-fetched anyway."

"Lot of far-fetched stuff going down these days," he said, thinking back on the events of the last couple of months. "And remember, I didn't come up with the virus-taking-over idea. That was Jeanette's."

"Well, rest assured, there's no virus taking over Jeanette's mind. But she might believe there is."

"Maybe that's the engine driving the Holdstock cult—some sort of shared delusion."

"You may have something there."

"Yeah, well, whether I do or not, it's something for the NIH boys to handle, not me. Did you call Fielding?"

Kate's face clouded as she nodded. "Yes. He said not to worry. He's been in contact with them daily and what seem like interminable delays are simply the normal bureaucratic process."

"Why do I get the feeling you don't believe that?"

"Because he seemed so nervous. I could almost hear him sweating."

"Well, his reputation and his career could be at stake."

"Because of a mutation? I don't see how. I think I'm going to call NIH myself and see what I can find out."

"Good idea. And while you're doing that, I've got to meet the press."

"Sorry?"

"Long story."

Kate smiled at him. "Do you know how many times you've said that over the last few days?"

"Too many, probably. Someday soon we'll sit down together and I'll tell you a few of them if you want." *A select few,* he thought.

"I'd like that very much," she said.

"Then it's a date. But for now I've got to run. Call you later."

7

"Aw, shit," Joe said. "The kid's going for a walk in the park."

"Maybe he is, maybe he isn't," Stan told his brother in a soothing tone. Joe was as twitchy and fidgety as he'd ever seen him. Like he had roaches crawling all over his skin.

They'd hung around outside *The Light* offices all morning, watching for this reporter, this Sandy Palmer guy. They didn't even know if he was in the building, so they called inside and got him on the phone. That settled, they waited. He finally came out around 11:30 and ducked into the subway. Guy could have been going home, out for a haircut, or to visit his mama. No way to know. But wherever he was going, Joe insisted on following. The reporter had jumped on the Nine so they did the same. On the outside chance he might be on the lookout for a tail, they'd split up—Joe in the car ahead of him, Stan in the one behind. Stan noticed Joe keeping his left hand in his pocket the whole time. The kid ever saw that, Joe would be tagged; he'd have to back off and let Stan do the tail solo.

When the reporter got off at Seventy-second, Stan thought he might simply be returning to the scene of the crime. But no, he headed straight for the stairs.

Topside, Stan and Joe each took a different side of the street and gave him a block lead as he headed west along Seventy-first. Waste of effort. The kid was in his own world, loping along without a single look back.

Stan had joined up with Joe at the corner of Riverside Drive where they hung back as the reporter ambled into the park.

Stan tried to show Joe the bright side.

"This might be something. If you remember, we set up quite a few meetings in parks in our day."

Joe rubbed his stubbled chin. "Come to think of it, I do. So how do we work this?"

Stan surveyed the landscape. Riverside Drive ran at a higher level, bordered on its west flank by a low wall overlooking the greenery that sloped away below it.

"We split," Stan said. "You take the high road and I'll take the low road—"

"And I'll be in wherever-it-is before ya."

"Scotland. Keep your cell phone on and I'll call you if I think he's made me or I see him heading back up to the street. Then you pick him up and—"

"Shut up!" Joe hissed. He grabbed Stan's arm, his fingers digging in like claws. "There he is!"

"Who? Where?"

"Over there. Two blocks down. See him? In the baseball cap, leaning on the wall, watching the park."

Stan saw an average-looking guy. Nothing striking about him. Looked relaxed as all hell, taking a little fresh air while killing some time.

"You think that's our guy? Could be anybody."

Joe hadn't moved a muscle. His eyes were fixed on the baseball cap like a dog on point.

"It's him, Stan. I see him in my dreams, and I've been dreaming of this moment. You don't know how I've been dreaming of this moment." His breath rasped through his teeth. "The fucker! The *fucker!*"

"Easy, Joe. We've got to be sure. We—"

"*I'm* sure. God damn *fuck* am I sure! Know what he's doing? He's casing the park, watching this reporter make his entrance and checking him for a tail. If you'd gone down there he'd've spotted you and that would've queered it all. He disappears and the meet is off. But he's a dumb fuck. Figures if someone's tailing the reporter, whoever it is doesn't know what *he* looks like. Thinks he's sittin' safe and pretty up there with his bird's-eye view. But *we* know what he looks like, don't we, Stan. *We* know."

The longer Joe talked and the longer Stan looked, the more familiar this guy at the wall became. Stan was almost afraid to believe it *was* him, afraid he'd fool himself because he so very much *wanted* it to be him. Not as much as Joe, maybe, but still, some heavy debts cried out for payment—with tons of vig.

"You know, Joe . . . I think you might be right."

Joe was still staring. A heat-seeking missile that had found its target.

"Course I'm right." He reached into his jacket pocket. "I'm doin' him, Stan. Gonna splatter his IQ all the way to the river then take his head home as a souvenir! Make a soup bowl out of his skull and eat from it every fucking night!"

Stan gripped his brother's arm before he could pull his .38. The area was crawling with people.

"Too many witnesses, Joe," he said quickly. "What good's doing him if it's going to land us in the joint? Like you said before, we've got to send a message here. This is the guy that blew up our stash, our cash, and our reps. We got to do him in kind. Blow him to hell. A public blow. And then we can say, remember that guy who got blown to chili con carne back in June? That was the guy who blew our farm and wrecked Joe's hand. We found him and did him. Did him good."

He felt Joe's arm relax as he nodded, still staring at the guy.

"Yeah. All right. And not just him, but him and everything he owns and everyone around him. You don't mess with the K Brothers."

Stan knew it would never be the same. They'd never completely salvage their reps, but at least they'd have evened some of the score. That counted for something.

"How you want to handle this?"

"He's looking for someone tailing the reporter. But we'll be tailing him. We find out where he lives, then we do him. And no waitin' around, Stan. We do him tonight!"

8

Sandy checked his watch: 12:30. He'd been wandering around the park for half an hour now. The message had said same place, noon. The noon was clear enough. And Sandy had assumed "same place" meant same bench. So he'd waited there for a while, but no Savior. He wondered if he should call the Savior "Jack." He didn't know if that was his real name, but it was better than the Savior.

After fifteen minutes on the bench he'd got up and wandered around. Maybe "same place" had meant the park in general. But another fifteen minutes of trudging up and down a ten-block length had yielded no sign of the man.

Looked like he'd been stood up. What now? He'd threatened the Savior with the drawing, told him he hadn't got rid of them. Not true. He'd torn them up and flushed them down a toilet in one of *The Light*'s men's rooms. But he could print out another from the computer in minutes if he wanted to. But did he want to?

He remembered what Beth had said about *To Kill a Mockingbird*. Did he have a right to drag Boo Radley into the spotlight just for a story?

But the analogy didn't hold. He was here to do the Savior a favor—the biggest favor of his life.

Sandy checked his watch again. He'd give him another fifteen minutes, then—

"Hey!"

Sandy jumped, looked up, looked around—the Savior stood by a tree twenty feet away. He cocked his head down the slope toward the highway.

"Wait a minute or two," he said, "then meet me in the underpass."

Sandy watched him walk off, waited the requisite time, then followed. He found him waiting in the shadows of a concrete arch that supported a short span of the West Side Highway. Noise from the traffic above rumbled through the space.

"Look," Sandy said, approaching him, "before we go any further I just want to say—"

The Savior held up his hand for silence and scanned the park behind Sandy.

"If you're worried about my being followed, I wasn't."

"Probably right," he said. "Didn't see anyone tail you into the park, but you can never be sure about these things."

After a moment of narrow-lidded surveillance, he turned to Sandy. "What's the story, Palmer? We gonna play games, is that it? I thought we had an understanding: you get your interview, I never hear from you again."

He sounded pissed, and had a right to be, but Sandy had figured the best way to play this was not to allow himself to be put on the defensive.

"No games," he said. "I just don't think you were playing straight with me. I don't think you're working for the government, and I'm not so sure you were ever a Navy SEAL, either."

"True or not, what's the difference? You got your story, the paper's selling out—"

"How do you know that?"

His mouth twisted. "Had to go to three newsstands before I found a copy. Which means your bosses must be happy. You're a big shot now. Where's your gripe?"

Sandy resisted the urge to wipe his moist palms on his pants. This was a dangerous man and he had to be careful how he spun this. He'd mentally rehearsed his spiel for the last hour. Now it was show time.

"No gripe at all. It's just that I figured out the real reason you don't want your face in the papers, why you don't want anyone to know your name: you're a wanted man."

Bingo. The Savior had been scanning the park again, but when he blinked and stared at Sandy, he knew he'd struck pay dirt.

"You're nuts."

"Hear me out. I figure it had to be a felony. A misdemeanor

wouldn't put you into hiding. So you're either wanted for a crime or you've jumped bail or escaped prison."

"Got it all figured out, don't you."

Sandy shrugged. "What else can it be?"

"Should have known I couldn't fool you." The Savior shook his head and looked away. "The orphan part is true, but I made up the part about the cop telling me to join the army or go to jail. I've been in and out of trouble most of my life. Got picked up after knocking over a liquor store."

"A liquor store . . ." Sandy was afraid to ask the next question. "No one was shot, were they?"

"Nah. I just flashed a starter pistol. But that didn't matter; got charged with armed robbery. Couldn't plea down. I was only nineteen at the time. I wasn't going up for that, so I jumped bail and I've been on the run ever since."

"Are you wanted for anything else?"

The Savior didn't answer immediately. He was staring past Sandy again. Finally he pursed his lips and said, "Shit. Move back."

"What?"

He shoved him against the sloping concrete wall of the underpass. "Back!"

Sandy turned to see this guy about his own age in cut-offs and a T-shirt and a scraggly attempt at a beard racing a crummy looking bike full tilt down the slope toward the underpass. He clutched a gray hand-bag and kept looking over his shoulder.

His eyes widened as he entered the underpass and saw that it was occupied, but the Savior gave him a friendly, reassuring wave and said, "Hey, how's it goin'?"

"Not bad," the guy panted.

Then a lot of things happened quickly, too quickly for Sandy to process fully. Suddenly the Savior was moving, taking a quick step forward and kicking the bike's rear wheel. The guy lost control, hit the curb, and went flying over the handle bars. Sandy watched in shock as the Savior kept moving, following the man as he sailed toward the pavement, leaping as he landed chest first, and landing with his heels driving into the guy's upper back. The muffled crunch of breaking bones turned Sandy's stomach, as did the man's scream of pain.

What the *fuck*? Sandy thought.

"That was my mother back there!" the Savior shouted. He crouched beside the writhing man who was trying to rise but couldn't seem to get his arms to work. "You just rolled my *mother!*"

"Aw, shit!" the guy said, his voice a faint wheeze.

"My *mother!*" he screamed, his face reddening.

"Didn't know, man!" he groaned, every syllable wrapped in pain. "Didn't mean nothin'!"

The Savior turned to Sandy, his eyes wild. "Your turn to be a hero," he said, pointing to the gray handbag beside the man. "Take that back to the old lady he knocked down back near the top of the slope. Tell her you found it on the grass."

Sandy could only stare, stunned.

"Come on, Palmer. Move! I'll meet you over by the basketball courts." He bent again over the fallen man and screamed, "My *mother!*"

"I know, man," the purse snatcher grunted. "I'm sorry . . . like really . . . sorry."

He gave Sandy another look, then trotted out the opposite end of the underpass, leaving Sandy alone with the stranger. Gingerly he stepped closer, picked up the handbag, then beat it back to the sunlight and the park.

The Savior's mother? Was she in the park? Was this her bag?

He spotted a cluster of people near the top of the slope and jogged toward them. An old woman sat on a bench in the center of the cluster, sobbing. Her knees and hands were scraped, her stockings torn.

". . . just pushed me," she was saying. "I don't know where he went. I never saw him."

The Savior's mother . . . Sandy shook his head. Not likely. The old woman was black.

"Did you lose this?" Sandy said, edging into the circle around her.

She looked up and her tear-filled eyes widened. "My bag!"

"Where'd you get that?" said a beefy guy, eyeing Sandy suspiciously.

Sandy handed the bag to the woman, then jerked a thumb over his shoulder and stuck to the story.

"I was walking down by the highway and found it."

"Everything's here!" the woman said, opening her wallet. "Oh, thank you, young man! Thank you ever so much!" She pulled out a couple of twenties. "Let me reward you."

Sandy waved her off. "Absolutely not. No way."

The beefy guy slapped him on the back. "Good man."

Sandy made a show of checking his watch. "Look, I've got a meeting," he said to the man. "Will she be all right?"

"We called the cops. EMTs are on their way."

"Great." To the old woman he said, "Good luck to you, ma'am. I'm sorry this happened."

She thanked him again and then he was on his way down the sloping path toward the basketball courts, trying to process the events of the past few minutes. He'd led a sheltered life, he knew. His exposure to violence while growing up had been limited to a few schoolyard shoving matches. But all that had changed with the bloodbath on the train. His baptism of fire.

But in some strange way he found this new incident even more disturbing. The Savior had acted so quickly, with such decisiveness— one moment the purse snatcher had been cycling by, Sandy had blinked, and next thing he knew the man was flat on his face with two broken or dislocated shoulders and the Savior screaming at him about his mother.

What was *that* all about?

And more frightening had been the terrible dark joy in the Savior's eyes as he'd hovered over the downed man. He'd *enjoyed* hurting him. And he'd done it without the slightest hesitation. That was very, very scary. And even scarier was the thought now of dealing with him one on one.

Sandy began to sense that he might be in over his head, but he brushed it off. He wasn't here to threaten this man; he wanted to do him a favor.

But would that matter if he was dealing with a psycho? In an instant the Savior had changed from regular guy to mad dog. And why had he even bothered with the purse snatcher? If the Savior was a wanted felon, why would he interfere with a fellow criminal?

None of this made any sense.

He found the man leaning against the high chain link fence bordering the asphalt basketball courts. He started moving away as Sandy approached, motioning him to follow. Sandy caught up with him in a small grove of trees.

"Why here?" he said, looking around and noticing that they were partially hidden from the rest of the park. He was uneasy now being alone with this man.

"Because your picture's been in the paper twice this week. Who knows when someone will recognize you?"

"Yeah?" Sandy said, suddenly aglow. Someone recognizing him on the street. How totally cool would that be. "I mean, yeah, sure, I see what you mean."

Sandy sensed that Mr. Hyde had disappeared. The Savior seemed to have returned to Dr. Jekyll mode.

"So tell me," the Savior said. "How are you going to change my lowly criminal life?"

Sandy held up a hand. "Wait. You tell me something first: What was all that business about your mother? She wasn't your mother."

"She could have been. My mother would be about her age if she'd survived."

"Survived what?"

"Death."

Sandy sensed a big sign saying PROCEED NO FURTHER, so he switched to the other question that was bothering him.

"All right then, tell me this: why did you, someone who supposedly wants to avoid the spotlight, get involved in that?"

He gave him a puzzled look. "How could I not? If he'd taken off the other way I wouldn't have run after him, but he was passing right in front of us. To let him sail by would be . . . like . . ." He seemed to be searching for the words. "It would make me into an accomplice— an accomplice in rolling a little old lady. Uh-uh."

Sandy stared at him and experienced a flash of insight that seemed to point the way toward getting a handle on this man.

"I think I understand you now," he said, nodding. "You can't tolerate disorder yet you're trapped in a world where everything is spinning out of control."

"I'm not trapped anywhere."

"We all are. But you're doing something about it."

"Are you crazy?"

"Not at all. Look what just happened. A robbery. That's wrong. A prime example of the random disorder afflicting our lives."

"That *is* life. Been happening every minute of every day since some cave man decided he didn't feel like hunting and tried to steal his neighbor's brontoburger."

"But you made sure this one didn't happen. You reordered the disorder."

"Are you on drugs or did you run out of your medication? You make it sound like I'm out patrolling the streets trolling for wrongdoers. I'm not. This went down right in front of me. And he passed right by me. And I knew what I could do at no cost to myself. Period. End of story. End of discussion."

"But—"

"End. Of. Discussion."

"You ever heard of Nietzsche?"

"Sure. The music guy, right?"

"I doubt it. He was a philosopher."

"Jack Nitzsche? Nah. Used to play piano for the Stones."

"Friederich Nietzsche. Friederich."

"Fred Nitzsche? Who's he? Jack's brother? Never heard of him."

He's putting me on, Sandy thought. He's got to be. But his expression was deadpan.

"He's been dead about a hundred years," Sandy said. "I studied him in college. You really must read him. *The Will to Power* will crystallize so much of who you are."

"Crystallize . . . just what I need right now. To get crystallized. Look, forget philosophers and get down to you and me. What do I have to do to get you out of my life?"

Sandy felt as if he'd been slapped. "Hey, look, I'm trying to help you here."

"I think we both know who you're trying to help."

"Damn it, I can bring you in from the cold."

The Savior laughed. "You can *what?*"

"Are you wanted for anything besides that liquor store robbery?"

He stared at him. "Where's this going?"

"Just tell me."

"No."

"You're sure?"

"I haven't exactly been trying to draw attention to myself."

Sandy's mind raced, barely keeping up with his thumping heart. This was exactly what he'd hoped for. One crime—a felony, yes, but years ago when he was a teenager. Now he's grown, living on the fringe, but keeping his nose clean. A fugitive, an outcast, but when law-abiding citizens were under the gun, when their lives were in deadly peril, who stepped into the breach and saved them? This man, this criminal.

Oh, dear sweet Jesus, this has major motion picture written all over it. Got to secure the rights.

"I can get you amnesty!" Sandy blurted.

The Savior squatted and dropped his face into his hands. He rubbed his eyes. "I don't believe this."

He's overcome with emotion, Sandy thought.

"I can!" Sandy said. "I can start a campaign. Look at the lives you saved that night. How can they *not* grant you amnesty?"

"Very easy," he said, looking up at him now. "They just say no."

"They won't be *able* to say no. You don't know the power of the press. I'll *make* them bring you in from the cold."

The Savior rose to his feet again. "How do you know I don't like the cold? Maybe I'm a goddamn polar bear!"

"I don't believe that. Because nobody wants to be a nobody when they can be a somebody—a really *big* somebody!"

"You're wasting your time. And mine too." He turned and started moving off.

"Wait! You can't walk out on this! It's the chance of a lifetime!"

"For you, maybe." He didn't even look back. "I'm out of it."

Alarmed, Sandy started after him. He had to talk to him, had to change his mind. And then he stopped as he realized he didn't need his cooperation to do this. He could singlehandedly create a ground-swell of sympathy for the Savior . . . and he wouldn't have to stretch the truth in the slightest.

First, a piece telling how he'd spoken again to the Savior, and how the man had confessed that his real reason for not coming forward was that he's a wanted felon. Sandy would say nothing of the crime—didn't want the cops to scoop him by using police records to identify the Savior before he did—but would portray him as a decent man guilty of a single youthful mistake, who'd escaped prosecution years ago, but last week had repaid his debt to society in spades, repaid it in a manner far more fruitful than incarceration, repaid it with saved lives instead of lost years. Next he'd get testimonials from other survivors—starting with Beth. Then he'd interview the mayor and the police commissioner and the DA and put them on the spot: what about amnesty for this hero? Will the one bad deed he committed as a teenager live on while the enormous good he did wind up interred with his bones?

The words weren't just flowing, man, they were gushing!

The whole campaign was taking beautiful shape in his mind. He could see the other major papers being forced to take up the issue— whether pro or con, who cared?—and from there the debate would spread to the national news magazines like *Time* and *Newsweek*. If he could get this ball rolling it could carry him into *People* Magazine.

And once he achieved amnesty for the Savior, it would be up to the man himself to accept it or reject it. Either way, Sandy's debt to him would be paid.

He headed back to the subway, excitement spurring him to a trot. He couldn't wait to get started.

9

"Are you okay, Jack?" Kate asked.

He'd returned to Jeanette's apartment straight from the park and hadn't been able to sit still.

"A little edgy, that's all," he told her.

Not a little edgy—a *lot* edgy. Even maximum edgy didn't quite cover it. He felt like a pin cushion. All the while in the park he'd had this feeling of being watched but had never been able to spot anyone who seemed interested in him. The feeling had followed him back to Jeanette's.

He stood at the window now, watching the street, scanning for any-one who looked like he didn't belong. Saw a couple of guys having a smoke outside the print shop, another pair unloading rolls of fabric and lugging them into the wholesaler shop. But no lurkers.

He chalked up the feel to Palmer's crazy plan.

The kid had no idea what was involved here. An amnesty for him would mean coaxing the IRS, the BATF, and the FBI to sing harmony with the New York State Attorney General and the DAs of most of the five boroughs. Right. And the Jets are going to win the next six Super Bowls.

And Nietzsche? And "in from the cold"? Where did he come up with this stuff? That kid had to get out more.

Jack turned away from the window. "What did you hear from NIH?" he asked, anxious to move the talk away from his mood.

Kate shook her head. "Nothing good. Everyone I talked to was very closed mouthed."

"Meaning?"

"I couldn't find anyone who would admit that they'd heard from Dr. Fielding, and couldn't find anyone who'd admit that they hadn't."

"Typical bureausaurus run-around."

"That's what I figured but . . ."

"But it just doesn't feel right."

She nodded. "Exactly."

"You think Fielding might not be telling us everything?"

"Not sure. But that's the vibe I'm getting."

Jack had to smile. " 'Vibe.' How seventies."

She shrugged. "That's where I spent my teens." She reached for the phone. "I've had enough of this tiptoeing around. I'm going to call Fielding and ask him point blank—"

Jack gently gripped her arm. "Point blank tends to work better face to face. Where's his office?"

"NYU Medical Center."

"Along First Avenue?" That was due east from here—Twenty-seventh would take them right to it. "Road trip?"

"Why not. We'll pay Dr. Fielding a little surprise visit." She started toward the door, then stopped. "But what if he doesn't want to talk? What if he stonewalls us?"

Yeah, he might try that. But Jeanette was important to his sister, which made her important to Jack. No stonewalls today. Jack would be along to see to that.

"He'll talk," Jack told her. When she gave him a strange look he added, "People just seem to open up to me. It's a gift. You'll see."

10

"Yeah," Joe said, "but how do we know if that's where he lives? Maybe he's just visiting."

Stan Kozlowski chewed the inner surface of his cheek as he stared at the ornate apartment building on West Twenty-seventh. This had to be the sixth time Joe had asked that same question, and Stan was just as much at a loss for an answer now as the first time.

They'd followed their guy here after Riverside Park. Not so hard. He hadn't seemed to be on the lookout for a tail, but they'd taken every precaution, giving him so long a lead one time they almost lost him. They'd seen him go into this building. Since they couldn't follow him inside, they'd found a shady spot on the same side of the street and kept watch on the entrance.

"Only one way to find out," Stan told him. "Tail him everywhere he goes, and wherever he keeps coming back to, wherever he spends the night, that's where he lives."

"You hope."

"Since we don't know his name or anything about him—"

"We got that whisper that his name might be Jack."

"A 'might-be' doesn't help us. And Jack isn't exactly a rare name. Don't see how we've got much choice except to watch and wait."

"I can't wait, Stan. Been waitin' too long already."

"Just hang in there, Joe. A week ago we had no hope of ever seeing this guy again. Now we've got him in our sights."

"*Ka-pow!*" Joe said, grinning.

"Ka-pow is right. We—hey, isn't that him?"

Yes. Definitely him. And he wasn't alone. He had his arm around a blonde.

"Shit," Joe said softly as they pressed back against a wall. "He's got a babe. Ain't that sweet."

"If she's a live-in, bro, we may have found his crib. But let's keep on him, just to be sure."

"Oh, yeah," Joe said, grinning as he rubbed his scarred hand with his good one. " 'Cause we want to be *sure*."

Stan watched the couple turn and head for Sixth Avenue. This was kind of fun. And the best part was that he hadn't seen Joe enjoying himself this much in years.

11

"All I can say," Dr. Fielding said, spreading his hands in a helpless gesture, "is be patient."

Kate watched the light glisten off his gelled black hair as he sat behind his desk in his cluttered office on the third floor of the Solomon and Miriam Brody Center for Clinical Research. Kate knew the marble halls of this two-story, brick-faced building well. She'd been here enough times with Jeanette.

Fielding had looked rattled when they'd barged in—Jack had not accepted any excuses from the receptionist—but had settled back into his self-assured role of physician-priest. Kate was familiar with the type; she'd met enough of them in her work.

He'd sworn he'd been in touch with NIH daily, and that he was as anxious as Kate for their help.

"But she's getting worse by the day," Kate said, keeping her voice calm though she wanted to scream.

"I know, I know." He shook his head mournfully. "But we're dealing with a bureaucracy the size of the Pentagon."

An overstatement, Kate knew. So did Fielding, apparently. He glanced at Jack—something he'd been doing repeatedly. Maybe because Jack had announced upon entering that his sister had some questions and hadn't said a word since. He'd simply sat and stared at Fielding. Kate found his basilisk act unsettling; she could only imagine how Fielding felt.

Abruptly, Jack came to life. He slapped his hands on his thighs and stood.

"Well, I guess that's it then." He extended his hand to Fielding. "Thanks for your time, Doc."

Fielding rose and they shook hands. "I'm sure we'll have this all straightened out soon."

"One more question," Jack said, still holding Fielding's hand. "Why are you lying?"

"What? How dare—"

Jack's grip shifted and suddenly he was holding Fielding's thumb, bending it, twisting it. Fielding groaned as his knees buckled.

"Jack!" Kate said, stepping toward him. "Dear Lord, what are you doing? Stop it!"

"I apologize for the strong-arm stuff, Kate," he told her. "If we had time I'd find another way. But since time is tight—"

"I'll call security!" Fielding gasped. He brought his free hand up to try to break Jack's grip but that only allowed Jack to trap his left thumb as well. "The police!"

"Fine." Jack spoke softly, calmly, as if giving a passerby directions to the nearest subway. "But that won't stop me from dislocating both your thumbs and putting a three-sixty twist on each of them. You're a doctor. You figure out how long it'll be before you can use them again, if ever. The cops may come, but you'll have to live without opposable thumbs. A lower life form."

"Jack, please!" She'd never imagined her brother like this—an irresistible force, implacable, glowering with the threat, the *promise* of violence. He was frightening, terrifying. "He doesn't—"

"Truth!" Jack said, voice rising as he gave both thumbs a quarter twist. "You haven't called NIH, have you. Not even once. Am I right?"

Fielding whimpered as sweat beaded his livid face. Finally he nodded.

"You bastard!" Kate said.

Jack looked at her. "The B-word?"

Kate ignored him and stepped up to Fielding's desk. Just a heartbeat ago she'd felt sorry for the man—she hated seeing anyone hurt—but now she wanted to grab his brass pen set and brain him. It had taken Jack a mere thirty seconds to melt away Fielding's mask, reducing him from distinguished colleague to weasel.

"Why not?" she cried. "Explain!"

"Please?" he panted, nodding toward his trapped hands.

Jack released the left, but kept a grip on the right. "We're waiting."

Fielding took a deep breath. "The vector virus didn't mutate."

Kate was stunned. "But if there's no mutation, why—?"

He looked away. "It's a contaminant."

Now she understood.

"So what?" Jack said. "Either way, Jeanette's got the wrong bug in her brain, so—"

"He can't be blamed for a wild mutation," Kate told him. "Not unless he exposed the virus to ionizing radiation. But a contaminant . . . he's wholly responsible for that. No excuses there. A contaminant makes him look very bad."

"You slug," Jack growled. "Just for the hell of it I ought to—"

"No . . . please . . ." Fielding whined.

"Jack, don't."

Jack shoved Fielding's hand away, sending him back into his chair where he cowered.

Kate closed her eyes and gave herself time to pull her turbulent thoughts together. She knew the next question but hesitated to ask it, feared the answer. But someone had to.

"What is the contaminant?" she said.

"That's just it. I don't know. It's unlike any virus I've ever seen. Seems to be in a class by itself."

Oh, no. Kate's stomach lurched. "How did this happen?"

"I'm baffled," Fielding said. "We keep all the cultures under lock and key, with a sign-in, sign-out procedure."

Jack said, "You mean someone would want to steal a virus?"

"No, of course not. It's simply to insure that only authorized personnel—people who know the protocols of handling viruses—come in contact with the cultures. It's designed to prevent the very thing that happened: contamination."

"Looks like your people need a refresher course," Kate said.

She noticed an uneasy expression flash across Fielding's face. "What's wrong?"

"Wrong?" Fielding said. "Nothing."

"Tell her," Jack said. He interlaced his fingers and popped his knuckles. Fielding jumped at the sound.

"We had, er, something of a breach in the security procedures."

Jack leaned closer. "What kind of something?"

"An unauthorized person gained access to the viral cultures."

Kate felt sick. "Some sort of terrorist?"

"I doubt that. I might never have known if I hadn't learned about the contaminant. I went back and checked the sign-in records and found a name that didn't belong."

"Anyone we know?" Jack said. "Like Holdstock, maybe?"

"No. I found only one entry, dated months ago." He sifted through the papers on his desk and came up with a Xerox of a sign-in sheet. He pointed to an entry he'd circled in red. "There. 'Ms. Aralo.' But we have no one named Aralo in the institute, let alone with clearance to the viral lab."

"Wait a minute," Jack said, grabbing the sheet and staring at it.

"What's the matter?" Kate asked. "Do you know her?"

He shook his head. "Never heard of her. But something about that name . . ." He stared awhile longer, silently mouthing the name, then handed it back. "Forget it. Whatever it was, it's gone. Probably nothing."

But Kate could see it still bothered him.

"Well, if you remember anything, please let me know immediately. No one here remembers a thing about this person, not even who allowed her to sign in."

"Do you think this Aralo woman contaminated them?"

"I have to assume so. She signed for my adenovirus cultures. But I keep asking myself why. What purpose could anyone have in contaminating cultures used to fight brain tumors?"

"Some professional rivalry?" Kate suggested.

Fielding shrugged. "I'm not exactly breaking new ground here; more like fine tuning a protocol."

"How about germ warfare?" Jack said.

Fielding smiled for the first time since they'd arrived—a small, condescending twist of the lips. "With an adenovirus? Highly unlikely."

Jack glared and spoke through his teeth. "I meant the contaminant."

Fielding's smile vanished. "Also unlikely. It doesn't seem to cause any symptoms."

"Other than personality changes," Kate said.

"If that. We can't be sure. But even if it does, that's not a terrorist scenario. They want *terror*—something of epidemic proportions like *ebola* where people are dropping like flies in pools of bloody excrement. From what I've learned so far about the contaminant it isn't air or fecal borne."

"Then it's blood borne?" Kate said, feeling a chill.

She glanced down at her palm. The puncture wound had healed. But had something entered through that little break in her skin?

"I believe so," Fielding said. "If only Jeanette or Holdstock or one of the others would cooperate, I might have a handle on it. I'd love to see if they've formed any antibodies. It's a strange virus that can occupy the cerebrospinal fluid—at least I'm assuming that's where it's concentrated—without causing any sign of encephalitis or meningitis."

"Which are?" Jack said.

"Anything from fever and headache to paralysis, seizures, coma, death."

Jack looked at her. "Jeanette looked pretty healthy this morning."

"Physically, she's been fine," Kate said.

But what about me? she wondered.

She felt okay now, but she remembered mild aches and chills and a headache yesterday and the day before.

"That's what's so puzzling," Fielding said. "There seems to be virtually no immune response—at least nothing that's clinically apparent. If only I could get a sample of blood . . ."

"We're going to let NIH worry about that," Jack said. "Aren't we."

"And the CDC," Kate added.

Fielding paled. "Look. I'm Jeanette's best hope. I'm way ahead of everyone on the contaminant. I've already started testing virucidal agents against it."

"And?" Kate said, praying for some good news.

"No luck so far." He licked his lips and spoke quickly. "But at least I know what doesn't work, and when I find one that does, I'm sure I can reverse the effects on Jeanette and the others. I've already started laying the groundwork for a polysaccharide vaccine against the contaminant."

"Good," Jack said. "Now the big boys can pick up where you left off."

Fielding pressed his palms together as if in prayer. "Please give me a little more time. I can do this faster than those big bureaucracies. They'll take forever to start meaningful research."

"Forget it," Jack said.

Kate opened her mouth to agree, but a wave of indecision swept over her, clogging the words in her throat.

Maybe Fielding's right. Maybe he can do more alone than those lumbering bureaucracies.

No. That was ridiculous. She had a duty to let NIH and the CDC know about a new virus that causes personality changes.

The indecision mounted . . . Why not give Fielding some time? With such low danger of contagion, why not wait . . . for Jeanette's sake. Just a few days . . .

She shook her head. Where did these crazy ideas come from?

"Kate?" Jack said.

She looked up and found Jack and Fielding staring at her. Fielding's face was hopeful, Jack's expression said, You can't be having second thoughts about this.

And that look broke through the wall of indecision.

"Call them now," she said, pushing out the words. Pain lanced through her skull as she spoke them.

"Right," Jack said. "I see you've got a speakerphone. Use that. We'll listen."

"No, please. I—"

"If you call CDC," Kate said, fighting to control her voice, to keep from screaming at this man, "you can salvage something of

your reputation. If I have to make the call, I'll tell them how you refused to report a wild contaminant, and then you can kiss your career
good-bye."

Fielding made the call.

Kate sat with Jack, listening to the speakerphone as Fielding wove
his way through the CDC maze until he found the right someone in the
right office who could handle his problem. Dr. Paige Freeman, who
sounded as if she couldn't be over twelve, gave him specific instructions
on how to overnight the sample to Atlanta.

Kate personally oversaw the sealing, packing, and shipping of the
culture. They even waited for the FedEx man to pick it up.

Dr. Fielding had been subdued during all this, but his resolve appeared to stiffen as they were leaving.

"It's not fair, you know. I always follow strict anti-contamination
procedures. I can't be held responsible if someone deliberately contaminated the culture. It's just not fair!"

"You believe in fair?" Jack said. "I suppose you believe in Santa
Claus and the Tooth Fairy too. You think fair just happens? It doesn't.
You want fair, you *make* fair."

Kate looked at Jack, surprised by his sudden intensity. What was
he getting at?

But Fielding seemed to understand. He nodded, saying, "I still say
I'm your friend's best hope. I've got a head start on this and I'm going
to keep after it. If I'm going to get stuck with the blame for the contaminant, then I might as well take the credit for discovering how to
control it. You watch. Before the CDC has even begun to roll, I'll have
the solution for you."

Kate thought him overly optimistic but didn't want to discourage
him.

"Thank you," she said.

"And if I could just get a sample of Jeanette's blood," Fielding
said, "it would certainly speed the process."

"We'll see what we can do," Jack told him.

After they'd left Fielding's office, Kate asked, "How do you think
we're going to get blood from Jeanette?"

He shrugged. "You'd be surprised. Lots of ways to get blood."

Kate sighed and let it go. At least the experts were on the case
now. She knew the Center for Disease Control, despite its worldwide

renown, was neither infallible nor omnipotent, but it had access to the best virologists in the world. She felt confident that a solution was on the way.

But just as her spirits began to lift, they dipped. Would she need treatment too? Although she had no way of knowing for sure, and did not want to believe it, Kate suspected that Jeanette had infected her with the rogue virus.

Why? Why would Jeanette do such a thing to her? She shuddered at the thought of an unidentified organism taking up residence in her body, invading her cells and multiplying. What could it be doing to her?

12

Stan paid the cabby and joined Joe at the curb.

"What do you think they were doing over at that medical center?" Joe asked.

"Beats me."

They'd followed their guy and his woman over to the East Side, hung around First Avenue for what seemed like hours, then tailed them back here to their starting point.

"Think he's got cancer or something?"

Stan didn't remember a sign on the building that said anything about cancer. What was going on in Joe's head?

"How would I know? And what difference does it make?"

"Because if he's got the Big C, maybe we don't do him right away. Maybe we wait and watch him rot for a few months, then do him."

They stood way up toward Sixth near a framing place where they had a long view of the front of the apartment building. Their guy hadn't gone in yet. He hung outside the front door talking to his lady.

"That'd sort of be like putting him out of his misery, don't you think?"

Joe kept staring at their guy. "Maybe, but I don't want no lousy tumor putting him away. We gotta do that. We gotta be the ones that sign his death certificate. Ain't that right?"

Stan wondered if Joe meant 'death sentence' but didn't get to ask because suddenly Joe was grabbing his arm.

"Shit! What're they doin'? They're splittin'!"

Their guy had wrapped his arms around his girl in a clinch that had the look of a good-bye hug.

"Get moving!" Stan said. "Other side of the street. Follow him if he takes off."

Although he worried about Joe losing control while tailing this guy, he couldn't risk going himself. Stan still looked pretty much the same as he had two years ago. This guy would recognize him if he spotted him. Joe, with his extra forty pounds and semi-beard had a better chance of going unnoticed.

Joe was on his way. "What're you gonna do?" he said over his shoulder.

"Follow her inside. See where she lives."

"Excellent!"

Sure enough, the couple disengaged and their guy started walking away. Stan got moving, quick-walking along the street side of the parked cars as the woman turned toward the front door of the apartment building. She keyed the lock, pulled the door open, and stepped inside. Stan dodged to the sidewalk and dashed for the door, catching its edge with barely an inch to spare.

As he stepped into the vestibule he spotted the elevator standing open at the far end, but it was empty. Where the hell . . . ?

Directly to his right he saw a door marked STAIRWAY swinging closed, and heard footfalls echoing. Keeping at least a flight between them, Stan followed her up to the third floor. As he stepped out into the hallway he spotted her to his left, moving. Stan turned right and ambled down the hall in the opposite direction. He fished in his pocket for his keys and dropped them on the carpet. While stooping to pick them up he watched her out of the corner of his eye, saw her disappear into a doorway.

When her door had closed, he reversed and hurried toward it.

3C.

Pleased, Stan headed back to the stairway.

Now we know where *she* lives, he thought. Let's hope that's where he lives too.

13

That feeling again.

Jack did a slow turn, giving the small, crowded platform of the Twenty-eighth Street subway station a full inspection.

Somebody watching him. Could feel it. Trouble was, the Friday afternoon rush hour was just getting started and he was surrounded by a horde of possible suspects.

The question was who? Probably some member of Holdstock's cult. Jeanette and Holdstock he'd recognize immediately, and maybe a couple of others, but not all. One of them could be standing beside him right now . . . or behind him . . .

That possibility pushed Jack back from the edge of the platform.

Why follow me?

To keep tabs? Or find out where he lived?

The notion jolted him. That was where he was headed now: a stop home to run a few errands, then return to Kate's later with the car, in case they needed to take another trip to the Bronx.

The uptown 9 rattled into the station then, and the crowd pressed forward. Jack held his spot, watching for the slightest hint of undue interest in the commuters eddying around him.

Nothing.

But the watched feeling persisted.

Keeping to the rear of the press, Jack shuffled with the rest toward the nearest open door. He squeezed aboard backward, the tips of his shoes barely inside the door line, and waited. As soon as the doors began to move he stepped back onto the platform. He turned and scanned the length of the train as all the doors slid shut, watching for someone else making a last-second exit. But everyone stayed put as the doors closed, sealing all the passengers within.

The train began to roll, rumbling out of the station. Jack watched the windows, searching the visible faces for signs of surprise or anger. He saw only boredom and fatigue.

Had he let the train go by for nothing? Maybe. He knew he had paranoid tendencies—with good reason, he always insisted—and this wouldn't be the first time he'd expended extra time and effort because of a vague suspicion. He considered it time and effort well spent. Never be too busy to walk that extra mile . . . just in case.

And he was going to do a little extra walking right now—over to Eighth Avenue to catch a train there.

Started to move, then stopped, noticing something.

The feeling of being watched . . . gone.

14

Stan had found a spot on Seventh Avenue to wait for Joe. He'd just settled himself onto a shady bench near the Fashion Institute when his cell phone rang.

"Lost the fucker," said Joe's voice.

Even through the tiny speaker Stan could feel the heat of his brother's barely suppressed rage.

"He spot you?"

"Couldn't have. I kept my distance and he never even looked at me. Fucker must have a sixth sense or something. You pin down his apartment?"

"Sure did. Three-C. Checked the mailbox downstairs. Says the place belongs to 'J. Vega.' "

"J. Vega, eh? 'J' as in 'Jack'? I like it. You keep an eye on the door so we know when he comes back. I'm goin' home to put a few things together."

"What few things?"

"I'll show you when I get back. See you soon."

Stan hit the OFF button. If Joe wouldn't discuss the few things on the phone, that meant they weren't legal. But Stan had a pretty good idea of what Joe was going to put together. Something that went *boom*.

15

Kate approached the door cautiously. Who could be knocking? No one had buzzed from the vestibule. She peeked through the keyhole, half-expecting to see Jack. Instead she found a heavyset man in coveralls.

"Yes?"

The voice filtered through the closed door. "Bell Atlantic, ma'am. We got reports of line trouble all through the building. Any problems?"

"No. I don't think so."

"It's with incoming calls."

She wished he'd speak louder. Did he say incoming calls? How would she know if an incoming call hadn't got through? What if Jeanette or Jack—or, dear lord, one of the kids—were trying to get through to her.

Kate reached for the knob, then hesitated. She'd heard horror stories about situations like this—rapists posing as servicemen. She slipped on the chain latch and opened the door a few inches.

He looked convincing with his gray coveralls and toolbox.

"Can I see some ID?"

"Sure."

He unclipped the badge that hung on an elastic tether from his pocket and handed it through. It certainly seemed authentic, and identified the man as Harold Moses, Bell Atlantic employee. But the photo . . .

Kate looked up again, comparing the picture to the real thing.

"I know, I know," he said with a sheepish grin. "I quit smoking and I'm the size of a house."

The smile did it for Kate—the same as in the photo.

"Is there any way you can come back later? It's not my place and—"

"Well, it's late and if I don't do it today it could be another week. We've got trunk line problems all over the city."

No incoming calls for a week? Kate unlatched the door and handed back the badge.

"Okay. I guess you'd better check it out."

"Only take a couple of minutes," he said, stepping past her and looking around the front area.

Immediately Kate wished she hadn't let him in. She hadn't sensed it when he was in the hall, but now, enclosed in the same room with him, she found him frightening. He seemed so tense and he radiated . . . something. She couldn't put her finger on what it was but it seemed malevolent, as if his overstuffed coveralls were bursting with rage instead of flesh. And those narrow eyes, darting everywhere, as if searching . . .

But when he spoke he was all business. "How many phones you got, ma'am?"

"Three," she told him. She wanted to run out into the hall but kept her cool. "One in the kitchen and two more in the bedrooms."

He placed his toolbox on the kitchen counter and she noticed for the first time that he wore an oversized work glove on his left hand—only his left.

"Okay. I'll work through this one; but I'll need you on one of the others."

"Any particular one?"

He shrugged. "Your choice."

He barely looked her way, didn't seem at all interested in her. Kate began to relax. This strange business with Jeanette seemed to have shifted her imagination into high gear.

After an instant's hesitation she started for the bedroom. "Okay. What do I do?"

"Just pick it up and keep talking. Don't dial—just talk. Count from one to a hundred if you want. Anything."

He waved his left hand as he spoke and Kate saw that some of the fingers of the glove looked empty and others looked stretched to the limit.

Wondering if his deformity was congenital or accidental, Kate entered the bedroom; she picked up the receiver and started counting.

She heard the kitchen phone come off the hook. "That's good," the serviceman told her. "Keep it up. Don't stop."

Through her receiver she listened to him whistling softly as he rummaged through his toolbox. She heard tape rip and wondered what he was doing, but the phone cord didn't stretch far enough to reach the door. She looked around for her pocketbook and saw it on the dresser. At least she knew he wasn't pilfering her wallet.

After three minutes or so she heard a series of beeps through the receiver, then the man's voice.

"Okay, ma'am. All set."

Kate hung up and returned to the front room to find the man snapping the clasps on his toolbox.

"That's it?"

He nodded. "Yours was okay. Have a nice day."

"You too. Thanks."

As she closed the door behind him she wondered at her earlier apprehensions. Just now he'd seemed a different man, calm and serene, as if he'd been relieved of a great burden. Almost . . . happy.

How silly she'd been.

16

Joe opened the rear door of the car, dumped his toolbox on the floor, then dropped into the front passenger seat.

"Done!"

Stan looked at him. "Fine. And now that it's done, you mind telling me just what it is that's done?"

Half an hour ago Joe had arrived in this stolen Taurus and parked it downstream from the apartment building. He'd looked like a new man—showered, shaved, and dressed like a serviceman. He'd been coy, refusing to say what he was up to until he'd done it.

"Left a little gift for our guy. I was afraid I wasn't going to get in, what with that obsolete Bell Atlantic ID from the old days, but she bought it."

"Lucky. How big a gift?"

Joe grinned. "A brick."

"A *whole* brick?"

"Damn right."

Stan closed his eyes. Before the Feds had closed in they'd managed to salvage part of their stash of army-issue C-4—foot-long bricks, two inches wide and an inch thick, neatly wrapped in olive-drab cellophane. Lovely stuff. Stable enough to play catch with, still soft and moldable at minus-seventy degrees, no extrudation even at one-hundred-seventy.

In Nam he'd come up with other uses for it beyond explosions. Starting fires, for instance. Cut an inch-thick slice off a block, put a match to it, and instant fire. Stank but it burned hot enough to ignite wet wood. One thing you had to remember, though, was if you wanted to put out burning C-4, you drowned it. You did not—repeat, *not*—stomp on it. He once saw a guy lose the front end of his foot trying that. Stan even learned the meaning of detonation velocity, and that C-4's was a devastating 8,100 meters per second.

And Joe had set a whole brick of it in that apartment. Shit.

He pressed the buttons that raised the windows and swiveled toward his brother.

"Joe . . . an old building like that . . . you just might bring the whole thing down."

A beautiful building . . . a shame to mess it up.

"Yeah, maybe. But probably not."

"At the very least it'll take out most of the third floor and both apartments above and below his, and blow off the whole front of the building."

Joe stared at him. "And your point is . . . ?"

"He hasn't come back yet. He might not come back before it blows. It might not even be his place."

"Oh, it's his all right. His girlfriend told me it wasn't her place, so that means it's his."

"All right, let's say it is his place. What if he's out all night? If the place blows without him there, then we've tipped our hand. He'll know—"

"He'll know that his girlfriend is dead and that he's next." Joe's voice dipped to a cold rumble. "Let him stew awhile, let him suffer a little, let him be scared, wonderin' when the next shoe's gonna drop. I almost hope he doesn't come home in time. I want to be in the crowd and see his face when he finds what's left of his building."

"It's not our style, Joe. We always placed just the right amount in just the right place to get the job done with a minimum of collateral damage. We were *surgeons*, Joe."

"Yeah, well, this is a special case. This will send a message that if you mess with the Kozlowskis you die. And not only do *you* die, but your family and friends and neighbors die. You mess with the K brothers you invite a whole shitload of death and destruction. So think twice. Think three times. Better yet, don't think about it at all."

Stan sighed. No talking to Joe on this.

He glanced in the rearview mirror where he had the apartment house entrance framed. The car seemed far enough away to be safe from the bigger chunks of debris. And it would be downstream from the explosion, which meant they'd be able to cruise away immediately after the blast.

He watched a black Crown Victoria pull into a space directly in front of the doorway. He had to smile. Here was a guy probably thanking his lucky stars for finding such a primo parking spot. He wouldn't be thanking anyone if his car was still there when Joe's bomb blew.

"Joe!" Stan whispered when the driver stepped out of the car. "Take a look!"

Joe did a casual one-eighty in his seat, then jerked up straight when he recognized the man on the sidewalk.

"Yes!" He started punching Stan on the shoulder. "Yes-yes-yes-yes!"

"When does this go down?"

"Soon," Joe said softly. "But not soon enough."

17

"You let him *in*?" Jack said, not quite believing this.

Kate shrugged. "He had a Bell Atlantic ID, with his picture and everything. What was I supposed to do?"

Jack didn't want to go into how easy it was to fabricate photo ID. Someday he'd show Kate his extensive personal collection. But maybe it was all right. Maybe the guy had really been from the phone company and Jack was making more out of this than he should. But the fact remained that Terrence Holdstock seemed to know too much about what went on in this apartment. Maybe one of the bugs had gone bad and he'd sent someone to replace it.

"All right, what did he do while you were here? Tell me exactly."

"I . . . I don't know *exactly*. You see, he needed someone talking on one of the extensions while he . . ." She flushed as her voice trailed off. "Boy, that really sounds dumb, doesn't it."

Jack wanted to shout *Yes!* But this was Kate, so kept his voice level.

"It's okay. You simply don't have a fine-tuned sense of paranoia."

"Like you."

"Like me. How long was he alone in here?"

"Five minutes tops."

Jack looked around the front room. This wasn't good. The guy could have hidden any number of bugs in a zillion places, or—

Wait. Kate had said the guy carried a Bell Atlantic ID. Bell Atlantic didn't exist anymore.

He motioned Kate closer and cupped his hands around her right ear.

"Ignore anything I say out loud from now on," he whispered. "Got it?"

She gave him a puzzled look but nodded.

"Only five minutes?" he said aloud. "I guess he couldn't have stolen anything significant in that time. Nothing missing, right?"

He motioned for Kate to chime in.

"Missing? No. Everything's here."

The best thing would be to go home and retrieve his bug detector for a 5-to-1,000 MHz sweep of the room. And he might yet have to do that. But for now a simple visual check would have to suffice. All he needed to vindicate his paranoia was to find a single bug. After that it was like being a little pregnant—didn't matter how many more there were, he'd know they were under surveillance.

Which could work to his advantage by allowing him to spread some customized disinformation to the listeners.

He turned on the radio—loud—and started with the kitchen wall-phone. A seemingly obvious place, but only to someone looking for a bug. He disassembled it but found nothing. A search of all the lighting fixtures and the undersides of the counters and cabinets yielded nothing either.

Time for another perspective: he lay on the floor and slithered around like a snake, looking for anything that didn't belong. His joints felt a little stiff, his muscles sore. He wondered why. Hadn't done anything strenuous lately. And it felt kind of good to lie down. If he had a choice between a nap and hunting for bugs right now, he knew which one he'd take. But he had to keep looking.

He glanced at Kate who was staring at him as if he were crazy as he wriggled out of the kitchen into the dining area, checking out the underside of the chairs, the table—

"Holy shit!"

Jack's saliva drained away as he stared at the bomb duct-taped to the underside of the table. And no question it was a bomb—fine wires running from a tiny travel alarm clock to the ends of a block of either Semtex or C-4.

"What is it, Jack?" Kate said.

Looked for the readout on the alarm clock but it was dark. Had the battery died? Couldn't risk it. Might already be too late. Had to get Kate out of here as fast as—

Wait. Nothing sophisticated here. In fact a pretty basic piece of work. Could see the ends of the blasting caps jutting from the plastique. All he had to do . . .

"Jack, what did you find?"

Jack dried his hands on his pants and reached up to the bomb. His fingers trembled as he gently tugged the caps from the plastique—the one in the left end came loose first, then the right. As they fell free, dangling from the clock, Jack ripped the plastique from the underside of the table and rolled away.

Panting, sweating, he lay on his back with closed eyes, pulling himself together.

"What is *that*?" Kate said.

Jack sat up and looked at the block. As soon as he saw the olive drab wrapper he knew it was C-4.

"Enough plastique explosive to make a real mess of this building."

One of Kate's hands flew to her mouth while the other fluttered behind her, searching for a chair. It found one and she dropped into it.

"No!" Her blue eyes were wide in her ashen face. "You can't . . . you must be mistaken!"

"I wish I were."

"But that looks like modeling clay."

Jack lay the C-4 on the floor and reached back under the table. He found the little clock, ripped it free of its securing tape, and held it up.

"And here's the timing device."

He placed the clock on the kitchen counter, found a carving knife, and chop-severed the wires to its two dangling detonators, scarring the Formica in the process. Had to be done. Blasting caps can do some mean damage on their own.

Kate had risen from the chair. She eyed the timer like she might a snake. She opened her mouth to speak but no words came out.

"I know," Jack said. "Who and why, right?"

She could only nod.

"Let's think about that," he said.

Possibilities were buzzing through Jack's head like a swarm of killer bees. He retrieved the brick of C-4. Holding that in one hand and the timer in the other, he did his thinking out loud.

"Here's the situation: We've got two people living in this apartment at the moment, one of them acting real strange. The other resident and her brother hear the strange one say some weird things, things they maybe weren't supposed to hear. The strange one's cult leader arrives out of nowhere and removes her from the premises. A couple of hours later someone calling himself a phone repairman shows up, maneuvers himself into being alone in this room, then leaves. Immediately after that we find a bomb. Let's guess who the target might be."

Kate slumped back into the chair, shaking her head. "No. I can't believe it. Jeanette would never—"

"She's not really Jeanette anymore, is she. But for your sake let's give her the benefit of the doubt and say that she may not have known. But that doesn't change the fact that someone wants you, and perhaps me as well, out of the way. Permanently."

Someone wanted to kill his sister. Even the hint of such a thing should have sent him into a wall-punching rage. But the brick of army-issue C-4 in his hand cooled him, chilled him. Reminded him of a pair of brothers he'd been hired to deal with a few years ago. What were their names . . . ?

Kozlowski. Right. Stan and Joe Kozlowski. They'd put the arm on somebody who hired Jack to take the arm off. And he had. Found the K brothers' stash and torched it.

The stash had been chock full of C-4 bricks exactly like this one. Lots of domestic bombers made their own; not hard to do if you don't mind working with red nitric acid. The international set tended to favor

216 F . P A U L W I L S O N

Semtex, usually of Czech origin. But the K brothers had built their rep with ultra-reliable U.S. military-grade C-4. Word was that Joe K had hijacked a truckload in the nineties, enough to stock them up for decades. Jack was sure that other bombers had sources for army C-4, but still . . . this olive-drab wrapped brick bothered him.

Could I be the target?

Didn't seem possible. This wasn't his place. And the Kozlowskis had vanished. With just about every law enforcement agency in the US looking for them, they'd gone to ground and no one had seen or heard from them in years. Everything else pointed to Holdstock and his cult, but Jack couldn't bring himself to get on that train just yet.

"What do we do?" Kate said.

Good question. He looked at the little travel clock. The LED display had been disabled. Why? Only reason he could think of was so the glow from the numerals wouldn't give away the bomb's location.

Which could mean the bomb had been timed to go off later, after all the lights were out. Later . . . when odds were highest that the occupants would be home and in bed.

But what time had it been set for? The answer might be important.

Jack stepped to the window and looked down at the street. Watched the cars and the pedestrians cruising through the fading light. Someone down there might be the bomber; then again, the bomber might be miles away. But Jack would bet that, come the moment of the blast, the bomber—or the one who'd hired him—would be nearby, watching, waiting. Because this amount of C-4 was gross overkill. Irrational. Something more than simple murder going down here. Jack could all but feel the raw emotion radiating from the brick of plastique in his hand.

He turned to Kate. "Will you be all right if I leave for a little while?"

"Do you have to go?" He could tell from her eyes that she didn't want to be alone here.

"I think so. It could be important."

"Okay. Just don't be long."

"I won't." He'd disappeared on her once; he wouldn't again. "By the way, you haven't noticed anything around the apartment about escape routes during a fire have you?"

He needed to find a way to leave unseen.

18

"*Nu?* You're thinking maybe the Kozlowskis?"

The innards of the travel alarm clock lay spread out between them on Abe's work bench. The Isher Sports Shop was officially closed but a call to Abe had brought him back. Since disassembling a bomb timer was not something either of them wanted a curious passerby to witness through the store window, Abe had suggested they move to the basement.

"That's just it," Jack told him. "I *don't* think it. It's against all logic. But my gut keeps saying otherwise."

"So listen. A man shouldn't ignore his *guderim.*"

They sat in a cone of light, surrounded by Abe's true stock in trade—things that fired projectiles or had points and sharp edges or delivered blunt trauma. Unlike the chaotic arrangement on the upper floor, these items were carefully shelved and neatly racked.

Jack watched as Abe's stubby but nimble fingers resoldered the tiny wires from the display to the circuit board. Jack was no good with electronics. He could use the equipment, but the innards baffled him.

"There!" Abe said as the display lit with the time.

"Neat," Jack said. "Now check the alarm."

Abe pressed a button and *3:00* appeared.

"Three A.M.," Jack said with a sick coil in his stomach. If he hadn't found this today, tomorrow he'd have awakened without a sister. "The son of a bitch."

"You have a next step in mind?"

"Not yet."

Abe stared at him. "You don't look so good. You feeling all right?'

Did it show? He felt tired and achy. Irritable too.

"I'm okay. Nothing that can't be cured by a good night's rest and finding the guy who made this."

"Well, while you're figuring how to do that, I should tell you that I ordered your new back-up pistol. Should be here in a few days."

"I don't know, Abe. I'm having second thoughts about giving up the Semmerling."

"Listen, schmuck, a .45 that small stands out too much for a guy who shouldn't be noticed. Like a signature, that pistol."

"Wait," Jack said as a thought detonated in his skull.

"What?"

"Just stop talking a minute." Realizing he'd snapped, he added, "Please."

Like a signature . . . like all his jobs, Jack had tried to work his fix on the Kozlowskis from the sidelines, looking to move in, cripple them by blowing their stash, and then take off without ever making direct contact. But it hadn't worked that way. They'd shown up at their farm when they were supposed to be in the city and he'd had to shoot his way out. He'd used his Glock mostly, but he'd needed the Semmerling at one point. The Kozlowskis had seen the Semmerling, and seen his face . . .

And if they read the papers . . . and saw mention of a tiny .45 . . . and decided to follow the reporter who claimed he'd been in touch with its owner . . .

"Damn him!" Jack pounded the workbench with his fist.

"Who? What?"

"Sandy Palmer! He damn near got Kate killed! I ought to wring his scrawny neck!"

He explained to Abe.

"Possible," Abe said, nodding. "Very possible."

"What am I going to do about him?"

"The reporter? I think maybe you should worry about the Brothers K first, don't you?"

"Them I can handle—especially now that I know who I'm dealing with. But Palmer . . . I think he sees me as some sort of cryptofascist comic book character. He was quizzing me about Nietzsche today—can you beat that?"

"Nietzsche? Have you ever read Nietzsche?"

"No."

"Don't try. *Also Sprach Zarathustra*? Unreadable."

"I'll take your word." He pounded the bench top again. "What a nightmare. Palmer's like a junkie—he'll keep biting my ankles until I lose it and strangle him or he slips up and exposes me. He thinks he's got this idea that I can make his career. Thinks he wants to be a great journalist, but what he really wants is to be a *famous* journalist."

Abe shrugged. "A product of the zeitgeist. But listen: sounds to me like he admires you. If he sees you as some sort of comic book hero, then maybe you should play to that. Comic book heroes have boy side-kicks, don't they?"

"You mean, if I'm Batman, let him think he's Robin?"

"More like that boy reporter who was always tagging along after Superman." Abe snapped his fingers. "What was his name? Timmy . . ."

"Jimmy Olsen."

"Yeah. Get Jimmy Olsen's focus off you and onto something else."

"Like what?"

Abe shrugged. "I should know? You're Repairman Jack. Me, I'm just a lowly merchant."

"Yeah, right."

At least it was an approach, a possible way out of this mess. But Jack didn't have the faintest idea how to make it work. Yet. This would take thought. In the meantime, he had to deal with the Kozlowskis.

"Okay, lowly merchant. Show me your wares. I've got a feeling I'm going to need some specialized equipment to help me through the night . . ."

SATURDAY

1

"It's quarter to three, Jack. Aren't you ever going to sleep?"

Exhausted, Kate leaned in the doorway of the bedroom. Jack was a silhouette against the window overlooking the street.

"Not tonight, I'm afraid."

He turned toward her and she jumped when she saw two glowing green spots where his eyes should have been. Then she remembered the strange headgear he'd donned before turning out the lights and mumbling something about *night vision.*

He'd brought it back from his trip, coming and going via the roof somehow. He'd been gone almost two hours—the longest two hours of her life. When he'd returned he'd said almost nothing, and seemed even grimmer than when he'd left. He didn't look good. Pale, a glassy cast to his usually clear eyes. She chalked it up to stress. More than enough of that going around. She wondered how she looked to Jack. Probably worse.

At least the bomb was gone. He'd said he'd left it back at his place.

"Can I make you more coffee?"

He lifted his mug. "I'm set, thanks. Why don't you go lie down, close your eyes, and try for some sleep."

"Someone tried to bomb us! Someone wants us dead! How can I sleep?"

"I've got the watch. Nothing's going to happen while I'm here, I promise you. You're tired; sleep will come if you let it. Trust me."

She did trust him—more than anyone. And she was desperately

tired. She needed sleep but even more she needed the escape it offered from the gnawing anxiety that had seeped into her.

She stepped back into the bedroom and crawled under the covers; she lay flat on her back, folded her hands between her breasts, and closed her eyes.

I'll pretend I'm dead, she thought. Why not? That's what someone wants.

Lord, what a thought. What had happened to her life? Facing the fact that she wasn't the all-American soccer mom she'd always thought herself to be had been tough, but she'd finally come to accept being bent in a straight world. She'd thought her life was turning topsy-turvy then, but that was nothing compared to this past week.

And poor Jeanette . . . where was she now? What was she doing?

Are you thinking of me, Jeanette? she asked the dark. I think of you constantly. Does a single thought of me ever cross your mind? Or are you so taken with this cult that nothing else matters?

And Kevin and Elizabeth . . . she'd been away from them too long . . . had to get back to them . . . she's . . .

. . . *floating* . . .

No. Not floating. Flying. She has multiple transparent wings jutting from her shoulder blades, vibrating in a buzzing blur, propelling her through a hive-like structure, a glowing golden maze of myriad stacked hexagonal tubes that stretches away in all directions, reaching into infinity.

And in the air about her, a hum, myriad voices joined in singing a single note.

As she flies on she sees that the tubes are not empty. People within them, faces staring out at her, strangers, but calling her name.

Kate . . . Kate . . . Kate . . .

Who are these people? There seem to be millions of them, but with only half a dozen different faces. She's never—

And then Kate recognizes Jeanette reaching for her from one of the tubes, smiling, calling her name. Kate turns toward her, but as she nears, Holdstock lunges from an adjacent tube, clawing for her. Kate veers away and comes face to face with another Jeanette . . . and another . . . thousands of Jeanettes calling her name, the sound so loud, deafening.

Kate . . . Kate . . . Kate . . .

She flees, soaring through the hive at blinding speed, zigging and zagging, dodging this way and that until she sees an opening in the wall. She flashes through into the outer darkness. It's cold and lonely out here, especially after the warmth and light of the hive, but darkness or no, she knows she must keep going, must flee those voices that never tire of calling her name.

Kate . . . Kate . . . Kate . . .

The voices slow her, pull her back, prevent her from reaching escape velocity. Finally her outward momentum ceases. For a single heartbeat she pauses, suspended between the hive and open space. Then she begins falling backward. She turns and sees the hive from away and above. It's blue and brown and cloud swirled . . .

It's Earth . . .

2

"Fuck!" Joe shouted. He pushed back in the passenger seat and began kicking the dashboard. "Fuck! Fuck! *Fuck!*"

"Easy, Joe."

Stan checked his watch again: 3:14 and no explosion.

"He must have found it!"

"Think about that, Joe. You think he'd still be up there if he found a whole block of C-4 in his apartment? No way. He'd be heading for the hills."

"So you're sayin' I fucked up, is that it?"

Stan heard the menace in his brother's tone. Had to tread carefully. Lots of pride at stake here. Better simply to lob the question back.

"Joe, no rig you've ever made has ever misfired, right?"

"Right."

"But something did go wrong tonight. What? What's different about tonight?"

"Nothin'! I made the simplest damn fucking rig ever! I always keep in my head what you told me when we first started out: Keep it simple—the more bells and whistles, the more chances for a malfunction. So I had *no* bells and whistles. And I used two detonators instead of one, just for insurance."

"You said you disabled the display. Could that—?"

"Naw, I triple checked it, reconnecting and disconnecting. The clock advanced each time. The alarm stayed set for three. The rig was sweet. He found it. I tell you, Stan, the fucker found it."

Stan didn't want to mention Joe's scarred-up hand and how he was pretty sure that was why his rig had failed. Hard to solder fine wires when one of your hands looks like melted wax.

"So let's go back to my question: what's different about tonight?"

"I told you: Nothin'!"

"But there is: how you're burning up. Every time we've done a job it's been business, pure and simple. Never emotionally involved. Never knew the people on the receiving end. But tonight's not like that. We want this guy. And when you get emotions involved, things go wrong."

"That wasn't it, Stan. I—"

"How big a hard-on you got for this guy, Joe? Think about it."

Joe sat silent, staring out the windshield. Finally he shook his head. "Shit." His voice was laden with disgust. "I fucked it up."

"It's all right," Stan told him. "The night's not over yet." He started the car. "You get out and wait here. Watch the place while I go cook up something."

My turn now, he thought. And this time no mistakes.

3

Jack sat huddled under a blanket, fighting to keep his eyes open. Four-thirty-five and he felt miserable. Must have picked up a flu of some sort. Great time to get sick.

First he'd been wracked by chills, and just when he'd reached the point where he feared he'd never be warm again, he'd broken out in a drenching sweat, so profuse he'd had to snag a towel from the bathroom to dry off.

The aftermath was weakness and lethargy. Too weak to keep standing at the window, so he'd pulled up a chair. Down the street, to the left, his Viper-1 night goggles had spotted a Taurus pulling away at 3:20 or so, leaving a man standing in the deep shadows of the sidewalk. But even at maximum magnification he remained a featureless blur.

A Kozlowski blur, Jack was sure.

This was why he'd remained on watch: for a moment like this, to confront the bomb setter face to face.

Problem was he was in no shape to confront anyone. An arthritic old lady in a wheelchair would be a challenge right now. The Kozlowskis would mop up the street with him.

All he could do was watch and wonder. He knew the man in the shadows was watching the apartment house door; but where had the car gone? What was the driver up to?

And then the Taurus was back.

Jack stiffened. When had that happened? He flipped up the night goggles and checked his watch: 4:50. Must have dozed off. Damn!

There, almost directly below, a man crossing the street, moving away. Getting into the driver side of the Taurus.

Jack's heart began hammering. Where'd he come from? Had he

been in the building? Set another bomb, a bigger one, in the lobby maybe?

He watched the Taurus. It stayed put. Good sign. A bomb in the lobby big enough to kill the people in a third-floor apartment would take out half the block. But their car was parked in the blast zone.

That meant a smaller bomb, if any. But where?

He'd have to go down and check.

That was when the second bout of chills slammed him . . .

4

"What if the fucker sleeps till noon?" Joe said from the back seat where he'd stretched out.

Stan yawned. He still sat in the driver seat, eyes on the mirrors, mirrors on the Crown Vic.

"Then we get him at noon."

Long night. When was the last time they'd stayed out till sunup? The sky was brightening but the streets remained quiet. The city started moving a little later on Saturday mornings.

"Yeah, well, whenever it is, let's hope we have better luck with your rig than mine."

"We will, Joe. Because I stayed cool while I was making it. And I kept it simple."

Stan liked to call it the Kozlowski Kar Krusher. A quarter brick of C-4 sandwiched between a remote electronic detonator and an aluminum-insulated refrigerator magnet. He wasn't the first to rig one, he was sure, but he'd perfected it to the level of art.

Too bad it wasn't legal to sell them. He'd often imagined an infomercial for the Kozlowski Kar Krusher . . .

Got an annoying neighbor? An in-law who's making you crazy? A boss who's on your ass all day? A wife who's taking you to the cleaners in divorce court? Sure you do!

And you probably thought you just had to put up with it, just had to grin and bear it, right?

Well, think again!

The Kozlowski Kar Krusher changes all that! It's so easy! And safe too! Reduce your problems to rubble in just three easy steps! Here's all you do:

First, identify the car of the one who's darkening your days.

Second, walk by the target car and stop to tie your shoe. While you're kneeling, simply slip the rig under the car and let the magnet attach itself to the frame. No need to get in the car or under the hood, no dicking around with ignition wires. Simply place the Kozlowski Kar Krusher under the driver side, the passenger side, the rear compartment, the gas tank: the choice is YOURS!

Third, just straighten up and walk on.

And that's IT! Blow the bastard or the bitch to hell whenever you want! What could be easier, or more fun?

But that's not all!

If you're dealing with a suspicious type who has a remote start on his car, or a cowardly type who sends someone else out to start it while he's safe in the house, no problem! The Kozlowski Kar Krusher has got you covered! YOU are in control. Just wait till the human blot on your existence is in the car, then press the red button on the Kozlowski Kar Krusher Remote Detonator (batteries not included) and BOOM! Bye-bye bitch! Bye-bye bastard!

But wait! There's more!

Why blow up the car in front of the target's house? Why be so ordinary? The Kozlowski Kar Krusher allows you artistic expression, lets you choose the venue of your enemy's demise! How does mid-span on the Brooklyn Bridge sound? Or right in front of City Hall? Or better yet, in your ex-girlfriend's driveway! With the Kozlowski Kar Krusher you don't simply eliminate the problem—you make a statement!

The Kozlowski Kar Krusher! Regularly $119.99, but now, for a limited time only, get two for $200!

Wouldn't that be something, Stan thought. Wouldn't that be a pisser.

He shook himself out of his reverie and checked the Crown Vic again in the mirror. He'd attached the rig under the driver side. When it went, the C-4 would shred the car and leave nothing recognizable of whoever was sitting inside.

Stan had decided to take no chances. As tempting as it would be to follow the guy around and wait till he was near a cop car before hitting the button, Stan knew getting cute could backfire. A traffic glitch could put the rig out of range of the detonator, or a stray transmission from a two-way radio on the wrong frequency could set it off when they were too close. Keep it simple, stupid, and blow the guy to hell right there in front of his own building.

He stiffened as he saw the apartment building's glass front door swing open. A man stepped out and leaned on the door as it closed behind him.

"Check this guy out," Stan said. "Is that our boy?"

Joe's head popped up, looking through the rear window. "That's him all right. That's the fucker. Looks like shit, though. Like he's been smokin' rock all night."

The guy did look a little wasted as he slumped there looking up and down the street. That was what had made Stan unsure about him a moment ago. Here was a guy who'd been moving like a cat yesterday, but this morning he looked like a tired old hound.

Stan glanced at his watch. "He's an early bird."

"Nah," Joe growled. "*We're* the birds. He's the fuckin' worm."

Stan pulled the remote trigger from his shirt pocket. It was shiny and black, the size of a cigarette pack. He extended the transmitter aerial but left the little hinged red metal guard in place over the button.

As he watched the guy step away from the building, digging in his pants pocket as he moved, Stan thought, Please be going for your car keys.

And he was. A keychain appeared in his hand; he selected one and stuck it into the lock.

"Gimme the button," Joe said, thrusting his good hand over the back of the front seat. "I gotta do this. I just gotta."

"Just wait a sec. We're in no hurry here. Plenty of time. He's ours when we want him."

"You think I don't fuckin' know that?" Joe said, voice rising. "Just gimme the button!"

The guy had the door open and looked about to duck inside, but then Stan saw him step away from the car and go back to the apartment door.

"We missed him!" Joe shouted. He started pounding the seat back. "Shit!"

"Easy, Joe," Stan said as he looked around and spotted a young black woman striding their way along the sidewalk. Her route would bring her within a few feet of their car. He stuck the trigger back into his pocket. "Keep it down. We got company. We don't want nobody remembering us."

"We shoulda done him soon as he opened the car door," Joe hissed.

"Uh-uh. Worst thing is to blow it too early. We only hurt him instead of killing him now, we might never get another chance. He probably forgot something. He'll be back."

Sure enough, a minute later the guy appeared again.

"All right, so I was wrong."

As Stan removed the trigger again from his pocket, Joe snatched it from him.

"Damn it, Joe—!"

"It's all right," Joe said. "I'm cool, I'm cool. I'll wait till he's sealed in, I promise."

Stan didn't like this. Something about the whole setup was gnawing at him. He didn't like Joe with the trigger, but that wasn't it. Maybe it was the way the guy was standing inside his open car door scanning the street, like he was looking for something? Did he suspect?

Stan glanced around for the black girl—gone. Nobody else on the street now—no cars, no pedestrians . . .

As the guy slipped behind the wheel and closed the door, he heard the button guard click back and Joe say, "Now, baby, *now!*"

And in that instant Stan knew what was wrong and he reached for Joe's hand, screaming, "NOOOOOO!" as he tried to keep his brother's joyful thumb from jamming down on the button.

5

The explosion rocked the pavement as the car dissolved in a dazzling cloud of flaming debris. Jack ducked below his dashboard in case a piece came flying through the windshield. His big car was well insulated, muffling much of the sound, so his ears weren't ringing when he stepped back onto the sidewalk to survey the damage. A deep hole smoked in the pavement where the Taurus had been parked; the cars fore and aft of it were crumpled and burning, sending up dark twisting spirals of smoke. Shattered glass, twisted metal, and fuming pieces of plastic were strewn everywhere. The blast had broken auto and building windows up and down the street; alarms blared and rang and whooped; an unfortunate tree near the blast had been stripped bare and its leaves were still fluttering back to earth.

Jack closed his eyes against a wave of weakness and nausea—not because the bomb had been meant for him, but because he was almost too sick to stand. If he'd felt this bad a few hours ago he never would have found the bomb.

Good thing he'd pushed himself then. Sneaked down to the street via the fire escape of a neighboring building and crawled along the gutter to his car. His Viper goggles had allowed him to spot the bomb on the undercarriage. He'd removed it and, again with the aid of the goggles, made his way to the Taurus. Recognized Stan Kozlowski behind the wheel; took a bit longer to peg the heavier man with him as brother Joe. At that point it took Jack about a nanosecond to decide what to do. These guys were too dangerous to leave running around.

So he'd attached the bomb to the Taurus's underbelly and crawled away.

Barely made it back to Jeanette's where he collapsed with an alarm clock next to his ear. Just after sunup he'd staggered down to the street, hoping he'd be the only one up and about. On a mostly commercial block like this he should have been, but he'd spotted this black woman approaching the K brothers' car, so he'd gone back inside until she passed.

Okay. No more Kozlowskis—no more bombs for Kate to worry about. Looked up. Jeanette's windows had escaped damage. Saw Kate's strained face through the intact glass directly above, looking down. He waved that he was okay.

"What happened?" said a voice behind him.

Jack turned and saw a fiftyish fellow in jogging shorts and a NYAC sweatshirt.

"I don't know," Jack said. "I stopped to tie my shoe and next thing I knew I was flat on my back."

The man looked at him strangely. "You don't look so good. Are you okay?"

Jack ran a shaky hand across his face—the chills were back so he didn't have to fake the tremor. "If my lace hadn't come loose I would have been right down there by the blast. I'd be . . . dead!"

"Oh, man, talk about luck. I'd frame that shoelace if I were you." He looked around. "Anyone call nine-one-one?"

Just then the sound of sirens filtered through the morning.

"I guess so," Jack said.

"I'm going down for a closer look," the jogger said.

"I think I'll stay right here."

The braver souls and the too curious were filtering out of the Arsley, but otherwise the street remained deserted. Jack edged away, back up toward Sixth Avenue. When a howling pair of blue-and-white units screeched onto the street, he slumped himself into a doorway, head down, allowing himself to look as ill as he felt. As soon as they roared past he was up and moving again, heading east, but not quickly enough to raise suspicion.

On Sixth he walked down to the Twenty-third Street subway station and hopped the first train heading uptown. The car was almost empty and it felt good to sit down. Another chill shuddered through him.

How the hell did I catch this? he wondered. Flu season's long gone.

After listening yesterday to Fielding talk about the contaminant in his cultures, a viral infection now was unsettling. But he remembered

Fielding's mention that the contaminant didn't cause any symptoms. That was comforting, because Jack had symptoms aplenty.

Needed to get home, needed major rack time under a pile of blankets.

6

"The phones haven't stopped all morning," George Meschke said. "The response has been wild, beyond anything I imagined."

Sandy sat in his editor's office, leaning back, his ankle resting on his knee. Last week he'd have been on pins and needles, hoping he wasn't going to get chewed out about some little mistake. Now he was totally relaxed. Chillin' with the bossman. Because he was in the catbird seat. Circulation was soaring. Ad revenues this week alone had been equal to the entire first quarter's.

And all because of one person, Sandy thought. *Moi.*

He said, "I knew my amnesty idea would strike a chord."

"But what a chord!" Meschke said, running both hands through the few remaining stands of hair atop his head; his thick mustache was the same shade of gray. "It's Saturday morning and people have already read the story and are burning up the phone lines! Amazing!"

Equally amazing, Sandy thought, glancing around at the otherwise deserted editorial area, is that it's Saturday morning and I'm at work. And what's truly mind-blowing is I'm glad to be here.

"They should be calling City Hall," he said. "That's where it'll do some good."

"Speaking of which, you need to talk to City Hall yourself. I know it's Saturday, but see if you can track down the mayor and the DA and the police commissioner for their reactions. We need something for Monday." Meschke rubbed his hands together and grinned like a little kid. "Can you imagine? We've just had a Saturday issue, now we'll have another on Monday. Four issues of *The Light* in one week! Who'd have believed it?"

Monday edition or not, Sandy was not anxious to do those interviews. Any other time he'd have been chomping at the bit, but after this morning's issue he knew he wasn't going to be the most popular guy with the city brass, not after putting them on the spot like this.

But that's the game, he told himself. They of all people should know you can't make an omelet without breaking a few eggs.

"I'll see who's still in town."

"We've got to milk this, Sandy. Every extra issue we put out brings in more advertisers and more readers, many of whom—we hope—will stay with us when we go back to weekly."

Back to weekly . . . suddenly he was depressed.

"And I want you to know," Meschke said, lowering his voice and leaning forward, "I talked to Harness about you. How you deserve recognition for what you've done for the paper. He's ecstatic about how things are going and agrees completely." He winked. "Be prepared for a surprise in your next paycheck."

"A bonus?" Sandy said. "Cool!"

But his thoughts were ranging ahead. Calvin Harness was the publisher and major stockholder. No doubt he was ecstatic because the bigger profits and higher profile from Sandy's articles enhanced the chances of *The Light* being bought up by one of the big national chains. Harness would clean up. Meschke's stock options would put him on Easy Street as well. But Sandy . . . what did he have?

Time to get out the old resume, he thought. Bring it up to date and start sending it out. Strike while the iron was hot. But until he wrangled himself an offer at one of the big three in town, he'd have to find ways to keep his name in the news.

And the only way he knew to do that was the Savior. He had to push the amnesty for all it was worth, find a way to make it national.

But how . . . ?

7

Hot.

Jack kicked off the covers. The chills of an hour ago were gone. Now his skin seemed to be steaming. Sheets were soaked, sweaty T-shirt and boxer shorts plastered against him.

Thirsty. Mouth parched, lips flaky as he ran his dry tongue over them. Needed something wet. Tried to sit up. Almost made it half way. Flopped back onto the soggy pillow. Tried again with the same result. Last time he'd felt this weak he'd been bleeding to death . . . last summer . . . sitting in a chair in the next room . . . and the last time he'd had a fever like this had been directly after that . . . from infection in the wounds . . . Doc Hargus had pumped him full of antibiotics and pulled him through, but it had been tough going.

No wounds this time, just dying of thirst. And water, lots of icy bottles of gloriously wet Poland Springs, lay stacked on the bottom shelf among the beers and Mountain Dew in his fridge just a dozen or two feet away in the kitchen.

Might as well be in Westchester.

This was scary. Sick and sweating without taking in any fluids . . . he could wind up dehydrated . . . leaving him weaker still . . . a steady downward spiral . . .

Jack closed his eyes, gathering strength for another try.

"Here," said a voice.

He turned his head and started at the sight of an older woman standing at the side of his bed. She was thin, her thick black hair streaked with gray and pulled back into a bun, wearing a gray sweatsuit with pink piping. Couldn't see her feet but he'd bet she was wearing sneakers.

236

Questions about who she was and how she got into his locked apartment rose in his brain but were pushed aside by the sight of what she held in her hand.

A glass of water.

"Drink," she told him. She rolled the *r*.

Jack was already reaching for it as she spoke. The glass was wonderfully cool against his palm. He raised his head as far as he could and gulped it down, spilling precious drops in his haste, then let the enormous weight of his head drop back.

"More," he rasped. "Please."

"In a moment," she said. Her accent . . . Russian. Take Natasha Fatale, add thirty or forty years, stick her in a jogging suit . . . this was her. Where was Boris?

And then Jack saw the dog sitting beside her, an enormous purewhite malamute. It cocked its head and stared at him.

Hadn't Kate said something about an old woman with a Russian accent and a dog . . . the woman who'd given her Jack's number?

He tried to raise himself up on his elbows but sagged back. The water had left him less thirsty but no stronger.

"Who are you and how'd you get in here?"

"That does not matter. You must—"

"It sure as hell does matter. This is my place and my door was locked—quadruple locked."

"Listen to me," she said urgently. "You must fight infection and you must win."

"Only a flu of some sort."

"If only that were so. Is not flu. Is same virus that is in the others, in your sister's lover as well as in your sister herself. Is in you too."

Fielding's virus? The contaminant? Never mind how she knows about it; if she's right . . .

"That can't be. Fielding said it doesn't cause symptoms and it's only spread through blood."

"And did you not bleed yesterday?"

"No. I—"

Oh, hell. Holdstock. The scratch on my hand as he passed by on his way out of the apartment with Jeanette.

"Jeez, did you say Kate . . . ?"

The woman nodded; sadly, he thought. "Four days ago."

"Wait. If I was infected only yesterday and already this sick, why didn't she—?"

"She cannot fight it. None of them can fight it."

"You're talking crazy. If she couldn't fight it she'd be sicker, and she's fine."

The woman shook her head. "Only you can fight it."

"Yeah, right," he said. He closed his eyes. All this talk was exhausting.

"Do not speak," the woman said. "Save strength and listen: virus will spread. It will infect many, and the many will infect many others. There will be war between those infected and those not, war such as we have never seen, turning man against woman, parent against child, child against parent, brother against brother."

"It didn't happen with AIDS so why—?"

"Is different. Virus will spread like wind. All harmony, all trust will vanish as uninfected kill infected, kill those they merely suspect of being infected. But infected will fight back, striking from within, spreading their disease. The bloodshed, the death, the hatred, the terror—this planet has seen terrible things but never on such a scale. For there are so many more of you now, and no one—*no one*—will be spared."

"What's so bad about this virus? What does it do to you?"

"That is no matter. Virus is not end, virus is simply means."

"Means to what?"

"To what I have told you: war, hate, death, fear, pain, destruction."

"Who the hell wants that?"

"The Adversary."

Jack forced his eyes open and looked at her.

"And who's that? The devil?"

She shook her head. "You know. You have met. Adversary feeds on human misery, on discord, on chaos. Virus will create feast."

No doubt about it, the lady was a loon. And she'd invaded his home—brought her damn dog too—and Jack was powerless to make her leave.

But she had another glass of water in her hand. He took it and gulped it down. Maybe she shouldn't leave.

"How do you know all this?"

"I watch. Always I watch."

"Why tell me? I'm just one guy. Go to the government."

"Government cannot stop virus. Only you. You *must* stop virus. You are only one."

"I couldn't stop a lame kitten right now."

"You must. Is war and you are warrior."

"I don't join armies."

"Is no army. Just you. And one does not join. Is chosen. Others go before you. All dead except one, and he is too old. You have been chosen."

"Like hell I have."

"Stop virus before it spreads, or all you love will perish." She turned and headed for the bedroom door. "I leave you now."

Jack felt the temperature drop. No . . . more chills. He pulled the covers back over him.

"Lady, who are you?"

She and her big white dog stopped at the door and looked at him. "I am your mother."

Nonplused, Jack struggled for a reply. She was nothing like his mother. Finally he resorted to a simple statement of fact.

"My mother's dead."

"She was your birth mother," she said. "I am your other mother."

And then she was gone.

Jack felt a shiver of fear slip among the fever chills. He knew he'd imagined the woman, but her words had struck resonances that still rang through his brain. Her warning about something that fed on misery and hate . . .

And then the phone rang. Jack snaked a wavering hand over to the night table and wrapped his fingers around the receiver.

"Hello," he croaked as he shuddered with a chill.

"Jack, is that you?" Gia's voice. "You sound terrible."

"Sick," he said. "Fever. Delirious. Wouldn't believe the hallucinations I'm having."

"I'm on my way."

Good, Jack thought as he heard the click on the other end. Gia will know what to do.

He tried to hang up the receiver but didn't have the strength.

8

Kate jumped at the sound of the key in the door, thinking, Jack's back. Thank the Lord.

She'd been a wreck all morning. Jack had tried to ease her mind by telling her that the bomb he'd found had been meant for him, not her. Had he expected her to be relieved that her brother was some madman's target? Well, she wasn't. But he'd said he had a good idea who the bombers were and how to protect himself and her from them.

At least that had allowed her to go back to sleep. But then Jack had been up at dawn, looking terrible, all sunken-eyed and exhausted, saying he had to go out and instructing her to stay away from the windows and not worry if she heard a loud noise.

A few minutes later a car exploded on the street below.

Not Jack's, thank the Lord. His was still out there when she'd looked, and he'd waved up at her. She'd hoped he'd come back up, to tell her he hadn't blown up that car. She didn't want to believe he'd done such a terrible thing. Even if someone had been trying to kill him, he'd endangered everyone on the block.

But he must have done it, must have known it was coming. Why else would he have warned her to stay away from the windows?

But then instead of returning, he'd walked off.

He hadn't told her where he was going, but it didn't matter. He was back now.

But it was Jeanette who stepped through the door. And Holdstock. And others, six more men and women of varying ages, trooping in, all smiling at her with the open friendly faces of old friends. She knew them, she'd seen them through Holdstock's window.

Jeanette had brought her cult home.

"Hello, Kate," Jeanette said, beaming. "I've asked some friends over to meet you."

Kate swallowed. "That's nice."

They didn't seem threatening—if anything their expressions virtually glowed with amiability. So why then did she feel this cold dread seeping up from her stomach?

"I was so worried about you," Jeanette said, taking Kate's left hand and pressing it between both of hers.

Kate felt rather than heard a strange hum in her head, a faint, faint echo of Jeanette's voice.

"Were you? Why?"

"Why, the explosion, of course. When I heard about it and realized it had happened right on our block, I wanted to fly here. But then I learned that no one had been hurt except two men with criminal records, and I was so relieved. But still, I didn't think you should be alone."

That odd hum continued, but Kate sensed that she truly had been in Jeanette's thoughts, and that warmed her.

"That's nice, but—"

"So I brought my dearest friends to keep you company. You remember Terrence, don't you?"

Holdstock stepped forward, smiling warmly as he offered his hand. "I know we didn't get off on the right foot, but I'm sure I can make amends for that."

Kate didn't want to shake hands with this man, but how could she snub him with a radiant Jeanette still clutching her left hand? She extended her right, Holdstock grasped it—

—and the hum in her head grew louder.

Something wrong here! She tried to pull free of Holdstock but his grip was like a steel clamp.

"Let me go!"

"Don't be frightened, Kate," Jeanette said, smiling reassuringly while clutching Kate's other hand. "It's all right. Trust me, it's all right."

"No!"

The others were moving forward. Holdstock held out his free hand and one of them, a woman, took hold of it—

—and the hum in Kate's head increased—

—and then someone took the woman's hand and stretched out his hand to another—

—and the hum in Kate's head further increased, a roar now, like the ocean, and her heart was a panicked rabbit, battering itself against the cage of her ribs, trying to break free—

—and someone took his and another took hers and the roaring doubled and tripled and she felt her strength slipping away and through her blurring vision she saw Jeanette free one of her hands from gripping Kate's and reach it out to another hand, the last free hand in the world, and Kate saw them touch, closing the circle—

. . . and suddenly all is peaceful.

Kate's vision blurs as she descends into a deep pool of tranquillity, leaving no ripples, no trail of bubbles as she sinks.

There, says a soft, sexless voice that seems to come from within and without, from nowhere and everywhere. **Isn't this better? Isn't this wonderful, the most wonderful feeling you've ever known?**

And it is wonderful, a feeling of complete acceptance, of absolute belonging, of soft arms lovingly enfolding her and drawing her to a motherly bosom.

Her vision clears and she sees the others, the eight who've formed the hand-holding circle of which she is now a part.

Is this why Jeanette was sneaking off to the Bronx? she wonders. Is this what she was experiencing when I watched her through the window?

The Everywhere Voice answers. **Yes. That was when The One Who Was Jeanette was like you and could experience oneness only by touch. Now that she is of the Unity she is with us always, dwelling within the oneness.**

Kate isn't sure she follows that but it doesn't matter. What does is this glorious feeling of peace, of belonging. All the anxieties and un-certainties these past few years about the course of her life and where it will lead her, all the fears about revealing her true self to the children are gone, vanished as if they've never been. She can barely remember them.

Unconditional love and acceptance, simply for being. This is the way all of life should be, all the time.

And it will be.

No, Kate thinks. You've got it wrong. It's human nature to fear what's different.

Human nature can be changed.

Kate is about to laugh at the absurdity of this when a thought strikes her. The Voice reminds her of Jeanette's, but Jeanette's lips haven't moved.

"Who are you?" she says aloud. "Whose voice is this?"

It is us, all of us. The Unity.

"Then why do you sound like Jeanette?"

Because that is who you feel most comfortable listening to. But it's not the One Who Was Jeanette. It is all of us.

Kate looks around and sees the eight of them, Jeanette, Holdstock, and the rest, nodding in unison.

Kate senses an alarm bell trying to ring, to warn that this is all wrong, that she should not be conversing with voices in her head. But the cotton-thick ambiance of peace and harmony smothers it, and all that seeps through to her is confusion.

"I don't understand."

We have been united. We are one. We are the Unity. We know each other as no others have known us, even more intimately than we have known ourselves. Every thought—

"You can read each others' minds?"

We *are* each others' minds. We share every thought, every emotion.

Kate feels a twinge of fear. Is she crazy? Are they?

Don't be afraid.

And now a stab of terror. They know what she's feeling!

You need not fear the Unity. We love you. You are our sister.

"But why me? And how—?"

And then Kate knows.

The virus. The mysterious contaminant in Fielding's cultures.

Yes! It brought us together, repairing the faults in our brains, linking our minds into this glorious Unity.

"And me?" She looks at Jeanette. "I was infected, wasn't I. Why?"

You were following the One Who Was Jeanette, spying on her—

"I was concerned!"

And we sensed that. But we also feared that your loving con-

cern might turn into interference, and since we are at a delicate
stage of development, we brought you into the Unity.

"But I wasn't asked! You had no right!"

The niggling alarm sounding within Kate has escalated, clamoring
through the swaths of bliss, but still so faintly.

It was never a matter of *if*, Kate; merely a matter of *when*.

"What do you mean?"

**We are the future, Kate. You are witnessing the conception of
a new day for humanity. This is where the new world will begin—
with us, with the nucleus of the Unity. And you will be part of it,
Kate—a part of the Cosmic Egg that fuels the Big Bang. As we
gather more and more minds to expand the Unity—**

"Wait. Gather how?"

Infiltrate their nervous systems, just as we've done with you.

"You're not going to ask them either?"

Of course not. They'd never agree.

"How can you justify—?"

**We know what is best, Kate. The Unity is the future. Dis-
connected intelligences running loose are the past. Now that we
exist, they are as relevant as dinosaurs: too prone to conflict,
too inefficient.**

"We haven't done so bad. Look at the diseases we've conquered.
And now that we've mapped the human genome, there's no telling what
miracles we can accomplish."

**But at such a cost! War, racism, hatred. And no matter what
your science can do, it cannot mend the basic flaws in human
nature.**

"You've got something better?"

**Yes! A world where all minds are united, where differences
in race and gender no longer matter because all minds are
equal."**

A vision takes shape before her eyes, a sunny landscape checkered
with fields of wheat and corn. And closer in, people working those fields.

**A world where hate and suspicion disappear because every
thought is known, every lie is exposed.**

The vision shifts to a factory where contented workers operate weav-
ing machinery and clothing production lines.

Where no one is a stranger and no one is an outsider because no one is excluded. Because all are one.

And now Kate sees a cluster of buildings, a classic Midwest small town with people walking on the sidewalks and in the streets, dropping off produce and picking up clothing. And though no one's smiling, no one looks unhappy; merely intent, industrious.

The Voice glows with anticipation. **Won't that be a wonderful world?**

"World? That's not a world. That's a hive."

A long pause as Kate feels her thoughts and feelings being sifted. Then . . .

We understand. You are not yet far enough along for full integration. But as days pass you will learn, Kate. You will come to appreciate our benefits, just as you will come to accept our inevitability . . . the Great Inevitability.

Inevitability . . . she wonders about that. She thinks about Fielding and about the CDC and NIH and feels those thoughts sucked from her mind, like a shucked oyster slurped from its shell.

Yes . . . Dr. Fielding . . . we owe him much and yet . . . he knows so much about us . . . too much perhaps. We heard what he told you yesterday.

Suddenly she's listening to Fielding's voice repeating his parting words in his office yesterday . . .

If I'm going to get stuck with the blame for the contaminant, then I might as well take the credit for discovering how to control it. You watch. Before the CDC has even begun to roll, I'll have the solution for you.

Startled, Kate says, "Did you just take that from me?"

We could have, but no . . . we were there, listening ourselves.

In my head . . . listening. Kate is too stunned to respond.

You had an opportunity then to help the Unity, Kate. You did not have to insist on Dr. Fielding immediately contacting the Center for Disease Control. We tried to tell you, tried to make you see that bringing in government agencies so soon was not in the Unity's best interest, but you wouldn't listen.

Kate remembers her unaccountable indecisiveness yesterday, the difficulty she had telling Fielding to make the call.

"You were influencing me?"

Merely trying to let you see our side.

Kate is reeling. Her thoughts are no longer private. How much longer will she be able to call her thoughts her own, her actions her own? How long before she's doing things against her will? How long until she *has* no will?

You see, Kate? There's the problem: will—too many wills. You shouldn't have to worry about your will or our will. Within the Unity there is only one will. It makes life so much simpler.

But Kate senses something . . . a subtle shift in the Unity's mood, a hint of uncertainty. And she realizes that this oneness of theirs is a two-way street. They can see into her mind, but she can also see into theirs. Not clearly, not deeply, but enough to gather impressions.

"You're afraid, aren't you."

A dark ripple through the enveloping bliss. **No. Of course not. We are the future. We are inevitable. We have nothing to fear.**

But Kate can't be sure whether that's true belief or merely wishful thinking.

"What if Fielding finds a virucide that works against you? Or better yet—a vaccine? What happens to your inevitability then?"

He will not. He cannot. He hasn't enough time.

"He's got plenty of time. You're hampered by your nature. You're a blood-borne infection. It'll take decades—"

Kate gasps as a wave of joyous anticipation washes over her, blotting out her fears and suspicions in a surge of pleasure as intense as an orgasm.

Not true! You'll see! We will prevail! We will sweep across the globe. And you will be a part of it!

"No. Because if Fielding doesn't stop you, I have a feeling someone else will."

You're speaking of your brother? The Voice laughs. **How can he stop us when he will soon be one with us?**

Kate feels her knees sag. Not Jack! How? When?

Yesterday morning. He seemed too resourceful so the One Who Was Terrence scratched him with a pin dipped in our blood.

"*No!*" she screams and kicks and twists and wrenches her trapped hands, taking the Unity by surprise, breaking free, breaking contact, and abruptly the bliss and peace and belonging vanish, replaced by a void filled with fear and anguish.

Vision blurs, dark splotches expand before her eyes, merging, engulfing her.

9

"Is Jack gonna be all right, Mom?"

Disembodied voices echoed faintly around Jack. He tried identifying them but his mushy brain was having difficulty focusing.

The last one, a child's voice . . . what was her name? Vicky. That was it. But she sounded as if she were at the far end of the Lincoln Tunnel. He tried to open his eyes to find her but the lids weighed tons.

"Of course, honey," said another voice, female, older . . . Gia's voice. But she sounded even farther away—the Jersey side of the Holland Tunnel. "He's been sick like this before. Remember last summer?"

"I don't like to think about last summer."

"I know you don't. But remember after all the scary times were over and he was hurt and sick and we nursed him?"

"Yes."

"Well, this is like that time."

"But Jack had a doctor then."

"So to speak."

Even in his delirium agony Jack had to smile. Gia had never had much faith in Doc Hargus.

He felt the once cool, now warm washcloth peeled from his forehead.

"Here, honey. Go run some cold water over this again."

Over the fading patter of Vicky's retreating footsteps Jack heard Gia's voice, low and close to his ear.

"Jack, are you listening?"

"Nnnngh."

"Jack, I'm scared. You've got a temperature of a hundred-and-four and I don't know what to do for you."

He managed to put two words together. "Dc Hrgs."

Doc Hargus had had some run-ins with officialdom over the years, so his license wasn't exactly current. But that didn't mean he didn't know his stuff, just that it wasn't legal for him to practice. Jack had entrusted his life to him before, and he'd do it again.

"I've called him three times." He could hear the tension in Gia's voice. "All I get is his answering machine, and he hasn't called back."

"Mnth zit?" Jack said.

"Month? Don't you even know? It's June."

Hell. Hargus went to Arizona every June to visit his grandkids. So much for help from him.

"I'm scared, Jack. You looked like you were in a coma before."

Coma? As in comatose? With this fever, more like coma-toast.

"I'm going to call an ambulance."

"Nuh!"

"Please, Jack. I'm afraid you're dying!"

Couldn't go to a hospital. Too many questions, too many bean counters prying into the nooks and crannies of his life in search of money.

"Nut dine. Nuh husptl."

"I can't take this any more, Jack. I just can't sit here and watch you boil inside your skin. I'm getting help."

As Gia rose Jack slid his hand across the covers and clutched her arm. Not hard enough to haul her back—no way he had the strength for that—but the gesture stopped her.

Had to think. Couldn't let her wheel him into an ambulance.

Abruptly she pulled away. "Why didn't I think of this before? How dumb can I be?"

What was she doing? Wanted to cry out for her to stop. Please, Gia. No EMTs! I'll be fine. Just need some heavy rest. Don't do this to me! But his voice was gone.

His dread was swamped by the overwhelming fatigue that engulfed him and took him under again.

10

Kate came to on the couch with Jeanette next to her, holding her hand.

What happened? was the intended question but Jeanette answered before she'd completed the thought.

"You passed out."

Kate looked around. "Where are the others?"

"We . . . they left. A matter to attend to."

Did it really happen? Kate wondered, squeezing her eyes shut against a blinding headache. Or was I drugged or hypnotized?

"It really happened," Jeanette said.

Kate snatched her hand free and slid to the opposite end of the couch. This wasn't Jeanette. And she was reading her thoughts.

Could this be? Could a strange new virus change human brains and link minds? It was too bizarre. This sort of thing only happened on that Sci-Fi Channel that Kevin liked to watch.

And yet, if it wasn't real, what *had* she experienced a few moments ago?

And why this feeling now that her mind was no longer completely her own? Was it the power of suggestion . . . or real?

"We know how you feel, Kate."

"Do you? I doubt that."

"Fear . . ."

"More like terror."

". . . uncertainty . . ."

"How about betrayal, Jeanette?" Anger heated her face. "Do you feel betrayed? I know I do. I loved you, Jeanette. I trusted you."

She realized with a start she was using the past tense. "And you . . . you . . ."

"You'll thank us, Kate. In a few more days, when you're fully integrated, you'll bless that little pinprick in your palm."

"Never! And bad enough you infected me, but my brother as well! I'll never forgive you for this!"

Kate rose unsteadily. Never before had she wanted to hurt someone, but Jeanette's true-believer complacency made her want to hit her. Or worse.

"But you will. And so will Jack. In a few days you'll come to see—"

"A few days! Is that all? It took you much longer!"

"A mutation in the virus lets it spread much faster now through a host system. We—"

" 'We'? 'We' who?"

"Sorry. Once you're part of the Unity it's difficult to think of yourself as an 'I.' All of them are with me now and I am with all of them, even though we are miles apart."

"You referred to yourself as 'I' earlier when you walked in here with the others."

"That was so as not to alarm you."

"Maybe you should keep it up. Because right now I'm *very* alarmed."

"Okay, okay," she said soothingly. "I've been where you are, Kate. I fought it at first. I was so frightened, but it was only fear of the unknown. Now that I'm fully integrated, it's wonderful beyond description."

"But where are you going with this, Jeanette?"

"You know. We showed you. A transformed world."

"But what I saw was not all that transformed."

"What you saw was not the important part. It was what you didn't see that truly matters."

"You're talking in riddles."

"Think back, Kate. Did you see cattle farms? Did you see streets full of cars? Did you see jet contrails marring the skies?"

"So?"

"The Unity will change the way we live. Humanity will have a healthier lifestyle in a healthier environment. The first things to go will be the animal farms. Existing livestock will be consumed while we convert all the fields now devoted to feed grains to vegetable farms for humans."

"A race of vegans!" Kate preferred vegetables to meat but liked to have the option of fried chicken once in a while.

"Not at all. Wild animals that are caught will be consumed, but cattle, pig, and chicken farms will be a thing of the past. Too inefficient. It takes seven pounds of feed corn and soy to produce one pound of pork. So much simpler and healthier to eat the grains directly. Less waste that way. And speaking of waste, the cattle required to feed the average American family its annual supply of beef produce a pile of manure larger than that family's house. The methane released and the manure runoff into streams pollute the environment. All that will stop."

Now this *was* consistent with the old Jeanette—she'd often railed against what she called "the institutionalized animal cruelty of agribusiness," but her objections had always been on ethical grounds; this sounded more like simple pragmatism.

"There will be no need to travel within the Unity. You are everywhere everyone else is. And the environmental benefits from that are as enormous as they are obvious. Clothes, food, building materials will move on the rails and highways, but not people."

"But you showed me factories, so I assume there'll be industry."

"Only certain ones, the ones that provide the necessities: agriculture, clothing, housing."

"But what about business—banking, finance, international trade?"

"For what purpose? To sell stocks? To lend money? No family, no matter how large—and in the world of the Unity, families will be very large—will go without sufficient food, clothing, or shelter. What more will they need?"

"How about art, literature, and entertainment for starters?"

"No one will feel a need for those things. After all, what practical purpose do they serve? Whatever artistry you wish to express will be instantly appreciated by the entire Unity."

Kate felt her exasperation growing. "What about relationships?"

"The Unity is the ultimate relationship. You felt just a hint of it. The closeness, the 'oneness'—you've never felt such an intimate bond; it far surpasses what can be experienced with a mere individual."

That stung. "Meaning me?"

"This is different. This goes beyond what an unintegrated mind can grasp."

"Then what you and I had is gone?"

Jeanette nodded. "What we had was a procreative dead end."

"What?" Kate couldn't believe she'd heard correctly. "What did you just say?"

"There is no homosexuality in the Unity. It does not serve our purposes."

If she'd had any hopes that the Jeanette she'd loved might still exist somewhere, this quashed them. Kate backed away from her, toward the center of the room. She didn't want to ask but she had to know.

"What purposes?"

"To bring all minds into the Unity, of course. And then to create a perpetual flow of new minds to keep expanding the Unity. Since homosexuality is not procreative, it is counter to that goal."

"And so you wipe it out?"

"Nothing is wiped out. It simply is not a consideration that will arise within the Unity."

"Never mind considerations, what about feelings? What about love?"

Jeanette gave her a quizzical look. "Love? The Unity is love, complete and unconditional. It is bliss that increases every time a new mind is added. No one will need love outside the Unity. The only need will be the craving to add new minds, more and more, expanding our billions."

Kate backed further away from this puppet that had once been Jeanette, edging toward the kitchen. But something within wanted her to stay close to her and was making it difficult to move, the same something that was trying to soothe her riled emotions, calm her fears, ease her anger.

But she forced her legs to move, to inch toward the kitchen.

"That's not a human agenda, Jeanette. That's a *viral* agenda. It's aimed at one thing: more hosts in which to replicate. A virus is a parasite—the ultimate parasite. It can't even reproduce on its own. It enters a cell, co-opts the cellular machinery, then reprograms it to create copies of itself so it can go occupy more cells. That's what this whole plan is about, Jeanette: creating more hosts for the virus."

Jeanette followed her, a missionary trying to convert a heathen. She reached out but Kate avoided her touch.

"You don't understand, Kate. An outsider cannot possibly understand the Unity."

Kate felt as if she were wading against a current in chest-high water as she fought her way into the kitchen toward the microwave, and fought the anger-and fear-numbing tranquillity forcing its way through her mind.

"Oh, but I do. I understand perfectly: the Unity is the virus. In taking over your brains it's imprinted its agenda on your minds—or on your uber-mind or whatever it is. Be fruitful and multiply . . . and multiply . . . and multiply—and create nothing else. That's a virus's code of ethics, and that's what you're spouting."

Jeanette moved closer, her expression intense.

"Think of it, Kate. No nations, no borders. No me and not-me, no mine and not-mine—the sources of all conflict. Nothing can belong to anyone when everything belongs to everyone. The Unity future—"

"—is a sterile existence, Jeanette!" Hard to speak now. Her words slurred, her thoughts sludged. And Jeanette was closer, still reaching for her. "You want to turn humanity into a homogeneous mass of content, well-fed, healthy bodies in a healthy environment where we can breed like rabbits. You say you'll do away with livestock, Jeanette, but the truth is you'll *become* livestock!" Kate whirled, punched random buttons on the microwave over control panel. "And I refuse to live like that!"

Kate hit START.

And suddenly her mind cleared, her limbs freed up.

"Thank goodness!" she said. She turned to Jeanette. "Now we can really talk."

But Jeanette stood facing her, shaking her head and smiling ruefully.

"If you're looking for the old me, that won't work anymore. Not on me. I'm fully integrated now. The old me is gone, shucked like a worn-out skin. There's only the new me now."

Kate felt her breath clog in her throat. "Oh, no."

"The Unity doesn't understand why, but the vibrations caused by microwaves interfere with oneness in the unintegrated, causing the Unity to become blind to you. But it's only temporary. Once you're fully integrated, nothing can come between you and the Unity."

Kate's vision blurred as tears filled her eyes. Jeanette was gone, replaced by this . . . drone.

"Don't cry, Kate. I've never been happier. And you'll be happy too. Don't waste tears on the old me, and don't fight for the old you. The battle is already won. In a few more days the new, better you will emerge triumphant. And as for this . . ."

She reached past Kate, unplugged the microwave, then slid it off the counter and let it smash on the floor.

". . . don't waste your time."

Immediately Kate sensed that her thoughts were again no longer completely her own.

"Jeanette—"

The phone rang. They both stared at it, waiting for the fourth ring when the answering machine would pick up. Kate heard a beep, then a woman's voice.

"Oh, Kate. I was hoping you'd be there. I—"

Kate snatched up the receiver. "Yes? Who is this?"

"Oh, I'm so glad you're in. This is Gia. We met—"

"Yes, of course. I remember you. Jack's friend." She sensed the strain underlying the other woman's voice. "Is something wrong?"

"It's Jack. He's sick."

Her gut clenched. "How sick?"

"A hundred-and-four temperature. Delirious. Shaking chills alternating with drenching sweats. I don't know what to do."

"I'll be right over. Wait—I don't know where he lives." Gia gave her an Upper West Side address. "Don't leave him. I'm on my way."

"Your brother is sick," Jeanette said—a statement, not a question. Her expression was troubled.

"Yes. No thanks to you and your virus."

"But . . . this is not right. The virus does not make one sick. It slips past the immune system and—"

"Well, my brother's has thrown up a roadblock."

At least Kate hoped that was what it was. Those symptoms could indicate any number of infections, pneumonia among others.

She hurried to the bedroom where she changed into khaki pants and a chambray shirt. She gathered up the stethoscope and diagnostic kit she'd brought along in case she needed them for Jeanette—that was a laugh—and stuffed them into her oversized shoulder bag.

"Good-bye, Jeanette," she said, more from reflex than anything else, as she headed for the door.

Jeanette said nothing. She still stood where Kate had left her in the kitchen, staring at the wall, her brows knitted.

11

"Take another breath, Jack," Kate said. "Deeper this time."

Clad only in damp boxer shorts, he lay sprawled on a rumpled double bed. Jack didn't respond so she had to be satisfied with listening to his tidal respiration.

Kate pressed the diaphragm of her stethoscope more firmly against the perspiration-beaded skin of his mid back. She hadn't realized how sleekly muscular her brother had become. His almost total lack of body fat left the muscles close to the skin. The way he dressed gave no hint that this sort of body moved within his clothes. Men in Jeanette's end of town who had bodies like Jack's tended toward tank tops and skin-tight muscle shirts; their object was to attract attention; Jack's seemed to be to deflect it.

She strained to hear the crinkling cellophane rales that would signal fluid in the alveoli. She heard none.

"No sign of pneumonia," she said.

Gia sighed. "Thank God."

Not necessarily good news, Kate thought. Means we're dealing with something else. And if Jeanette had told the truth, that something else was most likely the contaminant virus.

"What do you think it is?" Gia said.

Kate looked at this pretty blond woman and thought back to the night—Lord, had it been only two nights ago?—that she and Jack had come over. Kate might have found herself attracted to her if not for everything that had been happening. She remembered how she'd been struck by the easy camaraderie between Jack and Gia, the way they laughed with each other and, when listening to Gia speak of Jack, how deeply she cared for her brother.

And now she saw the near panic in Gia's eyes, and thought, You're so lucky, Jack, to have someone who loves you this much. Don't ever lose her.

She decided to tell Gia part of the truth. "It's most likely a virus."

"Is it catching? Vicky's been in and out, helping me. Bad enough Jack's this sick. But Vicky's so little. What if—?"

"She should be fine."

Kate had met the dark-haired, blue-eyed child on the way in and her pigtails had made her ache for the days when Lizzie had been that age. Life had seemed so simple back then.

"I hope so," Gia said. "I've had to change his T-shirt three times. Finally I stopped. He pulls the covers over himself when he chills and throws them off when he sweats."

"That's part of the infection-fighting process."

But why is his system fighting it when mine didn't?

Kate felt a tug in her mind, a nanosecond of scrambled thoughts, and then a question leaping out before she could stop it.

"Has he ever been sick before?"

"This sick? Yes, once."

"When?"

She couldn't control her voice!

"Last summer. After . . ."

Kate tried to lock her throat, succeeded, but not before she said, "After what?"

"I don't know if I should go into that. Maybe Jack should tell you."

Now Kate herself wanted to know what Gia was talking about but was determined not to let the Unity hear the answer. She sensed fear and uncertainty in the Unity and that worried her. What might they do to wring the answer out of Gia?

She fought to regain control of her voice, and squeezed her eyes shut with the effort.

"Kate, are you all right?"

She felt beads of sweat pop out on her forehead . . . and then suddenly she was back in the driver seat . . . but she could still feel other hands reaching for the wheel.

"I'm okay. Just a bad headache."

"Oh, I'm sorry. Can I—?"

"You know what?" Kate said. "On second thought, it might be better, for Vicky's sake, if you go."

"Oh, no." She was shaking her head. "I couldn't leave Jack. I'll just keep Vicky in the other room and—"

"I'm concerned that if you catch whatever this is you might pass it on to her, and then . . ." Kate let the sentence hang and watched Gia chew her upper lip. She added, "I'll look after him, Gia. I've had a bit of training in this sort of thing."

"I know." She shrugged, her expression unhappy. "But I still feel like I'm abandoning him."

"I promise to watch over him as if he were a member of my own family."

This earned a smile. "Yes, I guess I can count on that, can't I." She sighed. "Okay. I'll take Vicky home. But you'll call me as soon as he comes out of this, won't you?"

Kate sensed increased efforts in her head to make her stop Gia from leaving but she beat them back.

"Of course."

Gia started for the door, then stopped and turned. Keep going! Kate wanted to shout. She didn't know how long she could hold out.

"Just one thing."

"You really shouldn't stay here any longer."

"I know, but I just want to warn you that Jack might not be too happy to find you here."

"I don't understand."

"It was my idea to call you over. When I told him he didn't respond, so I'm not sure it got through."

"Why would that be a problem?"

"He's a little quirky about this place. He . . . well, he doesn't like anyone to know where he lives. Hardly anyone does. And as for being here, Vicky and I are the only regulars. This is his sanctum."

"But I'm his sister."

"But you didn't know the address, right? I had to give it to you. See what I mean?"

"I think so."

"So if he's upset that you're here, don't take it personally."

Kate glanced at the sprawled sleeping man. "Strange guy, my brother."

Gia's lips said, " 'Unique' is more like it," but her eyes seemed to say, *If you only knew.*

Minutes later, when the door had closed behind them, Kate felt the pressure ease. The Unity was still desperate to know how Jack was reacting to the virus, but must have realized it could only watch and wait right now.

Was this what it had been like for Jeanette—fighting minute to minute, losing ground inch by inch? Maybe not. At least Kate knew she was in a war. Jeanette had probably had no idea. Most likely she wrote off any early alien feelings or thoughts as part of the healing process, a side effect of the tumor's shrinking. And when finally she'd realized that her mind was being usurped, it was too late.

When will it be too late for me? Kate wondered.

She thought of what was developing inside her head, the Unity virus running free through her brain, inserting its own genes into more and more of her brain's neurons until it had nibbled away everything that was her and replaced it with someone else, someone with viral ethics, another drone like Jeanette.

That possibility pushed up a bubble of acid to the back of her throat. She had to find a way to stop it. And bring Jeanette back. But first she had to save herself.

She looked at Jack. If his immune system truly was fighting the virus, it would be producing antibodies. If she could isolate those glob-ulins and inject them into her own bloodstream . . .

Her excitement died aborning. If-if-if . . . even if it were true, the process would be lengthy. She'd be a born-again member of the Unity by then.

She'd have to find another way. Maybe Fielding would come up with something. Whatever happened, Kate sensed that Jack would be the key. But everything was stuck on hold until he pulled through this, if he did.

She checked him again—still sleeping but less sweaty—then wandered into the dizzying clutter of his apartment's front room. She stopped when she saw something that looked like a gun on an end table. Dear Lord, it *was* a gun. She stepped closer. Did Jack own a gun? Obviously. Kate hated guns. Bad enough for her brother to own one, but she couldn't believe he'd be so careless as to leave it out like this with a child around. Gia's little girl could have—

Wait. It had a red plastic handle and the rest of it looked made of tin. The knob of a power dial bulged from the side next to a pair of words framed by lightning bolts etched into the metal: *Atomic Disintegrator*. Kate smiled and shook her head. A toy raygun—no, a cap gun. Ancient, too.

She did a slow turn. Look at this stuff. What did he do, go through flea markets and pick up everything that wasn't nailed down? And none of it seemed less than fifty years old. A Daddy Warbucks lamp, a Dick Tracy alarm clock—*lots* of clocks, all old, none working. Framed certificates and more clocks, their pendulums arrested in final swing, hid the walls. She stepped closer to check out the certificates—all from clubs and secret societies devoted to the Shadow, Captain Midnight, Doc Savage . . . what on earth did he see in this junk?

The only thing she could find that belonged in the Twenty-first Century—or in the latter half of the twentieth, for that matter—was the computer monitor atop the oak rolltop desk. And a vaguely familiar-looking black object resting on the monitor. Kate leaned in for a closer look and stiffened when she recognized the timer clock from the bomb Jack had found yesterday. She knew it was the same clock by the four cut ends of the wires snaking out from its casing. The only difference now was that the display was lit, showing the time.

And next to it were those silvery little AAA-battery-size things with the rest of the cut wires that had been attached to the clock. What had Jack called them? Blasting caps. But where was that clay-like explosive?

She checked the rest of the desk top and hunted through the room but didn't see it. Must have hidden it away. She didn't like poking through Jack's desk drawers but she'd feel better if she knew the explosive was here too. She suspected that Jack had used it to blow up that car this morning, and she hated the thought.

But the drawers in the old rolltop held nothing but papers and video catalogues. She made a point of not reading any of the papers and moved on to the equally old oak secretary. And there in the top drawer, next to what looked like another toy gun, she found it—still wrapped in cellophane, with the empty holes where the blasting caps had been inserted.

What a relief. When he recovered, maybe Jack could explain how that car exploded, but at least now she could be sure this stuff hadn't been used. Meanwhile, she didn't want to have to look at that timer and the blasting caps whenever she was in this room, so she put them in the drawer with the explosive.

As she wiggled the drawer to push it back in it slipped out of the desk. She stood there holding it, wondering why it was so shallow— only half as deep as the base of the secretary. She peered into the slot and saw what was obviously a false rear wall.

Curious, Kate replaced the drawer and angled the secretary away from the wall. She felt around the weathered rear panel until she found a recessed catch. A gentle tug released the board; it fell toward her, revealing a hidden compartment with three shelves.

And on those lay at least half a dozen pistols of varying shapes and sizes and finishes, extra clips, boxes of bullets, knives, blackjacks . . .

A miniature armory.

She stared for a dry-mouthed moment, then replaced the panel and pushed the secretary back against the wall. She opened the drawer again and took out the tiny pistol she'd seen before. Heavy . . . too heavy for a toy. She dropped it back in and shoved the door closed. Shaken, she retreated to the center of the room and stared around her.

She had to face it: Jack was a gun nut or worse. Some sort of criminal. Had to be. What other reason could he have for owning all that weaponry?

Who was her brother? What on earth had he become?

She'd thought he was exaggerating when he'd said his closet was deeper and darker than hers. Now she knew he wasn't.

And yet . . . he was still her brother. And despite all this damning evidence, she sensed a core of old-fashioned decency within him. A man you could trust, a man whose word meant something.

Was that the key to all this pulp era junk? Memorabilia from a time before he existed, relics of an antiquated obsolescent code of honor to which he still hewed?

Or was she reading too much into this? Not every idiosyncrasy had to have deep psychological overtones. How did the saying go? Sometimes a cigar is just a cigar. Maybe Jack simply thought this stuff was cool—or "neat," as he liked to say—and picked it up whenever he came across it.

Kate heard a sound from the bedroom and stepped back inside. Jack was tossing back and forth under the covers, moaning, mumbling, whining. He seemed frightened.

She watched him closely, wondering what terrible sort of nightmare would scare a man like Jack . . .

12

. . . Jack looks up as the girl in the middle of the store check-out line coughs. He watches from the rear as people ahead and behind her back away.

"Just a cold," the girl says, her voice slightly muffled by her surgical mask.

Everyone in the store, including Jack, wears a surgical mask. Jack loves the style—not only keeps out germs but hides the face. And the store is packed. Rumor got out that the place managed to get in a shipment of produce and people are buying up as much as they can carry. Jack left Gia and Vicky back at his apartment where they're safe from infection and ventured out alone. His cart—and it is truly his because he pushed it to the store from home—is loaded with corn and

peaches and tomatoes that look like Jersey beefsteaks. He managed to
snag some canned beans and a box of fusilli from the nearly naked
shelves as well.

Good haul, he thinks, happy with his finds. Food shipments are so
sporadic these days, what with survivalist groups hijacking trucks for
themselves, so you take what you can find. Looks like Italian on the
menu tonight. Gia can whip of some of her famous red gravy and—

"She's one of them!" cries a heavyset woman in a turquoise sari
directly behind the girl with the cold, backing farther away from her.
"I saw her pull out the bottom of her mask before she coughed!"

"Just a cold." The girl has wide blue eyes and short black hair. "I
swear it's just a cold."

"I saw her too," says the black man behind the saried woman.
"Pulled the mask halfway off her face!"

Jack has a feeling he might have seen it too, but only out of the
corner of his eye, so he doesn't say anything. The girl's been tagged
twice. A third won't change her fate.

Sensing where this could be going he angles his cart out of this
particular line and backs it toward the rear of another. But he passes
that and keeps on backing away, edging closer to the exit doors.

The checkout girl is signaling to the deputy but he's heard the
commotion and is already on his way over. He's a thin little guy, and
in any other situation he might be hesitant, but he's wearing the tan
uniform of a duly deputized NYC militiaman, he's got a testing kit, and
he's armed. And his strut says I'm official so don't mess with me.

"What's up?" His mouth is probably set in a grim line but the
surgical mask hides it.

The cashier points to the girl. "They say she coughed outside her
mask. On purpose."

"Is that so?" The deputy's eyes narrow as he reaches for the se-
rology tester clipped to his belt. "Okay. Gonna need some of your
blood."

"Just a cold," the girl says, backing away.

"If that's all it is, you can go on about your business—after the
test."

Jack, who by now has edged into a corner near the furthest checkout
counter, notices how the deputy doesn't say what happens if it's not
just a cold.

"No!" The girl rips off her mask. "No blood test! We spit on your blood tests!"

Then she charges into the crowd around the cash register and starts spitting—not on the blood test but on people. Terrified shoppers scream and try to flee but there's no room to run. The deputy has his pistol drawn but it's plain if he shoots he's going to crease a load of innocent bystanders.

Suddenly Jack sees something flash in the girl's hand—an old-fashioned straight razor—and knows what's coming next. So does everybody else.

"She's a kamikaze!" someone screams as panic takes charge.

Jack watches the girl ram the point of the blade deep into her throat and rip it sideways. Then she throws her arms wide, tilts her head back, and begins to spin. There's a certain grace to her movements, and it might be a beautiful thing to watch except for the scarlet stream arcing from her throat in a spasming geyser that sprays everyone in a ten-foot circle.

It's a brief dance. Her legs falter, her knees buckle, and she collapses to the floor, a crumpled waxen lump centered in a crimson spin painting.

But though the dance is done, the audience is still reacting: the screamers trapped at the row of checkout counters keep pushing back, deeper into the store; those just entering do a quick about-face and rush back to the relative safety of the streets. Jack, positioned in the no-man's land between, opts for the street and rolls his laden cart though the swinging doors. He'll settle up with the store tomorrow. Could be an hour, maybe two, before the mess is cleaned up in there. He wants to get back home.

Six months ago a scene like that would have blown him away. Now . . . he feels nothing. Had the dubious distinction of being on hand for two other kamikaze deaths before today's, but never this close. The Hive's MO is pretty much the same all over: find a crowded place and try to spread the infection surreptitiously—the cough, the sneeze, smearing a little saliva on vegetables—but if caught, go down in a glorious spray of body fluids. Pure pragmatism: sacrifice one of their number for the opportunity to infect dozens more.

The Hive is relentlessly pragmatic. That's the key to its success.

Half a block from the store he stops and unties his mask; he pulls

off his windbreaker and drapes it over the cart. The November wind
slices at him but his flannel shirt blunts its edge. He removes the Glock
from the nylon small-of-the-back holster and positions it in plain sight
atop the jacket. Then he starts moving again.

This gray, sullen, blustery fall day matches the bleakness Jack
feels. He wishes the sun were out—to warm his skin, and maybe even
take some of this chill off his soul. But sunlight would bring out more
people—maybe they think it's healthier, that the extra UV will kill
germs—and Jack prefers the streets damn near deserted like this, especially when he's hauling a load of food. Even so, his senses are on
full alert.

Ahead he sees a familiar face, a nodding acquaintance coming
his way.

"Hey," the guy says with a grin, eyeing Jack's cart. No way he can
miss the Glock. "Leave any for me?"

"Plenty," Jack says. "But you might want to wait awhile. A kamikaze did her thing in there."

"Shit!" the guy says. "They don't know when to quit, do they. They
know we've got the vaccine. Why do they keep trying?"

"Just because they've got lots of brains doesn't mean they're smart."

The guy doesn't think this is funny. Neither does Jack, but it's better
than talking about the rumor that the vaccine isn't what it was cracked
up to be, that it's been failing all over the country. What's left of the
U.S. government says these are lies spread by the infected to demoralize
the uninfected, but no one knows who to believe.

"Guess I'll just go down to the store and wait outside till they clean
things up."

Jack waves good-bye and watches him go. Once he's sure the guy's
not going to do a spin and jump him from behind, he resumes his walk
home. Knows he's always been a bit paranoid, but six months ago he'd
have kept the Glock holstered and wouldn't be worried about being
jumped for his food. As the saying goes, you're not paranoid if they're
really out to get you. And they are. Oh yes, they are.

As Jack walks along he can feel the threads of the social fabric
tearing, parting one by one.

Trust is gone, because anyone, your best and oldest friend, your
dearest, closest relative, could be carrying the virus. Bad enough they're

infected—that's not their fault—but less than a week after their inoculation they become someone else, someone dead set on infecting you.

Compassion is a memory. Sure, feel sorry for the victims of the virus—*after* they're dead.

Jack doesn't know about the rest of the country, but the tenuous sense of community that existed around the Upper West Side is atrophying. You'd think it would be the other way around, a community of the uninfected linking arms and closing ranks against the contaminated. But not when yesterday's uninfected ally could be today's infected enemy.

Jack figures he can extrapolate the local to the national, even to the international, and that means the whole world's going in the toilet—old social orders fragmenting while a new world order expands, relentlessly, irresistibly, geometrically, a rolling snowball of humanity with an unquestioned singleness of purpose.

Strange mix of feelings roiling through him these days. He's spent most of his adult life hiding from the social order, rejecting it, damning it. But despite its toxicity, now that it's on the brink of ruin he finds himself rooting for it, hoping it will find a way to hang on. Because the Hive is even more toxic than the world order it hopes to replace.

Not so much worried about himself—being a ghost in the Hive machine will be more of a challenge than his existence in the American social engine, but he'll manage it. His piercing concern is for Gia and Vicky and the jeopardy they face. They're not cut out to live in the cracks, and the Hive is too vast and pervasive for Jack ever to defeat on his own. Hates to admit it, but he needs help to protect the two people he cherishes. He knows he can't expect it from Democrats and Republicans, but maybe some genius in the medical establishment will come up with a killer app.

And most daunting is that deterioration to the current state has taken a mere five months.

First the virus mutated into an airborne form, then the original tiny nucleus of the Hive fanned out to all the New York travel hubs—LaGuardia and JFK airports, Penn and Grand Central Stations—to spread the virus. From there the bug raced across the country and around the world. Tens of millions were incorporated into the Hive before hardly anyone even realized it existed. Initially the two parties in Congress saw the Hive as a potential constituency and vied with each other to see who could grant it more special rights and entitlements. But after a majority of the politicians became infected, debate stopped.

By the time most people began to appreciate the enormity of the threat, it was too late.

The CDC's initial approach to containment was an influenza model, which proved ineffective. First off, folks with influenza know they're sick and so do the people around them; secondly, flu victims feel lousy and just want to get better. For Hive folk the infection's a party and the more the merrier.

And they were everywhere, contaminating water supplies, infiltrating food processing plants and dairy farms. People became afraid to eat anything they hadn't heated to a boil or prepared themselves.

As he pushes along the sidewalks, Jack wonders as he often does about his sister. Kate exited his life as quickly as she'd entered it. He searched for her but she stayed on the move, spreading the virus with the rest of the Hive vanguard, and he never caught up with her. But just last week he tried calling her office in Trenton and learned she was back in practice. She'd refused to take his call and he'd hung up sick at heart. He thinks of Kate as a pediatrician, with trusting parents, fearing their children might become infected, bringing them to her to be vaccinated against the virus. And Kate making sure if they aren't infected when they enter her office they damn sure are when they leave. All it takes is plain saline in the vaccine syringes and a little of the virus on the tongue depressors . . .

The thought of Kate betraying those children, breaking her oath to do no harm, negating the decent caring person she once was fills Jack with impotent rage. He wants to hurt, maim, kill, make someone pay, but how do you even a score with a virus?

He wonders if he should take a ride down to Trenton and . . . do something. But what? Put down the fouled thing that used to be his sister? The old Kate, the real Kate would want him to do that. Beg him to.

But can he? Take a bead on his own sister—even if she's not really his sister anymore—and pull the trigger? Can't imagine that.

Jack picks up his pace as he nears his block. Two old cars are

parked nose to nose, blocking the near end of the street; he knows two
more junkers are similarly situated at the far end—knows because the
whole setup was his idea. Sometime last month he went door to brownstone door talking—usually at a safe distance through windows or from
the sidewalk—to neighbors he'd never bothered to meet despite years
on the block, planting the idea of the block sealing itself off. Someone
with better people skills picked up the ball and organized the residents,
breaking the watch into shifts. Now no outsider enters the block unless
accompanied by a resident.

Jack nods to a guy he knows only as George, standing behind one
of the cars with a sawed off twelve gauge resting against a thigh. As
George waves him through, an NYPD blue-and-white goes by, two cops
in the front. Passenger cop's gaze lingers on Jack and George, then
slides by. Can't miss the Glock or the sawed-off, but he doesn't react.
The tattered remnants of officialdom are no longer worried about armed
citizenry—the unseen danger of the virus is a far greater threat to the
city. And besides, not enough police to go around as it is. They were
the Hive's first target: call the cops out to a domestic dispute, infect
them, then form a fifth column within the ranks to infect the rest.
Uninfected cops stayed home until the blood tests were developed.

The vaccine and the blood tests—cheap little home kits, like preg-
nancy tests—are the final fingers in the dam against rising tide of the
Hive. If they should fail . . .

Jack drag-bounces the cart to his third-floor apartment—his fortress
islet within the atoll of his closed-off block—and knocks on the door;
he has a key but Gia's so edgy these days he figures it'll go easier on
her nerves if he doesn't just barge in.

"Oh, Jack!" he hears her say through the door, and he knows she's
got her eye to the peep lens, but he detects a strange note in her voice.
Something's up.

And when she opens the door and he sees her red eyes and tear-
streaked face, he knows it.

"What's wrong?"

She pulls him inside, leaving the cart in the hall, and closes
the door.

"The test!" she sobs. "Vicky and I—we're positive!"

Jack's heart drops. Gia's been obsessed with the virus, and rightly so, to the point where she's been testing the three of them every day. Jack's been buying kits by the gross, figuring if it gives her peace of mind, then fine, do it twice a day if you want.

But in the back of his mind he's always dreaded the possibility of this moment: the false positive.

"No." His tongue is an arid plain. "No, that can't be. There's got to be a mistake!"

She's shaking her head, fresh tears spilling onto her cheeks. "I just repeated it. Same result."

"Then it's a bad batch."

"Same batch as yesterday."

Jack can't accept this. He moved them here so he could protect them, keep them safe. They've been under his wing, rarely leaving the apartment.

The sick feeling in his stomach worsens as an appalling thought hits him like a runaway train: Is it my fault? Did I bring it home?

"Do it again," he says. "All three of us this time."

Gia nods and wipes her eyes. "Okay." She turns and calls, "Vicky!"

"What?" says a little girl's voice from one of the back rooms.

"Come in here for a minute, okay?"

"But I'm watching a movie!"

"You've seen that movie a hundred times already. Come here just for a second, okay?"

"*The Parent Trap* again?" Jack says, trying to look cheerful as Vicky mopes in.

"And I was just at the good part where they find out they're sisters!"

"That the nice thing about videos—you can stop them any time and pick up later right where you left off."

Gia has seated herself at Jack's rolltop. "Let me have your finger, Vickie."

A groan, an eye roll. "Not again!"

"Come on. One more time. Jack's doing it this time too."

"Oh, okay."

She walks over to Gia and presents her finger, flinches as her mother stabs the tip with a microlancet, and allows a drop of blood to be milked onto the circle of absorptive paper in the center of the test kit card.

"There," Gia says with a smile Jack knows is forced. "Was that so bad?"

"No. Can I see my movie now?"

"Sure."

As Vicky hurries off, sucking her tiny wound, Gia's trembling fingers squeeze a drop of reagent from its bottle onto the bloodied circle. She glances at her watch, puts the card aside, and looks up at Jack.

"Your turn."

Jack allows his finger to be subjected to the same ritual. Barely feels the prick. Soon his blood sample is doused in reagent and waiting for ten minutes to pass.

And Gia's makes three.

The wait feels interminable, with Gia pacing back and forth, rubbing her hands as if scrubbing them, a beautiful young blond Lady Macbeth working at a stubborn stain. Jack opens his mouth twice to say something, anything to soothe her raw nerves, but can't think of a damn thing that isn't lame or inane.

Finally she looks at her watch and says, "Time." But she doesn't move. "Jack . . . will you? I can't . . . I just . . ."

"Sure, Gi."

Jack steps to the desk, flips the three cards over and, carefully maintaining their sequence, lifts the rear panels. One by one, the flip side of the absorbent paper is revealed, and around the blood spots on the first and third cards . . . a blue halo. Around the second, only a ring of moisture.

Jack closes his eyes and feels the room rock around him.

Can't be. This isn't happening. Got to be a mistake. We've all been vaccinated, we all eat the same, drink the same, and I'm the one who's in and out, I'm the one with all the exposure. It should be me, not them.

He opens his eyes and looks again, begging for a different outcome. But nothing has changed: two positives flanking a negative.

Gia is staring at him. "Well?"

Jack swallows. "Positive." His voice is a hoarse rasp. He quickly gathers up the cards. "All three."

"Oh, Jack," Gia sobs, floating toward him. "Not you too!"

She flings herself against him and they stand there clinging to each other, Gia weeping, Jack's throat too tight to speak.

He crumples the test cards in his fist. Can't let Gia know. If she learns he's negative she'll blame Vicky's infection on the only other person the child could have caught it from: her. She'll never accept that she could have caught it from Vicky. Gia will assume all the guilt, and it will crush her.

And Jack's negative will open a gulf between them—she'll recede from him, fearing that a kiss, a caress, even a word spoken too close will infect him, and Jack couldn't bear that, not now, not when she needs him most.

"Christ, I'm so sorry, Gia," he manages. "I must have brought it home."

"But how can that be? We took every precaution. And the vaccine . . ."

"Doesn't work. That's been the word on the street lately. Now we know it's true."

She buries her face against his chest and sobs again. "Vicky . . . I can't bear the thought . . ."

"I know," he says, pulling her closer against him and feeling a sob building his own throat at the thought of Gia and Vicky becoming meat puppets controlled by the Hive. "I know."

What now? he asks himself, trying to corral his panicked, skittering thoughts. What can I do?

He hasn't heard of anyone beating this infection. But that doesn't mean no one ever will. There's always a chance for a breakthrough, for a wild card.

Look at me—I should be infected but I'm not. Maybe that means something. But how to find out?

Abe. Abe knows everything.

He releases Gia and looks her in the eye. "It's not over."

"What do you mean?"

"When I was talking to Abe yesterday he mentioned something about a new breakthrough."

"The days of breakthroughs are gone," she says dully.

"Gia, if there's anything in the pipeline, anything at all, Abe will have a line on it. I'll call him right now."

He grabs the cell phone and punches in Abe's number, something in the past he never would have considered doing, but a lot has changed in five months. He waits through a dozen rings—Abe doesn't believe in answering machines—then tries again. Still no answer. Abe's always in this time of day. Maybe he's in one of his black, ignore-the-phone moods. He's been having more of those lately.

"Looks like I'm going to have to go see him," Jack says. He doesn't want to leave Gia but time is critical. The fact that they've just turned positive means she and Vicky are in the early stages. If something can be done, the sooner the better. "I won't be gone long. You'll be okay?"

Gia nods wordlessly.

"Gia," he says, taking her by the shoulders, "we're going to beat this." And he knows he sounds like a hack actor in a bad soap opera but he can't stand seeing her like this. He's got to give her some hope. "Have I ever let you down?"

"Jack . . ." she says, and she sounds so tired. "This is different. This isn't something your methods can fix. The best scientific minds in the world have tackled this and they've all come up empty. Every time they think they have a solution, like the vaccine, the virus mutates. So what can you do?"

And when she puts it like that, what can he say? No reason to think he can offer Gia and Vicky a chance when the big brains can't. But still he's undeterred.

"Maybe I suffer from terminal hubris. And maybe I can't stand by and just let this happen. I've got to do something."

He doesn't say that guilt has pretty much taken him over. He brought Gia and Vicky here to protect them, but the bug got to them anyway. So even if it's not his fault, he feels responsible.

"Then do it," Gia says, without a hint of enthusiasm, "but don't expect me to hope, Jack, because as much as I want to, I can't. I'm looking at the end of everything I am and you are and whatever we might have been, and the strangulation of everything Vicky could be."

"We're not through yet."

"Yeah, we are. Our futures end in a few days. If it was death, I could accept that—at least for myself. But this is a living death . . . and . . ."

Her voice trails off, and her gaze slips off Jack and settles somewhere in space.

Jack has never seen her like this. What's happened to her indomitable spirit? It's as if the virus has already changed her, reached inside somehow and snuffed out an essential spark.

He holds her in his arms again and kisses her forehead. "Don't write us off. I'm going over to Abe's and see what he knows." He releases her and backs toward the door. "I should be back in an hour or so. I'll call if I'm going to be any later. Okay?"

Gia nods absently. "I'll be here. Where else can I go?"

Jack turns at the door and sees her standing in the middle of his front room, looking like a lost soul. And that's so un-Gia he has second thoughts about leaving. But he's got to see Abe. If there's any cause for hope, Abe will know.

Free of the cart this trip, Jack makes good time through the empty streets toward Amsterdam Avenue, not sure if he is fleeing the dark reality of his apartment or running toward a ray of hope. Soon he is standing before the Isher Sports Shop. The lights are on inside but the front door is locked. That's not right. He bangs on the glass but Abe doesn't appear.

Worried now—for years Abe has been a heart attack waiting to happen—Jack pulls out the defunct Visa card he keeps in his wallet for moments like this. Looks up and down the street, sees no one near enough to matter, and uses it to slip the door's latch. Abe's never devoted much effort to protecting his street-level stock, but it would take a Sherman tank to get into his basement.

"Abe?" he calls as he steps inside, relocking the door behind him. "Abe, it's Jack. You here?"

Silence . . . and then high-pitched cheeping as something pale blue flutters overhead. Parabellum, Abe's parakeet. Abe always cages the bird when he leaves, so he must be here.

Jack's apprehension intensifies as he heads for the rear, toward the counter where he and Abe have spent so many hours talking, solving the problems of the world time and again. And then as he rounds a corner piled high with hockey sticks and the counter hoves into view, he stumbles to a halt at the sight of all the red—the counter puddled with it, the wall behind splattered.

"No," Jack whispers.

Gut in a knot, he forces himself forward. Not Abe. Can't be Abe.

But who else's blood can this be?

He creeps toward the counter, edges around the side, looks behind—

It's Abe, on his back, white shirt glistening crimson, head cocked at a crazy angle, throat a ragged hole, torn away by a blast from the sawed-off shotgun lying by his knees.

Jack spins away, doubles over, sick. He doesn't vomit but wishes he could. Rage steadies him. Who did this? Whoever tried to make this look like a suicide didn't know Abe, because Abe would never . . .

After a while Jack straightens, staggers to the back of the store, finds an old tarp, and drapes it over Abe's body.

The blood . . . still so wet . . . couldn't have happened more than twenty, thirty minutes ago.

If only I'd left a few minutes earlier I might have been here in time to . . .

And then he sees something on the far corner of the counter. The square of a virus test kit. He steps closer. A used kit . . . and the blue halo says it's positive.

Jack sags against the counter. "Aw, Abe."

And he understands: Abe saw no hope for himself. That means Jack will have none to offer Gia and Vicky.

He sits a long while, feeling lost and paralyzed as he stares at the test card. Finally he pushes himself into motion. Can't leave Abe here like this. What's he do? Call the cops? Will they even come? And if they do, there'll be an investigation and someone will find the armory in the basement. And all the while Abe's body will molder in a drawer in the morgue's cooler.

No. Can't have that. Jack knows what he has to do: come back tonight with the car and take Abe's body to Central Park. No cops, no inquests, just a quiet private burial for his oldest and dearest friend.

But what about Abe's family? The only family Jack knows of is a daughter in Queens. Sarah. Jack's never met her; he hid Gia and Vicky at her place during the rakoshi mess last summer, but she was out of town then.

Jack reaches for the blood-spattered Rolodex and flips through it. Abe used a computer down in the basement but stuck to old-fashioned methods up here on the main floor. An ache grows in his throat at the sight of Abe's crabbed handwriting and for a moment the letters blur. He blinks and tugs on the "S" tab, and there it is: simply "Sarah" and a number.

He calls the number and when a woman answers he asks for Sarah.

"This is she."

"I . . . I'm a friend of your father's. I'm afraid—"

"Yes, we know," she says. "He's dead."

Jack's alarms go off at the *we*. "How can you—?"

"We were hoping to get him to the point where we could stop him from such tragic foolishness, but those damn tests are so—"

Jack slams down the receiver. He can imagine how it went down. Sarah stops by with a peace offering. They've never gotten along, but these are extraordinary times and maybe they should bury the hatchet. She's brought something sweet, something her father can't resist, something heavily spiked with the virus.

And later, when Abe's blood turns positive, he knows he's a goner and knows who made him that way and it's all too much for him. Never would have believed it of Abe, but no telling what a person will do when the whole future goes dead black without a single glint of hope—

Jack's breath freezes in his chest as he remembers Gia's ten-mile stare when he left her and now he's heading for the door with his heart tearing loose. The phone rings and he knows he should ignore it but doubles back on the slim chance it might be Gia. She knows he's here, maybe she's trying to reach him.

"Jack," Gia says in response to his barked hello. "Thank God I caught you."

"What's wrong?" The preternatural calm of her tone sends screams of warning through him. "How's Vicky?"

"Sleeping."

"Sleeping?" Vicky is *not* a napper. "Is she sick?"

"Not anymore. She's at peace."

"Christ, Gia, what are you saying? Don't tell me you—"

"I didn't have enough sleeping pills for both of us, so I gave them all to her. Soon she'll be safe."

"No!"

"And I've got one of your guns for me, but I didn't want to use it until I called you to say good-bye—"

The phone slips from Jack's fingers and he's dashing for the door, bursting onto the sidewalk, and sprinting east when he glances up and skids to a halt at the sight of a giant face staring down at him. It's the Russian lady but she's grown to Godzilla proportions.

"NOW DO YOU SEE?" she cries, her booming voice echoing off the buildings. "NOW DO YOU UNDERSTAND? THIS WILL BE IF YOU DO NOT STOP VIRUS NOW!"

What does it mean? That this is all a dream? No. Much as Jack wishes it were true, he knows it's not. This is too real.

Averting his face from her giant, blazing eyes, he starts running again, down the center of a treadmill street with cardboard buildings sliding by on each side to give the illusion of forward progress, but he's getting nowhere, and no matter how much speed he pumps into his legs, no matter how he cries and screams at the top of his lungs, he's no closer to home than when he started . . .

13

"Kevin's being a real dickhead about it, Mom."

"Elizabeth Iverson, that is no way to talk about your brother. And where did you pick up that kind of language?"

"I can't help it, that's what he is. And I don't care if he comes. Who wants him around anyway."

Kate clung to her cell phone as she peeked into Jack's bedroom— he was still tossing this way and that under the covers—then returned her attention to Lizzie. With everything that had happened, she'd missed her morning call to the kids. Just as well; they both slept in on Saturdays. She'd waited till after dinner to check in.

All she'd wanted to do was touch base with them before they went out with their friends, but had wound up in the middle of a sibling contretemps. She should have seen it coming, but this was the last thing she needed now: Kevin was refusing to go to Lizzie's recital on Monday. Lizzie was acting tough but Kate could tell she was hurt. Ron had never been good dealing with arguments between the kids so, exhausted though she was, Kate had been designated referee.

She sighed. "Put him on."

"I said, I don't care!"

"Lizzie, please put your brother on."

A few seconds of muffled sounds, then a sullen, "S'up, Ma?" from Kevin.

"What's up yourself, Kevin? Have you got something better to do Monday night?"

"Aw, Mom, I hate that music, you know that."

"No, it's not Polio, I'll grant you that," she said, referring to her son's favorite band, perpetrators of cacophonies he referred to as "slash metal" or "thrash metal" or some such unlistenable noise. She realized that every generation needed music that rawed their parents' nerves, but *please*. "The music's not the issue, however. Your sister's feelings are."

"You heard her. She doesn't want me to go."

"That's just a defense because you hurt her feelings. We've always done things as a family, Kevin. Even after the divorce, how many of your soccer games did your father and Lizzie and I miss? Very, very few. And just like your soccer tournament, Kevin, we're planning to attend this concert as a family. Family includes you."

"But Ma, the flute! Of all things, the *flute!* It's so whipped!"

"It's Lizzie's big moment. She's performing a solo she's been practicing for months and we should be there to share it with her. Are you telling me you can't spare two hours out of your busy schedule to attend her concert? Think about it, Kevin. In the grand scale of things, is two hours on a Monday night such a big deal?"

"No, but—"

"Sleep through the concert if you must, but be there for her."

"Sleep? That music's deadly. When it's over and you find me dead in my seat, how will you feel?"

"Don't worry. I know CPR. I should be home by mid-afternoon Monday. I'll come over to Dad's and we'll all go together. As a family. I'd like to count on that, Kevin. Can I?"

A long pause, then, "I guess so."

"Great. See you then. Love you."

"Me too."

She broke the connection and took a deep breath. Another domestic crisis averted. She empathized with Kevin; her own musical tastes were mired in sixties and seventies pop and she found classical music as trying as he did—except when Lizzie was playing—but the concert was a family thing, not a music thing, and she had to keep the family together. That was her mission, a responsibility that possessed her. Because the divorce had been her doing.

She rose and checked Jack again. He'd finally stopped moaning and lay deeply sunken in sleep; his skin had been cool and dry for almost two hours now.

"Looks like you made it, Jack," she whispered, stroking his matted hair. He might spike another fever around four A.M. or so, but she sensed that his immune system had the upper hand now. "Looks like you beat it."

But beat what? she thought as she wandered back to the front room. Exactly what infection had he been fighting all day? She hoped it was the contaminant. That would mean it was not as invincible or as "inevitable" as it seemed to think.

But the possibility existed that Jack had caught some other virus and his symptoms had been due to his body's war against that.

Only time would tell.

Kate yawned and stretched. Not much sleep last night. She was tired but doubted she could sleep. Not after what she'd been through today, not after learning that something calling itself the Unity was hell bent on erasing her personality, her individuality, her very self.

She felt a sob build in her throat. I don't want to die!

And that was what integration with the Unity would be: death. Sure, her body would live on but the person inside would be obliterated. All her values, the little things that made her who she was, gone. She would no longer care about the music, the paintings, the movies she now loved because they'd serve no practical purpose in expanding the species. And Kevin and Liz would be downgraded from the two most cherished beings in her life to a pair of potential hosts who shared some genes with her, valued only for their capacity to breed more hosts.

She had to see Fielding again—first thing Monday morning, before she headed home. Maybe he was right. He'd said he was Jeanette's best chance; maybe he was hers as well. The Unity clearly was concerned about Fielding. And whatever made it uneasy could only be good for her.

Come to think of it, she hadn't felt the Unity tugging at her thoughts for the past few hours. Too occupied with something else? She wondered what it was up to. No matter. As long as it wasn't bothering her.

But if sleep was out of the question, at least she could lie down and rest her eyes now that Jack was over the worst.

She stretched out as best she could on the couch and laced her fingers atop her chest. Usually she looked forward to the next day, but not tonight. Would the Unity try to take over again, try to use her to wrest the secret of Jack's resistance from him?

Kate closed her eyes. She had to prevent the Unity from stealing what was hers—what was *her*. But how?

The question trailed her into sleep . . .

14

"You don't look like you're having much fun," Jay Pokorny said.

The four of them—Sandy and Beth and Pokorny and his longtime girlfriend Alissa—were standing at the long bar near the front of Kenny's Castaways on Bleecker in the Village, having a few drinks. The bar ran along the left side of the front section; tables cluttered the rear floor where a small stage huddled against the rear wall. Kenny's had been Pokorny's idea—something about a new band they had to hear. But here it was eleven already and still no music.

"So far it's just a bar," Sandy said.

He felt a nudge in his ribs and turned to see Beth smiling up at him. God, she looked great tonight.

"Be nice," she whispered.

He winked at her. "Okay."

"Yeah," Pokorny said, "but wait till you hear this chick in the band. Name's Debbie something. She's this little thing that looks like Betty Boop, but when she opens her mouth to sing—wow."

"Well, I hope she opens her mouth soon."

As much as Sandy liked live music, he wasn't crazy about bars. Especially a bar this packed and smoky and hot. Wasn't the AC working? None of which helped his lousy mood. He was hoping loud music and Beth's company would help him forget a strike-out day.

He hadn't been able to track down the police commissioner, but had cornered the mayor at a fundraising luncheon. He'd ducked Sandy's questions, rambling on about how it was a complex issue and how he'd have to know the details of the crime and run it past the Corporation Counsel and maybe a few judges. Yadda-yadda-yadda. Not much to write about there.

He checked his cell phone to make sure it was on. Yeah, it was, and no new calls. This sucked. Totally.

"Hey, Palmer," Pokorny said. "That's like the fifth time you've checked that phone since we got here. What's up? Expecting another call from the Savior?"

Sandy yielded to an instant of shock, then forced a laugh. "Yeah, right."

Truth was he'd placed two calls to the Savior today, and neither had been answered. Was the guy going to stiff him now?

A girl with lime Kool-Aid hair must have overheard Pokorny's Savior remark. She was leaning back from the bar, craning for a look at Sandy.

"It's you!" she said, her eyes widening with recognition. "You're the guy from the paper, aren't you. The one who was talking to the Savior."

Sandy shrugged, embarrassment and heart-singing joy tugging him in different directions.

"Damn right he is," Pokorny said. "That's Sandy Palmer himself, ace reporter and subway survivor."

Pokorny's sarcasm was lost on the green-haired girl who turned excitedly to her friend. "Kim! Kim! Look who's here! It's that reporter from the subway, the one who talked to the Savior!"

In less than a minute—less than half a minute—Sandy found himself with his back to the bar, enclosed in a tight, steadily thickening semicircle of men and women, all about his age. Pokorny and Alissa were been quickly elbowed out of the way but Sandy kept his arm around Beth's shoulder. This was a little scary.

They started asking him questions, general ones at first—what was it like, how did he feel, tell us how it really went down—then moving on to specifics like how much blood there was and what the Savior's voice was like and what kind of gun had he used. He pretended he hadn't heard that one.

He'd covered all this in his articles and lots of these people seemed to have read them, but that didn't matter. They wanted to hear him tell it, listen to him speak the words. Straight from the horse's mouth, so to speak.

And Sandy gladly obliged.

He felt a tap on his shoulder. When he turned, the bartender shoved a Bass Ale into his hand.

"On the house, mac."

And that started a flood of freebies as other people started buying him beers. But he didn't need alcohol. The recognition, the instant acceptance, the sea of rapt faces hanging onto his every word already had him higher than a kite.

This is what it can be like, he thought. Everywhere I go—*Right this way, Mr. Palmer. Never mind the line there, we'll have a table ready for you in a moment. Meanwhile, we're chilling a bottle of champagne for you now, compliments of the house.*

It's like a drug, he thought. No, it *is* a drug; a truly bodacious high. And I can see why people get hooked on it. Because there's nothing better than this. Nothing.

And then it occurred to him that Beth had been on the train too. She deserved a little attention. And he wasn't greedy. He could share the spotlight.

The question was, did Beth want this known?

What a question. How could she not?

He raised his hand and pulled her closer. "I'd like to introduce Beth Abrams. We met on the train that night and we've hardly been apart since, which proves that even the darkest cloud can have a silver lining."

The burst of applause and cheers, and the grins from the encircling crowd swept over him in a warm wave. He glanced at Beth and found her smiling up at him.

"That was sweet," she said.

She leaned toward him and they kissed, sending the crowd into another outburst of whoops.

"We're a hit," he said into her ear as he hugged her. "Maybe we should get an act together and take it on the road."

He was only partly kidding. If he could feel just one tenth of this every night . . .

Another tap on his shoulder. He turned and found a fellow about his age but all in black with a closely shaved head and a stud through his left eyebrow.

"Anytime you want to ditch this scene," he said in a low voice, "let me know."

"I don't get you."

"I'm talking about going some place very cool."

"This seems pretty cool." At least at the moment. Certainly a lot cooler now than when he'd arrived.

"This is nothing. I'm talking about a club. An exclusive club."

"Exclusive, huh?" He didn't have much money on him. The cover here had been only five bucks. In some of those clubs, "exclusive" was just a euphemism for overpriced-up-the-wazoo. "What's it called?"

"It's not called anything. I'm talking about a place so exclusive it doesn't even have a name. Doesn't need one."

"I don't know . . ."

"Don't worry. I can get you in. You'll be my guest. I think the regulars would like to meet you and your lady."

"Who might these regulars be?"

"Big names who wouldn't want me talking about them. But you've heard of them—everybody has. We're talking household names. You've seen their faces on the screen—the big one, not the little one. And if not their faces, then you've seen their names in big letters. You don't look like the fashion magazine type, but if you check out the Victoria's Secret catalog now and then you've seen some of the ladies' bodies."

Sandy had heard of such places: celebrity hangs for supermodels and movie people—stars, directors, producers—who wanted a place where they wouldn't be ogled and hounded for autographs.

And this guy's inviting me. Me! Shit, I don't believe this!

"All right," Sandy drawled with maximum cool. "I suppose we can check it out." He turned to Beth. "Come on. We're leaving."

"Where are we going?"

"A special place where we can have a little peace and quiet."

"Okay by me. I'll find Jay and Alissa and—"

"They're not invited. Just us."

"You think that's right?"

The truth was, he hadn't thought about it.

"Believe me, Beth, you'll want to be in this place."

"Fine, but the least we can do is say good-bye. I'll go find them."

As he watched her thread through the thicket of people, he thought, I'm out on the town with my conscience.

Which, all things considered, probably wasn't such a bad thing.

15

She thought she'd fallen asleep, but now Kate is up and walking.

She's outside. Where? Somehow she left Jack's and is walking the street. But not Jack's street. It's much wider, with houses instead of brownstones. She's in Queens, in a place called Middle Village.

Somehow she knows that. But how? She knows nothing of Queens.

She feels a buzz of anticipation as she turns up the walk toward one of the houses. It's dark on the first floor, with a single window lit on the second. Up the three steps, across the front porch, she reaches her hand toward the bell—

No! That's not her hand! It's too big, the fingers too thick. And she doesn't own a ring that looks anything like—

She knows that ring. She saw it on Holdstock's hand. But how did she get it? And what's happened to her hands? She watches as one of them pushes the bell button, not with a fingertip but with a knuckle. Strange way to ring. And what is this undercurrent of dread she senses?

The door opens then and it's Dr. Fielding standing behind the screen.

"Terrence," he says. "What a surprise."

Terrence? Isn't that Holdstock's first name?

"I hope I'm not disturbing you, Doctor," she hears herself say in Holdstock's voice, "but I need your help."

"Come in, come in," Fielding says, pushing open the screen door. "As a matter of fact, I could use your help too. Maybe we can help each other."

As she follows him inside, kicking the door closed behind her, she begins to realize what this is: another one of those surreal dreams she's been having. What's the symbolism here? What conflict is her unconscious trying to resolve?

Then she sees it: Because he was the first to be infected, Holdstock represents the leadership of the Unity. She's terrified by the Unity's invasion of her mind and body, so her subconscious is dealing with that by turning the tables and portraying her as having invaded Holdstock's.

But understanding doesn't release her from the dream's iron grip. She's simply going to have to ride it out.

Fielding is leading the way. "Let's go to my study where we can talk."

Her dread increases as she closes on Fielding's back, fumbling in her—Holdstock's—coat pocket and withdrawing a slim wire with a wooden handle on each end. Although she's never seen one, Kate knows it's a garrote. And she knows that Holdstock made it himself this afternoon, spending an hour drilling a midpoint hole through each of two short lengths of doweling, threading electrical wire through, winding it around and around and triple-knotting it.

Kate from the outset disliked this dream, and hates it now, but she can't stop Holdstock from crossing his wrists and looping the wire over the unsuspecting Doctor's head, from wrenching back on those handles and cinching the wire tight around Fielding's throat, from twisting the wire against the nape of his neck to lock it in place.

A grunt from Fielding as he claws at his throat and tries to turn but she—Holdstock—she—Holdstock—dear Lord, she can't be sure— keeps a relentless grip on the handles and stays behind the frantically struggling doctor. She can see half of his panicked, wide-mouthed face as it darkens toward blue, see one of his baffled, bulging, blood-engorged eyes as it pleads for mercy, for air, for life.

And Kate wants to scream but she's mute, tries to loosen her grip on those handles but cannot.

And now Fielding is kicking and spasming and clawing and twisting madly, slamming the both of them against the dining room table, doing anything within his fading power to break free, but Holdstock's body outweighs his by at least fifty pounds and Kate uses that to hang on, a homicidal rodeo rider on a doomed horse.

Stop it! Oh, dear God, let the poor man go!

But her cries are silent, her pleas unheeded.

And now Fielding's legs give way and he drops to his knees. Kate goes with him, directly behind, maintaining her relentless tension on the wire. His frantic movements slow, his body sags to the side. But Kate stays with him all the way to the floor, never letting up, shoving him onto his face and jamming her knees into his back and hanging on through the terminal spasms as the cells in Fielding's oxygen-starved brain and myocardium fire randomly, agonally, and then finally, not at all.

A stink fills the air as Fielding's sphincters relax. That's the sign she's been waiting for. Kate unwinds the wire and pulls it free. She jumps as Fielding sighs—a flat, atonal sound. But it's only the trapped air in his lungs escaping past his vocal cords. Gripping the table she hauls herself to her feet.

She stares down at the corpse of what had once been a brilliant man. Her dread has changed to remorse, deep regret . . . such a waste.

Heading for the door, she stuffs the garrote in one pocket and pulls a glove from another. She pulls on the glove and uses that hand to open the front door and close it behind her.

Kate is weeping inside as she walks back down the street, pursued by regret and remorse, and perhaps even a trace of guilt that is not her own.

SUNDAY

1

"Did last night really happen?" Beth said, her lithe body snuggled against his under the sheet.

Sandy stroked her bare shoulder. "Last night? That was this morning, babe. And I can't believe it's only eight and we're awake already."

They'd stumbled in around five, too wired for sleep, so they'd stripped and made wild, wild love. Sandy didn't know about Beth, but last night had been the best of his life—not that he had a whole lot to compare it to.

"I don't think I slept at all—I mean, I know I closed my eyes, but I don't think I slept a wink. Did it really happen? Was it a dream or was that really Leo DiCaprio with his hand on my shoulder? Was that really us in that club?"

"That was us," he replied. "And that's going to be us from now on."

On the way to Tribeca in the cab, the mysterious fellow they'd hooked up with at Kenny's told them his name was Rolf—he pronounced it strangely, as if he'd stuck an umlaut over the *o*—and how he knew all sorts of interesting people, and how his hobby, his mission in life was putting interesting people together with other interesting people.

That turned out to be a major overstatement, but Rolf had not been exaggerating about the club. Its entrance was an unmarked red door on Franklin Street. He'd had Sandy and Beth wait in the cab while he talked to someone inside the door. Finally, after what had struck Sandy as more of a negotiation than a conversation, the three of them were passed through.

Through the course of the next few hours Sandy learned that Rolf's day job was managing an ultra-exclusive accessories department in Blume's where he met the rich and famous, and his real talent seemed to be an ability as a hanger-on to parlay his acquaintanceships into entrees to exclusive scenes; he'd used Sandy's celebrity as a wedge into the nameless space, a place he'd never be admitted to on his own.

Once inside Rolf led them up a narrow staircase to a low-lit room with a small bar and lots of comfortable chairs grouped around low tables. It had taken all of Sandy's will to keep from gawking and tripping over his own feet as they followed Rolf to the bar.

He left them there and Beth's nails had been digging into Sandy's upper arm as she whispered, barely moving her lips: "Did you see who was in the red chair? And over in the corner—don't be obvious—is that who I think it is?"

It was.

Rolf meanwhile circulated to a few tables, bending and whispering in ears. Minutes later he'd returned and said, "Bobby would like you to join him at his table for a drink."

"Bobby?" Sandy said. "Bobby who?"

"De Niro, of course."

Oh, shit, he'd thought. I can't do this. He's . . . he's fucking *De Niro* and he's going to see right through me! But then he thought, Wait. Has De Niro ever been trapped in a speeding subway car with a murderous psycho blowing away everyone in sight? Fuck, no.

But Sandy had. So what was so scary about Bobby De Niro?

"Okay," Sandy had said, cool as a cube. "Let's go."

And so they'd had a drink with De Niro while Sandy told the story, and during the telling other famous faces had gathered around, listening, nodding, murmuring approval and awe.

And then Harvey Weinstein had drawn Sandy aside, talking about working up a piece for *Talk* with an eye toward developing the article into a screen property. Sandy could barely speak, just kept nodding, agreeing to anything, everything, his gaze always drifting back to Beth, deep in filmspeak with De Niro and DiCaprio.

"I still can't believe I spent the night talking about my student film with Robert De Niro—who kept telling me to call him 'Bobby'! How could I call him 'Bobby'? The word wouldn't pass my lips."

"I heard you calling DiCaprio 'Leo'."

"That's different; he's my age. But Robert De Niro . . . he's a god. He's *Mister* De Niro. And he's going to help me with my film! Lend me equipment! Let me use his AVID! Pinch me, Sandy."

He did. Gently. "There. And we're still right here together. You're on your way, Beth."

"And I owe it to one person. The Savior."

Sandy was a little miffed. He'd thought she was going to name him.

"The Savior didn't get you into that club."

"Not directly, but if not for him, the only place I would have been last night was six feet under."

Sandy couldn't argue with that. A small part of him kept insisting that he would have found some way to survive, but when he took a hard look back on that scene on the Nine . . . no way.

"Do you really think you can get him amnesty?" Beth said, stroking his arm.

"I think so." He hoped so. "I'm going to try like all hell, but the decision won't be up to me."

It won't be up to anybody if he doesn't get back to me, he thought.

And what if he didn't get back—ever? A sick feeling wormed through Sandy's gut. What if he'd scared the Savior with the amnesty talk, what if he'd picked up and left town? If the Savior was off the map, so was Sandy. How interested in Sandy Palmer would Harvey Weinstein be a few weeks from now when he literally was yesterday's news? No *Talk* article, no film development . . .

"You've so got to get this amnesty for him, Sandy."

And once more he was struck by Beth's different perspective.

For him? No, I'm doing it for me.

2

"What day is it?"

Kate jumped at the sound of Jack's hoarse voice. She turned from the TV and found him leaning in the bedroom doorway with a blanket draped over his shoulders. Dull-eyed and unshaven, his hair sticking out in all directions, but he looked so much better than yesterday.

"Sunday."

He shuffled into the front room and dropped into the recliner. He closed his eyes and let out a deep breath as if the short walk had exhausted him.

"I've been sick for a week?"

"No. Just a day."

"Feels like a month."

"You were pretty sick yesterday. Delirious at times."

"You should have seen it from my side. You wouldn't believe the nightmares."

Should she tell him about her own dream? If that was all it had been, then why bother. But if not . . .

Kate shuddered. She'd been up half the night trying to reach Dr. Fielding. She hadn't expected anyone to answer his office phone at four A.M. on a Sunday morning, but since his home number was unlisted she'd tried anyway. Finally she'd pulled out her cell phone—long since blocked to caller ID to keep patients from phoning her instead of whoever was on call for the group—and called 911; she flat out told the police to check on a Dr. James Fielding in Middle Village because he wasn't answering his phone and she feared, well, something awful.

She'd been flipping back and forth between the local TV chan-

290

nels ever since, looking for some mention of the murder of a respected medical researcher. So far nothing. She prayed it would stay that way.

"You didn't happen to make any coffee, did you?" Jack muttered.

"Just some instant, but you should be drinking something like Gatorade to replenish your fluids and electro—"

"Coffeeeeeeee," Jack intoned, sounding like a muezzin calling the faithful to prayer. "Coffeeeeeeee."

"Jack—"

"I've got a splitting headache from caffeine withdrawal. This is not to feed a habit, this is a medical necessity. Coffeeeeeeee!"

"For crying out loud," she laughed, heading for the kitchen. "All right. I'll get you some. Just stop that moaning."

"You know what?" Jack said from the other room as she filled an eight-ounce measuring cup with water and stuck it in the microwave. "Fever must make you hypersusceptible to suggestion. I dreamed about your mysterious Russian lady."

"Russian lady?" What on earth—? "Oh, yes. The one who gave me your name."

"Right. Dreamed she paid me a visit with her big white malamute."

Kate smiled. That was the breed—a malamute. She hadn't been able to place it. And then with a start she realized . . .

"Jack, I never told you it was a malamute."

"Sure you did. How would I have known?"

"Jack, *I* didn't know. I couldn't recall the breed. So how could you know?"

"Had to be from you, because the Russian lady's visit was all in my head. See that four-way bolt on the front door? Nobody gets in here unless I let them. So you must have told me."

Kate was sure she hadn't but wasn't going to argue.

"What did she tell you? In the dream, I mean."

"All sorts of apocalyptic stuff about the virus. Like if I—me and me alone—didn't stop it, the world as we know it would end in bloodshed, death, hatred, terror, all that good stuff."

Kate dumped two spoonfuls of instant coffee into a large mug. Not quite the communal agrarian paradise the Unity had pictured for her. Although the part about the end of the world as we know seemed right on the mark.

"What would make her think you could stop a virus?"

"Damned if I know. That's for guys like Fielding and the government's alphabet soup agencies."

Kate closed her eyes and took a breath. Yes, Fielding . . . if he's alive.

"But she said something even crazier. She said you and I were already infected."

Kate gripped the edge of the sink as the room seemed to tilt. "She told you that?"

"Yeah. And you know what? The Russian-lady delusion must have tripped a switch in my brain because that fueled an even weirder dream. Weirdest I've ever had."

Kate was almost afraid to ask. "How so?"

The microwave chimed. Her hand trembled as she removed the measuring cup and poured the water into the mug.

"Well, the whole dream was based on the idea that Fielding's mysterious contamination virus doesn't just cause personality changes, it links all the minds of the people it infects into one group consciousness—a hive mind. Isn't that wild?"

Kate, stirring Jack's coffee, dropped the spoon.

"Wh-what? What did you say?"

Jack was describing the Unity, describing it perfectly. But how could he know? And how could he know he was infected?

"A hive mind."

Was that how he knew? During the battle between his immune system and the Unity virus, could his subconscious have realized what was at stake and tried to warn him? No, she couldn't buy that. Too New Age-y. But somehow . . . Jack knew.

Feeling a bit punch-drunk, Kate carried the coffee into the front room and handed it to him quickly to hide her trembling hands, then lowered herself onto a nearby hassock.

"Tell me about it."

"It took place just a few months from now when we're in the middle of an all-out war between the infected and the uninfected."

A war. Yes, Kate thought, that's what could happen if the virus were easily spread—say, airborne. Thank the lord it isn't.

She listened to his chilling, tragic scenario with a lump in her throat. She didn't know this Abe Jack mentioned, but she'd met Gia and Vicky and was deeply disturbed by hearing of Gia overdosing her daughter.

"I don't know her that well, but I can't see Gia doing something like that."

"Neither can I," Jack said. "Like most dreams it's got Swiss cheese logic. Like where Gia got the sleeping pills; I never questioned it in the dream, but I don't think she's ever taken one in her whole life. Lots of things got by me, and the weirdest one concerned you."

Kate felt her insides tighten. "I was in your dream?"

"Not in person. But my dreamself was thinking about you as being one of the infected. It wasn't a shocking revelation or anything like that; more like something I'd known for a while."

Kate felt as if she were slowly becoming a block of ice. "Is that all?"

"Not quite. I was thinking awful thoughts about you, imagining you returning to Trenton and using your practice to infect all your kid patients.

Kate closed her eyes and fought a wave of nausea.

"Sorry for being such a sicko, Kate," Jack was saying, and his voice seemed to be coming from the far end of a long corridor, "but that was the dream, not me. I know damn well you'd never do something like that."

But that was what she found most sickening: it was exactly what she'd do. Because that was what the Unity would command her to do. And even worse, she'd *want* to do it. Once fully integrated she'd be an enthusiastic participant in anything that brought more minds into the Unity.

"Kate?" Jack's voice, echoing from somewhere. "Kate are you all right?"

She had to tell him. He had to know.

"Jack . . ."

But he was staring at the TV screen, pointing. "Holy, Christ, Kate! Look at this!"

Kate turned and saw Fielding's face, obviously a personnel file photo, on the screen.

Jack had grabbed the remote and was bringing the sound up.

"*. . . on a tip, police this morning found the body of medical re-*

searcher Dr. James Fielding in his home in Middle Village, Queens. Cause of death appears to have been strangulation. Police have no motive or suspects yet. In other news . . ."

Jack hit the MUTE button and stared at her. "What the hell?"

But Kate couldn't speak. Her throat had locked. Last night's dream hadn't been a dream. The Unity had murdered Jim Fielding, and she'd been there, could still feel the handles of the garrote against her palms.

"Jack, I'm infected!" she blurted.

He stared at her, wide-eyed. "What? How?"

"Jeanette."

As ill as he was, something fearsome flashed in his eyes and contorted his features. "I'll kill her!"

"No, Jack. It's not her fault. She—"

"How do you know you're infected? Are you sure?"

"Because . . ."

And suddenly Kate felt a surge within her, an invisible hand reaching through her mind and clamping down on her tongue, trying to paralyze it. The Unity was back—or maybe it had never gone away, maybe it had sat quietly within her, eavesdropping, monitoring her conversation, ready to react if she intended to say or do anything that might threaten it. And now it was pouncing.

Kate fought back, managing to push the words past her lips.

"Because the part of your dream about the hive mind is true."

"Can't be. That was fever. I was delirious."

"No, Jack. The hive mind spoke to me yesterday. Jeanette, Holdstock, and half a dozen more of Fielding's other patients are part of a single mind. And they're pulling me in too. They're in my head right now, trying to keep me from telling you this, but I guess I've still got enough uninfected brain cells left to resist."

Jack stared at her from his recliner, the rage in his face shifting to disbelief.

"They killed Fielding, Jack. They were afraid he might come up with a vaccine or a way to kill the virus."

"How . . . how can you know that?"

"Because I was there! I witnessed it through Holdstock's eyes."

That odd look on his face, worried for her, wondering no doubt how someone can seem sane one day and then suddenly lose her mind. She had to convince him, had to make him believe. Because if they killed Fielding, they just might kill Jack too.

"And Jack . . . that Russian lady . . . whether a dream or not, she was right. You're infected too."

3

Kate had lost it. That, or he was still running 104 and having another fever dream. Or . . .

Or it was true.

A year ago Jack would have snickered at the idea of a hive mind. But since last summer he'd come face to face with too many things he'd once thought impossible, so he couldn't just write this off. Especially when the source was someone as thoroughly anchored as Kate.

And even if this hive mind was a fantasy, he still did not want to be infected with Fielding's virus.

He felt lousy, too weak for a long, drawn-out discussion. Had to move this along.

"Okay," he said carefully. "First things first: if we're infected, how did we get that way?"

"With infected pins. Jeanette punctured my palm and Holdstock scratched your hand when he was here the other day."

The coffee went cold and bitter on Jack's tongue. He had never mentioned that scratch to Kate.

"How did you know about that?"

"The Unity told me."

She went on to describe yesterday's hand-holding session with Holdstock and Jeanette and the rest.

"You weren't imagining it?" he said finally, shaken because this was so much like his dream. "They were really talking to you . . . in your brain?"

Kate nodded. "Not just talking, showing me images of the future they envision for humanity."

"And you couldn't block them out?"

"No. In fact they're in my head right now."

Her words were a cold knife between Jack's shoulder blades.

"You mean they're here, listening to us?"

Kate's expression was bleak as she nodded. "Through me. And trying to keep me from telling you all this."

Revulsion stirred and crawled through Jack's gut as he tried to imagine the horror of what that would be like. He couldn't. His mind . . . invaded, violated, raped, and dominated . . . unimaginable.

"But Kate . . . you were never sick."

"That's because my immune system is like everyone else's, I guess. This virus can slip past the perimeter defenses and take control before it has time to react. But not in your case."

"What's so special about me?"

"That's what I'd like to know. Because . . ." With knitted brows Kate stopped and turned her head, as if listening.

"Something wrong?"

"The pressure just let up."

"What pressure?"

"The pressure to silence me . . . it's gone." Her eyes widened. "The Unity wants the answer too. You beat the virus, Jack."

"How do you know it wasn't some other virus I picked up—a summer flu or the like?"

"Oh, the Unity knows, Jack. Believe me, it knows. And it's afraid of you. You're a wild card, an aberration, an unexpected glitch in their master plan. Maybe you shouldn't say anything."

"Listen, we're related, so if I've got something inside me that can fight this, maybe you do too. You want to test my blood, it's yours."

"I don't have the equipment or the knowledge, but NIH and CDC do—you'll be invaluable to them. But the *why* still remains. Immune systems react to invading substances like viruses and attack them. It's a 'me' / 'not-me' reaction. Anything classified as 'not-me' must go."

"I like that."

"Sometimes it can overreact to innocent things like pollen, resulting in allergies, but the basic xenophobic protocol never changes. Viruses like HIV get past by invading the immune cells themselves, eventually destroying them; but this is ultimately bad for the virus since it then leaves the host open to every infectious organism that comes along. The Unity virus has a more practical approach: co-opt the immune system and leave it intact to function against everything but the Unity virus. That's what it did to me."

Jack squeezed his eyes shut. Aw, Kate. I can't stand this.

He said, "Why not me then?"

"I can't say. I can only guess that sometime in the past your immune system has battled something similar to, but not exactly like, the Unity virus."

"Why do you qualify it?"

"Because if you'd fought off something exactly like it before, you'd be fully immune and your system would have wiped out the virus as soon as it entered. Remember when you had chickenpox as a kid? The infection left you with permanent immunity: cellular guns loaded with varicella-seeking bullets. Should you get too close to a poxy kid and pick up some of the varicella virus, it's gobbled up the instant it hits your bloodstream, without your having an inkling it was there at all."

"But I got sick as a dog, so that means my guns were not loaded for the Unity virus."

"Right. But unlike my immune system, yours got put on alert by something about the Unity virus. My guess is a minor antigenic similarity. Maybe because of a previous infection, it recognized just one or two base sequences in its protein coat; whatever it was was enough to trigger an immune response, and your T-cells declared war."

Love those T-cells, Jack thought, but why should mine be special?

"The thing is, Kate, I'm almost never sick. I don't even get the usual infections, let alone special ones."

"Gia told me you were terribly ill last summer—just as sick as you were yesterday."

"Oh, that. That wasn't a bug I caught, that was from some infected wounds."

"Wounds?" Kate's brow furrowed. "Who wounded you?"

Jack was about to say, Not who—*what*, when it all came together, whipping his head around like a backhanded bitchslap.

"Holy shit!"

"What?"

How could he tell her about the creatures that had almost killed him last August, about how the gouges one of them had torn across his chest became infected, leaving him fevered up for days after? If some contaminant from those things had primed his immune system, allowing it to recognize the Unity virus, then that meant the virus was linked to them.

Was the same power responsible for those creatures also behind the virus? Was that what was going on here? He needed more information but didn't know where to find it.

"Jack, what's wrong?"

Could he tell her? Nope. His story was even more fantastic than hers. Sound like he was playing *Can You Top This?* And how could he explain what he didn't understand himself? All he knew was that they were dealing with pure evil.

Used to be Jack didn't believe in evil as an entity. But he'd come to know it was out there—no belief necessary, he'd experienced it— and very real, very hungry.

He pressed the heels of his palms against his eyes but it didn't slow his spinning mind. Couldn't worry about the big picture now. Had to stay focused on Kate and what was infecting her.

"Just a splitting headache," he lied.

"You were going to tell me about some wounds."

"There were nothing special."

"You don't know that. Something—"

"Please, Kate, we can worry about that later—"

"But I'm worried about it *now*, Jack!" she said and he saw tears filling her eyes. "I don't want to die."

"You're not going to die."

"Yes, I am! What's me, who I am . . ." She tapped her right temple as the tears spilled down her cheeks. "I'm dying in there, being eaten alive neuron by neuron. Soon I'll be gone, Jack, and I don't want to go. I've got too much left to do!"

Kate seemed to shrink, looking more like a frightened little girl than a professional and mother of two, and Jack's heart broke for her.

He struggled from the recliner. The effort, along with the change in position, made the room spin but he clenched his teeth and held on.

He dropped to his knees before his sister and put his arms around her, enfolding her in his blanket. She was trembling like a wounded thing.

He whispered in her ear. "I swear to you, Kate, that's not going to happen. I won't allow it."

"You don't know that. You can't say that."

"Yes, I can."

A cold resolve had taken shape within him, and Jack knew now what he had to do.

He waited till she'd composed herself, then sat back on his haunches, looking up at her.

"First we need to gather our facts. How many people in this Unity now—not including you?"

"Eight."

"Do you know their names and where they live?"

"No, I—" And then she stopped and cocked her head again. "I'll be darned. I do know."

"Great. Write them down and—"

"Why?" she said sharply. "So you can track them down and shoot them?"

Her words rocked him. "What makes you think I'd do something like that?"

"I found your guns, Jack."

Damn.

"That doesn't mean I'm planning to go out and shoot them."

But that was what was running through his head. Jack rarely believed in following the shortest course between two points, but with Kate at risk, the rules changed. He figured with Holdstock and the others dead there'd be no ubermind to control her. As the only surviving infected brain, Kate could remain Kate.

He hoped.

"Don't lie to me, Jack. And I don't know how you can even consider such a thing. They're not evil."

"Tell that to Fielding."

"The aggregate, yes—it's ruthless and will do anything to protect itself, but the individuals are innocent. They didn't ask to be infected. You heard Jeanette before she became fully integrated—she was terrified, pleading for help we couldn't give her. I'm sure they all felt that way but couldn't tell anyone. You can't kill innocent people, Jack."

Oh, yes, Kate, he thought, in this case I can. They threaten your existence. A choice between eight of them and one of you is no choice at all.

"Are you worried about them all, or just one?"

"Maybe I'm especially worried for Jeanette—I've lost her and I want her back. And I know her well enough to know she'd rather be dead than exist as she is now. But think, Jack: What if CDC or NIH test the virus and discover what to do? Jeanette and Holdstock and the rest can all be returned to their former selves. But not if they're dead. Could you live with that on your conscience, Jack?"

"One hell of a what-if, don't you think?"

"Maybe. But I know this, Jack: If you do something awful to them I will never speak to you again."

And if I don't, he thought with a deep pang of worry, you might never speak to me again anyway . . . because you'll be gone.

But to save her and then face her loathing . . .

At least she was sounding more like herself. She'd regained her composure, and the moral authority of an older sister.

Jack sighed. Might as well temporize. As if he had a choice. He was in no condition now to take any sort of action. In fact, just walking himself back to his bed would be an accomplishment. He'd need a day, maybe two to get his legs back. Question was, What could he do in the meantime?

"All right," he said. "I promise, nothing 'awful,' okay? But I've got to do something."

"Leave that to NIH and CDC."

Yeah, right.

"Holdstock seems to be the leader," he said. "Maybe—"

"You have to understand, Jack, there is no leader. That's why it calls itself the Unity—it's one mind and . . . oh dear, I just realized something. I had a dream shortly after I was infected, a landscape of coins with only the tail sides showing."

"Reverse—the head is the obverse side, the tail is the reverse." He stopped as he noticed her staring at him. "I know coins."

"Okay, only reverse sides showing, so that everywhere I looked I saw 'E PLURIBUS UNUM'."

" 'One from many'."

"Yes. I guess something in me knew what was happening even then."

"Back to Holdstock: you say he's not the leader, but he is the one who killed Fielding."

"His body was *sent* to kill Fielding. He had no say. He's an appendage, a tentacle on an octopus."

"Okay." He held up his hands, palms out. "You've made your point. What I want to know is why him?"

Kate opened her mouth, then closed it. She bared her teeth as if in pain.

"Kate! Are you all right?"

"The Unity . . . doesn't want me . . . tell you about this."

"What can I do?"

Jack held back a roar of frustration, wanting to grab and throttle whatever was mauling Kate's mind. But how do you tackle something you can't see?

"Because physically he's the largest member," she blurted, then gasped before continuing. "I've got it now."

"You're sure?"

She nodded jerkily. "Yes. They needed a body with the strength to overpower Fielding, and Holdstock was it."

"Why not just shoot him or stab him?"

"The idea was to leave as little evidence as possible. No noise, no bullet, no weapon, no bloodstains. Arrive, strangle him, leave, dispose of the electrical cord and wooden handles in separate locations on the way home."

"They told you all this?"

Kate shook her head, her expression bleak. "No. They didn't have to. I just . . . know."

Good plan . . . simple . . . grimly efficient. If the target knows you and doesn't fear you, it's perfect.

"Holdstock didn't touch anything?"

"No. Fielding opened the doors for him going in and he put on a glove going out."

"Think carefully, Kate. He touched *nothing*?"

"It all happened so quickly, I don't—wait." She winced and closed her eyes for a few seconds, then spoke through her teeth. "When he rose from the floor after the struggle with Fielding, he used the dining room table for support."

"Touched it with his bare hand, not his forearm or his elbow?"

"Put his hand flat on the tabletop—I'm sure."

"Well, well, well," Jack said.

A whole handprint, fingers and palm. Beautiful.

"Can you use that?"

"Can't say just yet." Telling Kate would be telling the Unity.

Jack couldn't guarantee that his newly conceived scheme would work but, short of executing eight people, it was all he had right now. Holdstock might not be the leader, but his murdering Fielding made him vulnerable. If Jack couldn't eliminate the Unity, maybe he could distract it, and maybe that would buy Kate time.

"Can I ask you, Jack," Kate said, her face grave as she stared at him, "why you have so many guns?"

"Because I can. Because I want to. Because they expand my comfort zone."

"You're not one of those NRA gun nuts, are you?"

"No." He smiled. "Those are citizens."

"I hate guns. Ron bought one back when we were still together. He said he hated them too but he figured some day he might not be allowed to buy one, so . . ." She shrugged.

"Smart man. I don't pretend to know the answers, Kate. I'm not in the business of solving society's problems, but trying to control violence by disarming potential victims strikes me as whacked-out insane."

"Is this some sort of Second Amendment thing with you?"

Almost laughed. "Not likely. Amendments, Second or otherwise, don't apply much to me. If it's any sort of 'thing,' Kate, it's a bad-guy/good-guy thing. As long as there's bad guys out there ready to stab, rape, shoot, bludgeon, and torture to get what they want, then their potential victims need a decisive way to respond. Guns weren't called 'equalizers' for nothing. The frailest woman with a gun in her hand is a match for any rapist."

"So I take it, then," Kate said slowly, "that if all the bad guys went away, magically disappeared, you'd give up your guns?"

"Not a chance."

Kate nodded. Didn't smile, but her eyes said, *Gotcha.*

Using an arm of the recliner for support, Jack pushed himself to his feet.

"Right now I'm too pooped to argue. Maybe after a nap . . ."

Shuffled back to his bedroom and collapsed on the bed. After resting a moment, he picked up the phone and punched in a number. He'd checked his voicemail before leaving the bedroom and found two messages from Sandy Palmer, boy reporter. Jack would call Gia, let her know he was feeling better and see how she was doing, then it would be time for Superman to call Jimmy Olsen and get him involved in something more productive than amnesty for the Savior . . .

4

Meet me at noon at the bar where you were told how to find me. I need your help.

The words bounced around the inside of Sandy's head. Especially the last four: *I need your help.*

He felt light and giddy, ready to laugh aloud as he hurried up Broadway. The Upper West Side was taking advantage of the sunny Sunday morning: dinks brunching al fresco, yuppie couples herding their kids along the sidewalk toward church or the latest IMAX offering.

Look at me! he wanted to shout. Last night I was shoulder to shoulder with the ultraglitterati, and this morning I'm answering a call from the mystery man the whole country is talking about, and he wants *me* to help him out. Don't you wish you were me? You all know you do! Say it!

This was so cool. Who'd ever dream life could be this cool.

The call had been a surprise. After Sandy had all but given up hope of hearing from the Savior, the man phones and *he* wants to meet. Because he needs help.

Help with what? Amnesty wasn't mentioned. Could he be in some sort of jam?

But back to cool: that was how Sandy was determined to be at this meet. Cool. Ultracool. Don't let the excitement show, don't buy right away into whatever he wants you to do. Think about it . . . check it out from all angles . . . weigh all the pluses and minuses . . .

Then jump in with both feet.

He grinned. Yes!

He'd forgotten the exact location of Julio's and made a couple of wrong turns before he found it. He stepped inside and it was déjà vu all over again: the dead plants in the window, the dark interior, the musty smell of stale beer, and at the bar, the same two hard drinkers who'd given him a hard time before. What were their names? Barney and Lou. Right. Everything exactly the same, like he'd stepped back in time: the same shots and drafts on the bar, and Sandy could swear Barney was wearing the same faded T-shirt. Did these two live here?

"Hey, meng."

Sandy glanced right to see the muscular little Hispanic owner strolling his way.

Julio said, "You've come to give me my share of the inheritance, eh?"

"What?" Sandy said, baffled.

Julio held up Sandy's original Identi-Kit printout and waved it in his face.

"The guy you were looking for, meng! I tol' you where he was, so now you give me my cut, right?"

What was this—some kind of shakedown?

"Th-that was just a joke."

Julio's expression was grim. "You see me smiling, meng? You hear me laughing?"

"Maybe this was a mistake," Sandy said, turning toward the door. "I think I'd better—"

Julio's sudden grip on his arm was like a steel manacle. "He's waiting for you in the back."

He gave Sandy a push toward the shadowed rear section; nothing rough about it, but firm enough to let him know which way he was going whether he liked it or not.

Behind him Sandy heard Barney and Lou snigger. Joke's on me, I guess. Ha-ha. Everyone's a comedian.

As he wound his way among tables laden with upended chairs, a pale form began to take shape behind a cleared table set with a large bottle of orange Gatorade. The Savior . . . his back against the rear wall. But he looked terrible. Even in this murky light Sandy could make out his sunken, half-glazed eyes and sallow skin.

"My God, what happened?" Sandy asked.

"Sit down." The voice was a weak rasp.

Sandy pulled out a chair and settled opposite him, as far away as possible while still at the same table. Whatever he had, Sandy didn't want it.

"Are you sick?"

The Savior shook his head. He seemed barely able to stay upright. "I was poisoned."

It took Sandy a few seconds to process the words. Poisoned? *Poisoned?*

"No shit! Who? Why?"

"Let me start at the beginning. You were right to doubt what I told you about doing undercover work for the government: all bullshit."

Am I good or am I good, Sandy thought with a surge of pride. He suppressed a grin and let a sage nod suffice.

"I make ends meet," the Savior went on, "by doing odd jobs for cash. One of those jobs is bodyguarding. Sort of a freelance thing, you know? Last week a certain Dr. James Fielding was referred to me. You recognize the name?"

Sandy had never heard of the man but didn't want to look dumb. "Sounds familiar but I can't place him."

The Savior sipped from his Gatorade bottle. "You may have heard it on the news this morning: he was murdered last night."

"Oh, man! And you were supposed to protect him!" Sandy put two and two together. "Is that why you were poisoned?"

The Savior nodded. "Fielding wouldn't tell me why, but for some reason he was afraid of a former patient named Terrence Holdstock. He said he didn't have enough to go to the police, but he feared for his life."

"Some sort of malpractice thing?"

"I'm not sure. I did a little investigating—in fact I was on my way back from doing just that when our friend on the Nine started shooting. What I learned is that this Holdstock is the leader of some sort of cult."

"A cult? I helped research a feature we did on local cults a while back but I never heard of him."

"It's a small cult, and relatively new. And get this: all members are former patients of Dr. Fielding."

"Oh, that's weird. That's really weird."

"Wait. It gets weirder. They drew lots and Holdstock won: he got the honor of murdering Fielding. And not by just any means—by strangulation."

Sandy leaned back and stared at this man. Yes, he'd saved Sandy's life, but he'd also lied to him. Was he lying again? Sandy prayed not. Few things on earth were sexier—news-wise, of course—than a murder cult.

"How do you know all this?"

"I can fill you in on the how later. What matters is Holdstock succeeded, and damn near offed me in the process." He lifted his Gatorade bottle. "I tend to drink this like water. But yesterday they spiked it with something that was supposed to kill me."

"Why kill you?"

"Because I knew too much. And I stood between Fielding and the cult. But they must have miscalculated the dose because it only put me down, way down, but not out. I couldn't move but I could still see, and I watched Holdstock strangle Fielding with an electrical wire garrote."

"You're an eyewitness? Oh, man! Oh, man, oh, man, oh, *man!* You can put this guy away!"

Sandy's mind was ranging back and forth, inspecting the story from all angles. If it was true—and please, please, please, God, let it be true!—and if Sandy could break the story . . .

But the Savior was shaking his head. "Not me. I'm not putting anyone away."

"Why not?" And then he remembered. "Oh, shit, yes. You're wanted."

"Right. And as if that's not bad enough, I left the scene—dragged myself away is more like it—and didn't report it. If I open my mouth I'm open to even more charges. That's where you come in."

Sandy sensed what was coming and he liked it. Liked it a lot. He leaned forward. "What do you have in mind?"

"Holdstock goes down." His mouth tightened into a grim line. "I took on a job and didn't get it done because of him. That hurts my rep. I work on referrals and this will be bad for business. But even worse, he damn near killed me in the process. So he's going down."

"Where do I come in?"

"You must know cops. You call one of them and tell him. I'll be a confidential source, someone who witnessed the murder but can't get involved. I saw your name in *The Light* and figured you're the one to call."

Something about this bothered Sandy. It was too easy, too pat. If this didn't pan he could end up looking like a gullible fool. But why would the Savior dupe him? What did that gain him?

Unless he was crazy, a complete paranoid who'd dreamed this whole thing up.

Which would make him an *armed* paranoid.

Or even worse, what if he'd killed this doctor himself?

Sandy felt his buttocks clench. He'd better be very careful what he said right now, and how he said it.

The murder was easily verifiable, but what about the rest?

He cleared his throat. "I'm all for helping you, but I can't just call up the NYPD and say, 'So-and-so did it.' "

"Holdstock. Terrence Holdstock. Lives in the Bronx. I'll give you his address."

"Great. But I'll need more."

"You can tell them about the electrical wire garrote. I'll bet they've figured that out by now but haven't released it."

"That'll help. But if there's no known motive, what do we have to connect Holdstock to this doctor, besides being his patient?"

"How about a handprint at the scene of the crime?"

Sandy straightened in his chair. "You're sure about that?"

The Savior nodded. "Holdstock covered his tracks, very careful not to touch anything in the house, but I saw him lean on the dining room table right after he finished with Fielding."

"*Now* you're talking."

Sandy's thoughts raced ahead. Worst case scenario: This is all a load of bullshit. If so, the worst that can happen is the cops think I'm just a reporter who got a bum steer from a wacked-out source. I can live with that.

How about best case scenario? If it's all true . . .

Sandy had to grip the edge of the table to keep from soaring away. *If it's all true it means he'll be instrumental in exposing not only a murderer but a murder* cult. *He'll be all over the front page again. But more than a brighter spotlight, this new story will earn him real credibility. His amnesty campaign for the Savior will make his bones in advocacy journalism while this murder cult story will simultaneously establish him as a major investigative reporter. No one will be able to call him a flash in the pan or a lucky one-hit wonder. Sandy Palmer will have* arrived.

Harvey Weinstein can develop the subway massacre into a studio property, but Sandy could see the murder cult story going up for auction.

Hold on, he thought, reining in his fantasies. *We're not even to first base here yet.*

"All right," Sandy said. "I'll run it up the flagpole with some cops I know and see if they salute."

The Savior squinted at him. "You're going to *what?*"

"I'm going to run with it. But I've got to ask: what do you want out of this?"

"Besides anonymity? I want Holdstock in Rikers getting passed around the showers like a party favor."

Sandy shuddered. "You have to know this might mean I can't devote as much time as I'd like to your amnesty cause."

"Told you I'm not interested in that."

Maybe not, but I am.

But even if the Savior should skip town as Sandy had feared this morning, he still had this murder cult to keep him hot.

"You should be, but right now I guess we've got a hotter fish to fry." He pulled out his notepad. "Okay, let's get some of these details down so I have my facts straight when I call the cops . . ."

5

Kate came out of Jack's kitchen when she heard the door open. He looked terrible as he stumbled across the front room like an exhausted homing pigeon flapping toward its roost. She followed and watched as he tumbled face first onto the bed she'd just made up. She'd opened the window to freshen the stale, sick air.

"Jack, are you all right?"

"Just swell," he said, his words muffled by the bedspread against his face.

"You could have fooled me."

"Imagine what's left of the Hindenberg on the Lakehurst tarmac after burning and crashing and you have the beginning of a hint."

"I was worried about you."

Those words startled her, not because they weren't what she'd intended, but because she wasn't saying them. A stormwave of terror smashed against her.

Someone else had control of her voice.

The words were true—he'd been gone awhile and she'd waited with growing concern—but the words weren't hers, and she couldn't stop them.

"Where did you go?"

Of course. That's what the Unity wanted to know. It had overheard him mention a countermove.

"Out."

"What did you do?"

"Nothing." He turned his head and looked at her with one eye, like a cat. "Is this a conversation or the title of a book?"

Kate tried to gesture to Jack, to let him know that she wasn't in command anymore, but her hands remained at her sides.

"If you're worried about the Unity listening in, it's okay. It's left me for the time being."

Lies! Jack, don't listen!

"Why would it do that?"

"I think it waited as long as it could for you to come back, then had to focus its attention elsewhere."

Jack rolled onto his back, staring at her, not quite convinced.

"You're sure?"

Kate felt her head nodding, tried to stop it—and succeeded. It worked! She wasn't completely helpless. But her voice . . . she still couldn't reclaim her voice.

"All right," Kate's voice said. "If you've still got your doubts—and I can't say I blame you—don't give me any details. But I'd like to know *something*. After all, I'm involved in this too—more than you."

Don't listen to me, Jack. It's trying to sucker you into revealing something.

He sighed and ran a hand over his pale face. "You've got a point there, I guess. Sorry."

"Well, then, how did it go? Were you successful?"

"I think so. I put some wheels in motion. We'll see if things turn out like I hope."

"Which is?"

Don't answer!

As Jack opened his mouth to reply, Kate willed her hands to move, to wave in the air before her.

Jack's eyes widened. "Kate? What's up?"

And suddenly her voice was hers again. She sagged against the bed.

"Oh, Jack!" she gasped. "That was the Unity! It took control for a few minutes there and I . . ." A sob burst from her throat. "It was awful!"

Jack sat up and gripped her hand. "But you fought them off. Keep fighting, Kate. We should know by late this afternoon if my plan works. Can you hang in till then?"

She nodded. "I think so. But don't tell me anything, Jack. Even if I'm in control, the Unity is part of me. It's always there, always listening."

His features hardened. "I shouldn't have let you talk me out of Plan A, damn it."

"Don't talk like that. You promised, remember."

"Promise or not, Kate, if Plan B doesn't work, it's back to A."

"It will work," she told him, and sent up a silent prayer that it would. "Whatever it is, it will buy me enough time for CDC and NIH to come up with a cure." If they can.

"It better." He flopped back onto the spread and closed his eyes. "And they'd better. Because if they don't, I'll use my own virucidal agent. Don't know about theirs, but mine's administered via nine-millimeter, hollow-pointed injection."

How could he speak so casually of killing eight people? Could he do that? Could her brother be such a cold-blooded murderer?

Looking at his features now as they relaxed toward sleep, she found it hard to believe. She touched Jack's cheek.

"Get your rest," she whispered.

She had an uneasy feeling he was going to need all his strength back, and soon. She'd sensed something while the Unity was controlling her voice. The same background of ecstatic anticipation she'd experienced last night, and something else: fear. The Unity feared her brother. It had feared Fielding, too, and look what happened to him.

Kate went to the front door and locked it.

And then an awful thought jarred her, stiffening her limbs with dread: How much of her would remain in the morning? Would she have enough of her own volition left to fight off the Unity and go home for Lizzie's concert? Maybe the distance to Trenton would attenuate its influence.

She prayed so.

6

"They didn't arrest Holdstock?" Sandy said into his cell phone. He wanted to shout but this was an NYPD detective he was talking to. "Why not? I served him up to you on a silver platter."

He'd called in his "tip" to McCann—the only NYPD detective he knew by name—who relayed it to the Queens precinct investigating the murder. Sandy had figured if the Savior's info was true, Holdstock would be locked up in no time. But when he'd called the 108th Precinct to confirm the arrest, he was told Holdstock had been sent home and no more. Unbelievable. He'd been trying to get hold of McCann ever since. Finally McCann had returned his call.

"You should get stuff appraised before you buy," Detective McCann said, his voice thin through Sandy's cell phone. "That silver platter of yours was mostly tin."

Sandy felt a twinge of nausea. Had he been set up?

He was seated in the dark in the front seat of a car he'd gone out and rented immediately after hearing the news. He was tempted to roll down a window for a breath of night air, but didn't. After what he'd seen a few moments ago, he wanted the windows up and the doors locked.

"What do you mean?"

"Had an alibi," McCann said. "Airtight, as they say on the tube."

"Who?"

"The seven other members of his cancer support group say he was with them at a meeting at the time of the killing. Hard to argue with that."

Cancer support group? What the—? Of course! The cult.

Sandy fumed. He should have foreseen they'd band together and cover for him.

"But the handprint—"

"Was just where you said it would be, and a perfect match."

That was a relief. At least he knew the Savior had been telling the truth about that.

"Well? Doesn't that prove he was there?"

"It does, but it doesn't tell us when. Holdstock says he must have left it there when he visited Fielding last Thursday."

"He's lying. He was there last night."

"He says different. It's not like they didn't know each other. Fielding treated Holdstock, and Holdstock says they struck up a friendly relationship."

"Bullshit. When was the last time your doctor invited you over to his house? And that's not a cancer support group Holdstock's been meeting with, it's a cult, and he's their leader."

McCann's chuckle grated through the little speaker. "You're a piece of work, Palmer. You come up with this interview with the Savior that says he's a former SEAL—which we're pretty sure now he's not—and now you come up with this eyewitness to a murder who says it was done by a cult. Where do you find these people?"

"I don't. They find me. And as for the cult, I'm sitting half a block from Holdstock's place now and believe me, this is a cult."

"Don't do anything stupid, Palmer."

"Not me. I'm just watching."

It was stuffy in the rental, the warm air tinged with the sour smell of old spilled coffee, but Sandy kept the windows up. His quick peek through one of Holdstock's windows had sent him scurrying back here with a bad case of the creeps. All those people sitting around the living room, grinning and humming as they stared into space. He shook off a chill and took a tighter grip on the phone.

"Listen, detective, every member of that cult is a former patient of Fielding's." Sandy hoped the Savior had his facts straight because he was going out on a limb here. "My source says they developed some delusion that Fielding had caused their tumors just so he could experiment on them, and so they decided to kill him."

"Let's put the cult aside and talk about your source," McCann said.

"The boys over at the One-Oh-Eight are still looking into Holdstock as a possible, but they're very interested in your source. They'd like to speak to him."

"Her," Sandy said.

That should throw them off. Sandy had been expecting this and figured he'd cover himself the same way he had after the Savior interview.

"Okay . . . her. She knew about the handprint and the electrical wire. Only way she could know that was to be in the room when the murder went down."

"She told me she was outside, looking through a window."

"The One-Oh-Eight boys say you'd have to be nine feet tall to see through the dining room window."

"Maybe she plays for the Liberty. I've never seen her, only spoken to her on the phone." Sandy smiled, happy with the way he'd slipped that in there.

McCann sighed. "Gonna run that on me again, are you, Palmer? No personal contact, everything over the phone, right? Well, listen up. The guys at the One-Oh-Eight think your source knows too much, and might be the killer himself."

"I told you she's—"

"Yeah-yeah, I know what you told me. But the killer wasn't a woman. It was a fairly strong guy. So if your source is really a guy, watch your back."

And then McCann cut the connection.

Sandy hit END on his phone and considered McCann's parting words. It had occurred to him before but now McCann had brought it up: could the Savior be the real killer and trying to use Sandy to divert attention from himself?

But why? Reading between the lines of his conversation with McCann he'd gathered that the cops in Queens had no suspects beyond what Sandy had provided. And Holdstock's print was there, just as the Savior had said.

And as for watching his back, if the Savior had wanted to harm him, the perfect time and place would have been at Julio's this morning: nobody had seen Sandy go in, and no one would have noticed if he never came out.

So far everything the Savior had told him about the murder had been dope. Still, you couldn't be too careful . . .

What Sandy needed was a story beyond the crime itself. He needed to link Holdstock and his cult to the crime. And since the cops weren't doing it, it was up to him.

That was why he was sitting here. In the dark. In the Bronx.

But hey, that was what investigative reporting was all about, right?

He stared at the lighted windows of Holdstock's place, partially visible through the trees along the sidewalk. He'd watch, but from here. No way he was going back to that window and listen to that humming.

Maybe he'd be lucky. Maybe they'd kill someone else tonight.

7

Kate yawned. Tired. She'd watched the eleven o'clock news for further word of the Fielding murder but it wasn't even mentioned. James Fielding, MD, pioneering medical researcher, had been reduced to a statistic.

Sic transit gloria.

She unfolded the couch in Jack's TV room, expanding it to a bed, then went through the apartment turning out lights. In the kitchen she noticed the dinner dishes still in the drainer. Might as well put them away.

Jack had awakened around five, feeling better but still far from a hundred percent. She'd heated a couple of the frozen entrees from his fridge and wanted to know if he lived on that stuff. He'd explained that like many New Yorkers, he rarely ate in.

They ate and talked about old times, warily avoiding the subject of Jack's activities earlier in the day. Jack had faded after dinner and headed back to bed, leaving Kate alone with her fears.

The Unity hadn't bothered her since this afternoon. It had stayed in the background, far in the background, all day, as if preoccupied. Which was fine with Kate.

She put the two dinner plates into a cabinet with their mates, but as she dropped the spoons and forks into their slots in the utensil drawer, her hand drifted to the side and gripped the black handle of a long, wide-bladed carving knife. She tried to pull away but her grip only tightened.

An icy hand clutched her throat. *No!*

She'd meant to say it, to wail it, but her voice remained silent.

Her hand lifted the knife and held it before her, twisting the blade back and forth to catch the light. Her left hand stroked the sharp cutting edge, then touched the point.

This will do.

The Unity! Speaking to her. But how? No one else was here. She'd had to be touching them before, holding hands with their circle to hear the Voice. How—?

And then she knew and she wanted to scream.

Yes, Kate. You are of us now and we are of you.

No, please, I don't want this! Please!

You will, Kate. The closer you move toward full integration, the more you will welcome it.

Don't I get a say?

Integration is inevitable. Arguments are futile, a waste of time, and time is everything right now.

With the knife held before her, Kate turned and began walking from the kitchen.

What are you doing?

Your brother is a threat to the future. Threats must be eliminated.

No!

Kate tried to stiffen her knees, dig her heels into the floor, hurl herself against the wall, but she moved relentlessly forward, turning the corner toward Jack's room.

She made no sound, but her words were a sob in her mind. *Please don't do this! Jeanette! Where are you? Stop this, I beg you!*

You are not doing this, Kate. We are all doing it. Together. As one. As we will do everything.

But you're not murderers! You're all decent people! You can stop this! There must be some other way!

We are one and he cannot be of us. He is not a host, and he threatens us, so he must be eliminated. He used what you told him this morning to put the One Who Was Terrence under suspicion. He is free now but the police may return. If the One Who Was Terrence is taken to jail he could be hurt, even killed, and then all our plans will have to be changed. All because of your brother. He must be stopped.

I can stop him. I can tell him things that will make him stop.

No. Too late. You've told him too much already. He won't trust you now.

She was in Jack's room now, standing over his bed. He lay supine before her, legs akimbo, deep in sleep. Her hand reversed its grip on the handle and Kate watched with escalating horror as it lowered the point to the fourth intercostal space just left of the sternum.

We're so glad you are a doctor. Your medical knowledge tells us the best place to strike.

God in heaven, stop this!

And then her hand was raising the knife high, and her second hand was joining and coupling with it. She felt the muscles tighten, readying a powerful two-armed thrust.

No! Kate threw every last fragment of her crumbling will into her arms. *NO!*

Sweat burst from her pores as the blade moved down an inch, then paused, suspended in a wavering hover.

It worked. She'd stopped it.

This is futile, Kate! You cannot overcome the inevitable.

Really?

Bolstered, she focused her energies more tightly on her arms. And slowly her left hand loosened its grip and fell away. And then the right hand, still clutching the knife, began to sink.

I will not kill my brother.

Panting, drenched in perspiration, she lowered the knife to her side.

A stalemate, Kate. For now. Your love for your brother overpowered us, but our love for you will overcome that. It is inevitable.

Love? Making a mannequin of me isn't love!

Love has many forms. The One Who Was Jeanette fought like a tigress against inoculating you with her blood, but she was more completely integrated with us at that time than you are tonight, and we prevailed. And now that she is fully integrated her love wants you to be with us.

Jeanette had fought them . . . like a tigress. Kate bet she did. She wanted to cry. She could imagine Jeanette kicking and clawing all the way down the hall and into her room, crying out in anguish as the pin pierced her palm. So tragic, and yet the knowledge of Jeanette's struggle warmed her.

This is only a temporary reprieve for your brother, Kate. You are not ours yet, but by tomorrow you will be more so. And then you will not be able to resist.

Tomorrow . . .

Tomorrow she would murder her brother.

She tried to shout, to wake Jack and warn him, but her voice was locked. She could restrain her arms from stabbing Jack but could not wrest back control of the rest of her body.

Tomorrow . . .

The word followed her as she was guided from Jack's room to return the knife to the utensil drawer.

Tomorrow . . .

Kate was walked back to the TV room where she lay down on the fold-out bed and closed her eyes, screaming without making a sound, not even a whimper.

MONDAY

1

I'm going insane!

Not at all, Kate, cooed the soft, sexless voice in her head. **Quite the opposite.**

Somehow, perhaps as a way for her mind to escape the horror of her situation, Kate had fallen asleep last night. Or perhaps the Unity had made her sleep. This morning she'd been awakened by the sound of a door closing.

For one glittering, hopeful moment, she'd cradled the possibility that last night might have been a dream, a nightmare even more horrific than participating in Fielding's murder. But then, despite her desire to sleep in, her body rose from the bed.

Kate had screamed, a ragged wail of terror and anguish that remained trapped inside her skull as her body walked to the kitchen where she found a note from Jack.

> *GONE TO MEET SOMEONE.*
> *BE BACK SOON.*
>
> J

Since then she'd been seated here on the edge of the fold-out bed, staring at the wall for what seemed like hours. Hours of nothing.

Hardly 'nothing,' Kate. With each passing moment you are becoming incrementally further integrated into the Unity.

Even her thoughts weren't her own.

You're lying. I don't feel any different from last night.
We don't lie. We don't have to.

Kate had reins on the panic that had suffused her since awakening, but the sick cold horror of her plight was a throbbing undertone through her consciousness, steadily interrupted by blasts of helpless frustration.

She had to call NIH and CDC, had to impress upon them the urgent need for a solution, had to tell them about Jack and the antibodies he undoubtedly carried.

She tried to reach for the phone but her hand refused to obey.

No. No calls to government health agencies. That would be counterproductive.

All she could do was sit. She was desperate for something, anything to distract her, even for a moment.

Can I at least read a magazine or paper or watch the news on TV?
What for?

How about to find out what's going on in the world?
What is happening out there does not matter.

Keep on thinking that way. I like it. Because that world out there is going to bring you down.

We think not. The history of "that world out there" begins a new chapter tonight.

Tonight? The utter confidence resonating through the voice troubled her. *What happens tonight?*

Something *wonderful*. We had to wait for The One Who was Jeanette to be fully integrated, and then for the bonds of unity to mature. Tonight, finally, it will be possible.

But what?

You are not yet ready to know. When you are further integrated you will understand.

Another of your inevitabilities?

Yes! The Great Leap that will make the Great Inevitability possible.

Kate didn't like the sound of that. *Tell me.*

When you are ready. Right now you will watch as we remove a threat to the Great Inevitability.

Oh, no. Did they mean Jack?

Yes. Your brother. We must do what you would not.

No! Please!

Watch.

Jack's TV room slowly faded from view . . .

. . . and Kate is walking along a New York street. She's crossing an avenue; somehow she knows it's Amsterdam. And then with a start she recognizes Jack walking three-quarters of a block ahead. She's behind him; the sun is locked above the rain-laden clouds, but she knows he's heading west.

Jack stops at a corner and swivels, looking around. As he turns toward Kate she makes a quick turn to the right, stepping between two cars and crossing the street, keeping her face averted from Jack as she moves. Only this isn't Kate's body; the arm that swings into view isn't hers—too scrawny, too old looking.

Kate gasps because suddenly she's watching Jack again, but from a greater distance and an entirely different angle—looking at his back. Somehow she's shifted almost 180 degrees, and a distance of two blocks, instantaneously.

Then with a shock she realizes what's happened. The Unity is following Jack and has shifted its viewpoint from one member to another. She's in a man's body now—can tell from the hairy wrist protruding from the jacket sleeve before her—and watching through the side window of a double-parked car as Jack turns her way and continues his trek.

No! Leave him alone!

We cannot. He is even more of a threat than Dr. Fielding. We regretted killing the doctor; he, at least, was a potential host. Not so your brother. There is no place for him in our future.

Viral ethics . . . anyone who won't help increase their numbers is disposable.

Please. I beg you.

We need peace for the Great Leap. To achieve it we need time for the eight of us to be together, isolated, undisturbed. Your brother is bent on disrupting us, fragmenting us. We cannot allow that.

She has to stop this!

Frantic, Kate tries to rise to her feet but her legs won't respond. She has to warn Jack, but even if she can reach the phone, how will she contact him? She's seen a cell phone and beeper on his dresser during her stay, but she doesn't know the numbers.

As the Unity—the perfect surveillance machine, each component in constant contact with all others, covering all possible routes—ranges around Jack in cars and on foot, Kate screams her frustration and bangs intangible fists against the walls of her flesh prison, all to no avail. She is a ghost in her own machine.

2

Beth, looking great in an exercise bra and running shorts, put down the special Monday edition of *The Light* after reading Sandy's story, her expression puzzled.

"I thought you told me there was a murder cult involved."

"Legal wouldn't let me use it. They said hearsay from a single source was not enough. Too far out on a limb. We'd be just asking to be sued. Damn!"

"It's still a good story."

"Yeah, but no staying power. Without the cult hook it's just another murder. I need some way to pump this into something that matters."

Beth looked at him. "Doesn't the death of a medical researcher who was trying to make the world a better place matter enough?"

"Well, it matters, yeah, but—"

"I'm sure it matters to his wife and son."

"Ex-wife."

Beth shrugged. "Still . . . something like that shouldn't happen to anyone. But when it's someone who was trying to find a cure for cancer, it seems doubly tragic."

She was right, as usual. Maybe that was the angle he'd have to play for now—until he could substantiate cult activity.

But even without that angle, this issue was special because it also ran his advocacy piece continuing the amnesty call for the Savior. Both in the first three pages. Which had led Pokorny to quip that soon Palmer would be writing the entire paper.

Sandy finished his coffee while Beth went back to work on the treatment for her film. He leaned over and kissed her.

"Got to go. Meeting somebody at nine, then the DA later on. I'll catch you later."

A short, shoulder-to-shoulder ride on the crowded Nine, followed by a quick walk, and he was back in Riverside Park. He and the Savior had arranged to meet at nine this morning to follow up, but the Savior had set the spot ten blocks uptown from their previous encounters.

He'd also told him to make sure he wasn't followed. That was an unsettling thought, but Sandy kept an eye out and couldn't find a hint that anyone was tailing him.

With rain threatening, the park was almost deserted. Sandy had his pick of empty benches. He chose one under a tree—in case it started to rain—and sat down. The Savior appeared a few minutes later, and sat on the far end of the bench.

"You look better," Sandy said. He still lacked the vitality of the man he'd first encountered here, but at least he didn't look like death warmed over. "That poison must be working its way out of your system."

"What?" the Savior said. He twisted his body back and forth, doing a full scan of the park. "Oh, yeah. I'm up to maybe seventy-five percent." He slumped back and rubbed his temples as if he had a headache.

"Holdstock walked," Sandy said. "Despite the handprint."

The Savior shrugged. "Figured that would happen. His cult buddies alibied him, right?"

"Right." He explained his dilemma about not being allowed to use the cult angle. "I mentioned that Terrence Holdstock was questioned, then released, but couldn't go beyond that."

The Savior said, "You've got to. There's a big story there."

"Yeah but I can't squeeze more ink out of it without an angle."

"Fielding was strangled. Can you imagine what that's like? Eyes bugging out, head feeling like it's going to explode. Nasty way to go. I think hunting his killer should be angle enough."

Sandy had to smile. "Do you know my girlfriend?"

"Should I?" he said, doing another body-twisting scan.

"Something wrong?

"You sure you weren't followed?"

"Absolutely." Well, not absolutely, but he was reasonably sure. "Why?"

"Got this *watched* feeling."

"Yeah?" Sandy glanced around. He saw a few people strolling above on Riverside Drive, but none of them appeared particularly interested in what was going on down here. "I don't."

"Had it since I left home, but I haven't been able to spot anybody. Maybe it's because I'm still not feeling right."

Or maybe you're scared, Sandy thought. I'd sure as hell be if I'd been poisoned.

"Worried they'll make another try on you?"

"The thought has crossed my mind."

Sandy wondered if hanging around this guy might be hazardous to his health. He glanced at his watch and rose.

"I've got a meeting with the DA about you."

The Savior's eyes widened. "Me?"

"Sure. Your amnesty."

"Forget that. Holdstock and his cult are the real story. You can bring in a murderer."

"And I can bring in a hero, too, if I can get you amnesty."

The Savior shook his head. "Holdstock. Not me. Holdstock."

"Don't worry. I'm on him right after I write up my DA tête-à-tête."

Sandy waved and strolled away, leaving the Savior on the bench, rubbing his temples again.

He started thinking about his meeting with the DA. First off, just being able to book such a meeting was a jaw dropper; he'd called at eight and they'd penciled him in for 11:30. A week ago he'd still be waiting for the call-back that would never come. Sandy expected no promise of amnesty, but no outright refusal either. A carefully clipped hedge. Fine. That would be a battle call Sandy could use to rally the troops and circle the wagons around the Savior.

While simultaneously trying to expose a murder cult.

It ain't easy being me.

He was going to need some fancy footwork to keep all these balls in the air, but he was up to it.

3

And now Kate, in a middle-aged woman's body, is moving down a grassy slope toward Jack. The younger man he was talking to has moved away, and that seems to have set the woman in motion. Jack's back is to her as he slouches on the bench.

Turn around! she screams.

But no cry is heard as she moves silently forward.

A dozen feet from Jack and picking up speed, the woman's right hand pulls a long, slim knife from her pocketbook.

Get up, Jack! Move! Get up and go! Anything but sit there!

But to her horror Kate senses another part of her urging the woman on, glorying in the imminent demise of a threat to the Unity.

No! That's not me! It can't be! I won't let it be!

The woman holds the blade low, pointed toward the left side of Jack's mid-dorsal region, ready to slip between the wooden slats of the bench and the bony slats of his ribs and into the posterior wall of his heart. She's almost to him now, the arm swinging back, preparing to thrust—

Jackieeeeee!

"Look out!"

A cry from somewhere behind, a man's voice, faint, distant, but enough to alert Jack. He leaps up from the bench and whirls just as the woman strikes, but her thrust stabs only air, and her momentum carries her forward, bending her over the back of the bench as Jack's foot lashes out, catching her under the chin.

A deafening *crunch!* and a blaze of pain in her throat and then Kate is unable to breathe. It's as if someone has clamped a vise on her trachea—no air moves either way. She sees Jack moving away as an impossible pressure builds in her chest and black and purple splotches swell and coalesce in her vision, and then she's falling backward and she wants to call out to Jack because she is dying . . . dying . . .

4

Jack hurried away down the path. Wanted to run but that would only draw attention. Not many people around on this dreary Monday morning but only a matter of short time before someone spotted the woman and dropped an emergency dime.

Glanced over his shoulder. Saw she'd finally stopped kicking and writhing. She lay flat on her back now, one knee bent over the other, the knife at her side, her clawed hands frozen at her throat. Never seen her before but he could guess who sent her.

Glanced up and saw Palmer at the railing overlooking the park, moving toward the stairs that Jack would take up to the street. Must have been him who shouted the warning. Now we're even, kid.

As Jack rounded a clump of shrubbery, he shot one last look at the supine woman. A couple coming up the downtown side of the path had stopped and were pointing at her.

He shook his head as he increased his pace toward the steps. How had he let her get so close? Must be this headache. Like a hammer and chisel chipping away at the inner surface of his skull.

He'd reacted instinctively when he'd seen the knife. Hadn't been aiming for her throat. Had intended a head kick but caught her as she was bending forward. Just as well, he thought, but Kate's words trailed him up the steps . . .

. . . *the individuals are innocent. They didn't ask to be infected* . . .

Yeah, well, that may be so, but it didn't make their knives any less sharp. If Palmer hadn't yelled, it would be Jack be on the ground back there and the woman walking away.

The Unity had just attempted Pearl Harbor. Jack was not going to give them a second chance.

At the top of the steps he found Palmer waiting, face white, eyes wild.

"I saw her! She climbed over the railing and jumped down to the slope!"

Jack grabbed his arm and pulled him along. "Keep moving."

"I recognized her! I saw her at Holdstock's last night! She's one of them!"

"Believe me now about Holdstock's cult?"

"Absolutely! But you . . . you hit her once and she died."

"Just lucky. Look, I don't know the lady's name but if you check her background I guarantee you'll find she was also one of Fielding's patients."

Palmer clapped his hands. Jack noticed his color had returned and his shock seemed to be fading into glee.

"This is perfect! Just what I need! This brings back the whole murder cult angle! Holdstock's already been linked to Fielding and placed in the house . . . I can link this woman to Holdstock . . . and now she's been killed while trying to commit murder—"

"Whoa! Murder who?"

"You."

"Uh-uh. I wasn't even here. I don't exist. Forget what she tried to do. Go with the fact that she's been killed. First Fielding, now one of his patients, all in less than forty-eight hours. And what do they have in common? Holdstock."

That should give the cops reason enough to haul him in again, Jack thought. Keep the Unity away from Kate.

Palmer skidded to a halt. "Right . . . right. Look, I've got to go back. I want to be there when the cops come. If we're in the right precinct, there's a good chance the detective on the case will be someone I know. I can put a bug in his ear."

"And maybe get an eyewitness slant on the story as well?"

Palmer grinned. "Damn right!"

"Go for it. But I'm telling you, if the cops don't pick up Holdstock, I'll be paying him a visit myself."

Palmer waved and trotted back toward the park. Jack headed east, thinking, You just might make it as big as you hope, kid—if you don't get killed trying.

Back at his apartment he found Kate standing in the middle of the front room, waiting for him. She looked frazzled, her clothes wrinkled, as if she'd slept in them. And then he realized that that was just what she'd been doing. Not as if she had a choice. The only clothes she had were what she'd worn over here.

"Someone just tried to kill me," he said, watching her closely for her reaction.

Her hand flew to her mouth. "Oh, dear Lord! Who?"

"Someone from the Unity ladies auxiliary."

"What happened to her?"

"I canceled her membership."

Something not right here. Kate hadn't asked if he was okay, and didn't want him to explain his last remark. But then, all she had to do was look at him to know he was unhurt.

Still . . .

God damn this! He was afraid to turn his back on his own sister!

Headed for the kitchen, mainly to busy himself in case his expression revealed his doubts, but he was hungry as well. Not much in the fridge except some wilted veggies left over from a ready-made salad he'd picked up at a take-out deli the other night. He grabbed a couple of carrot sticks.

"What are you going to do?" Kate said. She'd followed him in.

Munching on a carrot, he turned to her. "Of course, you realize this means war."

"What? I don't—"

"I'm not talking to you, Kate. I'm talking to the thing inside you. The Unity's in there listening, right?"

She looked flustered. "I . . . I don't know. They haven't been bothering me today. Maybe they were too busy attacking you."

"So you're still in control?"

"Of course."

As much as Jack wanted to, he wasn't buying. But he'd play it like he was.

"Great. But when you hear from them again, tell them they just made a big mistake. Massive retaliation coming their way. Not sometime in the future—today. Soon as I catch a few Z's."

Shoving the rest of the carrots into his mouth, Jack headed back to the front room where he settled into the recliner, leaned it back, and closed his eyes.

But not all the way. He kept the lids parted a hairbreadth, just enough to catch any movement in the room.

Definitely something different about Kate. She'd given him a full-fledged big sister lecture last time when he'd simply hinted that he might take direct action. This time, despite his issuing an outright death warrant, nothing. The attempt on his life could have changed her mind, but she hadn't offered even a token peep.

So he'd tossed down the gauntlet. If they used Kate to respond, he'd know.

Jack slowed and deepened his breathing, pretending to sleep. After a while he felt his muscles begin to relax, his thoughts drift, his eyes close all the way. Had to be careful here. The bad thing about pretending to sleep was sometimes it developed into the real thing.

But the chair was comfortable, and since his illness he never felt as if he'd had enough sleep . . .

And then Jack was bounding up from the chair and not sure why, but his nerve ends were tingling, his heart hammering. He blinked, looked, and shrank back when he saw Kate on the far side of the chair, his big meat-carving knife raised high in her trembling fist, her face impassive but dripping sweat. He glanced down and saw a glistening droplet on his left forearm. Must have dozed off . . . and that little bit of moisture alerted him.

"Kate?" His voice quavered with shock and dismay.

No answer, nothing in her eyes, but that raised arm looked as if it was at war with itself. They had her. The goddamn bastard Unity had her.

Quickly he stepped around the chair and grabbed her arm. He pried the knife from her fingers, then tossed it across the room.

"Come with me."

Her legs were stiff as he guided her into the kitchen. He didn't know why he hadn't thought of this before.

Keeping a tight grip on her with his left hand, he slammed the heel of his right palm against the door of his microwave once, twice, spider-webbing the glass.

Now Kate began to struggle, trying to pull away, crying, "No, Jack! Please don't do that!"

But he held her fast as he punched in a string of nines and hit the start button. As soon as the oven began humming, Kate stiffened, then collapsed against him.

"Thank God, Jack! Thank God!"

And then she began to cry, shuddering against him. He held her close as deep moaning sobs wracked her body. The sound, so full of fear and anguish, like the sole survivor of a train wreck that had taken the lives of all her family and friends, tore at his heart.

What was he going to do? How was he going to fix this?

5

It took Kate a while but eventually she managed to regain her composure. The sudden removal of the Unity's influence—like emerging from the deepest, darkest oubliette into sunlight and fresh air—had released a flood of emotion.

"I'm sorry, Jack," she said finally as she pulled away from him, but not too far. "I don't usually lose it but . . ."

"Nothing usual about any of this," he said, staring at her. "Are you all right now?"

Kate nodded but didn't really mean it. What did "all right" mean anymore?

"You mean, am I me? Yes. The Unity's gone . . . for the moment at least." Off stage now, but she could sense it hovering in the wings. "But it's winning, Jack."

His expression was stricken. "Don't say that, Kate."

"It's true. With every passing hour I seem to be a little less me and a little more Unity. It's like this virulent malignancy, metastasizing throughout my body, multiplying in every organ and tissue, crowding out the healthy cells until I'm all tumor."

"Kate—"

"I was on the verge of killing you, Jack! If you hadn't woken up . . ."

Her throat constricted around another sob as she envisioned that blade slicing into his chest, but she would *not* break down again. Time was too short.

"You were fighting it. I could see that."

"But what you couldn't see was that I was *losing*. Last night I completely stopped the knife, but—"

"Last night?"

"Yes! While you were in bed. Same knife, but I won. Today was different. It was stronger." She remembered her failing will, the resistance leaching out of her arm, and an ugly, tainted part of her whispering, *Yes! Do it! Do it!* "Another twenty or thirty seconds and . . ."

"Jeez."

"But the worst part is I'm starting to like it, Jack. It sickens me now, but when the Unity's with me . . . the love, the complete unconditional acceptance, the feeling of being part of something so much bigger and more important is like a drug, and the infiltrated part of my brain is succumbing."

"But you're okay now."

"Now. But I can't spend the rest of my life standing in front of a microwave."

His eyes hardened. "Don't worry. You won't have to."

She knew what he was thinking, but despite all she'd been through, the idea still appalled her.

"The Unity had it in for you before, Jack, but now that you've killed Ellen it will really be after you."

"Was that her name?"

Kate nodded. "The Unity is reeling from her loss. They want you dead; they may set a trap for you."

"Let them."

"They're seven, and they can follow you without you knowing it. Think about it, Jack: seven minds, each knowing exactly what the others are thinking, what they're doing, what they're going to do."

"But they'll be on my turf."

"I've got a better idea." This had just occurred to her. "Get me away from New York, get me as far away as possible."

"You mean where the Unity can't reach you?"

"Yes. There has to be a limit to its range. If I can go far enough, to where I fall off its radar . . ."

"If it can't find you, it can't rule you." As Jack reached for the phone his face lost the grim expression it had worn since he'd walked in. "I'll put us in the next two empty seats to California."

"Wait," Kate said as another thought struck her. "Once I'm away from the microwave, what's to prevent me from telling the first cop I see that you're trying to kidnap me?"

Jack's hand dropped back to his side. "Damn."

"We can go by car."

"Yeah, but what's to stop you from—"

"You can tie me up." She shook her head as his eyes widened. "Don't look at me like that. Just because I'm a lesbian doesn't mean I have bondage fantasies too. I'm serious. Bind me, gag me, put me in a burlap sack, toss me into your trunk, and take me far away fast."

"You're not kidding?"

"Jack, you can't imagine what it's like to feel your soul being engulfed. Once I'm out of range, I can wait for the cure."

"Let's think this through," he said slowly. "Let's say we get as far as Pittsburgh or Ohio tonight. How will we know if that's far enough?" He pointed to the cracked glass of the humming microwave. "I'm not buying a word you say once you're away from this."

"Simple. We'll bring the oven with us. Every time we stop, you find a place to plug it in and test me. If I still need it, we keep on moving."

He shook his head. "I don't like it, Kate. The idea of you in that trunk hour after hour . . ."

The thought of being tied up in such a small space terrified her, but not as much as surrendering to the Unity.

"It's a big trunk. Huge."

"I don't know . . ."

"You have a better idea?"

"No." He sighed. "All right. But I'll need to get some rope—soft rope—and since I don't stock body bags, I'll have to find something to wrap you in. And I'll want to get quilts to give you some cushioning."

"That means you have to go out and leave me."

He nodded.

The idea terrified her. "What if the microwave goes off?"

"I've set it for the max. The timer's got over ninety-nine hours left on it."

"Yesterday they were predicting storms for today. Are they still?"

"I think so."

"What if there's a power failure?"

"That almost never happens."

"But what if it does?"

The grim lines returned to his face. "I don't know."

"You do know: I become an enemy." And I lose control. And I stop being me. "We've got to try a test. I need to know how long I've got after the microwave goes off."

"I don't think that's such a good—"

"Please, Jack. We'll pause it for twenty seconds."

"Ten."

"Twenty, and then turn it back on. No matter what I say, turn it back on after twenty."

"All right," he said, shaking his head. "But I don't like it."

"I hate it." Her palms were moist already. "But I've got to know."

"Ready?" He placed a finger over the PAUSE/CLEAR button—"Here goes"—and pressed it.

As the oven's hum died, Kate watched the clock.

"Five seconds," Jack said, eyes on his watch.

Nothing yet.

"Ten seconds."

Still okay.

And then another sort of hum, vocal instead of mechanical, accompanied by a flood of loving warmth . . . even the air around her seem to take on a golden glow.

Kate, we've missed you so. Did he hurt you? You mustn't let him do that again.

A flood of disjointed thoughts and impressions swirled and eddied around the words as they flowed through her.

We need you, Kate. Now more than ever.

"Fifteen seconds," Jack said.

Why was he counting? she wondered. An instant ago he'd cracked the microwave oven's glass door and turned it on, but now it was off.

"Sixteen."

She sensed she had lost time. How much?

"Seventeen."

He must have started the oven and broken her contact with the Unity.

Yes, Kate. He took you away from us for a long time. Is he going to do it again? Is that why he's counting?

I don't know.

"Eighteen."

How long before he turns it back on?

I don't know!

Why didn't she know? He must not have told her.

He mustn't turn it on again!

She agreed. This was too good a feeling to lose. But then another part of her, a shrinking part, cried out to press the button herself.

"Nineteen."

She saw Jack reach for the start button.

Stop him!

"Wait, Jack." She gripped his arm. "Don't—"

"Damn," he said and hit the button.

N O O O o o o o . . .

Abruptly the hum and peach-glow warmth faded, replaced by the cold fluorescent reality of Jack's kitchen.

"It got you, didn't it," he said.

Kate nodded, fighting back a tide of depression. "Somewhere around twelve seconds."

"Jeez."

"But Jack, it was the strangest thing. Once the Unity came back I had no idea why you were counting. Neither did the Unity. Eventually it was obvious you were going to turn on the oven again, but I didn't know when. We'd agreed on twenty seconds but the memory was completely gone. The Unity appears to be blind to what I experience with the microwave running; so blind that my Unity self has no memory of it once the oven is turned off. It's like I'm two people now."

"So can we risk leaving you alone?"

"We'll have to, Jack. Just pick up what you need and get back here as soon as you can."

"I can just wait till the storm passes."

"No. Now's a good time. They've put you on a back burner to settle with later."

Jack's eyes narrowed. "How do you know that?"

"I'm not sure. The Unity doesn't communicate solely by words. Feelings are a major mode, but half-formed thoughts and what I guess you'd simply have to call *data* filter through as well. I got the impression it's put the 'Jack problem' aside while it deals with something else, something it considers momentous."

"Like what?"

"The Great Leap, whatever that is. They were planning on assembling this evening for it. They'd been so sure about it before, but now I get the impression that with the loss of Ellen this Great Leap doesn't seem quite as inevitable as they'd thought. I sensed a lot of confusion."

"Okay, but I still don't trust them."

"And I sensed something else, Jack."

"Like what?"

She rubbed her upper arms against a sudden chill. "Something outside the Unity, but connected to it. Not controlling it, exactly, but . . . nudging it."

Jack closed his eyes and sighed through his teeth. "The Otherness."

"The what?"

"Long story."

"You're not getting off with that again. If this involves me, I want to know."

He nodded, then, speaking rapidly, launched into a outlandish story about two huge opposing forces in conflict, with Earth and humanity as the prize.

"Cosmic dualism," she interjected when he paused for breath. "I never would have imagined you a believer in that."

"I'm not," he replied with a grim expression. "I'm a *knower*. There's a difference."

"But a war between Good and Evil? That's so . . ."

"It's not as simple as that. As it was explained to me, it's not a matter of good and evil, it's more like an endless conflict between a nameless force that's largely indifferent, and a truly evil one that some people have labeled the Otherness. But just so we don't start feeling too important, we aren't the big prize in this game; we're a tiny piece in an obscure corner of their cosmic chessboard."

"How do you know all this?"

"Because somewhere along the way I became involved."

"You? How?"

"Not my idea. Got drafted somehow. But if the Unity virus is connected to the Otherness, that means you're involved too. Someone once told me that the Otherness feeds on the worst in us, and if that's so, I can see now how it'll use the Unity to bring that out."

"But the Unity's goal is just the opposite. It wants to eliminate conflict by turning us into a single-minded herd of contented cows."

"But before it reaches that goal—if it ever does—it's going to spark a global race war between the infected and uninfected, just like in my dream. And that's when the Otherness will chow down."

The faces of Kevin and Lizzie loomed before her. "We've got to stop it . . . them."

"I know. And the first step is to put you out of range. Once you're safe, we stop playing defense."

He dragged a chair in from his front room.

"Here. Might as well be comfortable while I'm running my errands." He started for the door, then turned. "I'm locking the door. If anyone knocks, it's not me, so don't budge from that spot. I'll be back as soon as I can. Don't go away."

"Very funny."

After the door closed, she heard the multiple latches snap closed. Then she was alone with the humming microwave . . . and through the open windows in the front room . . . was that a rumble of distant thunder?

6

"I don't see how that's any of your business," the man told Sandy and stepped back to shut his front door.

Sandy put out a hand to stop it. "You know, don't you, that he was picked up for questioning about a murder in Queens?" he said quickly.

The door stopped, then opened wider.

That always got them.

Back in Pelham Parkway for the second time in as many days, Sandy had been knocking on doors up and down Holdstock's block, trying to get a handle on what the neighbors knew about his cult. Not much, it turned out. The few who were home on a Monday afternoon were suspicious and reluctant to talk, but tended to open up when they learned that the police were interested in their neighbor as well.

"You don't say?" the man said, stepping forward again.

"Yes. That was yesterday. And today a member of a group that meets in his house was found murdered in Riverside Park."

"No kidding?" He scratched his stubbled chin. "You know, I've seen a fair number of people going in and out of there lately. I'd heard he was sick and I just figured it was friends and family, or some prayer group or something."

"The police will be questioning him again today." At least that was what McCann had said. The new victim, Ellen Blount, had died on McCann's turf so now he was directly involved. "But besides extra visitors, have you noticed anything strange going on?"

"Like what?"

"Shouts, screams."

The man shook his head. "Can't say as I have."

That seemed to be par for the course. One lady had heard what she thought was chanting once, but that was it.

"Hey, there he is now," the man said, pointing over Sandy's shoulder. "Why don't you ask him yourself?"

Sandy turned and saw Terrence Holdstock hurrying down his walk to a green Accord parked at the curb. He got in and drove off with a squeal of tires.

"Wherever he's going, it looks like he's in a hurry."

"Thanks for your time," Sandy said and rushed for his own car.

Wherever *you're* going, he thought, looking after the retreating Honda, *I'm* going.

The first raindrops hit his windshield as he pulled away from the curb.

7

The rope had been no sweat—Jack had found some reasonably soft half-inch nylon cord he could use to tie Kate securely without hurting her. Neither were the extra-thick quilts—a bedding store had supplied those.

But the bag to hide her while he carried her from his apartment to the car, that had proved a problem. After searching from store to store he'd finally settled for a huge canvas duffel bag that would hold Kate with room to spare if she bent her knees. Once she was in the trunk, he'd open it and let her stretch out.

As he got rolling again the rain hit, and his thoughts veered toward the Otherness. Everywhere he turned these past couple of months he seemed to be bumping into something related to it. All seemed to start after that conspiracy convention back in April; he'd stood on the edge of a bottomless pit and sensed that some sort of torch had been passed to him. He'd written it off, but maybe that was what the Russian lady had meant by, *Is war and you are warrior.*

He hadn't signed up for anything, but she'd said something about, *One does not join. Is chosen.*

Chosen? By whom? Or what? What was happening to him? He'd shaped his life for maximum autonomy, but lately he seemed to be increasingly pushed and pulled by outside forces. Made him feel trapped, and that gave him a crawly sensation in his gut.

She'd said "the Adversary" was behind the virus. Was that her name for the Otherness? No, she'd said, *You have met.* That sounded like a person. Who—?

Jack's big Ford swerved as he realized: Sal Roma. He'd run up against Roma at that conspiracy convention, and damn near died as a result. That was why the mysterious unauthorized name on Fielding's culture sign-in sheet had seemed familiar. *Sal Roma . . . Ms. Aralo.* Cute. Just too damn cute for words. Jack already knew his real name wasn't Roma, and certainly Ms. Aralo wasn't either. So who was he, really? And how did he fit? As a tool? Or a player?

Not that it mattered now. What mattered was Roma was somehow pulling the strings that had put Kate in harm's way. And Jack already had witnessed the level of harm Roma could muster.

This changed everything. Taking Kate on a trip might turn out to be far too little way too late.

His search for the bag had brought him down to the West Thirties. Jeanette's apartment was only a few blocks away. Maybe he should swing by, just on the outside chance . . .

The downpour slowed traffic while the dark sky crackled with lightning. As he approached The Arsley he saw lights in Jeanette's windows. Maybe Holdstock was there with her. Maybe the whole gang.

Jack parked across the street and waited. If Jeanette or any other member of the Unity came out, he'd follow; if offered a chance to go in, he'd take it. Didn't have a plan yet; he'd play it by ear until one came along.

After about ten minutes a woman stepped up to the door and began fishing through her handbag. Jack jumped out of the car and was right behind her when she stepped into the lobby.

Smiled at her as he ducked into the stairwell. "Lousy weather, isn't it."

On the third floor, he pulled his Glock and quietly chambered a round as he stepped up to Jeanette's door. Inside he heard the phone begin to ring. It went on ringing. Whoever was there was ignoring it. Maybe he'd arrived in the middle of one of their seances or whatever they did. Wouldn't that be neat.

Pulled out his trusty defunct Visa card and slipped the latch. Eased the door open—if the chain was on he'd have to try another tack, but it wasn't. He slipped through, closed the door softly behind him, and looked around.

All the lights were on and he heard someone moving around in the bedroom. Sidled over to the doorway where he saw the tenant herself packing a suitcase—two, in fact. One with Kate's stuff.

Lifted the pistol and sighted on the back of Jeanette's head. He was cool, his anger confined. Here was the one who'd infected Kate, here was part of the group that had tried to kill him this morning. With her dead there'd be only six left. Maybe not enough to dominate Kate.

As his finger gently squeezed the trigger, the thought of Kate brought back her words . . .

. . . the individuals are innocent. They didn't ask to be infected . . .

And would Kate ever forgive him for killing Jeanette?

"Going somewhere?" he said without lowering the pistol.

Jeanette whirled with a gasp. "You! You're not with Kate?"

"You don't see her, do you."

Her frightened gaze settled on the Glock, then she took a deep breath.

"Scream," Jack said softly as she opened her mouth, "and I'll shoot you dead. Just give me an excuse."

Jeanette must have believed him. She paused, mouth still open, then said, "Where's Kate? What have you done with her?"

They don't know, he thought. *They've really lost contact. So why not throw them a curve?*

"She's waiting down in the car."

"You lie!"

"No. She found a way to kill off the virus."

"Impossible."

Jack shrugged. An idea was forming. "Believe what you want. I don't care. We were just stopping by to pick up her clothes. Which I see you've been so kind to pack up for her. Why?"

"She's going on a trip."

"To the Bronx for another hand-holding party? Those days are over. And the Unity's days are numbered."

"No! That can't be true!"

"Come downstairs and see for yourself. Say hello to your ex-friend."

Jeanette's lips smiled. A pretty smile. Too bad she wasn't behind it. "You're bluffing. I'll call you on it."

Jack's thoughts raced ahead as he followed her out the door, along the hall, and down the stairs.

Raining outside . . . cuts down the number of pedestrians . . . almost dark as night . . . if he can get Jeanette to the car maybe he can clock her on the head.

Trouble was, the Glock was mostly polymer, and didn't double well as a sap. But it was the best he had.

And once he had her, then what? Take her to Holdstock's? Pick him up too? That sounded like a plan. Start collecting members of the Unity in his trunk.

Collect them all! as the TV ads used to say.

But would that help?

Only one way to find out.

She paused at the apartment house entrance. Lightning still strobed the street but the downpour had died to a drizzle, prompting a few more pedestrians to brave the pavements.

Jack cursed silently. A lot of potential witnesses. Too many perhaps. Could he risk it? He'd have to play it by ear and decide when the moment came.

He pointed to his car across the street. "There. Kate's in the passenger seat. See her?"

Jeanette squinted though the gloom, then shook her head.

"Come on," Jack said, taking her arm and leading her onto the sidewalk. "Say hello."

He had her in the street, ready to cross, when headlights from a passing cab made it clear Jack's car was empty.

Jeanette pulled away and began screaming. "Rape! Rape!" She backed toward the curb, pointing a finger at Jack. "Stop him! Don't let him touch me!"

Up and down the block heads turned, looking their way. Feeling as if he were in a spotlight, Jack sidled across the street through a break in traffic.

"If you want us, you know where to find us," she said in a lower voice, then started running away, screaming again. "Rape! He tried to rape me!"

Keeping his head down, Jack turned and walked in the other direction. He went around the block. The rain picked up again and he was soaked by the time he returned to his car. He got in and pulled away.

Seemed to Jack like the Unity had issued a challenge. He'd accept it. But first he'd need a few supplies.

He headed uptown, toward Abe's.

8

Despite all the houses slipping by on either side, hundreds of them, Sandy felt like he was in the middle of nowhere. Maybe because most of the houses looked empty.

He knew he was somewhere at the Jersey shore, but that was all he knew. He'd heard of it—couldn't listen to much Springsteen without hearing of the Jersey shore—but had never been here.

He'd been following Terry—somewhere along the way he'd started calling Holdstock by his first name—for an hour and a half now: across the George Washington Bridge, down the Turnpike to the Parkway, and now along this spit of land with a bay—Barnegat?—to the right and ocean dunes far to the left across the wide, house-choked island that separated the north- and southbound lanes. They didn't waste a square inch of buildable space around here.

Right now he and Terry made up half of the cars on the road.

The whole area would probably be jumping come the weekend, and every day after July Fourth, but at the moment it had the pre-season lonelies.

What's this all about, Terry? Where are we going? Another murder, perhaps?

Part of him hoped yes, but another part prayed no. Because if he saw a killing about to go down he'd have to do something about it, wouldn't he? He couldn't just stand and watch it happen, then report it later. Like the Savior had said after he'd clobbered that purse snatcher: to do nothing would make him an accomplice.

But this Holdstock was a hefty guy, and Sandy a featherweight. He thought of the Savior's little Semmerling and wished he had something like it.

Maybe he's just going to plot his next murder, check out his intended victim. That I can handle.

Sandy called his apartment for the fourth time. On the last three his voicemail had picked up but he hadn't left a message. This time Beth answered.

"I'm glad you called," she told him. "I expected you back by now. Where are you?"

"Believe it or not, the Jersey Shore. A last-minute assignment."

"Not that murder cult thing, I hope."

He didn't want to worry her. "Something entirely different. But I won't make it home for dinner."

"Aw, and I just got in the fixings for my world famous bean burritos. How late are you going to be?"

"Not sure."

"Whatever. I'll wait up."

"You will?"

"Sure."

Someone to wait up for you . . . how great was—

He'd just passed a sign that said WELCOME TO OCEAN BEACH, NJ and now the blinker on Terry's Honda was flashing a left.

"Oops, gotta go," he said, poising his thumb over the END button. "Call you when I'm on my way back."

Sandy couldn't follow the car into the same turn—Terry would guess he was being followed—so he cruised past to the next left, then gunned across the inhabited median to the northbound lanes.

Sandy groaned as he saw the Honda turn north again. Was it heading back to the city?

What's going on? he thought. Is this all some wild goose chase?

But his sinking feelings reversed when he saw the Honda make a quick right onto one of the residential streets.

Sandy grinned. Looked like Terry Holdstock had reached his destination.

9

Kate sat on the kitchen floor, hugging her knees, her back against a cabinet. She'd been unable to get comfortable on the chair Jack had left her; this was better. She was listening to the storm and wondering about the future—if she had a future—and whether she'd ever see Kevin and Elizabeth again—

Oh, dear Lord! Lizzie's recital! It starts in less than two hours! I'll miss it!

She pawed through her shoulder bag for her cell phone but when she found it, the battery was dead. And the charger was at Jeanette's. She leaped to her feet and was reaching for Jack's kitchen phone when it began to ring. She snatched it up.

"How's it going, Kate?" Jack's voice.

"As well as can be expected." She didn't want to go into the recital business. How would Lizzie ever forgive her?

"The storm had me worried. I thought I'd give a call."

"Aren't you a good brother. So far, so good."

"Do me a favor, will you? Hold the phone up to the microwave."

"Are you serious?"

"I just want to know it's still running."

She did as requested.

"Satisfied?"

"At least now I know I'm talking to my sister. The other reason I called is I ran into Jeanette at her place."

"Jack, you didn't—"

"She got away. But she gave me an idea. If they're all gathering at Holdstock's, I might be able to work something that will give you a little more breathing room."

"What?"

"I'd rather not say. Not because you'll object to it—"

"But because you don't want the Unity to know."

"Well, yeah."

"It's safe, Jack. I know from experience the Unity has no idea what's going on while the microwave is running."

"I'd still rather keep it to myself. But I'll call you as soon as I get it done—if I get it done."

"Okay." She was unhappy not knowing but she didn't see that she had much choice. "In the meantime I have to call home and my cell phone's dead. Okay if I use yours?"

"Call away. Talk to you later."

Kate cut the connection and immediately began dialing Ron's number. They wouldn't have left yet. How was she ever going to explain this to Lizzy? What could she say to—

An ear-numbing crash of thunder shook the kitchen and the lights went out.

"Oh, no!" Panic spiked Kate's heart as she jumped to her feet in the suddenly dark kitchen. "Oh please, God, *no!*"

Twelve seconds before the Unity seized her again—and she couldn't see the clock. What could she do? She couldn't think, couldn't—

The overhead fluorescents flickered, almost died, then returned to full brightness.

Yes!

But the microwave remained off. Kate all but leaped on it. The clock display was blinking *12:00*. Never mind that. The timer buttons. Her trembling fingers found the numerical pad. Press them, jab them, stab them, any numbers, just get it going again: 8-8-8-8. Now START. Find START. There!

As her fingertip darted toward it—

The hum.

The warmth.

The glow.

The Voice.

Kate! You're still there? Tonight you must—

And then she hit the START button. If her finger had not already been on it, she might not have pressed it. Might never have tried.

As the oven hummed to life, Kate sagged against the counter, weak with relief. She sobbed. Once.

Too close. More unsettling was how quickly the Unity had gripped her. Kate hadn't been watching a clock but she was sure the oven had been off less than twelve seconds. Which could mean only one thing: she was becoming further integrated. The Unity's contact might be broken by the microwaves, but the virus was still doing its nasty work inside her head, invading more and more of her brain cells.

I'm lost, she thought. Without a cure, I'll be gone.

What had the Unity said? *You're still there?* It had sounded surprised. And pleased.

Kate closed her eyes and tried to sift through the residue that had seeped through with the words. Why surprised? And then she knew: Jack had lied to the Unity about her whereabouts. It must have thought he'd locked her away somewhere.

She realized with a start that it was glad to know where she was because it probably was sending someone for her. Not too much to worry about if they were. No one without a power saw and a sledgehammer was getting through Jack's front door.

And then she realized that the Unity had lied to Jack, sending him in the wrong direction. They weren't meeting at Holdstock's as originally planned. They needed a set amount of time in close contact for the Great Leap, and it had been decided—whether by them or for them, Kate couldn't be sure—to find an isolated location where they would not be interrupted. Or disrupted. Holdstock had become the object of further police interrogation, might even face incarceration—the thought of losing another member before the Great Leap terrified the Unity. Luckily they'd found the perfect spot, a place owned by another member. The exact location hadn't yet come through . . . all Kate could glean was something about "Joyce's rental property" . . .

But the word *tonight* . . . so laden with emotion . . . mostly anticipation about the Great Leap, but concern as well . . . and something
new there . . .

Kate closed her eyes, took a few deep breaths, and tried to relax
enough to let the residue seep to the surface where she could see it.

Slowly it came . . . tonight . . . the Great Leap . . . a mutation.

"Dear Lord!" she cried aloud.

Tonight the virus would mature enough to change itself, mutate
within all the members into an airborne strain.

And then the plan goes into motion: As soon as the mutation is
complete, all the members of the Unity will fan out to the transportation
hubs—Grand Central Station, Penn Station, La Guardia, JFK, and New-
ark airports—where they'll go from gate to gate, especially targeting
the international terminals, coughing, sneezing, touching, spreading the
virus far and wide. They will continue this day after day, week after
week, until the Unity has worldwide scope.

And from there it's a simple matter of geometrical progression.
Jack's nightmare will become reality . . . starting tonight.

She had to tell Jack! Had to stop them!

Kate picked up the phone from where she'd dropped it, then realized she had no idea of how to reach him. And even if she did, what
could she tell him? All she knew was that the Unity would gather at
"Joyce's rental property" . . . but where was that?

She did know the Unity wanted to bring her there.

And she also knew now that she could not outrun it. Distance meant
nothing. It wasn't like an FM signal where once you passed over the
horizon you lost reception. Once it got its hooks into you it always knew
where you were and what you were doing and thinking. Because you
were part of it. Just like putting your hand behind your back: it's out
of sight but you still know where it is and what it's doing.

Only microwaves interfered with the connection, and only tempo-
rarily. What would happen if she stayed by the microwave oven tonight?
Would her virus mutate anyway? She sensed it would not. But if not
now, then surely later.

And then she'd be like the rest, traveling around, spreading the
virus . . . going back home to infect Kevin and Elizabeth . . .

No! She would not be part of that.

She'd kill herself first.

But would that change anything in the long run? She was surprised how willing she was to die rather than spread this virus. But all she'd accomplish was the death of the only person not integrated into the Unity who knew what was going to happen tonight. The Unity would go on, the virus would mutate without her, and Kevin, Lizzie, the whole world would be sucked into her hell.

She couldn't allow that, had to stop them, was ready to die trying, but had no idea what to do.

With cold terror weighing upon her, she slid back to the floor and sat hugging her knees to her chest.

Please call back, Jack. You'll know what to do, I know you will.

10

Sandy peered around the corner of one of the plywood-box bungalows that were stacked up and down these sandy lanes like Monopoly houses. Luckily they were mostly empty; probably occupied during the summer and that was it. With barely a few yards of gravel and sand separating the houses, hiding places were scarce.

He'd parked near the end of a parallel street where he could hear the surf rumbling on the far side of the dunes. He'd moved between the bungalows until he found Holdstock's car parked in front of a bright yellow box, distinguishable from its neighbors only by its color. He'd been about to move closer when Terry emerged with a heavyset brunette built like a Rottweiler and the two had driven off in her car. Sandy had run back to his car to follow, but by the time he'd reached the highway they were out of sight. Since Terry had left his own car behind, Sandy had decided to wait.

Good thing, too. A few minutes ago the pair had returned with grocery bags.

Do I risk it? Sandy wondered as he eyed a lighted window on the east side of the tiny house, the only lighted window in sight. With the neighborhood so deserted, who'd know? Besides, nothing ventured, nothing gained.

He wished he'd brought a jacket, though. The salty breeze flowing over the dunes blew cool and damp. Faint flashes from the storm they'd left behind in the city flickered to the north. He hoped it stayed up there. He was chilled; he didn't need to be wet too.

Sandy decided on a circuitous route around to the house, removing his shoes for the final approach to minimize any noise on the gravel. The cold stones jabbed him through his socks but he gritted his teeth and kept moving. Finally he reached the window and peeked inside.

Eight chairs had been arranged in a circle in the front room. A small round table in the center was laden with cheese, crackers, chips, and dips. More than two people could put away. Obviously they were expecting company.

A party? Sandy thought. Is that why I followed Terry here—to snoop on a party? But then he supposed cult members had to eat like anyone else.

Hey, maybe they were planning an orgy. That would be cool. Then again, maybe not if Terry and the Rottweiler woman were any indication of the looks of the participants.

Sandy looked around for liquor but saw only bottled water. Okay, so it was an alcohol-free cult. But was it talk-free too?

The silence was deafening. No radio, no stereo, no TV. Terry and the woman sat in two of the chairs, staring into space, not speaking a word, seemingly unaware of each other's existence.

It gave him the creeps.

Lights flashed on the street—Sandy ducked into a crouch behind a nearby propane tank as tires crunched on the gravel. He heard car doors open and slam, shoes scuffing on the stones, the front door opening. He looked back inside and saw two men and two women enter. Neither Terry nor the first woman greeted them, or even acknowledged their presence. The newcomers said nothing as they helped themselves to the food and took their seats, leaving two empty. One of the newcomers placed a black-framed photo on one of the empty seats but it was angled so that Sandy couldn't the face.

Fascinated, he kept watching. This was the most bizarre scene he'd ever witnessed.

11

"*Nu?*" Abe said. "In such weather you're out? You're dripping on my floor. Even rats are smart enough to stay inside on a night like this."

Jack looked around. They had the store to themselves. The storm was keeping people indoors, and Abe did not encourage repeat business in his off-the-street sporting goods customers anyway.

"Got a bit of an emergency," Jack said.

"Before you go on . . ." Abe reached under the counter and came up with a paper-wrapped parcel. "See what you think of this."

Jack unwrapped it and found a tiny automatic pistol. He turned it over in his hands. He liked the feel of it. It ran maybe five inches from its muzzle to its concealed hammer, and couldn't have weighed much more than a pound.

"Looks like a .380."

"Correct," Abe said. "An AMT. Smallest U.S.-manufactured .380 ACP."

"So it's not a .45."

"Right. It's a backup. A .45 for backup you don't need, especially using those frangibles you like. And it's got a five-shot clip. Carry it with a round chambered—as you should—and you've got six shots. For you I've pre-loaded it. The first three rounds are your beloved MagSafe Defenders in .380. The last three are hardballs. Whatever you need you've got, and you can use the same ankle holster as the Semmerling. Like a glove it will fit."

Jack thought of his little Semmerling and felt a burst of irrational sentiment. They'd been through a lot together. He felt as if he were deserting an old friend.

"I don't know, Abe . . ."

"Don't be a shnook. The AMT gives you more rounds and is a true blowback autoloader. No more of this jerking the slide back and forth for every shot. And most important, I can get you parts—replacement barrels and firing pins I've stocked already. Can't say the same for the Semmerling."

Everything Abe said made sense. The Semmerling had to go. Reckless even to keep it around, let alone carry it.

"All right," he said. "You've sold me."

"The light he sees—at last! Give me the Semmerling and I'll dispose of it for you."

"Can't. It's back home."

For a disturbing instant he couldn't remember where it was, then it came back to him. In the top drawer of the secretary. He'd dumped it there the other day before he'd collapsed into bed with the fever.

"So bring it when you remember. *Nu*. What's this emergency then?"

"Remember that knockout gas you sold me last December?"

"The T-72?"

"That's it. Tell me you've got some more, or something just like it."

"Lucky for you I had to buy three canisters to supply you with that one." He stepped out from behind the counter and began to waddle toward the door to the cellar. "You're putting someone to sleep?"

"Seven someones, I hope."

"Seven? I should get you both cans. How are you going to do this?"

"Not sure yet. Lock them all in a closed room or a basement and break the vials."

"That'll work. As long as someone doesn't break a window. If someone should do that, what do you do?"

Jack sighed. Good question. But he was getting tired of this problem. Tired of worrying about Kate. Tired of pussyfooting around the obvious solution.

"Better throw in a box of nine-millimeter MagSafes while you're at it."

One way or another, he thought, this ends tonight.

12

Kate knew now what had to be done. The hard part had been deciding how to do it. But after solving that—in a stroke of inspiration—the decision as to who would do it was easy. Only one person in the world fit the job description: Kate Iverson.

The first thing she had to do was get to Jack's old oak secretary.

She rose to her feet. She didn't know the effective radius of the oven's microwaves. It couldn't be far. But just how far could she go without letting the Unity back in? She needed to know.

But first she had to blank her mind about what she was planning. She couldn't allow even a faint residue to remain for the Unity to pick up on.

That done, she took one small step away from the oven. Okay. No change.

Another . . . did the air seem a little warmer? The kitchen a little brighter?

A little further, half a step this time . . .

Kate? The voice was faint, as if heard through a wall. **Kate, are you there?**

Quickly she stepped back to the oven. Four or five feet, that was it. Beyond that the Unity waited. And the secretary was a good fifteen feet away. Still, she had to reach it.

She considered running to it, grabbing what she needed, then dashing back, but immediately discarded the idea. As soon as the Unity took hold she'd forget why she was out there.

The only solution was to move the microwave closer to the secretary. But how?

She checked the power cord. It was barely four feet long, not nearly enough.

She went through the kitchen, searching cabinets, yanking out every drawer until she found what she was looking for in the very rear of a catch-all cabinet next to the refrigerator: a pair of dusty, worn extension cords.

She stretched them out on the floor. The brown one ran a measly three feet, but the white was twice that. Nine feet of cord. Another three would be perfect, but it looked like she'd have to make do with these.

She connected them end to end, then plugged the combined cord into an open receptacle in an outlet by the microwave.

Now the scary part. She'd be taking a big risk, but not taking it would be a threat to everyone she cared about.

With the female end of the extension cord in her left hand, she grasped the microwave cord with her right. Taking a deep breath Kate unplugged the oven. As the whine of the transmitter wound down she jammed the microwave plug into the extension receptacle, missing on the first try because her hands were trembling so. Once they were together she darted to the front of the microwave and punched in 9-9-9-9. She hit START and—

Nothing. The oven's display was dark.

No! The kitchen was starting to warm, to glow . . .

What was wrong? Bad receptacle? Bad cord?

She switched the extension plug to the receptacle the oven had been using before and checked the display.

The LED was lit now, blinking *12:00*, and the humming warmth was enveloping her in its golden glow.

She felt as if she were moving underwater as she punched the numbers again, hit the START button . . .

And was dumped from the warm Unity amnion back into cold reality.

Kate leaned against the counter, waiting for her heart to slow. No time to dwell on what had happened. As soon as she caught her breath she wrapped her arms around the microwave oven and lifted it off the counter. Slowly, carefully—didn't want to pull out that plug—she shuffled her way across the kitchen. When she neared the combined length of the cords she knelt and gently placed the oven on the floor.

The secretary still seemed a dishearteningly long way off. She looked around. No other extension cord anywhere. She'd have to risk it.

Blanking her mind again, she took a step toward the secretary, then another. Now she was near the limit of the safe zone. She reached out toward the secretary's top drawer. No good. Her fingers were still a good twelve to fifteen inches away.

Kate edged her feet another half step away from the oven, then leaned toward the secretary. The hum began as her fingertips brushed the brass pull. She tugged on it, sliding the drawer from its slot. Two thirds of the way out it stopped, stuck. She pulled harder but it wouldn't budge.

Darn.

She leaned closer to get a look inside the jammed drawer—

The hum grew. **Kate? Kate?**

She jerked back. She'd have to move into the no man's land between the microwave and the Unity. But what if the Unity realized what she was reaching for? Her plan would be ruined. She'd have to fill her mind with something else.

A song. For some reason the inane lyrics of an old nursery song, "The Muffin Man" popped into her head: *Do you know the Muffin Man, the Muffin Man, the Muffin Man . . .* She'd sung it to Kevin and Lizzie— Lord, she'd even sung it to Jack when he was a baby.

Kate closed her eyes a moment, gathered her courage, then leaned again into the hum, stretching her hand, arm, and fingers to the limit while mentally chanting the tune.

Kate? Are you there, Kate?

Just get-ting a plas-tic box, a plas-tic box, a plas-tic box, just get-ting a plas-tic box—

Her fingers found a plastic object with corners and she snatched the little portable alarm clock back into the free zone.

Got it! And she'd kept the Unity from knowing what she'd done. At least she prayed she had.

Kate placed the clock and its dangling wires atop the microwave oven, then approached the secretary again. She chanted the same tune, changing a few words.

Just get-ting some bat-ter-ies, some bat-ter-ies, some bat-ter-ies, just get-ting some bat-ter-ies—

Her hands scrabbled through the drawer, grabbing everything they touched, and retrieved into the free zone the two little cylinders Jack had called detonators. And something else: the tiny pistol she'd seen the other day. She placed that and the rest on the microwave.

Now . . . the last thing, the most important item: the block of explosive. What could she call it—or rather, *think* it? It would have to be good because the explosive sat at the far edge of the drawer. It had weight and was wrapped in paper. And then she knew.

She stepped toward the secretary again, inches closer this time, into the hum, into a blush of warmth, into the voice . . .

Kate? Why do you keep fading in and out, Kate? We need you . . .

Just get-ting an ad-dress book, an ad-dress book, an ad-dress book, just get-ting an ad-dress book—

Her fingers closed around the long edge of something, an inch or so thick, waxy paper against her fingertips.

Kate? What are you doing?

Doing? Yes, what was she doing? Getting something from this drawer, obviously. But what?

Kate?

She leaned back, not to escape the voice, certainly not to escape that nice pool of warmth, merely to straighten her spine because it was uncomfortable and so awkward leaning over like that—

And she was freed.

And in her hand, the block of clay-like explosive.

Kate knelt beside the microwave and sobbed. Not with joy, not with relief, but with an aching terror in her bones. She didn't want to do this.

Kate allowed herself some self-pity for a moment, then began sliding the microwave back across the floor toward the cabinets. She had work to do.

She used a steak knife from the utensil drawer to strip the ends of the wires leading from the clock and the detonators. She twisted them back together and wrapped the splices with scotch tape.

Almost there. One more thing to do, the hardest of all, and then she'd be ready.

13

Jack cruised right past Holdstock's house on the first pass. He'd only been here once before, and he missed it in the dark. The pelting rain didn't help. Doubled back and found it, and realized why he'd missed it: not a light, not a sign of life.

Alarm bells clamored in his brain as he left the car and ran up the walk. Quick look though the front windows—not even a glimmer; around back—same story. A tomb had more activity.

Returned to his car and sat dripping in the front seat, staring at the dark house.

Suckered.

If you want us, you know where to find us.

Jeanette—or rather the Unity speaking through her—had misdirected him. Why? Just to waste his time? Or—

Oh, hell. Kate.

Grabbed his cell phone and dialed. Kept it for emergencies only and was always careful about what he said. This was an emergency.

Busy signal. Good sign. The Unity didn't seem to need phones to communicate and Kate had said she had calls to make.

Question was: did the Unity know where he lived? He had to assume that it had acquired most of Kate's knowledge, and Kate did know his address. Somebody from the Unity could be heading for his place now. He or she wouldn't be able to get in, but Jack would feel better being at Kate's side.

He gunned the car back toward the Bronx River Parkway.

14

Ron answered the phone. She could hear irritation battling with relief in his tone as the words poured through the receiver in a rush. "Jesus Christ, Kate, where have you been? Are you all right?"

"I'm okay," she said.

His voiced faded as she heard him say, "It's Mom. She's okay." Relieved murmurs from Kevin and Lizzie in the background, then his voice louder again. "We've been worried sick about you. Why didn't you call? It was like you dropped off the face of the earth. When you didn't show up this afternoon I started calling your friend's phone, your cell phone—no answer anywhere. We've been frantic. I was just about to call the New York police!"

"It's been terrible here, Ron," Kate said. "Jeanette's in a coma. I don't think she's coming out of it."

She wanted to tell as few lies as possible, but since no one would believe the truth, she'd have to stretch it. Jeanette—the real Jeanette—was in a coma of sorts.

"Oh," Ron said. "I'm sorry. But you could have called."

"And then there's my brother Jack."

"The long lost Jack?"

"I ran into him here and three or four days later he becomes seriously ill—high fever, delirious. So it's been one thing on top of another."

"Sounds terrible." His voice descended from anxiety to understanding. That had always been Ron's strong suit: understanding. "And you don't sound so hot yourself."

"I haven't been feeling quite myself."

"Still . . . you could have called. Are you still in New York?"

"Yes."

"Then there's no way you can make the concert." He lowered his voice. "Lizzie will be heartbroken."

"I know that, Ron. Don't you think I feel bad enough? Put her on, will you."

And then her dear sweet daughter came on and Kate pleaded for understanding and Lizzie told her it was all right, there'd be other concerts—she'd do a command performance for her mother when she came home—and Kate burst into tears and promised that as long as she lived she'd never miss another recital.

"You know I love you more than life itself, Lizzie," she said. "Never forget that, no matter what happens."

And then she spoke to Kevin.

"I feel so bad," she told him. "After my big lecture about doing things as a family, I'm the one who's not going make it. But if there was any way I could be there you know I would."

"Sure, Ma."

"So be there in my place, okay, Kev? Be my surrogate."

And then she told him how proud she was of him, how she loved him and wanted only the best for him, always and forever.

Ron came back on, his voice hushed. "Is something wrong, Kate? You sound so strange. You've spooked the kids."

"I don't mean to upset them," she said. "Maybe it's all the terrible luck Jeanette's been having. It's makes you think of all the good fortune you've had in your life. And the not-so-good things you've done. I'm sorry I messed up your life, Ron."

"You? No, it was—"

"Me, Ron. Me all the way. You're a good man and you'd have been better off if we'd never met."

"But then there wouldn't be Kevin and Lizzie."

"Yes, there's that. Our crowning achievements." She swallowed. "Are you happy, Ron?"

"Me?" He seemed surprised. "Not perfectly, but reasonably. Can't expect perfect happiness twice."

The remark bewildered her. "Twice? When was the first?"

"Maybe ten years ago when we were still building our practices and the kids were just starting school. I . . . I thought we were the perfect team, you and I, and the possibilities seemed limitless. I'd never been that happy before in my life. I'd never dreamed I could be that happy. And you were part of that, Kate. You made it possible. So don't ever say I'd have been better off without you."

Kate felt tears running down her cheeks. She couldn't speak.

Please don't ask if I've ever been that happy, she thought, because I don't think I've ever been truly, truly happy with my life.

Snatches of happiness with the children, the hope of it with Jeanette, but true happiness had always remained just around the corner, just over the next hill.

Finally she found her voice, and it sounded ragged. "You're a good man, Ron. A good father and a better husband than I was a wife. Don't ever forget that."

"I really don't like the sound of this Kate. You're . . ." He lowered his voice even further. "You sound depressed. You're not thinking of doing anything rash, are you?"

She had to end this conversation. Quickly. Before she broke down.

"Ron," she said in a disapproving tone, "after all these years, don't you know me better than that? It's just that I've never been away from the kids this long and what's happening up here makes you confront the idea of death, and I got to thinking, what if something happened to me on the way home? We never seem to take the time to tell the people we love how much they mean to us, and so I just wanted them to know how important they are to me, and how I'm sorry that I hurt you. That's all, okay? I'll be coming home soon. Oh, someone's at the door. Got to go now. Bye."

Kate thumbed the OFF button and knelt there on the floor, staring at the phone as she fought back another attack of tears. Lord, she didn't want to do this, but there was no other way. For Kevin, for Lizzie, and yes, for herself, she had to go through with it.

She froze her emotions as she picked up the alarm clock. Its two detonator caps dangled on their crudely anastomosed wires against her thighs as she set the timer for 10 P.M. The time was a guess, but an educated one. She'd gleaned enough from the Unity to know that its new meeting place was not close by, and that the mutation to an airborne strain would not be a few minutes' work. She assumed—prayed— she'd be in their midst by then.

She carefully reinserted the detonators into the holes they'd previously occupied, then emptied her shoulder bag and gently settled the assembly into its bottom. A dishcloth from the sink covered the bomb, then the rest of her stuff went back in on top.

She found a pen and a small pad and wrote Jack a quick note explaining the pending mutation and how she planned to stop it. She wasn't sure where she was going but if he could follow her and get there in time—before ten o'clock—maybe he could find another solution, one that would leave her alive to see Kevin and Lizzie grow up and eventually make her a mother-in-law, and a grandmother . . .

But at the moment this was the only way.

Now . . . where to leave the note? She didn't want it where the Unity could see it when it took over—that would abort her whole plan. She looked around and her gaze settled on the microwave, still on the floor.

Of course.

Kate lifted it back onto the counter, then slipped the shoulder bag strap over her head so it ran across her chest. She didn't want it to slip off.

She was ready.

Then she spotted Jack's little pistol. Might as well take that too. If it related to death and destruction she wanted it handy. She jammed it into the front pocket of her slacks.

Now the hardest part: turning off the microwave. Simply opening the door would do that, and it would give her a place to hide the note to Jack. The Unity would never look in there, but Jack would see the open door . . . at least she hoped he would.

With the letter in her right hand, she reached her left toward the oven door latch but her hand didn't want to go. It seemed to know the consequences. She forced it forward—just the opposite of fighting the Unity—and let her fingertips rest against the latch.

Isn't there another way? her mind screamed. There's got to be some alternative to this!

No. There isn't.

Kate pulled on the latch. As the door popped open and the microwave generator cycled down, she shoved the letter inside . . .

. . . and almost immediately the sound, the touch, the *presence* of the Unity floods in.

Kate! You're back! And you're alone! That means you're going to stay with us! This is wonderful, Kate. We've missed you so.

And she knows it's true. You can't lie in the Unity. The loving, welcoming acceptance flows through her . . . so wonderful. Why did she ever resist? She vaguely remembers being sad, being terrified, but about what? Of being alone? She can't imagine. She'll never be alone again.

She senses the One Who Was Jeanette outside on the steps, waiting by the front door to take her to the gathering. Kate loves her, but no more than she loves every other member of the Unity. Dimly she remembers loving her in a more carnal way, but that is past.

She unlocks the door to the apartment and walks down the stairs to Jeanette. Tonight is going to be so wonderful. The Great Leap will lead them toward the Great Inevitability and she will be part of it. She feels so safe and secure. This is where she really belongs. Anything less is not truly living . . .

15

The sudden outburst of cheers and applause startled Sandy.

His attention had been drifting. He'd been to boring parties in his life but this one took the cake and all the candles. Six people hanging out for hours and not one word spoken. And it wasn't that they were mutes or deafies; they didn't use sign language either. They didn't even hum as they had at the meeting he'd peeked in on the other night. *Nothing.*

The eeriness had worn off after a while, leaving him antsy for something to happen. And something was going to happen—he'd sensed the anticipation in their body language. And then again, maybe not. A certain tension in the air as well. Maybe something had gone wrong. Whatever was going on, Sandy had hoped he'd find out this century.

But then the sudden noise—real human voices—called his wandering thoughts back to the front room of the bungalow.

Grins, laughter, hugs all around—

What's going on? What did I miss?

And then they settled down again into that numbing silence. But the tension seemed gone. All Sandy could sense now was the anticipation.

So weird. Wicked weird.

Maybe they were planning on sneaking Holdstock out of the country, or moving the whole cult somewhere to avoid prosecution.

And then he noticed that someone had moved the black-framed photo from its empty chair to a side table. Sandy could see the photo now. He repressed a gasp as he recognized the face: Ellen Blount, the woman who'd tried to knife the Savior in the back.

With the force of a blow Sandy was reminded that these innocuous-looking people already had killed one man and attempted to kill another. And here he was in the middle of nowhere peeping on them. Was he crazy? He should turn around and get the hell out of here. These people were killers and if they found him spying on them they'd kill him too.

Go back to the car, watch from a safe distance, and be ready and able to move on an instant's notice. That was the smart thing to do.

But nobody got ahead by playing it safe.

And then he remembered what Savior had said: *If the cops don't pick up Holdstock, I'll be paying him a visit myself.*

Maybe he should give him a call and let him know about this. A visit from the man they tried to kill might liven up this party.

Sandy slipped away and headed down to the end of the block to check the name of the street so he could leave the address on the Savior's voicemail.

If nothing was going to happen on its own, maybe Sandy could *make* something happen.

16

A lead weight plummeted into Jack's stomach when he found his apartment door unlocked.

On guard, he leaped through and dashed to the kitchen.

"Kate?"

Empty. The microwave off, the cracked door ajar—paused with hours left to run. A knife on the counter but no blood.

"Kate!"

His bedroom, the TV room, empty. No sign of a struggle. Back to the door: no sign of a break-in. What the hell? It looked as if Kate had simply turned off the oven and walked out. But she wouldn't do that.

Obviously she had. Which meant she was wandering around the city somewhere under the influence of the Unity.

Panic nibbled at Jack. She could be anywhere. Why? Why had she done it? He stood by the silent microwave, staring at its cracked glass. He was about to slam it closed when he spotted the corner of a piece of paper inside. He yanked it open, grabbed the sheet, and read.

And read again, his tongue turning to parchment.

The virus . . . mutating to airborne . . . the bomb . . .

He darted to the secretary and found the drawer ajar and empty. The Semmerling gone too.

She'd reconstructed the bomb and turned herself into a Trojan Horse.

Jack's throat constricted at the thought of her sitting alone in his kitchen piecing the bomb together, the depth of desperation that had driven her to such an act.

Why, Kate? Wanted to scream it. Why couldn't you wait for me?

We could have fought this together! I could have fixed this if you'd just let me!

Ten o'clock . . . the note said if he can do anything, do it before ten o'clock. He glanced at his watch: 8:05. Less than two hours. But even if he had two days—he had no idea where she was.

"Kate!" he whispered to the note. "Where *are* you?"

He spotted the phone. She'd been using it. Maybe . . .

He checked his voicemail. One message. *Please!*

"Shit!" he hissed as he recognized Palmer's voice.

"FYI: your friend Holdstock and what's left of his cult have moved their clubhouse to number seven Starfisher Lane in Ocean Beach, New Jersey. You might want to come down and take a peek. It's weirder than you can imagine."

Jack was on the move as soon as the message ended. Superman's pal, Jimmy Olsen, had come though. Ocean Beach. He knew where it was. No need to pause to arm up. Had enough firepower. What he needed was time.

The Russian lady had said the Unity would cause war, hate, death, fear, pain, and destruction. If that was what they liked, that was what they were going to get.

17

Sandy sat in his car, out of the soggy salt wind at last, and wondered what to do. Almost two hours now since the celebratory outburst in the bungalow, and not another sound since. No movement either, other than to refill a soft drink or have another cracker or piece of cheese.

Bored did not even approach how he felt. He wondered if the Savior had picked up his message; and if so, was he on his way down. Sandy didn't want to miss *that*.

A flash of light on the neighboring street grabbed his attention. Headlamps, moving toward the cult bungalow. Immediately Sandy was out and heading that way. He arrived in time to see two women stepping up to the front door. It opened as they reached it. He ducked around to his old vantage point and peered through the window.

Of the two late arrivals, Sandy had seen the brunette before at the cult hum session, but the blonde was a newbie. They greeted her like a prodigal daughter, each taking a turn hugging her—and still not one damn word!

Finally they settled down, seating themselves in the circle of chairs. When only the blonde newcomer was still standing, everyone suddenly froze and stared at her. And she in turn was staring at something in her hand.

When Sandy recognized it he damn near jumped through the window. He'd seen that tiny pistol before.

18

Where did you get the pistol, Kate?

I don't know. I've never seen it before.

Kate stares at the silvery object in her palm. When she bent to place her shoulder bag under her chair she felt something in her pocket dig into her thigh. This is what she pulled out. So small, almost too small to be real, but it's made of steel and too heavy to be a toy.

Why did you bring it here?

I didn't even know I had it.

It must belong to your brother. He's a very dangerous man. But after tonight he will no longer matter. Put the gun down and take your seat.

She does as instructed, placing the pistol next to a half-empty bowl of potato chips.

Yes, it must be Jack's. He has so many pistols—she saw them herself. But how on earth did this one find its way into her pocket? She's glad the One Who Was Jeanette took her far away from her brother where he can't find her and break her communion with the Unity again.

Kate is only hours away from full integration, and that's close enough for her to aid us in the Great Leap that will lead to the Great Inevitability.

Kate knows now that the Unity was worried that the loss of the One Who Was Ellen would impair the transformation. Apparently a certain critical mass of viral-infected brain cells is necessary for collective consciousness, and an even larger mass to implement the mutation.

Imagine . . . a virus able to will its own mutation. Such a possibility was never even hinted at in virology texts. They'll have to be rewritten . . .

No, not rewritten. Tossed in the garbage. For no medical texts will be necessary when the Unity achieves the Great Inevitability. Disease will be a thing of the past. The Unity will brook no invaders—bacteria and competing viruses will be recognized upon entry into a body and killed off immediately. Under the Unity's direction all damaged cells or mutant cells starting tumors will be replaced with healthy ones. Genetic diseases will be a memory, for all defective genes will be repaired—a simple matter of replacing incorrect DNA base sequences with correct ones. Arteries will be swept clean, bones will be kept strong and, like all tissues in the body, will mend more quickly when injured.

The Great Inevitability will translate to a golden age of health and longevity for the human race.

Kate can hardly wait.

But first, the Great Leap.

She seats herself and joins hands with the One Who Was Jeanette to her left, and with the One Who Was Charles on her right, and the sense of Oneness overcomes her. She is important, she is part of something so much greater than herself, something that will transform this world into a paradise and she is here at ground zero, integral to the transformation that will make it all possible.

The air glows. Kate closes her eyes but the glow remains, for it comes from within, and she feels a giddy vertiginous whirl as her consciousness expands to the molecular level where she can feel the base pairs of the virus's RNA rearranging into new sequences that will allow it to seek new hosts, an ever-widening array of new members, through the air.

This is an ecstasy beyond anything she has ever experienced—

And then it is cruelly broken by a loud crash, like a door being kicked open, and a voice—

"Kate!"

And a rough hand on her shoulder, shaking her—

And now she's looking at herself through the eyes of the Unity, seated with her back to the door and there's a man standing over her—Jack.

A bolt of alarm—hers as well as the Unity's—shoots through her. Jack! He shouldn't be here! She has to get him out of here. He'll ruin the transformation . . .

And there's another terribly important reason he mustn't be here, but she can't quite recall it.

"Kate!"

And now Jack is breaking her grip on the One Who Was Jeanette, and the vision changes as her contact with the One Who Was Charles is severed—

"Kate, do you hear me?"

She opens her eyes and turns. "What are you doing here, Jack?"

His eyes are ablaze, his jaw set, his lips barely parted over clenched teeth. "Do I really have to tell you?" He grips her forearm and pulls her toward the door. "Come on, we're getting out of here."

"NO!"

Not just Kate's voice—a chorus, in her head and in her ears. The Unity is on its feet, hands raised in protest.

Jack pulls a pistol from behind his back, large and dark with sharp angles. He points it past Kate toward the members of the Unity.

"Who wants it first?"

The sight of the gun gives Kate an idea.

The little pistol!

Yes, Kate! Yes!

Guided by the Unity, she twists free from Jack's grasp and snatches the tiny pistol off the table. As she lifts it the voice roars in her head.

Shoot him! Destroy him!

Someone in the Unity knows guns and of its own accord Kate's left hand slides back the top of the pistol and lets it slide forward.

Point it at him and pull the trigger!

But Kate can't do that. Won't do that.

No. She's turning toward him. *I've never shot a gun and if I try I may miss.*

Shoot!

And if I miss he'll take it from me and we'll have no options.

SHOOT!

She faces him now and her arm raises the pistol toward Jack, but Kate bends it toward herself, jamming the muzzle against her throat.

No, Kate!

"Kate, what are you doing?" Jack cries, his face blanching.

The Unity tries to make her lower the gun but a more powerful force, a surge of strength from some well deep within the maze of protective instincts in the most primitive regions of her brain flows into her arm and bolsters its position.

Let me speak! I can make him leave!

Suddenly her voice is her own.

"Leave, Jack! Please."

"No." His eyes are fixed on her throat, on the spot where his little pistol presses into her flesh. His voice is a hoarse croak. "Not without you."

She sees his free hand edging forward, his body tensing, readying to spring.

"I know what you're thinking, Jack. Please don't try it. I swear to God I will end it right here, right now, if you make a move toward me."

His gaze moves down and lingers on her shoulder bag where it sits at her feet. Why is he staring at it? Then he looks at her again, his expression full of fear.

"Kate, please. Be sensible. Put it down and come with me. *Now.* It's important!"

Tell him you'll go with him later.

"Give me some time here, Jack, and then I'll go with you."

"It's got to be now!"

He looks so nervous . . . so afraid . . . of what?

"Later, Jack."

He licks his lips and looks past her. "They'll let you?"

Behind her, seven voices speak as one: "Return in two hours and she will be free to go. You may take her anywhere you wish."

The farther, the better.

Jack's eyes narrow. "Why should I believe you?"

"It's true, Jack," Kate tells him. "I wouldn't lie to you."

"No—"

"I'm not going to let you take me, Jack." She presses the muzzle deeper into her throat. "I can die now or I can go with you later. It's up to you."

Kate sees an agony of fear in her brother's face and hopes he will listen. She doesn't want to pull the trigger. Not because she's afraid of death—she will gladly die for the Unity—but because it will interfere with the transformation.

Suddenly Jack seems to relax, as if he's come to a decision. "All right. Two hours." He glances at his watch. "Jesus! It's 9:52!"

Alarm floods her. 9:52! Why does the time fill her with such dread?

"Go, Jack! Leave now and go far away!"

Her words—not the Unity's. Why did she say that? Why this blast of urgency to chase him away from here? She can't explain it but she knows he can't stay here. He must leave—*now!*

"I'll leave," he says quickly, backing toward the door. "But I'll be back at exactly 11:52 and I want to see Kate standing out front, waiting to go. If not . . ."

He lets that hang, then backs out.

Excellent, Kate, the Unity says as she lowers the pistol.

We told him the truth?

Of course. Once the Great Leap is accomplished, we want you to travel—far and wide, spreading the transformed virus everywhere you go. He will think he is thwarting us, but instead he will be doing our work.

Kate feels extra warmth envelop her.

You did well, Kate. You turned an enemy into an unwitting ally. We are so proud of you.

Kate basks in their approval.

19

What a scene!

Questions flooded Sandy's head in a mad rush. What the hell was that all about? The Savior had said he'd been hired by the late great Dr. Fielding to protect him from the cult, but who was the woman he'd tried to pull out of there just now? His girlfriend? And when she'd put that pistol to her throat—what a moment! Sandy could tell from her voice she'd been serious about pulling the trigger. And then when all seven of her fellow cultists had spoken at once . . . wow. His spine had turned to ice.

No one was ever going to believe this. He wished to God he'd brought a video camera.

The cultists were all back in their seats now with rejoined hands, and Sandy was about to move away from the window so he could go find the Savior, when the front door burst open. And again it was the Savior, gun in hand, but this time he didn't stop, didn't say anything. Moving like a giant raptor he swooped in, grabbed the blonde, and pulled her from the seat, then he threw her over his shoulder and dashed out the door.

Sandy stood frozen, gaping through the window, as shocked—and as mute—as the seven remaining cultists. A few heartbeats ago the blonde had been there, now she was gone. All that remained were her screams, trailing away in the night.

Aren't they going to do anything? He spotted the little Semmerling sitting on the coffee table where the blonde had placed it. Was one of them going to pick it up and go after them?

No. They just stood there in their broken circle. And then, unaccountably, they all began to smile. Sandy watched the Rottweiler woman pull out a cell phone and punch in a number, heard her say, "Dover Township Police? I want to report a kidnapping."

The Savior was going to be in deep shit now! Should he warn him?

20

"Sorry for the caveman act, Kate," Jack said to the screaming, kicking, clawing woman of his shoulder, "but this is the only way."

He glanced over his unburdened shoulder to make sure none of the others was following. The street behind him remained empty.

So far so good. He knew he was still a long way from successfully pulling this off, but he had Kate now and he wasn't going to give her up.

The first part had been easy. He'd guessed Kate would have to put down the Semmerling to resume the hand-holding thing. He'd given her half a minute before going back for her. He could have started shooting but burdened with Kate he might have missed a few of the remaining seven. Better to let Kate's bomb do the work.

And right now he had to get them both away from here before it blew. In the unlikely event that any of the Unity survived, Jack would come back to mop up.

He'd parked on the highway shoulder at the end of the street. Only half a block to go. Get her into the trunk and take off, try to be as far away as possible when—

A deafening roar and then an angry giant slammed him in the back, sending him flying. He lost his grip on Kate. They hit the sandy road surface simultaneously, and then Jack crawled on top of her, as much to keep her down as to shield her.

As she shuddered beneath him in something like a epileptic fit, Jack glanced back at the fireball mushrooming into the sky, carrying with it the last traces of the Unity hive.

And then the debris, some of it aflame, began to fall around them.

"You did it, Kate!" he whispered. "You—"

Something heavy bounced off his shoulders and the back of his head . . .

Next thing Jack knew he was alone on the road. Sick, dizzy, he pushed himself to his knees, propelled by Kate's voice crying out somewhere behind him.

"Jeanette! Jeanette!"

He turned and saw her stumbling away, toward the inferno that had once been a bungalow. He rose and lurched after her.

Flaming debris lay everywhere—in the street, on roofs—and the bungalow where Kate had sat a few moments ago—gone. Nothing remained of the structure but its concrete foundation slab. Water gushed from severed pipes, steaming in the heat; the four cars that had been parked before it were twisted wrecks; a half dozen neighboring bungalows were ablaze.

He caught up and turned her around. "Kate!"

She looked dazed, and surprised to see him. "Jack? What are you doing here?"

"Is it you, Kate? Really you?"

She nodded, her tear-streaked face reflecting the flames. "Yes, but—"

Jack threw his arms around his sister and hugged her, barely able to speak trough the joy exploding inside him. Kate was back. He could tell. The Unity was gone.

"Thank God! I thought I'd lost you!"

"But where's Jeanette!" she said pushing back. "I have to find her!"

"You can't," he said. "You . . . won't."

"But I've got to!" she sobbed. "I did this to her!"

She tore away from his grasp. Jack watched her approach the flaming ruins only to be pushed back by the heat. He wanted to pull her away, spirit her back to New York, but he knew she'd never go until she was convinced there was nothing she could do.

He glanced down the road. Cars were pulling over from the highway to watch, to call for help, to run and see. Gawkers trotted up the narrow sandy street, drawn like moths to the blazing spectacle.

Turning, he spotted a dark crumpled form sprawled in the sand on the far side of the wreckage. What were the odds it was Jeanette? Almost nil, but he hurried forward, skirting the heat of the blaze, and the closer he got the more it looked like a person.

He knelt beside the scorched body. No, not Jeanette. Someone else—a male, face mostly torn away by the blast, clothes shredded by debris missiles, but still recognizable as Sandy Palmer. Where had he been hiding?

Poor jerk. Looked like he finally was going to get the fame he'd been chasing—HEROIC REPORTER DIES INVESTIGATING MURDER CULT!— but he wasn't going to be around to enjoy it.

"Oh, Jesus!" said a voice behind him. "Is he dead?"

Jack rose and glanced at the middle-aged gawker, but didn't answer him; more were coming up the street. He could hear sirens approaching.

Time to go. He looked around for Kate, saw her wandering on the far side, near a neighboring bungalow half consumed by flames. He started toward her.

"Hey, I wouldn't get too close to those shacks I were you," said another gawker. "Another one of these propane tanks could go any second."

Propane? Is that what they thought? Of course they would. But Jack knew the bungalow's tank had only added to the blast, not caused it.

And then he stiffened as he spotted the rusty four-foot tank on the side of the burning house where Kate stood, the flames licking at its flanks . . .

"Kate!" Get away from—!"

The blast was a pale shadow of the first—smaller burst of flame, barely a tenth of the noise and impact—and it momentarily staggered Jack. But it engulfed Kate and sent her flying. She slammed against the wall of the neighboring house and tumbled to the ground like a discarded doll.

As the gawkers screamed and ducked and fled, Jack pounded toward the still form huddled on the sand, repeating one word over and over in a moaning whimper, the only word his dread-mired brain could manage.

"No-no-no-no-no-no . . ."

When he reached her he saw that her hair was singed and her blouse scorched, but her clothes hadn't caught fire. He was about to send up a prayer of thanks when he noticed the blood . . . and the jagged piece of metal jutting from her upper abdomen.

He dropped to his knees beside his sister—not simply to be closer to her but because his legs refused to support him. His hands instinctively reached toward the bloody metal shard to remove it but paused, hovering, unsure, afraid of touching it, her, doing anything that might make things worse. Finally he grabbed her hand in both of his.

"Kate! Kate! Are you okay?" Dumb-ass thing to say—she was anything but okay.

Her eyes fluttered open. "Jack?" Her voice was a whisper in a shell. "Jack, what—?"

"Propane tank . . . it . . ." The words dried up and blew away.

He watched her gaze lower to her body and fix on the protruding scrap of metal.

"Oh, dear."

This helpless kneeling and watching was killing him. Jack needed to do something.

"Should I pull it out?" She's a doctor, he thought. She'll know.

"Better not."

"Okay, then," he told her. "It stays. Help is on the way. Hear the sirens? You're going to be fine."

She was gazing at him now. "I don't . . . think so." Her fingers squeezed his hand. "Jack, the dark . . . it's coming and I'm scared."

"You're gonna be—"

"Not for me. For you and Kev and Lizzie and everyone. It's coming, Jack. The virus is still in my brain and it let me see. The dark is waiting but it will be coming soon, and it's going to roll over everything."

"Kate, save your strength."

"No, listen. Only a handful of people are going to stand in its way, and . . . and you're one of them."

She reminded him of the Russian lady now. *Is war and you are warrior.*

"Kate . . ."

"Please look after Kev and Lizzie, Jack. Promise me you won't let it get them."

"I promise. Now hush."

He looked up and saw half a dozen staring gawkers and wanted to shoot them all.

"What are you looking at?" he shouted. "Get outta here! Can't you see she's hurt? Get help!"

He looked back at Kate and his heart stuttered when he noticed her closed eyes. But she was still breathing.

"Kate?"

She didn't open her eyes, didn't move her lips. "Jack." Her voice so tiny, barely there.

He could feel her slipping away. "Kate, don't go. Please, don't go . . ."

Suddenly flashing red lights everywhere—two cop cars, an ambulance, and a voice shouting, "This way! This way! There's a woman hurt bad over here!"

Jack leaned over his sister, his lips close to her ear. "Help's here now. Listen to me, Kate: I love you, and I'm not going to lose you. Just hang on a little longer and you'll make it."

And then the EMTs, two men and two women sheathed in coveralls and latex gloves, crowded around; Jack watched their expressions change from curious to grim when they saw Kate. He allowed himself to be moved aside as three of them skillfully worked to lift her onto a stretcher while a fourth spoke on a phone to a doctor in the local emergency room, taking instructions and advising him to have a surgeon waiting.

Jack followed close behind as they moved the stretcher—carrying it instead of wheeling it—to the idling ambulance, watched as they slid it into the back of the rig and crawled in after it.

"I'm coming along," he told one of the EMTs. He had this insane feeling that if he stayed nearby, holding Kate's hand, he could keep her alive by pure force of will.

"Sorry, sir. Against the rules."

Jack's hand itched to pull his Glock for emphasis; instead he grabbed the man's arm. "Maybe you didn't hear me: I'm coming along."

"Even if you were allowed, there's no room for you and you'd only get in the way if she crashes."

Jack backed off. The last thing he wanted was to be in the way. He looked past the EMT's shoulder and saw the others starting IVs in both Kate's arms and hooking her up to a heart monitor.

As they slammed the rear door a cop hove into view on Jack's right.

"Did you know that woman?" he asked.

Jack nodded, eyes on the ambulance as it began to move off.

"I'll need to ask you a few questions," the cop said. His shoulder patch read DOVER TWP. POLICE.

Jack began walking, following the ambulance. "I'm going to the hospital."

A hand grabbed his shoulder and turned him a quarter way around.

"Sir," the cop said, "I need some answers before—"

He broke off and stepped back. Jack was ready to kill then and maybe the cop saw that in his eyes. Jack forced a breath and held up an open palm: peace.

"I'm going to the hospital. You want answers, you can find me there."

He turned and hurried through the red-flashing night toward the highway and his car. The cop didn't follow. Maybe he had more pressing matters to attend to, like herding the gawkers away from the site to let the fire crews through, or unspooling yellow barrier tape like the other cop Jack passed.

At a trot now, Jack was maybe a dozen feet behind the ambulance when it reached the highway and turned on its siren. Through the glass side he saw the EMTs go into furious motion, one of them leaning over Kate and beginning rhythmic thrusts against her chest . . .

"No!" he shouted. "NO!"

His heart was a booted foot, kicking at his chest wall as he leaped into his car and took off after the rig. Jack followed it across the median, then south along the highway, across a bridge to the mainland and down a crowded highway, staying close behind and traveling in its wake as cars pulled aside to let it pass.

"Come on! Come on!" he shouted as they raced mile after mile.

Where was this goddamn hospital? Why was it so far?

And all the while he fought a panicked sense of unreality. This shouldn't be happening to Kate, not after all she's just been through. She's one of the good ones, the best of the good ones. This can't be happening to Kate.

Finally the hospital. He trailed the ambulance up to the emergency entrance where he saw a doctor waiting at the curb. Jack was out of his car and standing with hands and face pressed against the rig's side glass in time to see the doctor shake his head and turn off his flashlight after shining it into Kate's eyes.

"No!" Jack's voice was a whisper as he moved around to the rear to catch the doctor as he exited. "There's got to be more you can do!"

"I'm sorry," the doctor said. He was dark skinned and spoke rapid, accented English. "She's gone. The steel must have nicked an artery. Only surgery on the spot could have saved her, I'm afraid."

Again the sense of unreality washed over him. Feeling lost, dead inside, Jack slumped back against the side of the rig. Gravity seemed to double, triple as he watched them wheel Kate's covered body into the hospital. Somehow he found the strength to follow. Her limp form was transferred to a gurney in one of the ER's curtained-off examination cubicles.

"I want to stay with her awhile," he told a nurse with pocked black skin and graying hair.

"Of course."

When she was gone Jack lifted the sheet and stared at Kate's pale face. She looked so peaceful, almost as if she were sleeping. He felt a pressure building in his throat, readying to explode when he nurse popped back in.

"There's a policeman out here who wants to speak to you."

He wanted to scream at her to leave us alone, goddamn it! But he held back.

"Can I have a few minutes? And a pen and a piece of paper if you can spare them?"

She fished both out of her pocket and laid them on the bedside table.

"I'll tell him you'll be out in a minute."

When she was gone, Jack steadied the paper with a knuckle and wrote *Kate Iverson, MD, Trenton, NJ*. He pocketed the pen. He peeked through the curtains and saw the cop from the explosion scene sipping coffee and chatting up the ward clerk.

Jack returned to Kate's side and kissed her forehead, then bottled up his emotions. Leaving her here alone seemed like the rankest sort of desertion; he felt like a rat, but he couldn't stay. He checked out the cop again, then slipped out through the far edge of the curtains and walked the other way. Moving on autopilot he followed signs to the lobby and exited through the front. Found his car and got rolling. A parkway entrance ramp was nearby so he took it north. Saw a sign for a rest area and knew he had to stop or explode. Pulled into the lot and turned off the engine.

Kate . . .

The sense of failure was overwhelming. He'd just got her back and now she was gone. Forever. And it was his fault. If only he hadn't listened to her and gone ahead and done what his gut had told him to do. If only he hadn't saved that damn bomb. If only he'd got home sooner . . .

Jack rested his forehead against the steering wheel and sobbed.

Kate . . .

EPILOGUE

Jack watched from the trees until everyone was gone, then he walked down the slope to where two workmen, one white, one black, were readying to fill in the grave.

"Hey, guys, can you give me a few minutes alone here?"

The white guy squinted at him through the obscenely cheery morning sunlight. "Sorry, mister. The ceremony's over and we've got to—"

Jack had two twenties ready. He held them out. "An extra ten-minute coffee break's not gonna matter in the long run, is it?"

They looked at each other, shrugged, took the twenties, and walked off to a pickup truck parked fifty yards away.

Jack dropped to one knee and stared at the shiny metallic surface of the coffin nestled deep in its hole.

"Sorry I couldn't be here earlier, Kate. I tried, but they wouldn't let me."

The explosion had been eight days ago. Because it was a medical examiner's case and various criminal investigations were involved, it had taken officialdom a long time to release Kate's body.

Jack had driven down to Trenton with Gia for the wake, but kept going when he reached the funeral home. Not because he dreaded the scene inside, the pain in his father's eyes, the baffled shock and hurt of the niece and nephew he'd never known, but because of the guy with the telefoto camera in the car across the street.

Jack had had an eye out for just such a car.

He'd guessed that even a volunteer fire marshal would realize that no propane tank explosion could demolish a house like that, even if it was only a plywood bungalow. A bomb squad would be called in. Traces of C-4 would be found. Addresses of the victims would be established, and lo and behold, one of them lived on the same New York City block where a C-4 car bomb had killed two men just a few days before. And a second victim had been staying at the same address. An interstate conspiracy? Call BATF.

After that it was no stretch to suspect that BATF would want to catalog all the mourners at the Jeanette Vega and Kate Iverson funerals. A photo of Jack could be identified by residents of The Arsley and by the Dover cop at the blast scene, and then the bulletins would be out and the hunt would be on.

This morning he'd seen the car and the camera parked outside the church and again right here in the cemetery.

Bastards.

"Good blood runs in your family."

Jack jumped at the sound of her voice but knew from the accent who he'd see when he turned. The Russian lady and her big white dog stood behind him. He didn't know how they'd come up on him without his hearing them, but at the moment he didn't much care.

"What would you know about it?" he said.

"A brave, brave woman. She saved the world untold misery."

"And she went through untold misery at the end. How the hell did this happen?"

"Is war." She looked around at the sky, the grass, the surrounding pines. "War to destroy all this."

"And I'm a soldier, right?"

"More than soldier. Are weapon. And like weapon, must be tempered, honed, tested, positioned."

Jack glared at her. "I want none of this!"

"Choice is not yours."

"Then why me?"

"Who is to say?"

This was getting nowhere. But Jack needed very badly to know something, and maybe this woman could tell him.

"Is any of what happened to Kate my fault?"

"No. Fault not yours."

That was a relief, but not much.

"Then whose? Because this whole situation reeks. A woman my sister happens to love just happens to develop a brain tumor and during her course of treatment she just happens to become infected with a virus planted by one side in this cosmic war I'm supposedly involved in. Just coincidence? No way I buy that."

"Should not buy. Is not coincidence. No more coincidences for you."

The words jolted Jack. *No more coincidences . . .* the implications were disturbing enough, but the utter certainty in her voice squeezed the breath from him. He stared at this strange woman, unsure what to make of her.

"Who are you, lady?"

"Your mother."

"Stop that! You're not!"

"Is true." She pointed to the coffin. "And am her mother as well. I am proud of this one. All of world owes her great debt."

Jack turned back to the coffin. "You got that right."

Me most of all. He shut his eyes as they welled up.

He felt the woman's hand rest gently on his shoulder. Her tone was consoling.

"A tragedy. But war is fashioned of tragedies. More are to come. A spear has no branches."

Took a moment for Jack to realize he'd heard that before, but by the time he turned to ask her what the hell she was talking about, he was alone.

He shot to his feet and turned in a slow circle. She couldn't have made it to the trees in those few seconds, and none of the gravestones was big enough to hide her and her malamute.

Jack stood alone by his sister's open grave, haunted by the woman's parting words.

www.repairmanjack.com